PEACEMAKER

The Corona Rebellion 2564AD

Gordon S. Savage, Jr.

PEACEMAKER

The Corona Rebellion 2564AD

Copyright ©2016 by Gordon Savage.

All rights reserved.

Cover Design: Kirk DouPonce
Kirk@dogeareddesign.com
http://www.dogeareddesign.com/

Editor: Karen Reddick <karen@theredpeneditor.com>

ISBN: 978-0-9976820-1-4

10 9 8 7 6 5 4 3 2 1

Science Fiction | Adventure | Mystery

Dedication

To my darling wife, Carol, who has not only put up with me for over fifty years but also allowed me to enjoy spending the time to create this book. She has made my life what it is, and I'll be forever grateful.

Our job is to maintain the peace, but that means if some dumb sum' bitch won't listen to reason, our job is to slap him upside the head until he will.

~ Admiral George Scott Remington, Jr.
Commencement Speech
Class of 2543
Royal Naval Academy
Canberra, Australia

Chapter 1

Commander William August Colt looked across the tarmac at his next assignment. He had known what to expect, but even so, she was incredible. The *Invincible* was the latest carrier to join the fleet and also the largest. At nearly 350 meters in length she dwarfed most ships of the line and even from the guard shack her size was awe inspiring. She was currently wearing light and dark gray with black lettering, her peace mission colors. Her aft launch door was down as a ramp, and workers and vehicles streamed in and out loading supplies.

"Your gear is unloaded, sir. Have a safe tour."

Colt returned the salute. "Thank you, Petty Officer Estrada." He caught a fleeting smile before she turned. He sighed briefly and reached down to pick up the steering handle of his footlocker. A blaster bolt rasped past his ear, singeing his hair and throwing a fiery plume of dust and dirt in the air a few meters away. He reacted immediately, diving for the only cover available, a small drainage ditch between the parking spaces and the guard fence. Almost before he hit the ground another bolt took a notch out of the parking bumper along the ditch. Pieces of hot concrete showered down on him.

He raised his head to trace the bolt back from where he had been standing and caught a glimpse of movement on top of one of the buildings. He rolled out of the way as a third bolt shattered the bumper. A voice behind him shouted, "Keep down, Commander. I'll be there in a second." He turned his head to look back. Through the dust and falling debris he saw the gate guard, a burly marine, running toward him, with an M44 blast rifle in his hands.

"On top of the hangar at your ten o'clock," Colt shouted.

The guard swung around to face the hangar as another bolt sprayed harmlessly off his deflector shield. He aimed his rifle and then hesitated, "Damn. He ducked behind the crown of the roof." He activated his communicator. "Dispatch, there's a dropper on top of hangar 42A. See if you can pick him up on motion sensor or video and get a team after him. He's armed with a hand blaster."

The guard listened for a moment. "That's right. He took a couple of shots at Commander Colt. He must have been listening when the main gate called him in."

Colt raised his head to take another look. The rooftop was clear, but the guard signaled him to stay down. Finally, the guard said, "The shooter seems to be gone." He slung his rifle and walked over.

Colt felt the breeze-like touch of the shield as it passed over him. He stood up inside its protection, picked up his cap, and dusted himself off. "What the hell is going on? I'm not used to being shot at, especially on base and in peacetime!"

The guard was all business, "Sorry, sir. I can't answer that. Captain Wessler might be able to tell you something. She sends her apologies and requests you join her in her cabin as soon as you're aboard. I'll have your gear sent up."

Colt knew better than to try to get anything more out of the guard. Obviously Colt was supposed to go straight to the ship. He fought to control his thudding heart and wondered if the guard shack had a spare personal shield. He noticed the guard was again listening to his communicator.

"Copy." Then he said to Colt, "Whoever took those shots dropped off the top of the building and got inside before the peepers could lock a video cam on him. Chances are he's gotten away for now, but he's in no position to take any more shots at you." He deactivated his shield. "Now, could I see your ID, sir?"

Colt was still shaky when he left the guard gate, and his mind raced. This was supposed to be the big one. He was coming aboard the *HMS Invincible* as the deputy flight wing commander. The assignment would get him promoted to captain, and he had already been more than a little wound-up. Then he had been told to report to Captain Wessler, the ship's captain, and, of course, Petty Officer Estrada wasn't permitted to tell him why. Now someone was shooting at him. What was going on?

He picked up his pace and focused on the ship in front of him to steady his nerves. As he neared the personnel gangway, the traffic on the aft launch door ramp briefly cleared to allow an airborne ambulance access. He paused while it flew into the launch bay.

What was a civilian ambulance doing coming aboard a navy carrier? Someone must have been seriously injured if the sickbay couldn't handle it.

At the top of the gangway to the aft personnel airlock he came to attention and addressed the officer of the day. "Permission to come aboard, sir."

Chapter 2

The OD, an ensign who looked as if he didn't yet need to shave, replied, "Permission granted. Welcome aboard, Commander Colt. The captain is waiting for you in her cabin."

Colt headed forward, absorbing the familiar shipboard sights, sounds, and odors. As he passed a lateral corridor he got a glimpse of the three levels of the hangar bay. The tail of a Scorpion fighter caught his eye. The lettering on the vertical stabilizer, "LA," designated the 131st Attack Squadron. As he watched a tug backing it into a parking space, he wondered again about his assignment.

He followed the starboard passageway a short distance to the turbo lifts and was about to touch the call pad when the pressure hatch for the middle lift released and slid open.

A moment later he stepped out of the lift to a distinctly different atmosphere. Simulated oak paneling lined the walls, deep green carpet covered the passageway deck, and a brass sign read "Officer's Country." Colt made a mental note to see what the enlisted quarters looked like.

A few meters down the passageway he came to a door with a name plate that read, "Capt. G. M. Wessler." He touched the annunciator pad and a familiar voice immediately said, "Commander Colt, come in."

The door slid open long enough for Colt to step through. He halted at attention, "Commander William August Colt reporting as—"

"Can it, Gus. Come on in." Captain Gretchen Wessler walked up and extended her hand, "It's been a while. How are you? I understand someone tried to use you for target practice."

Wessler was an old friend, and Colt gave her a wan smile, biting off an urge to say, "It wasn't that funny to me."

"I'm sure you're wondering what's up," Wessler continued.

"Captain, I'm more than wondering. The gate guard didn't seem all that surprised. What the Hemlock is happening around here? People don't get shot at …."

Wessler held up her hand. "I'll tell you what we know in a moment." She turned to the civilian seated on the couch. "This is Bremerhaven Chief Constable Martin Hatcher."

He stood and offered his hand, gripping Colt's firmly, "Despite the circumstances, a pleasure, sir."

"I'll get back to why he's here. And, this is my aide, Mark Claiborne." Colt shook Claiborne's hand.

"Please have a seat, and help yourself to a cup of tea." She waited for Colt to pour his tea. She glanced at the constable. "There have been several incidents in the past few days. Mr. Hatcher is here because of a shooting in town last night. Oscar Hernandez and three of my other officers were badly wounded."

Colt nearly dumped the tea in his lap.

"Oscar is in critical condition. The ship's surgeon thinks he'll make it, but even if he does, he'll need extensive reconstruction. That's too big a job for sick bay so we're going to send him to the Naval Medical Center in Melbourne on a medevac Dart. Which brings me to why I wanted to talk to you right away: this means a change in your orders. As of now you will be replacing Hernandez as first mate of the *Invincible*."

This time he did spill his tea.

"But I was scheduled to be the deputy flight wing commander," Colt protested mildly.

"Ralph," she said, speaking of the wing commander, "and I have discussed this. His senior squadron commander is an acceptable fit for deputy. I have some good officers, but none are as well qualified as you. So, unless you've any real objections, I want you for the job."

Trying not to appear too eager Colt hesitated briefly. "As long as the two of you have agreed," he responded, "I don't have a problem."

"We'll announce it to the crew at the all hands at eighteen hundred," Wessler said.

"Now, as to why you were shot at. We believe it was for the same reason Oscar was shot. Someone wants to delay our next mission."

"I'm not that essential," Colt objected. "For that matter you could promote any number off your current officers to XO in a pinch."

"Apparently whoever is doing this doesn't know the navy that well."

Wessler changed the subject, "Meanwhile, Mark will take you for a situation briefing." The annunciator on her desk interrupted her. She touched a pad, "Wessler!"

"Captain, this is the gate. Miss Lisa Aaron of Interplanet News is here to see you. It's about the recent shootings."

Wessler sighed, "Send her in. We can't ignore the press. Looks like your briefing will have to wait, Gus. She'll undoubtedly want to talk to you. I think you'll find her interesting."

###

The reporter and her camera operator showed at the captain's door less than five minutes later.

After the introductions, Wessler motioned toward the couch. "Please have a seat, Lisa." She turned to the camera operator. "Yuri, the room is clean. Set up wherever you want." Then she walked around behind her desk and sat down.

Lisa relaxed onto the couch. She turned her attention to Colt. "So, Commander Colt, I hear you got a rather warm welcome earlier this evening."

Colt barked a short, nervous laugh. "I guess you could call it that. If it had been any warmer, I wouldn't be here now."

"What can you tell me about it?"

"I was approaching the gate when someone took a shot at me. He missed."

"Do you have any idea why someone would shoot at you?"

"The best guess is that it has something to do with the *Invincible's* next mission, which is apparently common knowledge on the street."

"And what is that?"

"I said it was common knowledge on the street. Unfortunately, I haven't had time to visit town and find out."

She laughed and turned to Wessler. "Captain Wessler, what is the *Invincible's* next mission?"

"It's not classified. How much time do you have?"

"You know the news business. I'll be lucky to get an eight second sound bite."

"We're going to Corona to help restore order. The loyalists have asked us to mediate a truce."

"So there is outright fighting there?"

"The information we have is that different rebel groups have taken over a few towns and are trying to take over several others. That information is sketchy; in fact, the best we have is from the live news broadcasts since the navy doesn't have an intelligence operation on Corona, and if Imperial Intelligence has one, it's not telling. The GNN newscast a few hours ago said the rebels are calling on the central government to secede from the Republic."

Lisa stood up. "Well, if the best information I can get is from a rival news organization, there's not much point in me wasting any more of your time, Captain. Thank you for seeing me."

She turned to Colt and flashed a brilliant smile. "It was a pleasure meeting you, Commander."

Colt returned the smile. "The same."

Wessler got up and followed her to the door. "When we get back, you'll have to stop by for a social visit, Lisa. We haven't had an informal get together in ages."

"Thanks, Gretchen. Give me a call."

When the door hissed shut, Wessler looked at Colt. "This policy of openness with the media …." She frowned. "I'm still not completely comfortable with it. Thank goodness I like her." She nodded at Claiborne. "Now, Mark will take you for that briefing."

Interlude

"This is perfect." Richard Quan smacked his fist into his other palm. "These natives are just what we need, Corey."

Annoyed, Corey Anne McKillip responded, "Don't call me Corey. My name is Maryanne Phillips. You make that slip in public and someone will start asking questions."

Quan was pacing in front of McKillip in her private office in First Landing, the capital city of the planet Corona. She held the impressive title of Minister of Defense in the planetary parliament, second in rank to the Prime Minister. She sat behind a cluttered desk, looking at an intercepted message on the display screen. The message was from Governor General Remarque to the Colonization Board reporting the discovery of natives on the planet.

Quan stopped long enough to glance at her. "Whatever. You've got a new face and new fingerprints and no one has any reason to run your DNA. As far as anyone here knows, you haven't done anything illegal."

"As far as they know."

"And no one can prove anything with Prochaska out of the picture." He paused his pacing again. "You want to hear what I have in mind?"

"Go ahead," but she continued to frown.

"As soon as the Colonization Board finds out about the natives, they'll relocate all the colonists."

"You're talking about millions of people. It won't happen. It would cost too much."

"That's the beauty of it. By law they have to." He started pacing again. "If the colonists declare independence and set up their own government, I'm betting the Republic won't spend the money to take back control and move them. In fact, the colonization laws specifically allow colonies to secede from the republic if the population approves it."

"There are too many things wrong with that idea." She ticked of the problems on the fingers of her left hand. "First, a majority of the citizens would have to vote in favor of seceding. One reason there haven't been any colonies that have seceded is most people are happy belonging to the Republic. Second, the Republic can't afford to allow colonies to secede just to avoid obeying laws that are inconvenient. They'd have to make an example of Corona."

Quan interrupted, "I disagree. I honestly don't believe the Republic would spend the money to relocate the colonists, much less send an expeditionary force to take the planet back."

"Assuming you're right, why should the colonists vote in favor of breaking away from the Republic? I suspect that even if they have to give up their homesteads, most people on Corona would still want to be citizens of the Republic."

Quan turned to look at her again. "You're the politician. Convince them."

She considered for a moment. "Okay. What do we have for leverage?"

"The third planet — what's its name? It's habitable and doesn't have natives. It even has colonists."

She answered his question, "Persephone. The planet is Persephone. But the whole damn world is a hothouse. Where it's not jungle or ocean, the desert is too hot to live in the open."

"Exactly," he smiled. "So where do you think the Republic would relocate the colonists from here?"

For a second she feigned shock. "That's just plain evil." Then she grinned, "And it's logical. It would drastically cut the cost to the Republic."

He put his hands on the desk and leaned toward her, looking directly into her eyes. "Do you think you'd have any trouble selling that?"

"Not in the least. I like it," she acknowledged. "There's nothing more unifying than a common fear." She hesitated, "But what if we can't achieve a majority."

"We'll make it a two-pronged attack," he answered. "Besides your persuasiveness in favor of seceding, we can organize a revolt. Convince enough people that the only way to avoid being evicted to Persephone is to forcibly break away from the Republic."

"But a military takeover isn't the same as a majority vote. The Republic would never recognize it."

"No, but a strong military position could favorably influence the vote."

"Intimidate, you mean."

He shrugged. "Call it what you want. If we play this right, it will give you the power base to ease you into permanent control."

"I like the sound of that," but she frowned. "What am I missing?"

He spoke slowly, as if to a stubborn child, "If we bring in mercenaries to 'guide' the revolt, they can form a cadre of loyal troops to keep the revolutionaries in line once the vote is taken. All you have to do is persuade enough of the citizens that the danger isn't over, that we have to be ready to repel the Republic in case they don't accept the vote."

She remained silent for a moment, frowning. Then she nodded and smiled, "Okay. So now I need to work up a convincing story and figure out how to get it out to the public without alerting the governor's office."

A few minutes later Quan stepped out of McKillip's office. He nodded vaguely at the receptionist as she said, "Good night, Mr. Quan." Once in the hallway he pulled out his communicator and opened it. "She bit," he said, and broke the connection.

Chapter 3

As Colt hung the last of his uniforms in the wall locker, he took a deep breath and shrugged his shoulders, trying to relax. He looked around his stateroom. His glance fell on a video frame on the desk. He picked it up and stared at the image. A young woman and a ten-year-old girl looked back at him. His face darkened and his eyes moistened. Five years and it still hurt. He could still remember their last conversation.

"You're going to miss Caitlin's first regatta, you know," Rachel had said.

"I know, and I hate not to be there, but this is an important assignment. It could be a big step in my career."

"Nursemaiding a royal for a year?"

"Having her signature on a glowing effectiveness rating would move me up the list better than almost anything." Of course, he knew that wasn't all of it. It was a whole year in close company with a real princess, even if all he ever said was, "Yes ma'am" and "No ma'am."

"Can't you put it off until after the race?"

"She's leaving tomorrow for her goodwill tour. I have to be on the ship. That's out of my hands. Besides, Caitlin will only get better. I'll get to see her race next year."

It hadn't worked that way. The shuttle Rachel and Caitlin were in crashed on approach to Perth Spaceport. "I'm sorry, Rachel," he whispered, "I should have been there."

He forced his thoughts to the briefing he had just received. The information about the situation on Corona really was as sketchy as Wessler had given the reporter. There had been sporadic incidents where citizens calling themselves separatists had taken over towns or cities. The fighting itself had been minimal, although there had been a few skirmishes. What hadn't been in the news reports was that the governor general had just reported to the Colonization Board that natives had been found on the planet. That put a whole new light on the situation there.

He wondered how the survey team that cleared Corona for colonization could have left out an important detail such as natives.

The Colonization Board would never have permitted settlers if they had known about them. Now, more than likely, they would have to evict all the colonists. That wouldn't sit well with people who had been there all their lives.

The AI announced, "Lieutenant Commander Orsini is at the door."

"Open," Colt responded.

A tall, heavyset lieutenant commander stepped in. He threw both arms around Colt and gave him a bear hug. When he stepped back, it was Colt's turn to be surprised. Tony Orsini had been Colt's last roommate at the Academy. He had put on weight since graduation, and every time Colt saw him he had lost more hair. But he still seemed to attract beautiful women.

"First Officer Colt, I presume." Orsini held out a bottle of bourbon. "Congratulations, Gus."

"Tony, how are you?"

"Great. I just got word that my third stripe has been approved," he said. He looked at Colt appraisingly. "How long has it been?"

"How about just last year on Ridgeway? Remember the casino in New Vegas where you left me to pay the bills?"

"What're a few hundred credits between friends?"

Orsini looked around. "So these are the first mate's quarters. Where are the glasses?"

"Try the sideboard," Colt pointed and then lifted a bubble wrapped package out of his footlocker. He carefully peeled back the wrapping.

Orsini pulled out two glasses from the sideboard and turned around. "Here we are — What's that?"

"My Colt .45. You've seen it before."

The revolver was mounted on a highly polished piece of Teakwood. At the bottom, a tarnished bronze placard read, "Colt 45 Peacemaker." Colt moved to an empty place on the wall and held the plaque up to it.

Orsini opened the bourbon and poured for both of them. Before he handed a glass to Colt, he asked, "Why not put it over your bunk? Then the inscription could refer to the gun or to you."

Colt looked at him.

"I mean, really. You've always been a peacemaker," Orsini continued. "I remember the time at the Academy when you broke up a fight between two upper classmen by flattening both of them. That's my kind of peacemaker!"

"I'd forgotten all about that." Colt thumbed the mounting switch and stepped back to look at the plaque. He turned to Orsini, "How are you doing these days?"

Orsini smiled. "Well, things have been looking up."

Colt continued to unpack his footlocker while Orsini waxed enthusiastic about his latest girlfriend. "She's fantastic! We're sharing quarters. She has some really interesting political ideas. We sometimes stay up half the night talking about them."

"She's not a Dissolutionist, is she?" Colt asked referring to a political party that seemed to be gaining favor back on Earth. They advocated breaking up the centralist government because the cost of maintaining a widespread republic was supposedly draining the government's resources.

"Yes, she is. I think it makes her even more interesting."

Colt made a mental note to spend some time talking to her about it. "Sounds like you walked into a good deal there," he said.

"Speaking of walking into good deals, remember what's-her-name, Peggy Walker? What a knockout. After you 'persuaded' Graf Fairbanks to get out of her apartment, you could have had her by just crooking your little finger."

"I was still broken up over losing Rachel and Caitlin." Colt stood silent for a moment as he thought about his dead wife and daughter. A look of intense grief flickered across his face, then he continued, "That was five years ago. I could use someone like Peggy now." He smiled wolfishly. "So tell me more about this girlfriend of yours."

"I saw her first," Orsini replied.

Chapter 4

"Captain on deck!" Colt announced. He came through the main hatchway onto the bridge, stepped to the side, and stood at attention facing Captain Wessler as she entered.

"Carry on," Wessler barked. She turned to Colt. "Gus, I'm going to introduce you around. Then I want you to command our lift off."

As soon as Wessler had said to carry on, one of the officers turned from her station and walked up to them. "Captain," she said.

Wessler nodded to her. "Gus, this is Lt. Commander LeBlanc. She's the chief navigation officer. She'll be your second in command on the bridge."

"It's a pleasure, Commander," Colt replied, shaking her hand.

Wessler walked him around the bridge. As Colt was introduced he took in the layout. A transpex canopy wrapped over the entire bridge. The captain's and the first officer's command station stood in the middle. The pilot and copilot sat directly ahead of the command station. The navigation station occupied most of the port side. A similar imaging system on the starboard side allowed the gunnery officer to direct the ship's weapons at hostile targets. Along the aft bulkhead were the tactical stations, engineering, communication, and the science station.

"Spock?" Colt asked, referring to a placard above the science station that said simply, SPOCK.

The science watch officer glanced at the placard. "Folklore, Commander. A legendary science officer of the twentieth century."

The engineering watch officer announced, "Preflight checklist complete, Captain."

"Places, everyone. It's show time!" Wessler turned to Colt. "Gus, take the con and carry on."

"Aye, Captain, I have the con." Colt addressed the pilot. "Lieutenant Yamamura, request clearance, please."

"Bremerhaven tower, *HMS Invincible* requests clearance for lift off."

"*Invincible*, you are cleared for immediate lift off."

Colt winced inwardly as he repeated the traditional, "Cast off mooring lines. Raise ship, lieutenant. Engineering, defense condition green, set colors to white."

"Aye, sir." The exterior colors of the *Invincible* switched from gray to white for in system peacetime travel.

Yamamura eased the ship off the tarmac, turning her until the steering bars in the flight director display centered on her assigned flight path. "Departing," Yamamura transmitted to the control tower.

"Roger, *Invincible*. Have you departing at zero four hundred. Contact departure control on 256.5 Megahertz. Bon voyage."

The communications officer entered the new settings as Yamamura applied forward thrust.

"Bremerhaven departure control, *Invincible* on outbound vector."

"*Invincible*, we have you in sensor contact. Cleared for Victor five trajectory to 10,000 meter release altitude."

Colt said, "All ahead five percent." He turned to Wessler. "Lift off was at zero four hundred, Captain."

"Join me in the Ready Room as soon as we go to overdrive. Carry on."

Captain Wessler walked rapidly off the bridge, Commander Claiborne following close behind.

The communications officer broke in, "Commander Colt, HMS Mercury reports they have been delayed by twenty minutes."

"Thank you, Lieutenant Soriescu, we'll continue to the rendezvous point and wait for them."

Moments later departure control announced, "*Invincible*, we show you passing ten thousand. Assume vector Kilo twelve for rendezvous with HMS Mercury, and contact them on three five three point two. You are released."

"Vector Kilo twelve. All ahead twenty-five percent," Colt directed. "Lieutenant Yamamura, contact HMS Mercury and forward our ETA."

The *Invincible* rapidly accelerated clear of the atmosphere and arced over into low orbit. Commander LeBlanc reported, "Intercept vector to the rendezvous point is nominal."

"Lieutenant Yamamura, you may assume manual control at your pleasure."

"Aye, sir."

"Commander, I'm picking up two flyers at the rendezvous point," LeBlanc announced. "No transponders."

Colt was immediately alert and suspicious. "Any evidence of armament?"

"The scans are being processed now, sir. Another thirty seconds."

"Roger. Yellow alert. Shields up." The ship's lighting switch to yellow, and the external color switched to black.

Lieutenant Yamamura spotted the flyers first. "Commander, I have visual."

Colt nodded. "Jeanette, those scans …"

"They're finishing now, sir." She paused briefly. "Each flyer is equipped with anti-spacecraft blast cannons."

"Thank you. Fire control, lock tractors on them and give me an acoustic link."

"Aye, sir. Locking. You have voice."

Colt touched the talk pad on the chair arm. "Unidentified flyers, you have five seconds to power down your blasters. Five, four, three, …" Both flyers exploded.

LeBlanc said, "Sorry, sir. The scans didn't show any explosives." She looked at her display and frowned. "Come to think of it, they didn't show life forms either."

"Someone was going to play nasty. What were they out here for?" He tapped the pad for the Captain's ready room and reported the incident. Then he turned back to LeBlanc, "Any debris worth examining?"

"Negative, sir." She hesitated. "Considering the attacks on shipboard personnel lately, perhaps we were supposed to bring them aboard before they blew. They could have done a lot of damage and delayed our departure."

"Good point." He added her comments to his report. Then he turned to fire control. "Mister Quayle, sweep up the debris and vaporize it. We don't want the Mercury running into pieces of it." Colt touched a pad on the chair arm. "Secure from yellow alert. Flight deck, prepare to accept the Mercury."

Several minutes later the Mercury slid smoothly into the flight deck, took Commander Hernandez aboard, and backed out of the hatch. Elapsed time, two minutes and sixteen seconds.

16

"Mercury is clear," Commander LeBlanc reported.

Colt grinned. "Let's see what this tub can do. Engage navigation vector and full shields. All ahead full."

"Have a seat, Gus," Wessler said as he walked into the ready room. "Any thoughts about why those flyers were there?"

Colt took a chair at the oval briefing table. "I suspect that Jean Marie was right. They were there to damage us so we couldn't continue our mission. The only other possibility I can come up with is that they were hoping to catch the Mercury by surprise and destroy it so we'd have to wait around before departing the system. Why they would want to delay us, I don't know."

Wessler nodded. "You can go ahead now, Lieutenant."

"Yes, Captain." The briefing officer, Lieutenant Rasmussen, touched a pad on his remote controller. Several images appeared in the display field. They formed a composite of GNN newscasts.

"The latest reports we've received from Corona show the conditions have continued to deteriorate. As you know most of our information comes from GNN broadcasts, although we have been getting sporadic information from the governor general's office. We do know that a group of citizens on Corona is engaging in civil unrest. Strikes, protests, and even some riots have created havoc on the planet. We've confirmed that while there have not been any significant battles, the Home Guard did fire on one riot, killing a high profile college student. If the information is correct, she was the daughter of Duncan McInerny, a prominent industrialist. The unrest is disrupting local businesses and travel, especially off-planet. The legislature was ordered into recess because half the legislators are supporting the rebels. As you know, the loyalists have asked us to mediate a truce."

"So there is actual fighting?" Colt asked.

"The information that rebel groups have taken over several towns appears to be an exaggeration. At least, we can't confirm it. The few towns we know they have taken over were uncontested. Some of our sources did indicate that the rebels are trying to assemble a united army, but we can't confirm that either. So far, we have no information from Imperial Intelligence, not even at the highest classification levels. The governor general's reports did say that some of the rebels are calling on the central government to secede from the Republic."

Wessler looked at the briefer. "Why do I get the feeling something is missing here?"

"Well, ma'am, there's been no new contact with the planet in over eighteen hours. None of the subspace transmitters in the system seem to be operating. Even GNN is off the air. No ships have departed the planet in the past sixteen hours, and the ones on the ground aren't responding."

"How many?"

"Six commercial carriers and at least thirty-two private cruisers."

"All without working subspace transmitters?" Colt asked. "I don't like the sound of that. I'd say it's clear the rebels have taken over at least part of the planet."

"I agree," Wessler responded. "However, we won't know for sure until we get there." She turned back to the briefer. "What's the military situation there?"

He touched another button on the remote. "The Home Guard is the only trained military force on the planet, and there aren't many of them. There are five battalions planet wide. There's one in New Perth, one in Johnstown, one in First Landing, one in Victoria, and one here at Kyoto. Each is equipped with a flight of Patton armored troop carriers, a Super Cobra flight, and six Hercules heavy transports. Every guardsman is issued a sidearm, the rifle platoon has M44 blast rifles, and the artillery platoon has 155 millimeter blast cannons and 75 millimeter mortars. Also, each platoon has an anti-spacecraft squad using 75 millimeter blast rifles with sensor directed fire."

"Considering that less than a fourth of the planet is settled, that's a pretty substantial Home Guard," Wessler observed.

"Yes, ma'am."

"Is there anything else we should know?"

"I believe you're aware that the GNN reporter on the scene is Princess Jana Stewart."

Colt almost sputtered. To cover his personal feelings he groaned, "Oh great, a royal. Don't get me wrong, I've met Jana, and I like her, but if she's out of communication, the royal family probably has their shorts in a knot back home."

Wessler smiled, "I guess we'll just have to put her back in communication."

Interlude

"Well?" McKillip looked up at Quan from her desk display.

He closed the door and walked over to her desk. "It isn't going to be as easy as I hoped," he admitted. "Do you know how many subspace relays and transceivers there are on this forsaken dirtball?"

"I can imagine." She leaned back in her chair and templed her fingers. "I gather we haven't put them all out of commission."

"Well, I ..."

"You said we could get this done quickly," she demanded. "How bad is it?"

His face turned red and he started to speak. With a visible effort he slowed his breathing and responded calmly, "GNN has its own transceiver, and the damn spaceport is cluttered with them. Every bloody citizen who has an overdrive equipped cruiser has a transceiver, and the First Landing primary relay is on the spaceport. That's the one the governor general uses if you'll remember."

"We need to shut down the spaceport anyway," McKillip reminded him. "How hard can that be?"

"The Home Guard has a company stationed there, and with all the skirmishes going on. They're on alert. We can't put a mishmash of untrained volunteers up against them. It would be a blood bath."

She sat silent for a moment. Then a grim smile formed on her lips. "What about a diversion. The rest of the local battalion of the Home Guard is scattered over the province putting out fires. If a mob of separatist militia moved on First Landing from the south, wouldn't that draw out the company that's on the spaceport?"

Quan brightened. "It might. Certainly most of them. If we have a mercenary platoon spearheading the attack, they can take on any Home Guard left at the spaceport." He smacked a fist into his palm. "That will work."

"Great. Now what can we do about GNN?"

Quan sobered. "That's a whole other problem. The reporter is Princess Jana. The governor general has a squad of guards in mufti around her at all times. It will be extremely difficult to separate her from the transceiver." He began pacing.

McKillip watched him without speaking. In a moment he stopped and turned toward her. "I've developed some contacts," he said. "Let me see if they can help us."

"What can they do?"

"For one thing they can identify the guards," Quan responded. "Then perhaps they can 'convince' them to turn their heads long enough for someone to get to the transceiver."

McKillip frowned. "We've been treading a fine line with this whole rebellion. I believe we can get away with it as long as it looks to be supported by a significant number of citizens. They won't spend a lot of effort tracking the leadership down. Especially if there's a clear cut vote in favor of seceding. On the other hand, if we put a royal at risk, they may not be so understanding."

Quan smiled. "Leave that to me. I'll see that there's no way to connect us in the first place and that the princess is taken care of."

Later, when he left McKillip's office, Quan called the private number. "I need a team to keep Princess Jana out of trouble."

Chapter 5

"Hey, Number One. Over here." Tony Orsini waved to Colt from a table near the port bulkhead.

Colt quickly made his way across the amidships mess hall to Orsini's table, noticing the attractive lieutenant who was with him. Both of them stood as he approached.

Orsini nodded at the lieutenant. "Gus, this is Lieutenant Magda Von Hagen. Magda, this is Commander Gus Colt."

She smiled brightly, "It's a pleasure to meet you, sir."

"Good to meet you, Lieutenant Von Hagen." He slid into an empty chair. "Sit, please."

"What are you doing in the crew mess?" Magda asked. "I'd expect you to be at the captain's table."

"Not my style. I want to know what's going on with the crew. That means I have to spend time with them whenever I can."

Magda showed a faint smile. "You mean you want the crew to believe you care about them so you make a show out of being where they work and eat."

"Magda—" Orsini started, but Colt raised his hand. "That sounds a bit cynical. You don't think it's possible that a senior officer cares about the lower ranks?"

"It's theoretically possible, but I've never seen it."

"I'm tempted to ask you if you have ever looked for it, but I can see this is an ideological discussion. I'd love to continue it; however, I need to get back to the bridge as soon as I finish lunch. Perhaps you and Tony could come by my quarters this evening after second watch mess."

"I'd like that."

Orsini cleared his throat. "Magda, I know you like a challenge, but I think you're out of your league on this one." He turned to Colt, "We'll be there. Shall I bring bandages?"

"I'll keep it bloodless if she will. I haven't had a real opportunity for ideological debate in ages, and I wouldn't want to inhibit it. Besides I suspect Lieutenant Von Hagen can hold her own. It sounds as if we should have an interesting conversation this evening," Colt said, smiling.

"How did you come by the name Barkley?" Colt asked.

His cabin AI responded, "Is that name unsatisfactory, sir? You can change it if you wish."

"Barkley is fine," Colt responded. "I was just curious how you came about the name."

"Like all the other Artificial Intelligences on the ship, I'm integrated into the ship's computer system, but as a model 1738N, I apparently converse more spontaneously than other models, and Commander Reynolds, thought I was similar to MP Barkley Samuels."

Colt grinned. Of course, Samuels was known throughout his career as a non-stop talker. If this Barkley was similar, he'd have to tone it down some.

Once Colt had finished instructing Barkley on his personal protocols, he called up the records on Corona. The planetary system had been discovered by telescope over 350 years before, but it was far enough from Earth that the first exploration didn't take place for almost another 150 years. Colonization began as soon as the Colonization Board cleared it.

The system was a treasure trove. The sun, Aurora, had four habitable planets. The third planet, Persephone, yielded large amounts of rare organic compounds. The fifth and sixth planets, Castor and Pollux, circled each other. The deserts on the far side of each held vast stores of easily accessible minerals.

The fourth planet, Corona, was so earthlike some scientists initially speculated that somehow it and Earth had been seeded with the same startup proteins. It rotated once every 24.6 hours, and orbited Aurora in just over two Earth years. From the beginning, settlers flocked to the smaller northern continent, where a year-round southerly flow kept most of the arable land green. Consequently, the bulk of the population lived there, and most of the available land was rapidly being settled.

Colt had started to read about the history of the settlement when Barkley announced, "Commander Orsini and Lieutenant Von Hagen have arrived." The AI opened the hatch as they walked up.

"Come on in, and make yourselves at home," Colt said. "Either of you care for tea or coffee?"

"You do have something stronger, don't you?" Orsini asked.

"The liquor is still in the sideboard, along with the Buzz-Off tablets. How about you, Magda. May I call you Magda?"

"Yes, sir. I wouldn't mind a cup of tea."

When Orsini had returned with his drink and everyone had settled in, Magda said, "If I may ask, Commander, where do you call home?"

"First, my friends call me Gus. While we may agree to disagree, I hope you'll consider me a friend."

Magda nodded, frowning almost imperceptibly, "I have to say that I'm not entirely comfortable calling a senior officer by a nickname, especially the XO."

"Well, you have my permission if you change your mind. I went through the same thing with Gretchen … Captain Wessler."

Colt continued, "As for my home, it used to be the Pacific Grove suburb of Monterrey Bay in North America. Since my wife and daughter died, I've pretty much lived shipboard."

"Tony told me about the accident. I'm sorry to hear it."

Colt glanced at Orsini before saying, "I appreciate that. It still hurts once in a while, but I've had to get on with my life."

Orsini interrupted. "Didn't we come here to discuss politics? I'm waiting for the bloodletting to begin."

Colt laughed. "Thoughtful adversaries should always start politely. It allows us to be nastier without the battle turning physical. I hope we won't see any bloodletting tonight."

"I'm prepared to make my point without being brutal," Magda agreed, smiling slightly.

"Well, let's get on with it," Orsini said.

Colt nodded, "I was going to work into this, but if it's all right with you, Magda, perhaps you can enlighten me on your views."

Over the next half hour Colt and Magda exchanged verbal barbs, with neither side willing to concede significant points. As the discussion progressed, Magda grew increasingly agitated. Colt could have easily wrapped up the argument but held off. He felt something was wrong with her responses but couldn't decide what it was. Then it hit him. He paused for a moment, looking at Magda quizzically.

"What?" She asked angrily.

Colt sat up a little taller. "I've been watching your eyes as we've talked. Your face and voice and body language have all said that you're passionate about Dissolutionism, but your eyes haven't shown the passion. I don't think you really believe what you're saying. What's going on here?"

Magda's face went pale. "What … well …I …." She sputtered. She stood up. "I'm sorry, sir, but I have to go." She almost lurched out the hatch, leaving Colt and Orsini behind.

"Now what was that all about?" Orsini asked.

"I believe I know," Colt answered, "but I think you'd better go after her."

Interlude

Quan stood with his hands clasped behind his back, looking out McKillip's panoramic window onto the busy street below. "Our agents weren't able to delay the *Invincible*'s departure. She'll arrive here in two weeks with a full complement of marines. We need to advance our schedule."

"I don't see how, Richard," McKillip disagreed. "The separatists are getting edgy about the idea of having to fight other colonists. A lot of them have friends who are loyalists."

Quan turned to look at her. "We'll just have to put more mercs in charge."

"Won't that mean pulling them away from guarding the subspace transmitter sites?"

Quan barked a short laugh, "Considering the condition of most of the sites, that won't be a problem. Even the weakest units could easily handle them without mercs. At worst they can plant charges and blow them when they surrender. We can pull most of the professionals out of the effective militia units and move them to the ones that are wavering. Leave just enough of them in the other units to maintain control."

"I don't think it'll be that simple." She got up from her desk and walked over to the window. "We need to account for Billy Hargety. He's become a bigger factor than we originally thought. In fact, he has become the de facto leader of the separatists. That wasn't supposed to happen."

Quan grimaced. "I know," he spat. "My information was that he was a buffoon that no one other than his close friends would take seriously. I apologize for underestimating him."

"You see the problem here, don't you? As long as Hargety has this much influence, we can't ignore him, and he doesn't know there's any reason to hurry."

"So we get rid of his influence."

"And how do you propose to do that?" She asked.

"He could have an accident."

"Wait right there!" She glared at him, unblinking. "I draw the line at murder."

He returned the stare. "What exactly do you call conducting a civil war?"

She continued to look him in the eye. "War. The casualties of war have never been considered murder victims. The other side always has the option of not resisting."

"Neither of those statements is accurate, but I will grant that we humans do make a distinction between war-time casualties and murder victims." He resumed looking out the window. "Never mind, I'll work something out."

He glanced at his watch. "I have a meeting in ten minutes. We'll talk more when I get back." He strode to the door.

"No murder," she repeated before the door closed behind him.

He called the private number. "We need to eliminate Hargety as a problem."

Chapter 6

"First Landing Control, this is HMS *Invincible*, come in please."

The speakers remained inexplicably silent. Ensign Bath turned to Captain Wessler and said, "I don't get it, ma'am. They're down there, but they aren't answering."

Colt, now sitting in the first officer's chair, turned to the communication station. "Lieutenant Soriescu, are you picking up anything?"

"Yes, sir," responded the communications officer. "The personal communicator system seems to be working normally. They just aren't answering traffic control radio. I can patch into the comm system if you know a number to call."

Colt looked at Wessler for direction. "We'd better go directly to the governor general," she said, touching a pad on her console. "Adrian Remarque." The number appeared on her screen. "There's the number, Lieutenant Soriescu. See if you can raise him."

"Yes, ma'am."

The comm had barely rung when the three dimensional image of a pale young man in a business suit appeared in the display screen, the governor general's crest floating above his right shoulder. "Governor General's Office. Mr. Wallace at your service. How may I help you?" His face seemed to brighten as he recognized the navy uniform.

"Captain Wessler of *HMS Invincible* calling Governor General Remarque."

"Yes, ma'am. Just a moment, please."

The crest briefly replaced his image. Seconds later Remarque appeared. A swarthy man with a neatly trimmed black mustache and a full head of black hair, he stood out in a scarlet ceremonial jacket with gold trim and a gold sash. "Gretchen! Thank God you're here!"

"I hope the ceremonial uniform doesn't mean you were about to surrender, Adrian," Wessler said.

"What? Oh, no, despite this bloody nonsense with the separatists, my daughter, Melanie, is getting married today. You didn't get the invitation?"

"I'm afraid not." She paused. "What's going on down there, Adrian? We can't contact approach control."

"Rebel troops are holding the port. It's a nuisance. The Home Guard has them surrounded, but we figured it was better just to wait them out since we have so little space traffic. It's been a standoff for the last three days."

"Shall I send down a platoon of marines?"

"I suppose that would be best. Please, instruct them to minimize casualties. These may be rebels, but they have a large percentage of the population on their side. We don't want to add more to their sympathizers."

"Gus, can you take care of that?"

Colt stood. "Aye, Captain." She signaled him to wait.

"We'll have troops on the ground in an hour, Adrian. If you have radio contact with the rebels, tell them they can surrender to the Home Guard or wait for the marines. I don't think the marines will be in a mood to play games."

Remarque nodded off-screen. When he turned back to the screen, he said, "The wedding is at 3:00 PM this afternoon. Will you be able to make it?"

"Sorry. Technically this is a hostile situation, so I have to keep the *Invincible* in orbit and on alert. Give Melanie my regrets, and tell her I'd be there if I could. Hopefully I'll be able to see her before she leaves for her honeymoon."

She spoke to Colt. "I'll brief the COC duty officer. You contact the marine commander and Captain Decker to set up the troops and the transport. It's time to stop the nonsense. Meet me in the ready room in ten minutes."

###

"Gus, I'm sending you with the marine contingent so I can get your take on what's going on down there." Captain Wessler paced thoughtfully in the ready room. "This whole thing doesn't feel right, and I want reliable information."

Colt frowned, "I'm not objecting to the assignment, but doesn't it suggest that you don't trust Lieutenant Camarotte?"

"I want Felipe concentrating on securing that landing field with minimum casualties. Your job will be to assess the rebel's operation.

What are they trying to prove? Are they combat ready or disorganized hooligans?"

"Okay. I'd better get going then. The landing craft leaves in twelve minutes, and I still need to get into my armor."

"Use a camera helmet. I want several feeds, and you can narrate yours as you go along." She paused. "When the operation is over, I want you to report to Adrian and fill him in on what you saw. Then find out what we can do for him. I don't trust standard comm circuits for sensitive information."

The landing craft touched down on an open pad near the center of the spaceport. As the fore and aft ramps were lowered, a few stray blaster bolts glanced harmlessly off the force field. The shooting stopped when the marines surged onto the surface and fanned out into combat positions.

Colt and the marines wore the same camouflaged armor. The carbon fiber shell could stop a charging rhino without a dent. The servos augmented normal movements so the user could run faster, jump higher, and carry a heavier load. The personal shield could withstand a blast rifle bolt. He checked that his shield was on full and followed the last squad out onto the tarmac.

As soon as he reached the ground, he looked back and gave thumbs up to the copilot. The landing craft immediately lifted straight up, climbing high enough to provide active surveillance of the battle area. As it moved into position, it began broadcasting a battlefield image to the ground forces.

Colt glanced at the battlefield display in his helmet and turned slowly around, scanning the space port with his video camera. Primarily built for private spacecraft, the field had everything from cabin cruisers to yachts and passenger liners, along with small craft hangars, scattered maintenance buildings and warehouses, the tower, and the subspace relay building. As he rotated, men and women in civilian clothes began coming out of the buildings and from behind the scattered spacecraft.

Colt narrated for his long-range transmitter, "The landing craft is in position, and I'm getting battlefield imagery, but it doesn't look like we'll need it. The rebels are coming out of cover with their hands in the air." At that moment the battlefield image flashed. "Whoa! What was that?" Another flash caused Colt to shout into the loudspeaker, "Hit the deck. Incoming." He dove for the ground, noticing that the rebels were looking around in confusion.

Before he could yell at them again, the ground twenty meters in front of him erupted in a shower of flames and asphalt. Several marines were lifted into the air and thrown outward. Colt jumped to his feet and dashed toward the downed marines.

As he ran, another explosion rocked the tarmac. This one came from the subspace transmitter building. The walls blew out, spraying shattered brickwork, and a rolling cloud of flames and black smoke lifted the roof into the air. It slammed to earth only meters from a private yacht.

A third, muffled explosion followed, and a dense cloud of smoke billowed up between two rows of buildings. It rapidly spread across the area where the flashes had originated, obscuring the scene in the battlefield image. Suddenly it made sense — a smoke screen. Colt started running toward where he had seen the flashes. "Peacemaker Zero One, max stun on where those flashes came from," he ordered to the landing craft. Simultaneously, the powerful stun beams sprayed from the landing craft, ionizing the air enough to be visible and saturating the target area.

"Still some hostiles left," Colt said into the long-range transmitter. "They're trying to use a smoke screen to get away."

Just as Colt charged into the smoke, a squad of marines fell in with him, weapons ready. Rounding a hangar, one of them yelled, "Down!" Colt was still on his way to the ground when a rocket propelled grenade flashed over him. The explosion erupted with a cloud of flames, dust, and smoke that rained shrapnel and brick fragments.

Looking up he saw an obscure shape flying through the smoke-filled air coming right at him. He turned to run, but a blow from behind slammed him to the ground, knocking his breath out, and something massive landed on him. His armor and personal shield kept him from being crushed, but the weight was so heavy that even augmented he could barely twist to see the mass of twisted metal lying on top of him.

He heard a brief exchange of blaster fire. Then a pair of armored boots appeared out of the smoke and dust, "Commander Colt, are you all right?"

"Yeah, get this damn thing off me."

"Hey, guys, over here!" The smoke cleared enough for Colt to see the squad of marines running toward him. With all of them lifting and pushing, the wreckage easily slid off him. He rolled out of the way and looked back where he had been. The marines were lowering what was left of an expensive Bentley Asteroid cruiser to the ground. "Thanks, men. Did we get them?"

"No, sir. They got away while we were blinded," Gunnery Sergeant Royer said.

He held up the mangled remains of Colt's blast rifle. "I'm afraid this thing is toast. At least you still have your hand gun."

Colt checked to confirm that the blaster was still attached to his armor. Then he called the landing craft, "Peacemaker Zero One, do you have our quarry on the heat sensors?"

"No, sir, the smoke seems to have obscured them."

"And you haven't seen any heat sources leaving the area?"

Lieutenant Camarotte's voice broke in addressing the sensor operator on the landing craft, "Girard, reprocess the IR data from right before the smoke screen started. Up the gain to pick up anything out of the ordinary."

"Good thinking," Colt acknowledged over the radio.

"Sirs, I have six very dim targets entering the next hangar down across from you through the middle door and disappearing from contact." Girard said.

"Sergeant Royer, get after them. I'm sending backup to join you, but don't wait." Camarotte said.

"I'm going to tag along to provide video, but this is your mission, Gunny. I'll catch up in just a second," Colt responded.

Before following the squad, Colt trotted over to the Bentley. Inside, the cockpit was completely demolished. "*Invincible*, did you get all that?"

"You sure know how to make an entertaining video, Gus." Captain Wessler responded.

###

By then the smoke had dissipated. The hangar across the tarmac had only one personnel entrance, and it was in the middle of the building. Royer hand-signaled to the squad to spread out and surround the building. He and Colt dashed to the hangar and hugged the front wall. Crouching down, they moved toward the personnel door. When they reached it, Royer twisted the handle, yanked the door open, and jumped back.

Immediately a blaster bolt rasped through the opening, striking the hangar across the way. The blast was powerful enough to take out a large piece of the wall and the front end of the flyer parked inside. "Damn!" Royer hissed. "That was heavy duty." He keyed the squad frequency, "Delta Squad, the rebels have an anti-spacecraft blaster. Keep out of the open as much as you can." He returned to Colt, "Even this armor with shields on full can't stand up to that. What are we dealing with here?"

"I don't know, but these buildings are mostly sheet metal. I think we'd better move."

Almost immediately Colt heard another blast, but this time inside the hangar. From the back of the building Corporal McCloud reported over the radio, "The rebels just blew out part of the back wall and are coming out of the building. Hey! They're wearing armor." A second later he added, "Uh oh, that guy is wearing a power pack and carrying an anti-spacecraft blaster. Pascal, Reubens, on my command shoot with me for the muzzle. Three. Two. One. Fire."

Colt and Royer started for the far end of the building. They heard the simultaneous blaster bolts from the other side. Then McCloud reported, "We got the muzzle of the blaster. It won't be of any use. Uh oh, here comes another one!"

This time there was the sound of a heavy blaster firing. Colt could see the flash and the resulting explosion in the battlefield display. A moment later McCloud announced, "That was too close. Gunny, we need to call in the heavy artillery."

Royer halted at the corner of the hangar and signaled for Colt to stay back. He called the landing craft, "Peacemaker Zero One, we need some heat on these guys?"

"We're moving into position now," the pilot responded.

Signaling Colt to wait, Royer checked around the side of the building. Then he dashed across the opening and plunged behind the cover of the next hangar. After rechecking between the buildings, he flagged Colt to come ahead. Colt followed Royer's lead and dove for cover as soon as he had crossed the gap. A bolt from a hand blaster struck the ground right behind him. Colt jumped to his feet and raced away from the corner of the building. When there was no further blaster fire, he stopped to check the battlefield image. "Corporal McCloud, I'm seeing three bright spots as well as the six dim images in my display. Can you tell what's going on?"

"I see three people in civilian clothes with their hands on their heads. Could be hostages."

"Peacemaker Zero One, did you get that?"

"Yes, Commander, we'll hold our fire."

Even though jogging was faster in the augmented armor than men on foot could run, the potential of hostages held the squad back, pacing the rebels as they ran between the hangar rows.

As they jogged, Royer called the platoon leader, "Lieutenant Camarotte, can we get somebody on the ground in front of them? Maybe borrow a flyer?"

Colt checked his battlefield image. The rebels had reached the end of the hangars. They paused briefly and then dashed across the open space to a warehouse, dragging the three civilians with them. As soon as they were inside, they vanished from the imagery.

Colt and Royer rounded the corner of a hangar and the warehouse came into view. They ducked behind a cargo module parked between the hangar and the warehouse. Royer called for the rest of the squad to stop. "Spread out and surround the building. Keep out of sight from the warehouse and keep your eyes open. Watch for snipers in the second story windows. When you're in position, call in."

Crouched behind the cargo module, Colt took in the situation. Royer shook his head, "The more I look at this, the less I like it. I get the feeling it's an ambush." He looked at the sky for a moment. On the tactical channel he transmitted, "Lieutenant Camarotte, if the backup has commandeered a civilian flyer, tell them to get on the ground and come on foot. Peacemaker Zero One, be sure your shields are on full."

Down on his stomach, Colt crawled to the corner of the cargo module. He stuck the top of his helmet out just far enough for the camera to get a shot of the warehouse. A flicker in the battlefield display caught his eye. At that moment the heat source flared and a blaster bolt ripped through the cargo module – anti-spacecraft blaster. The hole it left was only centimeters above his head. He quickly rolled away from the end of the module. Another blast ripped the bottom of the module where he had been.

Royer shouted, "Let's get out of here." He and Colt dashed for the hangar, keeping the cargo module between them and the warehouse. Another blast ripped through the middle of the module as they turned the corner of the hangar.

"Commander," Royer said, "If he wants to, that shooter can take out this whole building us with it." As if in answer to his statement another blast ripped into the hangar. "That was too close! Keep moving!"

As he ran, Colt said, "I think that's what they want. They want to make sure no one is watching what they do next."

"But we have battlefield surveillance," Royer replied.

"The landing craft can't see what's going on inside the building," Colt responded.

Another blast ripped through the hangar.

Royer pulled up. "You're right, sir."

At that moment Corporal McCloud called in, "Gunny, I'm hearing fire from the warehouse. Do you need support?"

"Someone is shooting at us with an anti-spacecraft blaster from a window on the second floor. See if you can take him down, but don't become a casualty yourself," Royer said.

Colt looked at the battlefield image and turned back toward the warehouse. "The heat source in the window has disappeared," he said. Being careful to stay behind cover, he ran back to the wreckage of the cargo module and dropped to the ground. As he watched, the delivery door at the end of the warehouse rolled up. As soon as there was enough clearance, a large van pulled out. Colt reached for his blaster, but it was missing. He quickly looked around and saw the blaster lying a few meters away. It had come loose when he rolled out of the way of blaster fire. He started toward it, but Royer reached it first and tossed it to him. By the time Colt got back to the corner of the module and could see what was happening, the van was almost out of range. Royer started to take a shot with his rifle, but Colt touched his arm. "Hostages," Colt said. He then called Lieutenant Camarotte, "Lieutenant, your display should show a cargo van that just left the warehouse. It may have the rebels aboard. Can you release the landing craft to follow?"

"Will do, Commander. Peacemaker Zero One, did you copy?"

"Yes, sir. Do you want us to take it down?" Camarotte said.

"Don't fire on it unless in self-defense. There may be hostages aboard. Do you have a tractor beam?" Colt asked.

"No, sir. Not this model. The *Invincible* does have a light tug for salvage operations."

"See if you can get it," Colt replied.

Captain Wessler broke in over the long range radio, "I've been following what's going on. The tug is being scrambled now. It should be down in fifteen minutes."

Royer immediately called his squad, "Delta Squad, converge on the warehouse. Don't let anyone leave until we can confirm they aren't the rebels. Be alert for heavy weapons."

Colt watched the pursuit in his battlefield display. The landing craft had no difficulty keeping up with the van. The speed governor on the van kept it at two hundred kilometers per hour, but it quickly crossed the open space around the spaceport. Once over the city, it headed for the commercial district. Before the tug could reach it, someone aboard the landing craft reported, "Six men in armor just bailed out of the van."

The battlefield display in Colt's helmet switched to live video and showed six armored rebels using personal field drive units to descend to the ground. As soon as they touched down, they ran inside a parking structure and disappeared from view.

The van continued straight ahead, apparently on autopilot. Colt switched over to the video from the tug as it swooped down on the van and hauled it in. Overpowering the van's field drive, the tug returned it to the spaceport and held it on the tarmac while a marine squad guardedly approached. There were no hostages.

Chapter 7

Governor General Remarque turned out to be a small man. The top of his head barely reached Colt's chin; still, he dominated the room. "Have a seat, Commander," he said, shaking Colt's hand. "I'm sorry you had to wait. The wedding ceremony ran a little long."

"That's all right, sir. It gave me time to get out of my armor and make sure I only had minor dings," Colt said as he took the indicated chair.

"I heard you were nearly crushed. I'm glad to see you're alive. With your help we have the rebels from the spaceport in custody. Unfortunately, they destroyed the subspace relay and all the other subspace transceivers while they held the port. What exactly happened, anyway?"

Colt described the battle. When he mentioned the RPG that was fired into the Bentley, Remarque asked, "Why the Bentley?"

"We think they were targeting the transceiver. As you know, sir, the Asteroid is a high end private cruiser — a small yacht really. That particular Asteroid had its own subspace transceiver, and the rebels apparently hadn't yet destroyed it."

"What about the rebels who got away? How did they manage that?"

"Once the rebels dumped their armor, they just walked away in the crowd on the street, and no one noticed them."

"What about those hostages at the spaceport?" Remarque asked. "Were they part of the rebel force?"

"That's what we were wondering, sir. They haven't been able to give us a really satisfactory answer. They claim their supervisors told them it was business as usual. Their supervisors claim they said no such thing. My guess is that the rebels made the calls that got them on the field just so they would have potential hostages."

"Any good news?"

"Yes, sir. We were able to get positive DNA samples from the rebel's armor. The Admiralty database matched six former military men and women. Their names are in the report on your desk. Interestingly, there is no record of them being on Corona, but I don't imagine that would be unusual. There's no reason to keep track of everyone who passes through. However, it does suggest that they're mercenaries."

Remarque nodded. "True, the only people who have to register are the ones who want to become citizens. Mercenaries sounds a little ominous though."

"Strangely, none of the rebels we captured seems to know anything about the other six. I'm not sure whether they're really ignorant or are just doing as they were told."

"I suspect it's irrelevant," Remarque replied. "We won't be holding them to interrogate them. They'll all be sent home — without their weapons, of course — as soon as we've identified them and slapped their hands. Of course we'll keep them on record so they can pay restitution after this is all over."

Remarque changed the subject. "Was anyone hurt during all this?"

"No one was seriously injured, sir," Colt answered. "One marine broke an arm and several of the rebels were struck by flying debris, nothing that won't respond to medical treatment."

"Good." Remarque looked at the report on the wall screen. "One thing I have noticed from all this is that the rebels have pretty well cut us off from the rest of the Republic. They even ripped the transceiver out of my personal yacht."

"That seemed to be one of their objectives," Colt agreed. "I'm sure that if you have anything that needs to go out, the *Invincible* can relay it. And I imagine we have enough parts to replace the spaceport transceiver or cobble something together to replace it. Let me check on that."

"I'd appreciate that," Remarque said.

He dropped his gaze from the report and looked at Colt. "So far there's been very little bloodshed from this rebellion, and I'd like to keep it that way," Remarque said. "But it's time to end it. I've put out calls to both sides for a truce and a peace conference. I'd like to see a strong navy presence."

"Yes, sir."

"Also, I'm formally requesting the navy to provide the transportation to pick up the various leaders from all parties. I want to let everyone know we're serious about stopping this useless rebellion, and having the navy on hand to keep the peace should show that."

"That sounds like our job all right," Colt agreed.

"Good. Mr. Wallace, my executive secretary," he indicated the pale man standing beside the desk, "will provide you with the names and locations of the leaders who need to be picked up."

Colt nodded, "We met over the comm circuit when the *Invincible* first called down."

"Good, as soon as we have the details worked out for the conference, we'll send them to you. In the meantime, First Landing has been secured. If your men and women need shore leave, they're welcome to come down."

"Thank you, sir." Colt stood and followed Wallace to the outer office.

As they walked down the corridor, Colt asked, "Are you a former SEAL, Mr. Wallace?"

Wallace stopped and looked at him. "How did you know?"

"Mostly a lucky guess. Your movements suggested someone thoroughly trained in unarmed combat, and you're in a good position to be an unobtrusive bodyguard."

Wallace resumed walking.

Colt continued, "I bring it up because your training may be needed. I'm concerned that Governor General Remarque is minimizing this situation. I don't think what we have here is a friendly game of bridge. I don't suppose I need to remind you to keep on your toes."

"Not at all. I'm concerned too, but as long as the *Invincible* is in orbit, I believe the rebels will mind their manners." Wallace ran his fingers over the keyboard of his desk console.

"I hope you're right," Colt responded.

Wallace picked up several sheets of paper from the printer. "Just in case, this is a printed list of the people we'll invite: names, head shots, coordinates, street addresses, and communicator numbers. I also transmitted a copy to the *Invincible*. Good luck, Commander."

Colt accepted the papers. "Thank you, Mr. Wallace. Keep your eyes and ears open."

###

Aurora had long since set and the inner moon, Selene, hung almost directly overhead just out of the planetary shadow when Colt strode out of the governor general's residence and walked down the stairs to Captain Wessler's personal flyer. He opened the right front door and climbed in. As he turned to the driver, he realized the man was unconscious.

A voice from the back seat said, "Well, Gus. How did it go?" For a split second Colt froze — his heart in his throat. Then the voice registered. He jerked his head around so he could see the man in the back seat.

"Bloody Hell! Fitz, you just about scared the life out of me."

Charles Fitzhugh chuckled. "Sorry about your driver, he'll be around in a few minutes. I just didn't want him to see me. I think you're right that the rebels don't believe this is a bridge game."

"You've got the big man bugged? I guess it shouldn't be a surprise. Can you tell me anything or is this a one-way exchange."

"Just to be on the alert. I do need your help though. Jana Stewart has been taken hostage, and I'm temporarily isolated from my secure link to headquarters. I need you to pass this on to Naval Intelligence." Fitzhugh handed Colt a nanodrive. "Make sure only you and Gretchen see what's on there. Otherwise, there'll be hell to pay."

Fitzhugh opened the left side door. "Well, I can't stick around to socialize. Maybe we can talk later. I'll look you up." And he was gone.

"Did you notice anything odd about Fitzhugh's report on the nanodrive, Gus?" Wessler asked.

"More like what wasn't odd about it," Colt replied.

He and Captain Wessler sat in the briefing room, examining the report Fitzhugh had given him. He looked thoughtful, "Dissidents have their hands on a Royal, and they aren't even making it public? That doesn't make sense. If they don't have her as a hostage, why not? There wasn't much information in the report."

Wessler nodded. "I think the answer to your question is that she knows something they don't want her to tell. If they made any demands based on having her, even to make it look like a simple kidnapping, they risk someone finding her."

"I can buy that, but it also suggests that something is afoot that has to happen fairly soon. They can't hold her for long, even incommunicado, without her family back on Earth demanding she be found." Colt lapsed into silence, his brow wrinkled.

Wessler looked at him expectantly. "I know that look. You've thought of something."

"There's something about this that's familiar. I'm trying to remember what it is."

"You mean about the kidnapping?"

"Yes. Wasn't Jana kidnapped about seven years ago?"

Wessler hesitated. "I vaguely remember that. It didn't amount to much. They found her right away, unharmed."

"Exactly, and they found her because of the way she left clues."

"Like her ring?"

"Not just her ring. When I was her liaison officer she talked to me about it. She left a lot of material, including a recording of the comm call she was following up on, in the safe at the hotel. There was nothing in this report about checking the safe."

"I don't suppose there was something encoded in the report?"

"I wouldn't be surprised, but I doubt it has anything to do with checking the safe."

"So we need to contact Fitzhugh. Do you have a way to contact him?"

Colt shook his head. "Chuck always seems to find me. I don't know how to contact him."

"Well, since Adrian wants us to provide transportation to bring the delegates together for this peace conference, we could use a liaison officer to go along. I'd like you to stand in and see if Fitzhugh contacts you."

"Sounds good to me, Captain."

"You might as well take charge of setting up the transport. I'll leave the details to you, but keep me informed."

Chapter 8

"Good afternoon, Commander Colt. I observe that your firearm plaque is no longer in your quarters." The AI sounded concerned. "Did you remove it while I was down for maintenance?"

"What the hell?" Colt stared at the blank spot on the wall where his Peacemaker plaque had been. "What happened to my forty-five?"

"I beg your pardon, Sir, your what?"

"My forty-five, the pistol on a plaque I had hung on the wall."

"That is what I was reporting, Sir. I was shut down for maintenance from 13:01 until 13:12. It was here before then, and it was no longer here afterwards."

"You mean you didn't see who took it?"

"Sorry, Sir. No. For some reason the room sensors were off at the same time I was down."

"Great," Colt growled. " Call the Provost Marshal for me."

"Provost Marshal." On the screen the petty officer who answered the intercom looked ready to yawn. His nonchalant attitude reminded Colt that the worst the shore patrol had to deal with on ships of the Republic in flight was usually a fight that got out of hand.

Colt clamped down a disciplined calm. "I'm Commander Colt, and I need to report a missing firearm."

The petty officer jumped to alert, "Yes, sir." He touched a pad on his desktop. "All right, sir, I'm recording. Could you start with your name, rank, and service number?"

Colt managed to remain composed as he provided what seemed like far too much trivial information. Finally the petty officer asked, "Now sir, could you describe the firearm?"

"It's a Colt model 1873 single action .45 caliber revolver, known as a Peacemaker."

"I'm sorry, sir, a what?"

"A .45 caliber handgun that shoots bullets. It can be just as deadly as a blaster if used properly. However, I don't believe anyone else aboard has ammunition for it."

The petty officer visibly relaxed. "I see, sir. Why would anyone steal it if it can't be used?"

"It's a collector's item. It's one of the early ones, and very few of them survived The Event."

"I see, sir. Is there anything else I should know about it?"

"The serial number on it is 357849."

"Very well, sir. I'll send an investigator to your cabin immediately. She'll have the paper work with her, ready for you to sign."

As soon as he broke the connection with the provost marshal, Colt forced himself back to work. He called up the details of the pickup. There were twenty-four delegations of two or three people each. Seven would provide their own transportation. That left three separate pickup runs for a C7 class shuttle with VIP seating. Colt contacted flight ops and described the mission. A few minutes later, Tony Orsini was on his screen. "Decker figured it was my turn to take one of the milk runs," he said.

Colt explained the logistics to Orsini and left him in charge of picking the rest of the crew, getting the seating installed, and loading any necessary supplies.

One of the civilian contractors on the *Invincible* was retired Master Chief Petty Officer, Harry Chapman. Chapman had a way with field drive generators that was legendary throughout the navy. Colt decided to take him along as insurance. He dialed Chapman up.

"This should be a routine passenger pickup, Harry, except these are all delegates to the peace conference."

"All VIPs, you mean."

"Yes, but you'll be along to make sure the drives are working, not playing nursemaid to VIPs. I want to get this over without a hitch, and I can't think of anyone better qualified to make that happen."

"Flattery always makes me suspicious," Chapman said. "So why are you on this run?"

"Courier duty."

"Pretty high-ranking courier, Commander."

"I know, but the details are sensitive, and I happen to be the best qualified to take care of them."

"Okay. Sign me up. I could use some shore leave."

The crew Orsini rounded up, including an honor guard of marines, looked to be a good one. Colt made only one change. He released the co-pilot since he planned to be in the right seat. Orsini conducted the briefing while Colt sat in the back of the briefing room.

At zero nine hundred hours Orsini backed the shuttle, Clermont, out of the hangar bay and into space. Wallace had insisted on a final briefing for the crew, so Orsini took the Clermont directly to First Landing spaceport.

They landed mid-afternoon local time. The Home Guard posted a security squad to look after the shuttle, and the liaison officer escorted the entire crew to the Home Guard hangar for the briefing. Wallace gave Colt a dossier that contained backgrounds on every delegate, including personality traits and conflicts. After the briefing Wallace introduced the Home Guard quartermaster who assigned everyone a room in the barracks next door and gave them chits for the mess hall in the barracks building. Colt released the crew with a reminder to keep on their toes and be ready for lift-off for the first run at zero four hundred hours local the next day.

Colt changed into his civvies, called for a cab, and headed downtown. He planned to spend the rest of the afternoon window shopping, making sure he was noticed in case Fitzhugh or someone working for him was watching. He was approaching a store entrance when he saw a familiar face coming from the opposite direction. She was tall and physically fit with short brown hair and green eyes. What drew Colt to look at her was that she wore no makeup and she walked with a distinct military gait. He couldn't place her, but something nibbled at him telling him she was important. He pulled out his communicator and began talking to it as if he were answering a private call. As he turned to look in the window of the shop, he surreptitiously ran a quick video shot of her.

The shop sold communicators and he pretended to study the models in the display window. The window also clearly reflected what was behind him as she walked by. A small tattoo on her neck caught his attention: marine special ops. Colt knew she wasn't from the *Invincible* because he had familiarized himself with the special ops squad.

An image flashed in his mind of former marine sergeant Nancy Hess. She was one of the six rebels who had escaped earlier from the spaceport. She had been given an other-than-honorable discharge for brutalizing a prisoner to get information that allowed her squad to rescue over a dozen civilians who were being held hostage. Colt wondered briefly why she hadn't fought the charge. She was known to have a quick temper and was believed to be working for New Castle Security, a somewhat unorthodox mercenary organization — unorthodox meaning no evidence was available that was acceptable in court.

Colt used his communicator to call Wallace. "I've just run into one of the six rebels who got away at the spaceport. I'm sending her picture now so you can confirm it. Her name is Nancy Hess."

Wallace responded, "I'm getting the video now. That's definitely her."

"Good. Send a squad of Home Guards to pick her up. I'll keep her in sight. Have the squad leader contact me right away. I'm headed south on Centennial."

Hess turned at the next corner and walked east. Mid-block she pulled out her communicator and spoke into it briefly. Putting the communicator away, she began walking faster. Colt continued to follow her, but he was careful to stay back as far as he could to keep her from noticing him. Colt's communicator announced an incoming call from the Home Guard. They were fifteen minutes from his current location.

Hess continued east, passing businesses of various sizes that lined the street. Then she turned south again. Colt became more and more uncomfortable as the number of people on the street decreased, making him feel exposed. A few blocks farther on Hess met a group of people on the corner and stopped to talk with them. Although it seemed innocent, Colt took pictures of the group and forwarded them to the Home Guard squad leader. He pretended to be examining a new model flyer in a dealership lot while he waited for Hess to move on. When she continued down the street, the group began walking his way.

He continued to look at the flyer until they had passed. Just as a harried looking salesman hurried up, Colt turned and headed south again. She was gone. He swore to himself as he started trotting toward the corner. Caution slowed him down before he reached it. Looking to the left and right he saw nothing but an empty street. Then he realized someone was approaching him from behind.

The group who had passed by him at the dealership was coming back. "Are you looking for someone, mister?" The tall man in front said. It had an edge to it.

Colt saw no point in lying. "Yeah, I'm looking for Sergeant Hess."

"Do you know her?" the man asked, a bit surprised.

"Only by reputation; one of the toughest soldiers on the market."

"Do you have business with her?" By then the group had surrounded him and Colt noticed several bulges that were clearly sidearms.

Colt decided that business was as good a cover as any. "That depends. I wouldn't want to be bidding against her current employer."

"Perhaps you should talk to her," a woman said, exposing a blaster.

"If she's willing to see me," Colt responded.

"Oh, she'll see you," the tall man said. "Put your hands on your head. I need to frisk you."

They took his communicator and wallet. The tall man pulled out Colt's ID. "Commander Colt, Royal Navy. Now, why would you want to talk to Sergeant Hess? You know you're on opposite sides, don't you?"

"She's for hire, isn't she?"

"When this gig is over."

The woman showed him Colt's communicator. "His last call was to the Home Guard with a picture of all of us talking."

The man tossed Colt's communicator onto the sidewalk. "You didn't expect to get away with this, did you?"

"I thought I was doing such a good job," Colt answered.

The rebel looked at him. "Oh, you were."

"Then how did you notice me?"

"Never mind," the rebel responded. "Let's go. We don't want to be here when the Home Guard shows up." He caught Colt by the arm and pushed him ahead adding, "Don't do anything stupid."

The commercial buildings ended abruptly and were replaced by older well-kept homes, most with mutated Earth trees surrounding them. A few blocks later the group led Colt up the driveway of a brick house enclosed by a tall, almost impenetrable hedge. They took him behind the house to an outside entrance that led directly into the basement. Downstairs, the tall man turned to one of the others, "Go sit on the porch and keep an eye out for the Home Guard." Then he turned to Colt, "Now what are we going to do with you?"

"For starters, you're going to let me talk to Sergeant Hess."

"Are they?" A woman's voice from the top of the stairs asked.

Colt looked up to see Hess descending the stairs with a faint smile on her face. "You do realize what kind of trouble you're in, don't you, Commander?"

"Trouble?" Colt returned the smile. "I'm here with a business proposition."

"With Home Guard as backup? I don't think so." She said.

"Tall and skinny here says you may be available after this gig. So, I'm in no hurry." Colt replied.

"All right, let's cut the crap." Her smile gave way to a frown. "How did you recognize me?"

"You left DNA in your abandoned armor. I must admit you have a fascinating military record. One blemish got you canned. Why didn't you fight it?"

"I did what I did. I disobeyed orders. I figured the hostages were more important than the creeps who were holding them."

"I can't officially condone what you did, but unofficially I can admire you for the results. But, that's not why I'm here."

"I assume you're really here about yesterday."

"True. But I do have a question. Do you know anything about why someone took a shot at me back on Alsace?"

"How is that relevant?" Hess asked.

"If you knew anything about it you'd know why it's relevant, which I suppose means it isn't relevant."

Hess shook her head. "Enough nonsense. What do you want?"

"You should be able to figure that out. By now you know that all the rebels we picked up yesterday have had their hands slapped and been sent home. You and your cohorts were a little more destructive, so I'm not sure how you'll be handled, but I can promise you we'll be fair."

"You seem to think you're in charge here," she said. "Look who are holding the weapons."

"It does give you a false sense of power, doesn't it? But before I take you in, I have one more question."

"Before you take me in …?" she sputtered.

"Yes." Colt continued as if unperturbed. "Why was it necessary to destroy all the subspace communicators? From what I understand, someone even broke into the governor general's yacht and wrecked his."

"Those were our orders. Even if I knew why, I wouldn't tell you," she said.

"I suspected as much. Well then, shall we go?"

"You act like you expect to get away with this."

Colt smiled. "It was worth a try."

She looked at him for a moment. "I like your sense of humor, but you present a problem." She turned to the tall man, "Tie him up. I'm going to have to contact my commander to see what to do about him." She headed back up the stairs.

The tall man pushed Colt into a wooden chair. Another man tossed him a roll of industrial tape, and he quickly taped Colt to the chair, securing his legs to the chair legs. For good measure he put a piece of tape over Colt's mouth. "That should hold you." He beckoned to the rest and led them upstairs.

As Colt's ears became accustomed to the quiet, he began catching snatches of the conversations upstairs.

" … get all the weapons into carrying cases …"

" … make sure we haven't left anything the Guard can trace to us …"

Then he heard Hess say something that chilled him, "I don't like this either but my orders are to torch the house with Commander Colt in it. Get everybody out of here. I'll set the fires."

Colt struggled against the tape, but it held firm. He could barely move. He looked around for something sharp. There was nothing in sight. He rocked the chair back and forth and noticed it wasn't as solid as he originally thought. Pushing back as hard as he could he managed to tilt the chair over, banging his head against the concrete floor.

After his head stopped swimming, he smelled the first traces of smoke and frantically began flexing the chair. Adrenalin gave him the extra strength he needed to wiggle the joints of the chair loose. The seat broke away from the back first. Then the front legs came loose, allowing him to roll over, but with his arms securely taped to the chair arms he couldn't push himself upright.

He paused for a second to catch his breath. Then he backed over his knees to get his weight far enough back so the rear chair legs would touch the floor. Before he could get his feet under him, a pair of hands caught his shoulders. He froze.

"Here let me help," Hess said as she helped him to his feet. "I don't kill people unnecessarily, orders or no. And this would be just plain cruel. Let's get you out of here." She urged him up the back stairs. "I'm going to leave your arms taped up so you don't try anything heroic."

Outside, she said, "Stay down and head toward the back of the lot. Some of the rebels I'm working with are trigger happy. I'd hate to have wasted my effort." She turned and raced around the house, dodging flames as one of the windows exploded outward.

###

As soon as he was clear of the fire, Colt stopped and watched as the interior of the house was engulfed in flames. The fire department arrived on the scene almost immediately and had the fire under control before the surrounding trees were more than scorched. One of the firemen saw Colt standing behind the house and approached him. "Here let me get that tape off you." As he worked, he asked, "Did you see what happened?"

"Yeah. I was inside. It was a rebel safe house. They burned it to get rid of the evidence."

The fireman signaled a policeman over. "This man says he was inside when the fire started. He says it was set by the rebels."

The policeman looked suspiciously at Colt. "What were you doing inside?"

"I was being held prisoner."

"Uh-huh. Could I see some identification?"

Colt frowned. "Okay, this is going the wrong way. I'm Commander William Colt of the HMS *Invincible*. Could you call Captain Savakis of the Home Guard and tell him where I am? He should be nearby looking for me."

The policeman looked skeptical but pulled out his communicator. A few minutes later Savakis and his squad landed nearby.

Savakis walked up. "Commander Colt, I'm glad to see you're all right." He produced Colt's communicator and wallet. "When we found these, we were afraid something drastic had happened to you."

Colt accepted them with thanks. "It appears I got a little closer to the rebels than I intended."

Chapter 9

After debriefing with Savakis and with Captain Wessler, Colt cleaned up and headed back downtown. Early that evening he found himself in front of Mama Louisa's café. It advertised genuine northern Italian cuisine. After looking the café over Colt decided it offered the privacy Fitzhugh would need for them to meet. Human staff rather than an AI ran the café. A waiter showed him to a booth in the back. As he read the menu, his communicator buzzed.

"Gus, the situation down there seems quiet for now, so I'm letting some of the crew have time off," Wessler said. "They'll be coming down in two of the C-7s in about a half hour."

"Anything I need to do?"

"No, I just wanted to keep you apprised. How are things going?"

"We're in place. The Home Guard is watching the Clermont, and I gave the crew the evening off rather than having them twiddle their thumbs in the barracks. We'll start our first run at zero four hundred local tomorrow."

"Any sign of Fitzhugh?"

"Not yet. He has a penchant for surprise. I don't expect to see him until he slides into the seat across from me."

"Commander, mind if I join you?" The voice came from behind him. He almost dropped the communicator as he jerked around. Harry Chapman stood there, looking somewhat bemused. "Did I interrupt something?"

"Have a seat, Harry. I was just talking to the captain. Excuse me for just a moment." He spoke into the communicator. "Anything else, Captain?"

"That's it for now, Gus. Keep me informed if anything happens."

"Will do. Out"

"You expecting trouble, Commander?" Chapman asked.

"No. But a couple of shuttles are coming down from the ship for shore leave. Wouldn't want something nasty happening."

"I'm not sure shore leave is such a good idea. My contacts tell me that there are rebels on every street corner. Something serious is going down."

"Nothing specific, I suppose?"

"Sorry, Commander, that's all they could tell me."

"Well, the conference is supposed to start tomorrow. They may be assembling in case it doesn't go their way. I suppose I should notify Wallace."

"Don't bother. I talked to some of his people. They know as much as I do."

"That's interesting. I wonder why he didn't brief us."

"Well, he did say to be alert."

At that moment a man looking suspiciously like Fitzhugh stepped in the front door, looked briefly past Colt, and walked back outside. Colt saw him but couldn't do anything about it with Chapman there. And he knew it was useless to go outside after him. "Damn," Colt said under his breath.

"Something wrong, Commander?"

"Oh, I had just hoped for once things would go smoothly." He grinned. "Did any of your contacts have anything useful to say about this café? I was about to order, and I haven't found anything on the menu I recognize. Where's good old pizza when you need it?"

Chapman stuck around until after the meal, listening to Colt's story of his encounter with Sergeant Hess and offering observations on the local situation. He even identified some of the rebels in the café. If Colt hadn't been so preoccupied with making contact with Fitzhugh, some of what he heard would have made him more than a little uncomfortable. He managed to show a polite interest, but it wasn't until later that Chapman's words soaked in.

As they got up to leave, Chapman said, "Well, Commander, it was a pleasure getting to know you. I'm going to head on back to the barracks."

"It was good talking to you, Harry. See you in the morning."

Chapman was flagging down a cab when Colt started down the street looking for a suitable bar. He immediately found McGinty's on the next corner. He swallowed a Buzz-Off tablet and pushed his way through the heavy wooden door.

McGinty's, as the name implied, turned out to be modeled after an old Irish pub. Dark stained wooden booths lined one wall, most of them full. The bar occupied nearly all of the other side. At the back hung a dartboard where several patrons played. The current champion appeared to be a young woman. As Colt walked in she was accepting money from a man who looked as if he was having a hard time being a good loser. Colt took a seat near the end of the bar so he could watch the action.

"What'll it be, sailor?" The publican had a strong Irish accent. Colt couldn't tell whether it was genuine or affected. The man leaned on his hands on the edge of the bar, looking Colt in the eye.

"I'll have a pint," Colt replied. "How'd you know I'm in the navy?"

"There've been a bunch of you in here this evening. You seemed to fit the mold. A pint of McGinty's comin' up." He walked to the pump and deftly filled the glass from the spout.

As the publican set the glass down, Colt pulled out his wallet, "What do I owe you?"

"Three quid."

Colt gave him a five credit note. "Keep the rest," he said. "Have you seen a lot of strangers in here?"

"Yeah, this is a great tourist spot. Of course, since the separatists started causing trouble, the number of tourists has really been down. You sailors are the biggest crowd of visitors we've had in months."

"Well, I'm glad we can help the local economy. My name's Gus Colt."

"Pleased to meet you, Gus Colt. I'm Seamus McGinty." He reached across the bar and accepted Colt's hand. "The navy comin' to town in force?"

"I'm afraid not. We're rotating some of the crew through on shore leave, but the *Invincible* will stay in orbit." As Colt spoke, a man slid onto the stool next to him.

"Seamus," the man said.

McGinty acknowledged the new arrival with a smile. "Dennis. The usual?"

"Aye."

McGinty looked at Colt. "Gus, this is Dennis O'Toole. Dennis, this is Gus Colt. I'll be back in a nod."

Colt turned to face the burly redhead and accepted his extended hand. Fitzhugh!

"It's a pleasure to make your acquaintance, admiral," Fitzhugh said.

"The pleasure is mine," Colt managed to respond. "You know, your name is familiar. I think Jana Stewart mentioned you as some of the local color."

"She would." Fitzhugh looked briefly annoyed. "How is Jana? I haven't seen her in ages."

"To be honest I don't know. I haven't seen her except on the news since I left Bremerhaven."

Seamus returned with another glass of McGinty's. "Your regular," he announced. "You two look like old friends."

"Common friend as it turns out," Colt said. "Unfortunately, neither of us has seen her recently."

Seamus eyed Fitzhugh suspiciously. "Another young beauty, I'd bet. Dennis, how do you do it?"

Fitzhugh took a swallow of his ale. "Pheromones," he said, wiping his mouth with the back of his sleeve.

McGinty laughed and walked away.

Colt turned to Fitzhugh. "You know, the last time I talked to Jana she said she was leaving something for me in her hotel safe. Trouble is I don't have time to check on it for now. It sounded urgent, but it'll have to wait until I get through with this chauffer duty."

"Chauffer?"

"Yeah, I'm riding shotgun on a mission to shuttle delegates to the peace conference," Colt responded.

"That sounds like a cushy job. Of course, cushy jobs can't be taken for granted, can they?"

"Well, there are the usual safety concerns, but we have great maintenance and a well-qualified crew."

Fitzhugh nodded. "I'm sure, but I was thinking in terms of the local opposition. There are rumors that they don't want a peace conference."

"I'm not surprised." Colt sipped his ale.

When Fitzhugh had finished his drink, he put the glass on the counter, and stood up. "Well, admiral, nice meeting you. Maybe you can give me a call sometime." He handed Colt a business card and waved to McGinty. "Seamus, I've got to run. See you next time." He shook Colt's hand and headed for the door.

Colt took another swallow of his ale, glanced at the card and put it in his pocket. Looking surprised by the time on his watch, he hurriedly got up. He gave McGinty a mock salute and headed for the door.

It had started to rain. Big drops spattered in the dust on the sidewalk, leaving splash rings. Colt flicked on his repeller field as the rain turned to a downpour. He stepped outside to flag a cab.

Two men came staggering down the sidewalk, singing drunkenly. The hairs on the back of Colt's neck stood on end. Without making it obvious, he changed to a fighting stance. The repeller field wasn't designed to keep out slow moving objects, and one of the men staggered into him. "'Scuse me," the man slurred.

Colt felt an arm tighten around his waist and immediately sprang away. Turning to face both men, he shifted into a crouch. A stainless steel blade glittered in one of the attacker's hands. The other attacker drew a blaster but held his fire. It was useless against Colt's repeller field. The knife was another matter.

The first attacker charged. Colt managed to parry the knife arm. The blow knocked the knife flying. With his outstretched left leg he tripped the man, sending him sprawling on his face in the street. Colt then turned back to focus on the attacker with the blaster. The man backed away as Colt approached when a sudden blow across his back sent Colt stumbling forward. He could see the muzzle of the blaster come up and penetrate the repeller, and he threw himself to the side just as the blaster went off. Heat from the bolt stung his cheek, and he heard the other attacker scream.

Colt swung his foot in an arc that connected with the shooter's stomach. The man doubled over. The blaster flew from his hand. He fell backward against the door to the pub and lay still on the sidewalk.

Colt turned to the other man. He was lying on the sidewalk clutching his arm. As Colt picked up the knife and blaster, McGinty stuck his head out of the pub.

"What the Bloody Hell?"

"Sorry for the disturbance, Seamus. Would you mind calling the constabulary?"

"I'll get right on it."

Colt propped both men against the side of the building. He checked the one man's wound noting that the blaster had grazed his arm, leaving a nasty burn, but had not done serious harm. Colt stood back and guarded the two until the police arrived. Several of McGinty's patrons stepped out of the pub to see what the disturbance was about, but they stayed clear of Colt.

He kept looking over his shoulder to make sure no one else was sneaking up on him.

Chapter 10

"Interesting fracas last night, skipper," Harry Chapman commented as he stood with Colt watching the crew inspect the Clermont.

"Which one?" Colt asked.

"There was more than one? I was talking about the group who tried to storm the base's main gate. What was the other one?"

"Oh, a couple of locals objected to me being on their streets. The constabulary said they were known muggers who had managed to escape prosecution up until now."

"I gather they got the worst of it."

"Yeah."

Harry took out the toothpick he had been chewing on and looked at the frayed end for a second. "I was thinking about that attack on the gate because it wasn't very effective — other than it drew the guards away from the Clermont."

Colt nodded. "That's why Orsini has the crew giving her an extra going over, even though the sensors don't show that anybody was able to get aboard."

At that moment the crewman who had been examining the keel called out, "Got something!"

The something turned out to be a stick-on limpet mine painted to match the Clermont's heat shield. Orsini called the bomb squad in to remove it. The amount of explosive in the mine turned out to be small. It probably would have penetrated the hull, but it was unlikely to disable the shuttle. Colt felt there was something wrong with that, but the remainder of the inspection turned up nothing else.

Orsini came up. "I don't know, Gus. The inspection is complete, but I have to admit I'm not happy. I get the feeling we're supposed to think that the explosive was that easy to find because the intruders were in a hurry. It would certainly look that way, but I'm wondering if it was a red herring."

Colt nodded. "You think there's another explosive on the Clermont? But the sniffers didn't find anything else, and the rest of the hull was clean."

"Yeah, I guess I'm just being paranoid."

"No, I get the same feeling. If we could sit here on the ground another day, I wouldn't mind field stripping this thing to be sure, but we don't have enough indicators that there might be another bomb. I think you've made a reasonable inspection, and we need to get going. We can't cancel this mission on intuition."

"I suppose you're right," Orsini sighed. He turned back toward the Clermont. "Chief Juneuil, let's saddle up," he shouted.

Colt followed the last crewmember aboard and closed the hatch before going forward to the cockpit. He slid into the right seat, attached his harness, grabbed his headset, and began prepping for takeoff. Pulling the checklist binder out of the pouch under the seat, he started reading it to Orsini. They quickly made the rounds of the small cockpit, checking switches, circuit breakers, controls, and displays. When they had finished, Colt keyed the intercom, "Cockpit check complete. Engineering?"

"Engineering, complete."

"Cabin?"

"Cabin, complete."

Looking at Orsini, Colt said, "Secure for lift off."

Colt switched to the ground control radio. "First Landing Ground Control, this is Diplomat Zero One for departure clearance."

"Roger, Zero One. Your flight plan is approved as filed. You are cleared to take off from your present position. Contact departure control on two five three point five."

"Thanks for your assistance. Going to departure control."

By the time the Clermont touched down in Woomera, Colt had started to relax. They were scheduled to pick up the final three teams of negotiators; one from a loyalist group and two from separatist groups. The first to arrive were separatists, and they were fifteen minutes late. The leader, Billy Hargety, was unapologetic. He stormed up the gangway and became outraged when the security guard stopped him and his three cohorts.

"What's going on, Sergeant?" Colt asked when he arrived to check on the disturbance.

The marine sergeant snapped to attention. "Sir, I have Mr. Hargety on the manifest, but not the other three men. Also, they are carrying weapons, which are specifically prohibited."

Colt quickly took in that all four men were wearing side arms. Hargety carried an especially nasty looking PPK Iridium blaster. Colt looked him in the eye, "Mr. Hargety. The sergeant is absolutely right. Is there some compelling reason for bringing three extra people along?"

"Mr. Dubrovich is taking the place of Fred Kim, my chief of staff, who is on the manifest. Mr. Yakullo is my communication expert, and Mr. Friedman is my lawyer. I can't be expected to make decisions without input from my associates."

"The last time I checked, the global comm system was functioning within reasonable parameters."

"Some of my associates don't have the utmost confidence in the planetary government at this time. They are concerned – and quite reasonably – that the Home Guard will trace the calls and try to pick them up. Whereas, if we contact them with a radio broadcast, receivers can't be traced."

"Let me see if I have this straight. Your other associates aren't willing to talk to you on the web because they're concerned the call will be traced and they will be arrested. Instead, Mr. Yakullo will go to the negotiations and act as a relay between you and them by encrypted radio. In other words, you aren't concerned about Mr. Yakullo being picked up by the militia. Is there any reason Mr. Yakullo couldn't stay in contact with you on the web and relay from here? That way he could perform the same function without taking up valuable space on the shuttle and at the negotiating table."

Hargety started to reply and stopped.

Colt continued, "Likewise, Mr. Friedman can advise you from here via the web, can't he? Now, as for the weapons, if you really feel you must have them with you, fine. However, while you are on the Clermont, they will be locked in the weapons case, and when you get to the conference, the Home Guard will hold them until you return home. Please hand them over to Sergeant Jiracek. They'll be returned when you debark back here."

Hargety fumed but removed his holster and handed it and the pistol over to Jiracek. Dubrovich followed suit. The sergeant quickly snapped open the handle of Hargety's PPK, dumping the iridium charge into his hand. Dubrovich handed over a pocket-size Franklin two-phase. Jiracek released the energy pack, adding it to the iridium charge.

"Get the link set up as soon as we leave," Hargety said to Yakullo, "I'll call you when I get there, and tell you how to proceed."

Colt backed out of the hatch and stood aside to let Hargety into the shuttle. "Your party was blocked for row two, seats E and F. As soon as the rest of the latecomers arrive, we'll be ready to go."

He turned to Jiracek. "I'll take your watch while you stow the pistol and blaster, Sergeant." He frowned at the Franklin as the sergeant moved past him. On full power, that little piece of nastiness could take out a big chunk of the shuttle's pressure hull.

The loyalists arrived almost as soon as Hargety and Dubrovich had taken their seats. Falconetti and his aide arrived together five minutes later. Both parties were without weapons or associates.

About fifteen minutes after leaving Woomera, Colt had to put down a near riot when the loyalists started tossing insults at the separatists. Standing at the front of the passenger cabin, he barked, "That's enough!" into the intercom, with the volume set high enough to make ears bleed. The voices subsided abruptly, and they all turned to look at him. Colt glared at both sides. "I feel like a nursemaid to a bunch of school kids. You're supposed to be here to work out an agreement … a peace agreement, and that's what you're going to do. Sergeant Jiracek, if anyone starts anything before we land, you have my permission to stun any and all of them, as you see fit."

He turned and stepped back into the cockpit, dropped into his seat, and slid on his headset.

He heard Orsini swear, "What the hell?"

Colt didn't have to ask what the problem was. He had heard the crash of static and the following silence on the radio. He triggered his microphone. "*Invincible*, this is Diplomat Zero One, radio check, over."

While he waited for an answer, he glanced at his other instruments and the sensor display. What he saw was chilling. The guidance beacon from the *Invincible* was off the air and the sensor scan through the volume where she was supposed to be showed nothing but a rapidly expanding cloud of hot debris and gas. He felt his gut twisting. He whispered, "My God! What happened? Where's the *Invincible*?"

He didn't have time to think about it. Almost immediately the Clermont's master caution light flashed on. At the same time the warning horn began blaring in his ear. From the right seat Colt shot a glance at Orsini. Only two lights showed on the panel: the master caution and a steady, bright red, main drive light. Then the shuttle dropped suddenly, just as the red light for the emergency drive flashed on. Both drives were dead.

Colt looked at the pilot. Orsini was frozen. Colt saw the wide eyes and the white knuckles on the controls. This was no time to coddle him. "Tony, get yourself together!" he barked. "Come on, man. Now!"

Orsini shook his head, and reflexes took over. He pulled the wing controls to fully extended, slapped the master caution light to shut it off, and began easing back on the control stick on his right armrest. As the wings deployed, the near free-fall sensation was replaced by planetary gravity. While Orsini worked to set up the glide, Colt had pulled out the emergency checklist. He rapidly read off the emergency actions while Orsini responded. "Master Caution – Reset. Fully extend wings. Establish optimum glide. Altitude permitting, select emergency landing site. WARNING: Do not attempt to turn back to the take-off site unless above 5000 meters altitude."

Colt tuned the radio to the standard emergency channel and quickly broadcast their situation and position. Traffic control acknowledged and asked for details. Colt scanned the instrument panel. All the gages were normal except the electrical power gages for the drives. Both the voltage and the wattage read zero. Colt stabbed the main drive power reset button. The gages didn't quiver. Colt keyed the radio. "The power to both drives is out. No other indication. Thirty two souls on board. I'll get back to you as soon as I can." He stood up and pulled open the doorway to the main cabin. He quickly spotted Chapman.

"Harry, we've lost all power to the drives. Get back to the engine bay and see if you can get us some juice."

Falconetti lurched up out of his seat. "We've lost power to the drives?" he shrilled.

"Sit down, Mr. Falconetti," Colt commanded. "Mr. Orsini has things under control. It won't help if you go into a panic."

Colt's voice stopped Falconetti. He slowly lowered himself back into his seat.

Colt returned to his seat and began looking at the ground for a suitable place to make an emergency landing. A discouraging vista met his gaze. Sharply mountainous terrain greeted him with towering peaks and ridges, steep sided canyons, and either large boulders or heavy tree cover almost everywhere. They would need more than half a kilometer of open space to put the shuttle down. As the seconds ticked by he could find only one area that looked remotely like a landing spot, a narrow valley with a short open field in it. "Tony, there's a valley about ten o'clock. See it?"

"I've got it." Orsini gently banked the shuttle to the left, steering for the valley. When he did, the valley dropped downward in the windscreen going below the glide angle projection in the head up display—a good sign. As long as it stayed there, they could make it.

A moment later Chapman called on the intercom, "No go, boss."

"What the hell happened, Harry?"

"Some kind of acid. It ate through both power busses to the drive units."

"Damn! Is there any way you can repair either buss?"

"There's some spare wire in here. I might be able to twist enough together to carry a little current."

"Give it a try. In the meantime we're going to work on putting this hummer down in one piece."

Colt toggled six short rings for the emergency landing warning. Then he keyed the intercom. "This is the first officer speaking. We have lost power to the main drive and are forced to make an emergency landing. This is going to be rough, so quickly stow any loose objects, make sure your safety harness is secure, and prepare for impact. I'll turn the warning bell on steady just before we touch down."

Directly below, a river rushed through a rock-walled canyon. The rim of the canyon reached up toward them as they rapidly approached. If they could clear it, the terrain on the other side looked less formidable. The ground sloped downward away from the canyon offering a short stretch of open meadow dotted with small trees. With luck they could walk away from the landing.

Orsini adjusted the heading as the wind shifted, keeping the flight path aimed at the open area. Colt watched the sink rate for a split second. It looked as if the shuttle would barely clear the ridge. The meadow might just be close enough to make it.

But the wind switched to a head wind, and Colt watched with dismay as the touch down point on the head up display began to move closer to the edge of the canyon. The touch down point kept moving back. Soon it reached the lip of the canyon and began creeping down into the canyon. They were too close to the ground to risk any but the smallest of corrections. The only choice appeared to be a desperate last-second attempt to pancake into the front side of the ridge instead of hitting it head on.

Colt tensed, ready for Orsini to pull the nose up at the last minute. Again the wind shifted. The touch down point started back up. The wind was now giving them a nudge from behind, but it wasn't enough.

Chapman broke in on the intercom, "We have a little power, but don't use much. Ease it on, and I'll yell if the wires start glowing."

The little bit of drive was just enough. The ridge slid by less than five meters under the shuttle. Orsini began easing the nose up, saving precious altitude and bleeding off airspeed. Branches scraped the bottom, but the craft cleared the trees at the edge of the meadow. The shuttle lurched. Then Chapman's voice came over the intercom, "I hope you don't need power anymore."

Trying to say it as calmly as if it would be a normal landing, Colt tripped the warning bell and called into the intercom, "Brace for impact!"

Chapter 11

Colt slapped the gear handle down. The landing gear slammed into place, and almost simultaneously the wheels hit the rough surface of the meadow. Despite full aft controls the force of the contact brought the front of the shuttle down hard, shearing off the nose gear. As Orsini fought to keep his feet on the rudder pedals, trying to steer around obstacles, the shuttle plowed through the hummocks of grass and small boulders, spraying dirt and rocks over the windscreen. They were slowing down, and full right rudder could no longer keep them going straight. The craft started a drifting turn to the left. The left wing smashed into a tree trunk, ripping most of wing off and spinning the craft around in a slow-motion pirouette. The tail slammed into a boulder, reversing the rotation. The impact bounced the nose of the craft several meters in the air and swung the right wing into a stand of trees. The trees shattered, smashing the wing against the fuselage. The shuttle scraped to a stop, still upright.

Colt glanced at Orsini to make sure he was okay. He looked dazed and his nose was bleeding, but he was releasing his harness. "All right!" Colt bellowed into the intercom. "Everyone get out of the shuttle and take cover, immediately! Let's move it!"

The crewmen opened the emergency exits, but many of the rattled passengers had trouble freeing their restraints. Orsini and Colt worked their way back through the cabin releasing seat belts and shoulder harnesses. At each seat they checked under the cushions, pulling out whatever survival gear they could find and passing it along to the crewmen at the exits. At the back of the cabin Colt opened the weapons locker and handed out the weapons, instructing the crew to hold on to them. Finally, when the last passenger had exited, he grabbed the first aid kit and jumped out the aft door. Orsini followed him.

They hit the ground next to Chapman and dropped into a crouch. Colt said quietly, "We may not have much time, Harry. Have you seen a good place to get under cover?"

"There's a small gulch about fifty meters that way," Chapman said, pointing into the trees.

"That'll have to do. Let's get everyone into it." He stood up and shouted. "Everybody, let's go! There's a gully behind those trees. Get in it and get down! Now!"

The frightened passengers hesitated, but the crewmen quickly prodded them into running. When everyone had reached the gully, Colt signaled to two crewmen to take up guard positions. Then he ran a check for injuries. They had been fortunate: a concussion, some serious bruises, and some cuts, but no broken bones. He left the first aid kit in the hands of Chief Petty Officer Linda Juneuil and crawled up the side of the gully beside Sergeant Jiracek to take a look. Just as he stuck his head above the edge, Jiracek said, "We've got company, sir. Looks like a troop carrier just over that mountain to the south." He pointed to a dark spot in the sky that was growing rapidly and handed Colt his binoculars.

Colt quickly spotted the craft. "That was fast," he said. "They were definitely ready for this. At least, there only seems to be one of them." He turned and called back into the gully, "Tony, get everyone under an IR blanket. Pronto!"

By the time he looked back, the troop carrier, a standard Patton armored carrier, painted mottled desert browns and tans with a sky blue belly, had become visible to the naked eye. The stubby cigar shape flew directly to the clearing, landing about seventy-five meters away. The doors on both sides split open, the bottom half dropping down to form a ramp and the other half swinging up over the top and out of the way.

With the doors open Colt could see through the craft. He counted sixteen armed men as they sauntered nonchalantly down the ramp doors. They were wearing civilian clothes, but each of them held a serious looking blaster, including a couple of heavy-duty anti-spacecraft units. The men quickly split into three teams and spread out. One group took cover in the scrubby trees and brush across the clearing. The other two began circling to the left and right to close in on the downed shuttle. The troop carrier closed its side doors and lifted off. It rose to about fifty meters and began hovering.

"I counted sixteen, five in the group to the west. Six to the east. And five in the group over in the tree line," Colt said.

"That's what I saw, sir," Jiracek said. "They don't seem to be very well trained," he added, watching them straggle across the clearing.

"Maybe we can take advantage of that," Colt said. "Stay here and let us know if they start getting too close." He slid back into the gully.

"Leslie! Juneuil! Buchanan!" He flagged the ensign and two crewmen over. "Ensign Leslie, have you ever led a squad in combat?"

She shook her head. "But I led the squad that took the commander's trophy my last summer camp at the academy."

"That should put you head and shoulders above these clowns. Follow me back to the top so we can all get a look. And keep down." Colt scrambled back to the rim with the other three close behind. "Okay. We have at least sixteen moving into the meadow to clean up. They have weapons, and they have the troop carrier as a lookout and for fire support. We have a few handguns. They'll check the shuttle first, which will give us a few minutes. What we need to do is isolate one group of them and take them out so we can get their heavy weapons."

"The group on the south is staying back in the brush for cover," Leslie said. "And this gully wraps around to that side about twenty meters west of them. It looks to be out of view from the carrier. If we head out now, we can get across while they're still concentrating on the shuttle."

Colt signaled Orsini over. "Tony, you're in charge here. Make sure these people – all of them – keep down and quiet. You're authorized to use force if necessary."

He turned back to the team. "Let's do it! Buchanan, you're point. Be on guard for a sentry watching the gully, and keep an eye on the carrier. Move out!"

Minutes later they had worked their way in behind their targets. Leading the way, Buchanan scrambled up the side of the gully. Then he kept watch as Leslie repeated the process. As Chief Juneuil moved to join them, she stepped on a loose rock. It gave way, pitching her forward noisily onto her hands and knees. Colt waved everyone to the ground and stuck his head up just far enough to see if anyone was looking their way. Their group of searchers were

66

squatting or sitting in the brush, intently watching the others work their way in on the downed shuttle. Colt gave the okay signal. Buchanan took a final look over the edge of the gully. Then he signaled to move ahead. They crawled out of the gully on their stomachs.

Through the brush and clumps of grass they could see all five of the searchers spread out along the tree line. One of the searchers stood up. "Hey, I've got to answer the call. I'll be right back."

Leslie whispered, "I've got him," and slipped into the brush. Colt nodded appreciatively at how quietly she disappeared. Moments later she appeared carrying two blasters. She handed one to Colt.

"That was fast," Colt said.

She held up a hypo-spray. "Somnolene. He'll be out for at least four hours."

Colt turned to the others. Gesturing as he spoke, "Juneuil, you take the one on the west end. Buchanan, take the one next to him. Leslie, since you have that hypo, take the one with the heavy blaster. You can get to him in spite of the energy pack he's wearing. I'll take the one on the far end. Check your watches. Hit them in one minute from my mark … Mark!"

The four spread out and moved forward quietly through the brush. Colt came up behind the man on the east end just as he turned his head to call down the line, "What's keeping Mike?" Then he saw Colt. His eyes opened wide and he started to swing his blast rifle around.

Colt brought his blaster into view, pointing it right between the man's eyes while holding the index finger of his left hand to his lips. He reached out with his left hand to take the blast rifle away. As he was motioning the man to lie down, he heard a grunt from his left. Ensign Leslie had taken care of the heavy fireworks. Then a yelp and the rasp of a blaster broke the quiet. The bolt had been fired skyward, but it was enough to alert the other search teams. They all dove into the deep grass. A moment later he heard Leslie whisper, "We've got all these guys secured, sir."

Colt focused his attention on the carrier. It started turning in their direction, its two forward cannons swinging ominously toward them. "Take out the carrier's guns," he shouted to Leslie.

From his left Leslie fired two quick blaster bolts from the heavy blaster. Each one took out a cannon, leaving blackened petals of metal in their place. The carrier slewed around and headed for the other searchers on the ground, the crew doors opening as it set down. The two groups scrambled aboard the carrier, climbing over each other in their panic.

"Sir, they're getting away!" Buchanan shouted.

"Let them. We can't stop them without destroying the carrier, and we don't have the manpower to guard them." Colt turned to Leslie. "Ensign, hit them with a couple of low charges when they get airborne to let them know how vulnerable they are."

As the carrier took off Leslie got in two quick shots, the widespread charges coruscating harmlessly off the closing crew doors. Then the carrier turned away at high acceleration. When it paused a few kilometers out, Colt said, "One more low charge amidships."

The charge sparkled across the closed troop doors. The carrier immediately accelerated away, ducking behind a ridge.

As the team trotted back, Colt reviewed the situation. It didn't look good. Whoever had sabotaged the Clermont had the foresight to send a cleanup team. They would certainly be back with a bigger team to finish the job and soon. The crew and passengers needed to get farther down the mountain and under heavy tree cover quickly. The IR sensors wouldn't be as effective if the quarry were in the trees.

He spoke into his communicator. "Tony, get everyone on their feet. We need to move out."

Colt half-slid, half-ran down the side of the gully, coming to a stop at the bottom. Hargety stormed up and planted himself in front of Colt. Hargety angrily demanded, "Sir! What is going on? The Royal Navy is supposed to be supporting peace talks, and you can't even keep us safe getting to them!"

"Mr. Hargety, unfortunately we don't have time for discussion right now. Our immediate need is to get off this mountain."

Leslie walked up. "Sir, the prisoners have been secured."

Colt turned to her. "Thank you, Ensign. Take another crewmember and bring up the rear. Keep an eye out for any returning air or ground troops." He raised his voice. "Buchanan, you've got point again. Find us a path these civilians can handle and take us down. Saddle up, people."

"You can at least arm us," Hargety grumbled.

"No, Mr. Hargety, leave the military functions to the military. Right now we need to move out."

The group straggled down the gully, grumbling. Where the gully finally broadened out and joined the valley, Buchanan found a well-worn trail. A few minutes later they entered a deep forest. The heavy leaf cover looked to be thick enough to shield them from sensor detection, so Colt called a halt.

"Ladies and Gentlemen, you're probably wondering why I asked you all together here." The joke did nothing to lighten the mood. "All right, it appears someone doesn't want us to reach the conference. If they were one of the two groups onboard, they were willing to sacrifice their own people. So, unless you have a suicidal bent, whether they were yours or not, you can't be very happy with them. You'll also notice they came looking for us. I'll leave it up to your imagination as to whether they planned to take us alive. At the moment we're out of their reach. The tree canopy will prevent their sensors from detecting us for a while, but I expect them to pursue us on foot as well as maintain an aerial watch. Our best bet is to get off this mountain and to a settlement before they find us. The nearest settlement is Sykesville, but if they really want us, they'll be waiting for us when we come out of the trees. Birchland is almost as close, but it's in the trees."

Hargety interrupted, "Birchland is also over a steep ridge, not down an easy to navigate valley."

"Interesting that you'd know our position so well, Mr. Hargety. You're correct. Getting to Birchland will take more effort, but it also will be safer."

"I'm not about to climb another mountain."

"You're certainly welcome to continue down this valley to Sykesville if that's your desire, Mr. Hargety."

Several other voices chimed in with comments such as, "I don't want to climb" and "I'm not wearing the right shoes for it."

Colt continued, "However, anyone who goes down this valley does so without weapons. It should be safe enough as long as the saboteurs aren't interested in killing you."

"Now wait a minute!" someone shouted.

"Look, we don't know what their purpose was, but I don't think these guys want us to talk to anyone anytime soon. I believe we stand a reasonable chance if we head to Birchland, but I'm not about to give up weapons to someone who might turn them on us. You have a choice, go with us or go unarmed."

Interlude

"Mr. Quan is here, Ms. Phillips," the receptionist announced on the intercom.

"Send him in."

Quan looked flushed, and he was out of breath. He strode rapidly across the room toward her desk. As soon as the door clicked closed he said, "We may have gotten a reprieve. I just heard that the *Invincible* was blown up."

"What?" McKillip surged upward from her chair. "That's horrible! Do you know how many people were on the *Invincible*?"

Quan looked unimpressed. "I heard it was over a thousand."

"More like forty-five hundred! What happened?"

"We're not sure. Space traffic control said they lost radio contact with it and the shuttle Natchez Belle around eight this morning. When they checked the volume with sensors, there was a cloud of ionized gas and nothing else. The governor general's yacht has been dispatched to get a closer look."

"The governor general? I should have been read in." McKillip sputtered. "After all, I am the defense minister, and that sounds like hostile military action in our space."

Quan glanced at her display wall. "Are you hooked into the defense net here?"

"No. It's not officially secure."

"That might explain it. Check the news stream."

" ... Once again, we are getting reports that say the *HMS Invincible* has disappeared from sensor coverage," the reporter said. "There has been no official confirmation. Stay tuned for more news as it becomes available. Now back to ... ."

The local GNN link was just starting on a repeat of the story, but they had no more information than Quan had been able to give. When they switched to a reporter who had dredged up irrelevant facts about the *Invincible* and her crew, McKillip closed the link. She rose from her chair. "Looks like I need to get back to the ministry office and find out if anyone actually knows anything." She looked at Quan. "Did you have anything else?"

"Just that we need to take advantage of this."

McKillip gave him a hard look and grumbled, "I suppose you're right. You figure something out while I check in with the ministry." She walked out of the office, leaving him standing by the desk.

Quan pulled out his communicator and flipped it open. "I need instructions," he said more to himself than to the communicator.

Chapter 12

The trip off the mountaintop produced a few mishaps. About an hour after they started, Falconetti tripped over a log and went sprawling. He landed badly, breaking his right arm. Colt called a halt from the forced march to give everyone a chance to rest and to take care of the man's arm. One of the marines used an auto-adjusting splint from the first aid kit to lock the broken bones in place. Falconetti complained vehemently, but they moved on.

The overhead canopy of leaves grew thicker as they descended, cutting out a significant amount of light. Sunset almost caught them by surprise. About the time Colt noticed the light turning orange, Buchanan reported a wide spot in the trail that looked suitable for camping. Civilians and military worked together to set up camp, although not without some conflicts. Several times Colt or Orsini had to step in to prevent a a fight from breaking out.

The conditions were rough and emergency rations weren't exactly gourmet cooking. However, Colt judged that the heavy tree cover would safely hide a small fire. He hoped the warmth of the fire would sooth brittle nerves. The trip down from the tree line had taken most of the afternoon, and he had faced a steady barrage of complaints. The loyalists wanted to know why the navy had let them down. The separatists wanted to stop and be picked up by what they believed to be other separatists. Even some of the navy crewmembers complained about not being ground troops.

"I don't know, Gus," Orsini commented, cradling the mug of coffee to warm his hands. "I can't shake the feeling that Hargety is trying to stir up trouble with the rest of the diplomats. It's like he wants to start a fight."

Colt lunged to his feet. "You may be right, Tony. At least, he's managed to start a fight." He nodded toward a group around another fire. Mackiewicz, one of the loyalists had just swung a left hook at Hargety, sending him sprawling. "Sergeant Jiracek!" Colt bellowed, heading for the fight.

Jiracek got to his feet immediately. Bringing two sailors with him, he trotted after Colt toward the battle. Before they could get there, Hargety got up and charged the other man. He came in at chest level, throwing his arms around Mackiewicz and driving him to the ground. One of the loyalists tried to drag Hargety off. A separatist spun him around and hit him in the jaw. Almost immediately several other punches were thrown. The ensuing melee involved almost all of the colonists, before the military arrived to break it up.

Several minutes later while Colt and Orsini pulled the last of the belligerents apart, Colt heard the sound. An armored troop carrier was descending into the woods nearby, coming down and crushing the brush in the last clearing they had passed. The troops would be on them in minutes. "Everyone, take cover. Now!"

He signaled for the crewmembers to spread out. Then he pulled out his blaster and dropped behind a boulder. Listening intently he heard three more troop carriers descending. That meant they would be outnumbered by about eight to one if all the carriers were full. He signaled for some of the crewmembers to cover them from behind and then settled in to watch the trail.

Moments later a single man wearing camouflaged fatigues walked into the clearing. His blast rifle was slung and his pistol was holstered. He stopped with his hands in the open when Colt shouted, "Stop right there!"

"Ah, Commander Colt, it's good to finally catch up with you. You made surprising progress today ,considering you were herding a bunch of civilians. You've been an admirable opponent, but now it's over. You must realize you're completely surrounded. It's time to surrender."

"No chance!"

"Oh, come now, Commander. Try to fight us and no matter how poorly my troops fight, some of your charges will be casualties."

"If we don't fight, all of them will be."

"To the contrary, if you surrender, your charges will all be taken home, safe and sound. I admit you and your crew will have to be imprisoned, but you'll be well taken care of."

"Why should we trust you after you destroyed the *Invincible* and tried to kill us?"

"Those were both regrettable lapses by my colleagues. They'll be facing suitable charges when the new government takes office. As to why you should trust me …" A bright, blue-white flash and a

74

clap of thunder signaled a blaster bolt that cut straight down through the trees, striking the ground near the center of the clearing. Bits of burning debris cascaded down through the freshly opened hole in the canopy. "If I had wanted you dead, you'd already be dead."

Colt stood up and signaled for the rest of the group to get up as well.

"A wise choice, Commander." A dozen rebels in camouflage stepped out from behind trees on the other side of the clearing, pointing blast rifles at the diplomats and crewmembers. "If you'd be so kind as to deposit your weapons in a pile over here."

Dubrovich, who had accompanied Hargety, walked into the clearing using the same trail the rebel leader had used. He had a military communicator in his hand. It wasn't hard for Colt to figure out the fight had been a deliberate effort to distract the navy personnel so Dubrovich could get away from the group and call for reinforcements.

The rebel commander walked to the center of the clearing. "Ladies and gentlemen, give me your attention, please. We have four transports but they are all full of personnel. We're going to leave one contingent here to watch over the rest of you while we take the others back home. That will take several hours and the crews have already spent a long day, so most of you will have to wait until tomorrow to be picked up. I regret the inconvenience, but you already have the start of a camp set up. If you'll help my men, you'll be comfortably set up in no time.

"Mr. Hargety, gather up whoever you want to go with you so we can get you out of here."

He turned to Colt, "I regret that we will have to restrain you and your crew, Commander, but you understand we can't afford to take chances with any of you." One of the rebel troops stepped forward with an efficient looking set of shackles.

Darkness had settled in. The light from the campfire barely reached Colt, but he kept checking to be sure the guards couldn't see him. Both of them were sitting by the fire, absorbed in conversation. The metal stake he was shackled to had cracked the rock it was embedded in. Straining to be quiet, he carefully worked the stake out of the rock. When it jerked free, he grabbed for it in midair, catching it just before it fell to the ground. The dangling cable had made enough noise that some of the nearby crew members glanced at him. He put a finger to his lips and checked the guards. Then he gathered up the cable.

Now came the tricky part. He made his way back into the shadows and over to Orsini who was nearby. Silently they both tried to free Orsini's shackles, but the stake held. He checked the guards again and worked his way through the crew. With each crewman he was increasingly aware that at any second someone would notice him and alarm the guards. Petty Officer Juneuil was the last. He had to work his way out to her on his stomach. As with the others the stake held. He murmured, "Sorry. I have one more idea." Keeping his eye on the guards, he worked his way back into the shadows.

He eased himself into a standing position and moved behind them, keeping well back. All the weapons that had been aboard the Clermont had been confiscated and carried out with the first group of passengers, the same with the communicators. The guards were the only ones left with weapons. Before long Colt realized that to get close enough to grab a weapon from either of them, he would have to come out too far into the firelight. Someone would see him. He swore under his breath.

Frustrated, he knew the best thing he could do under the circumstances was to escape. He began to back away from the fire, feeling for obstacles. For a moment he wished he could get to his shoes, but the guards had them by the fire. Not having shoes worked in his favor. He immediately knew when his foot touched the smooth surface of the trail. Without taking his eyes off the guards he began to inch onto the trail as he continued to back up. In a few seconds he felt leaves on his cheek, and in a few more seconds he had put a bush between him and the campfire. He resisted the urge to turn and run. As he slipped further into the darkness, he raged at having to leave his crew behind. He began planning his strategy to recover them.

Forcing himself to take his time, he slowly moved away from the camp. The shackles on his ankles made it impossible to take long steps, but he continued to put distance between himself and the guards.

76

As his eyes adapted to the darkness away from the fire, he began looking for a place to get away from the trail. When he came to a gap in the brush on the right side of the trail, he slipped through and began feeling his way through the underbrush. Something furry and cold scurried across his foot. He barely contained a yelp of surprise. Within a few meters he had to stop abruptly at the edge of a cliff. In the darkness he couldn't make out the bottom, but he could barely make out the branches of a tree several meters below.

He had started inching back toward the trail when he heard a piercing wail that sent icicles down his spine. The name banshee flashed through his mind. The largest predator on the continent was similar in appearance to an earthly cougar but slender and blindingly fast. It was known to hunt after dark, using its night-vision and speed to bring down much larger prey. It was also known for cleaning up its prey, rarely leaving enough blood to show that it had attacked. Its hunting shriek gave it its name. So far there had not been a reliable report of a banshee attacking a human, and remains were found of all the humans who had allegedly been attacked. Still the wail had frightening overtones, and he hesitated for a moment wondering if he should return to the campsite.

Then he heard the disturbance from the camp. The guards were already shouting about his disappearance. Within seconds something was crashing through the brush, coming toward him. His heart jumped into his throat. Frozen where he stood, he looked in the direction of the noise. When he saw the beam of a guard's flashlight swinging back and forth, he began moving as if in slow motion.

Colt looked around for cover, but the sweep of the flashlight showed that most of the plants were too sparse to hide him. He had to find a way to get over the edge of the cliff. Getting down on his stomach, he began feeling over the rim for a handhold. The light from the guard's flashlight swept near him, and he closed his eyes to keep it from blinding him. He found a root sticking out of the cliff's surface. Gripping it, he pulled at it with all his strength. It felt strong and anchored. The light swept by again. He eased over the edge of the cliff, disturbing a noisy cascade of dirt and rocks, and found himself hanging away from the face of the cliff. The root held, but he was sure the noise had been heard. Hooking his right arm through the loop of the root, he felt under the overhang with his free hand until he found another root. After checking its strength, he carefully transferred his weight to the new root. When he released the first root, the second one started to move. A small shower of dirt and rock fell away. The noise seemed deafening. He could see the guard's light swing in his direction along the top of the cliff. He tried to flatten himself against the cliff face and hold still, but the strain on his arm rapidly drained his strength. He slowly reached his other hand toward the root he was holding. The movement set off another cascade of dirt and rocks. He frantically searched for another handhold. Then he heard the root crack. At that moment the guard peered over the edge, blinding him with the flashlight. "Here, grab my hand, that root's about to let go."

The guard's words were prophetic, because the root broke loose at that moment. Colt grabbed for the face of the cliff but caught nothing but air. For a second he fell free. Then he struck an outcropping. The blow stunned him and threw him away from the face of the cliff into a tree branch. As he tumbled through the thickening growth, smaller branches whipped him and larger branches clubbed at him. The cable attached to his restraints snagged on a limb, nearly ripping his arms and legs from their sockets. When the branches ended, his back slammed into the ground and a shower of lights flashed before his eyes.

He had landed on a steep talus slope, scattering small pieces of shale. The fall through the tree had slowed his descent, and the angle of the slope warded off most of the force of the fall, reducing the impact but in his dazed condition he couldn't control his path. He bounced clear of the surface and began tumbling and sliding down the slope. For a moment he seemed to be slowing down. Then he slammed into the tree. Intense pain, then blackness claimed him.

Interlude

Quan jerked as the door to McKillip's outer office opened unexpectedly. "What the ... ," he barked as he turned to look. McKillip followed his gaze.

Dubrovich stood in the door, his face mottled with dark red splotches and his teeth clinched in unmistakable fury. McKillip stood up. "Welcome back, Mr. Dubrovich. You seem upset."

"You're damn right I'm upset! I didn't volunteer for a suicide mission, you bastards."

McKillip looked genuinely confused. "A suicide mission?" she repeated. "What do you mean? Please come in and tell us what happened."

"You know damned well what happened. You don't need a debriefing." He began walking toward her, fists clenched.

Quan subtly moved forward to intercept him, but McKillip continued to look puzzled, and Dubrovich stopped short. He asked, "You mean you really don't know?" He looked at his hands and unclenched his fists.

"You're the first person to report back after the mission," McKillip responded. "What happened?"

"The son of a bitch who sabotaged the drive motors on the shuttle took out both of them. We were almost killed. That pompous ass Dixon said it was planned that way."

McKillip showed her shock. "That's not possible. The plan was for the shuttle to have to return to Woomera when it lost one drive."

She glanced questioningly at Quan who shrugged his shoulders and said, "I don't know where Dixon got his information, but that's wrong."

"The hell it is. I heard the engineer say that both busses were melted by acid. That couldn't have been a mistake."

Quan frowned. "I see what you mean. That pretty well had to be deliberate, but it certainly wasn't supposed to happen." He glanced at McKillip and then turned back to Dubrovich. "Look, George, I can't blame you for being upset. I would be too. Let me run down what happened and why and get back to you."

Dubrovich growled, "Someone had better pay for this!"

McKillip cut off Quan before he could respond. "We'll get to the bottom of this and make sure that whoever was responsible is properly punished. You have my word. Thanks for bringing it to our attention."

When Dubrovich had gone, McKillip glared at Quan. "We're losing control, Richard. Find out what idiot gave the order for this and bring him to me, preferably alive. I want to personally ream him a new one," she ordered. "And tell Dixon he'd better learn how to keep his mouth shut."

In the hall outside McKillip's office, Quan called the private number. "Close one," he said, "And Dubrovich is no longer an asset."

Chapter 13

Something was sniffing at his face. At first he ignored it, but then he became aware of warm, fetid breath. Alarmed, he extended his vision to something hovering in the blackness in front of him. Two glowing, slitted red eyes glared at him inches from his face. A huge mouth opened. His heart jumped, and he shut his eyes again, trying to block the terror coursing through him. A gabble of sound came to him – voices, several voices. He realized his head was spinning. As the spinning slowed and stopped, he noticed through closed eyelids that it was daylight. The second thing he noticed was pain. Every part of his body hurt. The babble of strange sounding noises continued. He tried to open his eyes, but only the right one would cooperate. What he saw made him close it immediately. When he reopened it, a creature was still leaning over him, peering with wide-spread, bulging black eyes. He squeezed his one good eye shut and opened it again . . . a giant frog?

Along with the bulging black eyes, the creature's large flat head contained a wide mouth that appeared to split the head in half. Two spindly arms ended in three-fingered hands with opposable thumbs. Smooth, pale green, hairless skin covered its body, and Colt could see no discernible neck. The frog-like creature wore clothes made of drab cloth and carried some kind of a knife in a scabbard on its belt. The shaft of a metal tipped spear rested in the middle of Colt's chest. He couldn't tell anything from the creature's expression, but it was clearly examining him. He also noticed that when he had opened his eye the voices stopped.

The creature with the spear prodded him and made some kind of sound that seemed a cross between a howl and a trill. For no reason that he could discern he decided the sound did not seem hostile. Was it some kind of question? He tried to say something, but it came out as a violent and painful cough. He tasted blood and felt a wave of darkness sweep over his working eye.

As his coughing subsided he heard another voice quickly approaching from the distance. He got the impression it was somehow saying, "Get out of my way!" The small group of the creatures surrounding him separated to reveal an even shorter creature with darker, wrinkled skin. This creature wore clothes made of bright feathers. "Oh, great, the local witch doctor," Colt wheezed and started coughing again.

The dark skinned being knelt over him with something in its hand. The shock, when Colt understood that the "witch doctor" was holding a med-scanner, caused another round of coughing. The "doctor" signaled to one of the others, croaking and shrilling as if giving an order. The other creature turned and trotted off. It returned moments later with a knapsack. The dark skinned doctor pulled an unfamiliar looking laser scalpel from the bag and made quick work of the locks on Colt's restraints. He found his hands and feet free, and for the first time he became aware that the restraints had been holding him in a twisted position. The leather straps of the restraints had shredded the skin around his wrists and ankles. With the restraints gone allowing his body to relax, a wave of pain swept over him and his joints screamed. His stomach knotted, and despite how he hurt he rolled onto his side and retched.

When he could control his nausea, he rolled onto his back again. Then he reached up to touch his left eye, relieved to find that only a cake of dried blood was keeping him from opening it. Pressure on the cake caused a red spot to move around in the blackness that was all he could see with that eye. With luck it hadn't been damaged too much. Then he almost doubled over with another coughing spasm.

The doctor-being moved the med-scanner over his chest and paused midway down his rib cage on the right side. It reached into the knapsack and pulled out some kind of flexible black tube with dual eyepieces. When it pulled up Colt's shirt, he felt something cold on his side followed by a brief, sharp sting. Continuing to look in the eyepieces, the doctor maneuvered the tube and made occasional small sounds. In a moment Colt felt another stab of pain followed by another. Then it withdrew the tube and began using a microsuturer. That's when Colt blacked out again.

He woke to a gentle swaying motion. Although he still hurt, he could open, and see, with both eyes now. Patches of blue sky flashed above him between branches. He gradually realized he was on a piece of heavy cloth stretched between two poles. One end was dragging on the ground, and some large hairless creature led by one of the frog-like beings was pulling it. A piece of fur covered him, but he still felt cold. He began shivering, which brought on the cough. He noticed this time that he didn't taste any blood, and it didn't hurt as much.

He began to take stock of his injuries, counting the number of places he hurt. When he passed ten, he decided it wasn't worth the effort. In the process he realized that his right leg had been splinted and his chest tightly wrapped. He looked around to see if the doctor creature was nearby.

A small pale being walking beside the travois chirped shrilly when Colt began to move. The being leading the draft animal stopped the beast and echoed the chirp more loudly toward the head of the column. In a moment the doctor was again looking down at him. It said something that clearly had separated sounds, but Colt could make no sense of it. He tested his mouth and tongue at forming the sounds, but decided not to start another coughing spasm by using his vocal chords. On impulse he raised his right hand and gave a thumbs-up gesture. For a moment the doctor stared at him without changing its expression. Then it looked at its own hand, closed it into a kind of fist, and extended its thumb upward. It looked back at Colt. Without thinking, he nodded his head. It seemed to understand the gesture. It straightened up and said something to the driver. Almost immediately they were underway again.

The travois bounced along the narrow trail, causing occasional flashes of intense agony from his various injuries. Overhead the leaves of the canopy continued to become larger and closer together as the entourage progressed. Soon the leaves blocked out the sky altogether, leaving Colt with an uninterrupted expanse of green to watch. Boredom and fatigue took their toll, and despite the aches and jabs of sharp pain, he dozed off.

Seemingly only minutes later he awoke to a high pitched twittering. He opened his eyes to see two small versions of the beings looking down at him, from less than half a meter away. The green one chirped something in a voice noticeably higher in pitch than he had heard before. The brown one responded with what Colt immediately thought of as a giggle. Then both the beings disappeared from his field of view.

It dawned on him that he had been looking at children, surprisingly human-like in behavior despite their appearance. The presence of children meant they must be near their settlement. He strained to look around just as the procession turned a corner and broke into a clearing. Within the clearing he saw a village that seemed to consist of large mud-baked beehives. Under a canopy of branches and leaves the village would have been virtually invisible from the air or from orbit. Colt was struck by the odd contrast of the doctor's high technology equipment and the primitive nature of the huts and dirt streets of the village. Then he saw the wires running between the huts and the gleam of an incandescent light. Something about the inconsistency started gnawing at him, but he reasoned it was just the strangeness of the situation.

They stopped in front of one of the huts where a pair of the beings emerged and walked up to the travois. They looked subtly different, but other than the fact that one was brown like one of the children and slightly larger than the other, Colt had a hard time telling them apart. The doctor spoke to them and mimicked the thumbs-up gesture. Then the three turned to Colt and all gave him the thumbs-up. He almost laughed. His head was clearing, and he realized they were telling him he was safe.

Four of the beings lifted him off the travois and carried him inside the hut. At the direction of the brown being they laid him on a pile of animal furs on a raised platform away from the door. The doctor checked the wrappings around his chest and around the splints on his leg. Its expression remained inscrutable, but Colt concluded from its gestures and voice that it seemed satisfied. It spoke for several minutes to the two beings who seemed to be his hosts, and the three of them then walked over to him. The doctor recited what might have been the names of the other two, and each of them responded to the specific sound.

Carefully, Colt spoke his own name, "Colt." It came out hoarse and slurred, and the effort threatened to bring back the cough. Both beings tried to produce the same sounds. The green one said something that sounded roughly like "Cote." Colt responded with a thumbs-up gesture rather than risk starting another coughing attack.

Over the next several hours the two beings took turns sitting beside Colt. Whatever treatment the doctor had given him seemed to be working. The pain was receding and his thinking was becoming less muddled. As his head continued to clear he took in more of his

84

surroundings. The dome was a one room structure. One area seemed to be a kitchen. Another area seemed to be a sleeping area. The platform he was on surrounded an open hearth. The fire had long since gone cold, but half-burned logs lay on some kind of andiron. And the walls were covered with color. Murals showed scenes of open fields and mountains, of trees and flowers, and of a village and more of the beings.

While the beings sat with him both of them spoke frequently. As his thinking cleared, Colt decided they were trying to get him talking, perhaps to learn his language. In spite of the constant threat of another siege of agonizing cough, Colt stubbornly worked with them. He wanted to learn to speak as many of their words as they learned of his. He couldn't tell for sure because of their non-human facial expressions and gestures, but Colt came to feel they appreciated his effort.

Some words seemed easy: water, for instance. Colt managed to gesture that he wanted a drink. Then he identified the contents of the ceramic mug they brought him as water. However, later, after a dinner consisting of a soup that he found surprisingly good to human taste buds, he discovered that the water in the washbasin was called something else, and the water that spilled on the floor was yet another sound. He wondered if any of his translations made sense at all.

The day's events, the dinner, and the quiet after everything had been cleaned up hit Colt suddenly. He realized he had been running on adrenaline all day and the sudden relaxation left him groggy. He fell asleep while trying to figure out how he was going to find his crew and free them and wondering if there were other survivors.

When he awoke well after the sun came up the next day, he found that someone had covered him with blankets during the night. Before he opened his eyes, he catalogued how he felt. First, he didn't hurt nearly as badly as he had the night before. Many of the pains had subsided completely. Even his chest and right leg felt better, although his ribs still felt uncomfortable, and he felt inexplicably weak. *Nothing like having a little witch-doctoring*, he thought. Then he opened his eyes.

A being he had not seen before stared down at him. Smaller than the others, it was tan and its clothes had some vaguely human characteristic that Colt couldn't place. Its expression changed when it realized Colt was awake. The being danced around excitedly as Colt worked himself up on an elbow. The being paused and looked directly at Colt. To his surprise it spoke to him in English, "My name Uujii. You name Cote?"

Colt tested his mouth and found that it wasn't too dry. Carefully he said, "My name is Colt."

Uujii turned and ran, chattering to the adults, who stood next to the entrance. Their conversation lasted only a few seconds. When it returned to Colt, Uujii said, "You Colt. This Olowan." It gestured toward the green adult. Then, indicating the brown adult, it said, "This Ramaanii. Their home your home."

Colt carefully pushed himself to a sitting position. "Please give Olowan and Ramaanii my thanks."

Uujii made a sound, which Colt later learned to recognize as a giggle. It nattered briefly to the couple. Their expressions changed, leaving Colt convinced they were pleased but not certain why.

Up until then Colt's thoughts had been jumbled by the trauma of the fall and a deep fatigue. Now as he awoke fully, questions came flooding in. These people were obviously the natives the governor general had reported. Why had it taken so long to find them? The technology he had seen wasn't borrowed from the colonists, so there had to be some kind of manufacturing on the planet. How had the survey teams missed the plants and, for that matter, the power generators?

He listened intently for a moment. There wasn't a sound to indicate a power source for the electricity. The village was embedded in dense tree growth which made wind or solar power unlikely. Several other possibilities popped into his mind, but they all suggested a higher level of technology than was visible. He rejected them one by one. Every one of them would have been detectable. He mentally scratched his head. He'd have to check into it as soon as he could get around.

He frowned. It really didn't matter in the long run. The fact that the natives had somehow been overlooked by the colonization surveys was unfortunate, but made no difference. Their presence meant the colonists would have to be relocated – forcibly, if necessary. The realization struck him like a physical blow. Someone must have leaked the report the governor general had sent to the Colonization Board, which explained why the rebels were trying to break away from the Republic. Not that that would make any difference. They'd still have to be deported.

Colt looked at the small being next to him. How long had the colonists known about the natives? There must be some form of contact, because this little one spoke English.

When Uujii turned back to face him, Colt asked, "Where did you learn to speak my language?"

It squatted down next to him. "I meet others who teach me some words. I watch and listen from trees. I listen to radio. Do I speak well?"

Colt was startled to realize that he was talking with an adolescent, and, as he later confirmed, a female. She was obviously proud of her ability to speak English. "You speak very well. I hope someday I can learn your language as well as you speak mine," Colt replied.

Later that morning the doctor came in and sat cross-legged beside him. He ran the med-scanner over Colt's injuries, making noises to himself. Finally, he folded the med-scanner shut and looked at Uujii. He spoke to her for several seconds, finishing by nodding his head toward Colt. Uujii hesitated; then she spoke briefly to the doctor. He said something that sounded very much like what he said the first time. Uujii looked at Colt, "Doctor says you have ..." She held up her three fingers, "... broke bones ... here." She lightly touched his side. "And broke bone here." She touched his injured leg. "Doctor says you getting better."

"Healing," Colt said.

"Healing," Uujii echoed. "Doctor says tiny machines that fix you are working, but he must be careful since they are not made for your kind. Healing will take many days. He will be back later to make sure they continue to work."

Colt recognized that the "tiny machines" were nanites, microscopic robots. He was even more perplexed by the level of sophistication they represented. How could these people be so primitive and yet have nanotechnology?

He asked Uujii to thank the doctor. Then, when the doctor had left, he settled down to work on improving both her understanding of

English and his understanding of her language. To prepare for another assignment years before, he had taken a conditioning program in linguistic absorption. He dredged up those techniques now to help him quickly understand the words and structure of the local language. He learned words for various parts of the breakfast that Olowan offered him, and found himself trying to teach Uujii how to conjugate verbs. His hosts called themselves several different names that were all similar to Lodaanii, which, not surprisingly, translated to "people," although they referred to their ancestors as Nidacheen — which also translated to "people." The Lodaanii had a complex language, full of technical words for things that didn't seem to exist in the settlement, such as television. They did have a radio receiver that he later saw; however, he didn't see any evidence that they had the technology to make it, and it clearly wasn't of human origin. The more he learned about this community the more he was intrigued by the paradoxes it represented: an inexplicable combination of primitive and sophisticated. Was their technology supplied by someone else? Surely, there wasn't a third sentient race on the planet.

As the day progressed he couldn't help thinking about this conundrum. No one could really blame the current human population for keeping the Lodaanii secret, but had a survey crew found them and deliberately not reported them? How could the Lodaanii have such a combination of advanced technology and primitive living conditions? Were they a decaying civilization? The remnants of the industrial base needed to produce some of the technology he had seen should be detectable. None of it made sense, and it was distracting him from his language lessons.

He looked at Uujii. "Tell me about your people," he said. "Do it in Lodaanii so I can continue to learn the language."

For a moment a strange expression lingered on Uujii's face. Colt finally realized she was puzzled as she asked, "What is there to tell? We are the people. We live in the mountains. We thank the over-being every day that we have a good life."

"Have you always lived in these mountains?"

"There are stories that we once lived somewhere far away – the other side of the big water, but that cannot be true. How would we get here if that was so?" She looked at him, and the strange expression came back briefly.

Colt just nodded. "Where do you get your … ?" He couldn't find a word for technology. "Your radios?"

"We have always had our radios," she answered.

"What about your lights?" He pointed at one of the incandescent bulbs. "Araduii, the light maker and her mate make them. I was told we used to have lights that were cool to the touch, but they wore out and no one knew how to make them anymore."

The more questions Colt asked the more intrigued he became. He asked other Lodaanii similar questions. They all indicated the same thing: that no one knew where the technological developments had come from and many were failing as they wore out, and that no one knew much about their past. As far as Colt could tell their history started a little over one hundred local years before, roughly the time the first humans began settling the planet. That was a chilling thought. Had the early colonists destroyed the Lodaanii civilization and wiped out any evidence of it? He couldn't accept that.

As the day wound down, his thoughts turned to his own situation. He needed to get back to human civilization soon, not just to report in but also to find out how these people had been overlooked. And what had happened to the *Invincible*? Besides the shuttle crew, were there any other crew members on the planet when it happened? Where was the shuttle crew? Were they still alive? Were they being held prisoner somewhere? What could he do about it?

The more he thought about the *Invincible* the angrier he got. He had close friends aboard. The explosion could have killed over four thousand men and women. And you just don't go around taking that many lives without payback! He promised himself that whoever did it was going to get theirs. He needed to start finding answers, but that meant he had to get back to humanity. Right now he was far too weak to travel. He was feeling better every day, but he seemed to be getting weaker at the same time. When would he start feeling stronger, and how long would it take him to recover?

###

The following morning as Colt sat on the open floor of the hut stretching his injured leg, he looked up to see Uujii flanked by two adults.

"This Ahlonjii and Jomara," she said. "Mother and Father."

Using crutches the doctor had brought him earlier that morning, Colt struggled to a standing position. As soon as the wave of weakness passed, he attempted the half bowing gesture Lodaanii used when they met one another and briefly grasped each of them by a hand.

"Cote, I greet you." Ahlonjii said in broken English. Jomara spoke to Colt in Lodaanii.

"It is good to meet the parents of my amazing helper," Colt replied in Lodaanii.

He glanced at Uujii and saw what he guessed was the equivalent to a smirk. "I believe you have had contact with other humans — my people," he said to Ahlonjii.

"That is correct. I have traded with the beings in the grass sea at the foot of the mountains."

"I hope they were not too impolite."

"They are not Lodaanii, but most do the best they are able," Ahlonjii responded.

"I must thank you for allowing Uujii to work with me. She is very helpful, and I am learning much from her."

"Now if she would apply as much energy to her schooling," Ahlonjii said.

Colt smiled, briefly wondering what they thought of a human smile. "I understand that you want her to go to the human school in First Landing."

"Yes. She learns very quickly and our teaching equipment is wearing out. Many of the programs are no longer complete. The one she wants to study from is no longer working at all and the school in First Landing has it."

"What do you want to study, Uujii?" Colt asked.

"I believe the word is interspecies. I want to learn interspecies relations."

Her response staggered Colt. There were too many things about this village that didn't make sense, and now Uujii wanted to study a subject that the teaching equipment once had but was no longer

90

available, a subject that could not have been developed without contact with other sentient species. Yet the Republic had no record of a native sentient race, much less of one that had dealings with other races.

###

Over the next few days as the nanites worked to reconstruct his damaged body, Colt continued to feel better but remained too weak to leave the village. He fumed about not being able to strike out on his own to find out what had happened to his crew.

He spent most of his time with Uujii. When he felt able, he asked her to help him move to the front step of the hut. Sitting just outside the door, he could see much of the village. It occupied a roughly circular clearing with several large trees spread through it. The intertwined branches of the trees formed a dense canopy. Diffused sunlight filtered through, somehow sustaining a wide variety of plants. Small, colorful gardens grew near most of the huts. The bright red, yellow, and gold provided decoration as well as food. Near the center of the village, a few houses away, a brick platform held two square wooden columns that supported a large metal bell. Markings that might have been writing covered the bell, but Colt sat too far away to make out individual characters. On one side of the clearing he heard the splashing of a small stream. On all sides dense brush made it impossible to see any distance out of the clearing. Even the main trail took a quick turn once it left the village and disappeared behind the brush.

During the day Lodaanii coming and going kept the trail constantly busy. Occasionally a heavy cart pulled by one of the hairless draft animals would emerge from the trail, and the villagers would rush out to see what it carried. Sometimes they would exchange goods. Sometimes they would invite the driver in for a meal. And all day long passersby looked at Colt in apparent curiosity. Uujii helped him learn how to greet them, and to continue to develop his ability to speak their language. Despite the significant differences in the vocal cavity between humans and Lodaanii, he quickly learned to pronounce their words well enough to be understood, although he did occasionally get a sound from Uujii that could only be a snicker.

Chapter 14

Colt found more and more that Uujii reminded him of his own daughter. To help her with her English he told her stories. When he tried to explain about a boyhood fishing trip he took with his father, she surprised him by showing that she knew nothing about fish. In fact, Uujii laughed aloud when he first tried to describe them. Patiently he explained about creatures that live and breathe underwater. Although Uujii stopped laughing as he explained about gills and the oxygen captured in the water, he could see that she remained skeptical.

"I've always loved the water. I remember spending summers on the lake at my family's home in New Hampshire. In fact, I had my own sailboat by the time I was eleven."

As far as Colt could tell Uujii was more than a little puzzled. She said, "What is a sailboat?"

"It's a boat that uses a large piece of cloth called a sail to get the wind to push it."

"What is a boat?"

"It's a craft that floats on water and carries people."

Uujii was aghast. "You mean that people go out in the water on your world?"

"Sure. We travel on the water. We catch fish from boats. We …"

"You are making a joke, yes?"

Colt began to wonder if Uujii understood any of what he was saying. The next day he found a way to show her. His broken bones were knitting rapidly, and he was able to use the simple wooden crutches the doctor had presented him to move about the village, despite his weakness. As he gained mobility he could move farther and farther away from the hut where he stayed. About two hundred meters away, he found the small stream that the Lodaanii used as a water source. Colt and Uujii had walked down to the edge of the stream when Colt spotted a fish swimming vigorously against the current. He remembered her skepticism and pointed at the movement beneath the surface. "That's a fish," he said.

Uujii looked confused. He realized she didn't see it. Puzzled, he lowered himself onto his good knee, put one hand on a rock sticking out of the stream, and reached out across the water to where the fish swam. The fish didn't look very earth-like, but from what he had read he knew that native water creatures were harmless to humans and most had been found to be highly edible. Carefully he lowered his hand into the water. To his surprise the fish didn't seem to notice him. With a flick of his forearm he lifted the fish from the water and tossed it on shore.

Uujii gave out a shrill chirp and jumped back from the flopping creature. As it continued to thrash about she began to approach it curiously. "That was in the water?" she asked.

Colt nodded, a gesture she had learned to recognize. She continued to watch the fish with fascination. "But that is impossible," she said. "Nothing can live underwater."

Colt spotted a pool temporarily cut off from the main part of the stream. He caught up the fish and dropped it in the shallow water. "I told you about gills. It needs the water to breathe," he said. The two dorsal fins stood out of the water, moving about in the pool as the fish recovered from its open air exposure. Colt watched as Uujii traced the movement of the fins and slowly began to recognize the outline and movement of the fish beneath the surface. Then she began to see other creatures flitting about in the water. She was almost giddy with the discovery. "I see other fish," she said.

About that moment an adult Lodaanii shrieked, and Colt looked up. A short way down the stream a Lodaanii youngster thrashed about in the water. On the shore two adults frantically ran back and forth, flailing their arms and calling out, but not going in the water. The realization that the adults could not bring themselves to go in the water to save the child struck Colt like a blow. He climbed laboriously to his feet and hobbled to the spot as fast as he could on his crutches. He waded into the water, and by juggling his crutches he picked the child up. He carried the young Lodaanii to shore and handed him to his shocked parents. Then, as his weakness caught up with him, he sank to the grass beside the stream.

The parents and other Lodaanii gathered around him, asking concerned questions and offering to help him to his feet. When he was finally recovered enough to get back up, the parents effusively thanked him, and more Lodaanii gathered around them, whispering and pointing. One of the adults asked in Lodaanii, "Cote, how do you do this? Are you not frightened of the water?" Uujii translated for Colt.

For a moment Colt hesitated, wondering if the Lodaanii had some kind of taboo about water. Then he said, "My kind likes water. We are simply careful not to breathe it." Uujii translated. She added, "There are creatures in the water. I have seen them." The Lodaanii whispered among themselves again. One of the parents said in Lodaanii, "Your kind must have great charm. We are blessed to have you with us. Olowan and Ramaanii are twice blessed that you stay in their dwelling."

"And I am grateful for their hospitality—for all your hospitality," Colt responded. "Thank you."

Soon all the Lodaanii had returned to their own business. Some of the children gathered along the edge of the stream, pointing at movement in the water, until their parents shooed them away. Colt was perplexed. They had accepted his explanation without question so it wasn't a religious prohibition, and Uujii had responded positively to capturing the fish. But clearly the Lodaanii weren't comfortable with the concept of getting in the water, and they believed his lack of fear was mystical. He thought back to Olowan and Ramaanii's hut. They had running water and a sink. Was it "big" water that bothered them? For a moment he stood silently, leaning on his crutches. Then he limped to the pool where the fish continued to swim about.

As he carefully lifted it out of the water, Uujii asked, "Can I touch?"

An hour later Colt and Uujii returned to the village. As they entered the dwelling Ramaanii greeted him at the door. "Greetings, Cote. We hear you walked in water to save Aaguaar's life. The earth mother smiles on you, and because you stay with us perhaps she will smile on us as well."

"That is my wish also," Colt replied. Wearily he lowered himself to the mat he used for sleeping. "I didn't realize how weak I am."

Ramaanii handed him a mug of water, and then she hesitantly said, "You are very good with the young. Do you have a mate?"

"I had a mate," he answered. "She's dead now." He paused.

Sensing his discomfort, Ramaanii said, "I'm sorry for your loss. Would it be inappropriate to ask what happened to her?" Uujii struggled with "inappropriate" and finally gave up. "May she ask what happened?"

Colt took a sip of the water. "Several years ago I had a wife and a daughter. We lived beside the ocean, and my wife was a terrific sailor. She won several sailboat races." Uujii interrupted, "You told me about a sailboat, but I do not have the words for sailor."

"Well, a sailor is someone who works on a boat. When I say my wife was a terrific sailor, I mean she knew how to control a sailboat very well. It takes great skill to win a sailboat race, and she won many." He paused, closing his mind to the ache of the memory.

"When I am among my kind, I am a Peacemaker." He hesitated to say warrior because he wasn't sure how the Lodaanii would respond. "My duties often take me far away. One time when I was away from home, my wife and my daughter were traveling to a race being held in another land." Colt halted. How could he explain they were flying in a shuttle that crashed? "There was an accident and many members of the party were killed. My wife and daughter were among them."

Colt could see the shock in Ramaanii's face despite the species differences. "That is very sad," she said.

The following morning while Colt was sitting outside the hut, a young Lodaanii ran into the village. Between gasps for breath he shouted something that Colt could only interpret as "others" and "attack." The youth ran up to the hut of the chiefs, Malaakii and Lodaro. Malaakii caught him as he collapsed at the door. It was only then that Colt saw the arrow protruding from the youth's back. Malaakii shouted, "Others! Take cover!" as she lowered the young Lodaanii to the ground.

A male villager walking by the bell in the center of the village grabbed the rope and began ringing it frantically. When a blaster bolt sprayed off the bell, leaving a red glowing circle, the villager dove to the ground. Almost immediately the air was full of arrows and blaster fire.

Colt rolled into the depression beside the entrance steps. Peeking over the edge of the steps, he scanned the forest for movement. At first he saw nothing. Then he spotted one Lodaanii behind a blaster flash and another when an arrow took flight. The Others were apparently another tribe of Lodaanii. After a moment he could count twenty-three of them. He also noticed that so far, there had been no return fire from the village.

Another volley of fire sprayed the village. A blaster bolt glanced off the side of the hut, raining small chunks of hot stucco down on him. He looked up at the spot. The bolt had been incredibly weak. If the stucco hadn't already been cracked, it wouldn't have been harmed. With the next volley he noticed that the blasters and arrows weren't directed at Lodaanii. Instead they were bouncing harmlessly of walls and trees. Except for the youth who brought the warning there were no casualties among the villagers, and Malaakii had moved the young Lodaanii into her hut out of harms' way.

An amplified voice boomed something from the forest. Colt recognized a few words, including the name of Malaakii's mate, the other chief, Lodaro. He guessed that the voice demanded surrender. The village answered with a volley of its own weapons fire. Colt watched the Others drop to the ground as blaster bolts and arrows glanced off the trees and rocks around them. Again, he was surprised at how ineffective the effort was.

He heard the sound of someone running up behind him, but before he could roll over to check, Uujii plopped down beside him. She was breathless from running. "Colt, you are still injured. You should be inside where you won't be hurt again."

"Uujii, what is going on?" Colt asked.

"Others have captured Lodaro. They will take whatever they want from the village and give him back."

Suddenly, a Lodaanii, splendidly dressed in a brightly colored feather costume, appeared on the main trail into the village. He was surrounded by Lodaanii children, and he walked straight ahead as if there were no fighting. Colt realized it was the doctor. He walked straight to Lodaro and Malaakii's hut. None of the blaster fire or arrows came anywhere near him. The children followed him inside.

96

Apparently the doctor was immune to the fighting and was there to treat the injured Lodaanii.

A moment later Malaakii came out wearing a dark, formal robe. "Malaakii will surrender village now," Uujii said.

"Isn't there anything she can do?" Colt asked.

"If the village had a warrior, he could fight with a warrior from the Others until one of them gave up. If our warrior won, they would return Lodaro to us and leave. If their warrior won, the village would surrender."

"Where would they fight?"

"Our warrior would choose."

The firing had stopped when Malaakii came out, so Colt worked his way to his feet. He was leaning on his crutches as Malaakii walked past. "Malaakii, wait!" he yelled. "I will be your warrior and fight for your village."

Uujii stood shocked, almost unable to translate.

Malaakii turned to him. She was angry. "Cote, please do not joke!"

"As a Peacemaker I have been trained to fight, and even on my crutches I believe I can at least try to defeat their warrior, especially if I choose where we fight."

After several minutes of translating he finally convinced her. She turned to another dark robed Lodaanii stepping out of the forest. "Jontaro, my warrior would challenge your warrior."

"And who is your warrior?" Jontaro asked.

Colt was able to follow the conversation. He swung forward on his crutches until he stood in front of Malaakii. "I am the warrior," he said in Lodaanii.

Jontaro bent in a spasm of what had to be laughter. When he recovered, he turned angry eyes toward Malaakii. He said, "Do not treat me like a fool, Malaakii."

"Are you afraid to accept the challenge?" Colt asked.

Jontaro walked up to Colt and stood for a moment looking into his eyes. He then looked at Malaakii. "Is this being serious?" he asked her, in a cold voice.

"I am serious," Colt answered.

"I did not ask you, small mouth!" Jontaro growled. He swung a back hand blow at Colt's head. Colt parried with a crutch. Jontaro grabbed his arm in pain. Without waiting, Colt swung his other crutch around, knocking Jontaro's legs out from under him. He fell with a thud.

Gasps came from the surrounding crowd.

Shifting his weight to one crutch, Colt reached down to Jontaro, took his uninjured hand, and hauled him to his feet. "I challenge your warrior."

Jontaro was seething, but he said, "Choose your fighting place."

Colt used his free crutch to point to a small island in the middle of the stream. "There."

"What? That is not a fighting place."

"It is the place I choose."

"Lodaanii do not fight in places like that!"

"Why not? Is your warrior not brave enough to face me at a place of my choosing?"

Jontaro sputtered, "That is in water! Lodaanii do not go into the water!"

Colt looked at Uujii. He caught the subtle indication of a smile that said she knew what she had to do and would do it.

On his crutches Colt hobbled across the open space to the stream. All the village followed behind him. Colt stepped into the water, Uujii hesitated momentarily but clamped her mouth closed and warily put first one foot and then the other into the stream. Doing her best not to show her fear, she followed Colt to the island. At one point the water reached her knees and to fight the current she had to clutch Colt's arm. Then she continued on without help.

When they had both reached the island Colt turned and looked back. Malaakii and Jontaro had followed them to the edge of the stream. "Where is your warrior, Jontaro? Surely, if a child is this brave, your warrior is as brave."

Uujii poked him with her elbow. "Child?" She asked, under her breath.

"I'm still learning your language," Colt replied.

Jontaro tried fruitlessly to convince one of his warriors to step into the water. Finally, he drew a sword and threw it down. Colt watched with satisfaction as Jontaro stormed off, a proud leader who was thwarted because his warriors had refused to do what a child did. In a few minutes Lodaro, unharmed, walked back into the village.

Colt leaned down to Uujii, "You did well, little one. Shall we go back to shore?"

That evening Olowan had prepared a special meal, and both Ramaanii and he wore bright, festive clothes. As they and Colt ate they frequently looked at him with what he had come to interpret as smiles. In fact, he thought they practically beamed. They talked excitedly throughout the meal, and Colt could only understand part of it. His best guess was that they believed he had done something special for them although he had no idea what it was. He finally understood that they were having some kind of special ceremony the next evening and he was to be their guest.

At Uujii's insistent urging Colt struggled to his feet, leaning on his makeshift crutches, and hobbled out of the hut toward the village commons. If he understood correctly, Ramaanii and Olowan were celebrating because he had brought them some form of kismet. Uujii walked at his side, chattering incessantly in English. "This is great moment," she said. "Ramaanii and Olowan happy you decide to come. Even Chiefs Malaakii and Lodaro will be there."

In still hesitant Lodaanii Colt said, "This Rahana-Nikohbi dance does not happen often?"

Uujii giggled at his accent, "This is first time for Ramaanii and Olowan, and they have been mates for four years."

They had reached the commons, and Uujii looked around excitedly. She spotted another young Lodaanii, Esok, sitting by himself. "There is place by Esok where we can sit." She hurried over to the young male and spoke to him. He looked back at Colt who was working his way slowly toward the spot. Esok smiled. He climbed to his feet as Colt approached. "Welcome, Colt," he said in Lodaanii.

"Good fortune, Esok," Colt replied. Uujii and Esok shared a glance that Colt could not identify, but Uujii didn't giggle.

Esok and Uujii helped him get seated. Almost as soon as he had put his crutches together at his side, the crowd noises subsided. The two chiefs, Malaakii and her mate Lodaro, strode to the center of the dance circle. Malaakii carried a small torch, but Lodaro spoke. "Good Fortune, my children," he said. As he spoke, five of the village youths ran to the center of the circle carrying loads of dead branches, which they piled to form a council fire. Lodaro turned to look directly at Colt. "And Good Fortune to you, Colt. It is because of you that we have council fire to honor this Rahana-Nikohbi for Ramaanii and Olowan. Thank you." With that he bowed, and Malaakii threw her torch into the branches.

The villagers gave out a collective cheer, which took Colt by surprise. From the council hut on the far side of the dance circle Ramaanii and Olowan emerged, and again the villagers cheered. Ramaanii was resplendent in a ceremonial garment covered with multicolored feathers and a silver headband, while Olowan was equally striking in a skin tight jump suit of a shiny silver and black material. Once again Colt was struck by the inconsistency as he realized that the clothes were machine made, not skins or even rough home-spun.

As Ramaanii and Olowan approached the center of the dance circle, someone on the far side of the fire began a light, steady rhythm on a drum. They bowed toward each other, and a clay flute began to play. They began circling, bodies and feet moving in time with the music. A harp-like instrument joined in. They drew closer as they circled. With each step the music swelled. The tempo grew stronger. Soon many of the villagers joined in, clapping in time to the music.

Ramaanii and Olowan touched. Instantly the music stopped. For a moment they swirled in silence, dancing to their own inner music. Olowan touched something on Ramaanii's costume and it fell to the ground. A moment later Ramaanii touched Olowan's costume and it too fell to the ground. Then they separated.

The drum started up again, quietly and in time with their dancing. Part way around the circle another couple had joined the dance. They too bowed and began circling. Somehow their movements became part of the music without interfering with Ramaanii and Olowan's dance. Once again Ramaanii and Olowan came together. This time they held each other close, writhing sensuously as the music grew to a crescendo again and stopped. Colt was so entranced by the grace and beauty of the dance that he didn't realize what was happening until he heard the villagers gasp and then cheer. In the brief silence that followed. Esok leaned over toward Uujii and whispered to her. She giggled and turned to Colt. "Esok say he is looking forward to seeing a human mating dance."

Colt found himself with his mouth open and his face turning red. The whole village had turned out to watch Ramaanii and Olowan make love. He was glad Uujii couldn't read his expression very well. Still, if this was the way they did it, he wasn't going to judge a non-human culture. Surely, they did some of it in private.

As Colt continued to watch, three more couples joined the dance, smoothly flowing into the music. Colt himself could feel the attraction. The music's simplicity and subtle beauty were hypnotic. He found his head whirling with the dance. He lost track of time, unable to turn away. Then he realized it was over. And he had witnessed the whole thing, had even felt like a part of it.

The music slowly resumed, still intoxicating, but somehow different. Now the rest of the villagers got up from the grass and joined the dance. Uujii and Esok looked at each other, then at Colt. He realized they wanted his permission to join the others. He nodded. Uujii's smile would have been obvious even if he hadn't been observing her since he came to the village.

The dance continued until the sunrise began filtering through the trees. Somehow he had stayed awake through the whole event, never even feeling sleepy. Now, as the sun rose, the villagers began drifting away – dancers and musicians – a few at a time. Uujii and Esok walked back to him. "Good fortune, Colt," Esok said. "I must go home and rest."

"Good fortune, Esok."

Uujii lay down on her back in the grass. "I will rest here," she said. "Good fortune, Esok."

She rolled onto her side and looked at Colt. "Olowan and Ramaanii were very happy that you came," she said. "They will name the child after you."

"How soon will they know if they will have a child?" Colt asked.

Uujii looked obviously puzzled. "How could they not have a child?"

"Among my kind mating only causes children once in a while. That is not the way with Lodaanii?"

"Why would you mate if not to have a child?" Uujii asked.

Colt almost tried to explain but decided the question was rhetorical. Besides, he'd already embarrassed himself enough for one night. "So, when will the child be born?"

"In 293 days."

Chapter 15

"Good morning, Colt. Are you going to sleep all day?"

He opened his eyes and found Uujii peering down at him. "What time is it?" He asked.

"The sun is above the eastern ridge. The entire village is up."

Colt tried to sit up, but a wave of dizziness overcame him. Putting his hands close to his shoulders, he pushed himself upright. "Whew! I'm a little dizzy this morning."

"Are you not feeling right?" Uujii asked.

"I don't hurt very much, but I feel very weak."

Before he could say any more, Uujii had run from the hut. Colt didn't have the energy to call after her.

He forced his head clear. "Why am I so weak?" He asked out loud. He drew his crutches to him and with an effort made it to his feet. The room whirled about him, then slowed and steadied. As he stood there, he took inventory and decided he was definitely getting weaker.

Moments later Uujii returned with the doctor, and Colt told him of his concerns. "My bones and wounds appear to be healed, but I'm weak and dizzy."

The doctor gave the equivalent of a human nod. He ran the med-scanner over Colt, chirping disapprovingly at times. When he finished, he spoke slowly to Uujii who translated for Colt. "Doctor says little machines have fixed as much as they can. Now they are eating … something I cannot translate … from your blood."

Colt said, "Red blood cells?"

"Doctor says you must go to a human doctor very soon."

The doctor got to his feet and hurried out of the hut.

"Doctor is going to get volunteers. He says you must go now."

The whole village volunteered. The doctor picked a few stronger males and females, relenting when Uujii demanded to come along.

The trip down the valley felt much more pleasant than his first ride on the travois. They stopped at the edge of the forest, where a local farmhouse stood off in the distance. Colt tottered to his feet. One by one his escorts grasped his arm and said their farewells, disappearing back into the forest, until only Uujii remained.

Colt looked at her. Even though the Lodaanii faces were still difficult to read, he knew she was upset that he was leaving. He got down on the knee of his unbroken leg so he could look her directly in the eye. "Uujii, I'm not sure what is going to happen over the next several days, but I do know that if I can, I will be back. I have made many friends among your people and I am sad to leave them. Let me show you a gesture that we humans use to tell other people we care about them."

He gently reached his arms around her, and she hesitantly put hers around him. As he pulled her to him, for that moment he held his own special little girl. When they separated, he realized he had tears in his eyes. "I'm coming back for you, Uujii."

He carefully used his crutches to get back on his feet. He reached out and touched Uujii's cheek. "Good-bye for now, little one." He turned and began walking toward the open field, leaning heavily on his crutches.

The farmhouse sat across a narrow dirt road and a cleared field, about half a kilometer away. The way he felt, it would be tough, but he thought he could make it. Fifteen minutes later he was beginning to wonder. After half an hour he felt ready to collapse, but he made himself drag one foot after the other. Just a few more steps and he crossed the boundary between the crops and the house yard. He staggered and almost went down.

"That's far enough!" A woman wearing a worn, denim jumpsuit and a battered straw hat stood on the porch cradling a 16-gauge shotgun in the crook of her left arm.

"Looks like you're right," he managed to say, before he pitched forward into darkness, his face landing in the cool grass of the yard.

Colt stirred to the feel of soft clean sheets.

"It seems your guest is back among the living," a woman's voice said.

He opened his eyes to see a blonde, mature woman with a med-scanner in her hand. "I'm Doctor Lois Strauss. How're you feeling, Commander?"

He paused and took stock, "Weak, but better."

"Good. I had a bear of a time flushing those nanites out of your system. We knew the locals had medicine, but we didn't realize how advanced it was." She snapped the scanner closed. "The nanites fixed most of your injuries, but they were destroying your red blood cells. In fact, you were just about dead when Lindsay brought me here. Now that they're out, you'll be weak until your red blood count is close to normal, but you should be good as new in week or so. In the meantime …" She paused and looked over her left shoulder. "Looks like you have a guest for the next few days."

Another woman stepped into his view, the one who had come out on the porch with the shotgun. She was no longer wearing the battered jumpsuit. Instead she wore blue jeans and a shiny black t-shirt. Colt noticed she was quite pretty and looked her over appreciatively. Her oval face and high cheekbones perfectly framed her green eyes and wide, expressive mouth. Auburn, sun-streaked hair fell softly on her shoulders. He became aware that she stood almost as tall as he did and had a strikingly feminine figure.

"No way!" the woman exploded. "He's not my guest. He's Royal Navy!"

The doctor looked at her, "Lindsay, you know as well as I do he didn't have anything to do with Ed's death. You can't take it out on everyone who's in the navy."

"Still, he is navy," Lindsay grumbled.

"Yes, and he's human." She nodded at Colt. "From the med-scanner results I'd say he was injured nearly ten days ago, and very lucky to be alive." She looked at Colt. "How did you get in this shape anyway?"

Colt hesitated. "I was running away from a pack of rebel militia and fell off a cliff."

Lois caught the hesitation. "We're not rebels, so you don't have that to worry about." She glanced at Lindsay. "If you don't want him, I'll take him home with me."

"Oh, what the hell! Fine! He can stay till he's healed up." Lindsay didn't seem very pleased, and for a moment Colt wondered if he really wanted to stay.

Doctor Strauss didn't seem to notice. "Good," she said. "Tell me, you ride Sarah and Sampson, right?"

Lindsay looked puzzled, "Yes?"

"Your guest will regain his strength faster if he can get in an hour or so of riding every day. Riding will exercise his muscles without stressing them too much. "

"What?"

"You can get rid of him sooner. Just make sure he doesn't fall off."

"But, how do I get him on a horse?" Lindsay sputtered.

"You'll think of something."

For a moment Colt wondered if Doctor Strauss had winked at him. "You'll be all right here until you can travel, Commander." She pointed to a disk on his forearm. "I wouldn't do anything strenuous, such as getting out of bed, until your blood count reaches at least fifty on that counter. That won't take long, two or three hours, but do take it very easy for the rest of the day."

Colt slept through until the next morning. He woke feeling like he was going to live after all. A sound from the hall drew his attention, and a small freckled face peeked around the door frame.

"Hi. Who are you?" Colt asked.

A red-haired boy with bright green eyes eased into the room. "I'm Brady, and that's my bed. Who are you?"

"You can call me Gus."

"Is that your real name?"

"It's my real nickname. It comes from August, which is my real name."

"Mom says you're navy. Are you?"

"I am. Doesn't your mother always tell you the truth?"

"Yes, but she said it funny."

"Oh, I see. So how old are you, young man?"

"I'm four and a half."

"That would make you about nine in Earth years."

"That's what mom says."

"And what grade are you in school?"

"Summer third," Brady answered proudly. Summer meant he had started school in the summer, and third was equivalent to third year on Earth. "Do you have any kids?"

Before he answered, Colt levered himself up and put a pillow behind him. "I did have a little girl," he responded in a subdued voice.

Brady eyed Colt as if appraising him, "Is she grown now?"

Colt winced, "No, Brady. She died."

"Oh." Brady walked to the window and looked outside. "My daddy died," he said, his voice flat.

"I know. I am sorry to hear that."

Brady turned back to look at him. His eyes were emotionless. "What was your little girl's name?"

"Her name was Caitlin."

"Was she pretty?"

Colt had to pause a second to keep from being overwhelmed. "Yes, she was," he answered.

Brady walked over to the bed. "I bet you loved her very much. I loved my daddy."

"I'm sure you did."

Brady's eyes filled with tears. "I miss him … a lot."

Colt didn't say anything. Instead, he put his left hand on Brady's head and mussed his hair gently.

"Brady! Get away from there!" Lindsay stalked into the room. "I told you not to bother the commander!"

"He's no bother, Mrs. Hansen."

Lindsay ignored him and ushered Brady out of the room. "Scat!" she said, patting him on the rear. Then she looked back at Colt. She growled, "If I ever catch you touching my boy again—" She started out of the room.

Colt pushed himself up in the bed and called out, "Now, just a damn minute! You come roaring in here like I've done something awful or you expect me to do something really bad. I'll grant that you don't have any obligation to like me; that's your decision. But I would appreciate a little respect at least. I'm not your enemy."

Lindsay paused and looked at him, face blank. "No, you're not," she said without emotion. "I'll have your breakfast ready in a minute. There are clothes on the chair. If you want to eat at the table, put them on and join us." She turned and left the room.

Chapter 16

After breakfast Lindsay reluctantly helped Colt get ready for his riding lesson. Then she sent him to the barn while she finished her morning chores. Outside he leaned on his crutches and studied the barn's distinctive architecture. Its semicircular roof of corrugated metal rested on a half-meter-thick, two-meter-high wall of fused earth. The service doors at each end stood open to let the early summer warmth escape into the morning breeze. Beside each service door and along the sides of the building, smaller entries in the form of airlocks stuck out like warts. As he hobbled into the front of the barn, Colt noticed how heavily the building was padded. He could imagine that the six month long winters produced some harsh storms and the barn had to be well insulated to protect against them.

Inside the barn, stock enclosures of various kinds lined one side and stalls for the horses and cattle lined the other, each serviced by one of the entry locks. Most of the doors stood open with the animals in their outside corrals, except for one hen that strutted around loose inside the barn, clucking indignantly at the intrusion.

Lindsay came in behind him and walked to one of the stalls where a very large, heavyset black horse that Colt later learned was a draft horse, a Shire mare, stood. Lindsay quickly tossed a thick, russet colored pad with stirrups on the horse's back, and strapped it securely in place. She then led the horse out of the stall.

Lindsay was wearing jeans and a green plaid work shirt with her hair tucked into a white baseball cap that said "Egrets" in blue letters above the bill. As she walked up with the horse, Colt couldn't help but be drawn once again to both her face and figure.

"Are you going to gawk or ride?" Lindsay asked with disdain.

He looked at her for several seconds. Her face had started to turn red before he answered. "Look, I know you've suffered a great loss, and I'm sorry, but I had absolutely nothing to do with it. I'll get out of your hair as soon as I can because I have some things I need to do."

Lindsay didn't ask but he felt a need to continue, "I have to at least try to notify the Admiralty about what's going on here, and I need to find out what happened to my crew from the Clermont and see what I can do about them. In the meantime, it would be nice if you could at least be civil."

"You mean you need to tell the Admiralty and the Colonization Board about the natives," she snapped.

"They both already know about the natives," Colt responded. "That wouldn't be telling them anything new. I need to tell them that my ship was destroyed and that I, and my crew, might be the only ones left alive."

"Oh, I'm sorry." For a moment she dropped her eyes. When she looked up, she said in a quiet, but sullen voice, "Let's do this."

She led the horse to a platform along the front wall, and Colt followed her. She pointed at the stairs leading to the platform. "Up there, or do you need help?"

"I'll manage." He caught the handrail attached to the wall and laid his crutches on the stairs. Gritting his teeth, he forced himself to climb up to the platform. She watched, biting her lip. For a moment a smile flickered across her face when he reached the top.

"Before you mount up, say hello to Sarah."

Colt reached out and stroked the massive horse's neck. "Hello there, girl."

"Okay. Can you swing your right leg over her back? Take hold of her mane with both hands to steady yourself."

Colt reached out to grip the mane. "I've always wanted to try riding, but I never had the chance before. I didn't realize horses were this big." He leaned toward Sarah until he got his knee across her back and then slowly slid onto the riding pad.

Lindsay walked around to the horse's right side and helped guide Colt's foot into the stirrup. "Can you get the other side?"

Colt leaned forward and reached down with his left hand. A wave of dizziness swept over him, and he slipped forward, catching the horse's neck with his right arm.

"Hey!" she blurted. "I'll get it. Just don't fall off."

As Colt clung to the horse's neck, Lindsay led her away from the platform and came around to put his left foot in the stirrup. "There. Are you okay now?"

Slowly he straightened up. He hesitated before responding, "Yeah, that dizzy spell just took me by surprise."

"If you feel dizzy again, let me know right away. I'm not sure I can pick you up."

She led the horse out of the barn to a fenced enclosure. As she closed the gate, she said, "Lois says that to do this right I should have helpers on both sides of you to make sure you don't fall off. Since I'm all there is, you'll have to keep yourself on." She looked at him, noting his concern. "Don't worry. I'll keep it slow and easy. I don't want you falling off and getting hurt worse. Then I'd have to keep you longer."

Lindsay led Sarah around the enclosure for several minutes, allowing Colt to get used to the rhythm of the horse's movement. Then she stopped. "How are you doing?"

"This is surprisingly tiring, but I think I'm getting the hang of it."

"Well, don't get cocky. That's when you're most likely to do something stupid and fall on your …"

"I get the picture! Believe me I won't get careless."

"Okay. We'll make this a short one anyway. We'll go longer as your blood count gets closer to normal."

After half an hour Lindsay led the horse back into the barn and maneuvered her up to the platform. Colt very carefully brought his right leg across the horse's back and put both feet on the platform. Then with one hand holding Sarah's mane he slowly stood up and reached back for the railing at the back of the platform. Catching his breath, he said, "She was astonishingly calm through all this."

"They call draft horses 'gentle giants' for a reason." She started to lead Sarah back to her stall. "Wait there. I'll be back to help you get down."

When Lindsay returned, Colt was sitting on the platform with his feet on the stairs. "I believe I can do this on my own, but I figure it wouldn't hurt to have you close by, just in case."

She stood by the stairs, reaching up to hold his free hand as he made his way down the steps. As he neared the bottom, he stumbled slightly. She steadied him with the hand she was holding. He puffed, "Sorry, I'm not as strong as I thought."

"Lois said it may take up to a week for you to regain your strength, even with the riding."

He looked at her, and for a moment her face softened. He said quietly, "Thanks." She dropped his hand. "I'm just trying to get you out of here," she responded, but Colt noted she lacked the intensity she had before.

###

Later that afternoon, Colt poured the final helping of grain into Sarah's trough. The big horse eyed him warily and then cautiously moved forward to stick her nose into the trough. Colt reached out a hand to scratch between the gentle giant's ears.

"What are you doing?"

Colt jerked his hand back. Lindsay was standing in the doorway to the barn, her hands on her hips. With the bright outdoors behind her all Colt could see was her curved silhouette.

"I'm trying to earn my keep. I may be weak, but I can carry food to the animals."

"You don't know how much to give them!" She objected.

"Brady told me," he responded, trying to sound reasonable.

"Brady's not supposed to talk to you!"

"Why not?" He said, allowing anger to creep into his voice. He stepped toward her, resting his hand on the top rail for balance.

"Because you're..." She started.

" ... Navy?" He finished her sentence. He stopped half a meter in front of her. So close, he could see the tracks of the tears sliding down her face.

"Normally I wouldn't pry," he said, "but since you seem to tar me with the same brush, why do you blame Navy for what happened to your husband?"

She broke down sobbing. Instinctively, he reached forward and put his arms around her. He was surprised when she didn't resist and instead buried her face in his shoulder. "I don't. I'm sorry. I shouldn't be blaming you." She pushed back and looked at him. Her face was no longer angry. "It's not just losing Ed. He and I started this place, and it has been my home for twelve Earth years. Now that the Colonization Board knows about the natives, we're all going to be shipped off the planet. I don't want to give it up."

He stood in silence. He knew he couldn't truthfully tell her that she wouldn't lose the farm. In reality, he expected that all the

112

colonists would have to leave the planet. A fundamental law of the Republic said settlers didn't take planets away from native intelligences, but she already knew that. He didn't want to hurt her more by bringing it up. "I'm sorry." He dropped his arms to his sides.

For a moment she turned but didn't walk away. Then she turned back blinking away more tears. "I know you can't do anything about it," she said as if reading his thoughts. "That's why I'm angry. It's so unfair." Then she looked at the horses in their stalls, "Thanks for feeding the animals."

He followed her outside the barn where a frightened looking Brady ran down from the front porch.

"Mom, the news says there's fighting at Woomera!" At nine years he couldn't fully understand what it meant, but the report on the webcast caused fear and excitement. Lindsay ran to the house, and Colt limped after her as fast as he could. When he caught up, she was in the community room staring into the web screen, where men and women behind a barricade were exchanging blaster fire with an unseen foe. Two bodies lay smoldering in the background. Lindsay appeared to be fighting back nausea, her face ashen.

"What's going on?" Colt asked trying to catch his breath. She hushed him with her hand and continued to watch the screen as if she couldn't turn away. An on the scene reporter announced, "The news from Woomera is mixed as the separatists have surrounded the city. Intense fighting has taken place. Home Guard personnel still control most of the city, but so far they have not used their more powerful weapons. According to Colonel Randall Archer, the Home Guard commandant, the governor general has expressly forbidden using blast cannons and short-range missiles within the city."

The image switched to Archer who said, "We're trying to avoid civilian casualties. The bodies you see were rebel fighters."

The reporter reappeared. "Although we are in contact with the Defense Ministry, they aren't releasing casualty figures at the moment. Other sources report the casualties for Woomera at about a hundred dead and close to fifteen hundred wounded on both sides."

The screen switched to a man wearing what appeared to be a uniform. He was speaking but the voice-over continued, "In other news, separatist forces have taken Lexington. The local separatist leader, Daniel Cruikshank, was just on the air declaring the town had surrendered. He promised amnesty for all Home Guard troops and loyalist militia who surrender in the next hour. So far over 350 combatants have surrendered with approximately 80 still at large."

Over a map the reporter continued to talk, "A group of separatists trying to take Johnstown have been surrounded and have given up without a fight." Clearly the fighting was indecisive. Some cities and towns had been taken by the separatists, but others had successfully defended themselves. Still others had launched counterattacks with varying levels of success. So far the battles had not affected the people in predominantly rural areas, but they continued sporadically.

Lindsay turned away, "My God!" Then she looked at Colt. "You seem to be shocked by all this. I would think you'd be in your element."

"Just because I'm in the navy doesn't mean I approve of wars, especially meaningless ones." He concluded reluctantly, "People get killed in wars."

Lindsay looked surprised. "If you dislike war, why are you in the military?"

"My job has always been to enforce peace, not wage war. Yes, it can involve knocking someone's teeth in, but only when they've crossed the line. Admiral Remington said it best at my class' graduation: 'Our job is to maintain the peace, but that means if some dumb sum' bitch won't listen to reason, our job is to slap him upside the head until he will.'"

"But still, that does mean killing people."

"It does, but only to keep them from hurting the people I'm supposed to be protecting, and even then, only when absolutely necessary." He paused. "Of course, the job's a lot easier to do if the opposition knows you'll do whatever it takes when push comes to shove."

Lindsay considered that for a moment and sighed. "I suppose it isn't fair of me to blame you, or the navy for that matter, for what happened to Ed. I just keep thinking if he hadn't had to join the navy, he wouldn't have died."

Colt looked at her for several seconds before he spoke again. "If it doesn't hurt too much to talk about it, can you tell me what happened?" he asked.

Lindsay paused for a moment. "It's been two years and it still hurts," she said with a catch in her voice. "Ed and I came here right out of school. We took the post-immigration service option. Ed signed up for two years of military service. I served my two-year commitment as a free veterinarian."

"So Ed went into the navy?"

Lindsay nodded. "I had made enough as a veterinarian to pay off his debt, but he insisted he had an obligation. God! I hate that word."

She continued, "It was right after our ninth anniversary. Ed was protecting a group of Shaleen students from rioters when someone rolled a grenade inside his shield. He died instantly. I know it's not fair of me. I'm not wishing someone else had died, but why did it have to be Ed?"

"I'm sorry—" Colt began.

"Breaking News," the webcast blared. They turned back to the screen. The newscaster's monotone voice filled the room with ugliness, "There is news just in from Pretoria. Separatist forces have taken the city after several hours of fierce fighting. Home Guard Troops trying to protect the provincial capital were surrounded in Province Hall when a fire broke out. Only three of the troops were able to get out of the building alive. They were badly burned and have been transported to St. Mark's Hospital where they are listed in critical condition. It is also reported that several members of the provincial legislature were trapped in the burning building, including loyalist leader, Hiram Forsythe."

Colt looked back at Lindsay, "I wonder how many more will die before this thing is over. We humans never seem to learn."

Lindsay continued to stare into the screen. "What are we fighting for anyway? Do we want to steal this planet from its rightful owners?"

Colt played the devil's advocate. "There are those who would argue it's possible to share the planet."

"Yes, but the technically unsophisticated always end up losing out."

"I don't know about that. Before The Event, China had a habit of absorbing any group that invaded it. These natives seem to be as highly sophisticated as we are, just different."

"You're taking the separatists side?"

"Not really, but I figure I need to understand both sides of the argument."

"Ed was like that," Lindsay observed. "He'd get you into an argument and pretty soon he'd have you so twisted around you were arguing against yourself."

"He sounds like someone I would have liked," Colt responded.

"Yes," Lindsay said absently while glancing back at the webcast. "I don't know about you, but I need some air." She stood and walked out of the room.

Colt caught up with her on the porch. He stopped next to her and leaned both hands on the porch rail. They stood in silence surveying the countryside. To the west the sun slanted orange rays through clouds and mountains and scattered them across the fields. The mountains' dense forest walked up to the edge of the plain and disappeared. Colt remembered the report on Corona and could see how over the millennia, silt dropped by streams flowing out of those mountains had created the fertile farmland where Lindsay's home now stood.

Almost due west he could see the mouth of the valley he had followed to get here and a brief glint showed where the stream flowed. To the north, a range of granite stuck out of the valley floor looking like the dorsal fin of some gigantic sea monster. The plain itself swept to another range of mountains on the east and to the horizon in the south. Clumps of trees dotted the plains, lining the streams and the lakes, and appearing as islands in the midst of the cultivated land.

Standing there he became aware of her warmth and her faint but pleasant scent. As he looked back at her, one of the sunbeams splashed through the leaves of the Norcross Elms, dappling her face. Once again Colt was struck by her beauty.

Lindsay leaned against the porch rail, staring unseeing at the mountains. "Do you ever regret being in the navy?" She asked.

"If you mean am I happy being in the navy, the answer is, I am." He hesitated briefly. "If you mean have there been times when I've missed out on something important to me, definitely. I missed Caitlin's third, fifth, and sixth birthdays. I missed several wedding anniversaries. And I can't help but feel that if I had been there, Caitlin and Rachel somehow wouldn't have been on that flight when it crashed."

Lindsay stepped away from the rail and looked at him. The sunset glow lit the side of her face and highlighted her hair. Colt felt his breath catch. "Brady told me about your daughter. You lost your wife in the same accident?" she wondered. "Do you blame yourself for their deaths?"

He hesitated. "In a way I do. I made a decision that kept me from being home when the accident happened," he answered. "Of course, to be honest, I know if I had been with them, I would probably have been aboard the shuttle when it went down. Yes, it wasn't my fault, but things could have been different." He paused. "Unfortunately they aren't, and nothing will change that."

"Do you miss them?"

He looked away at the sunset. "Every day, and it's been more than five years."

When he turned back to her, she looked down and spoke in a low voice, "I guess I feel the same way about Ed. Only—" She moved back to the porch railing so she was standing next to him. For a moment she looked into his eyes, and her expression was unreadable. When she reached for the rail, her hand brushed his. Colt felt an electric thrill surge through him. For a split second he thought, Whoa! What's happening to me?

"Still looking at the sunset she said, "I know I shouldn't blame you for what happened to Ed. I apologize if – no – that I've been rude to you."

He smiled. "I understand what you're going through. No need to apologize. What say we start over."

She nodded. "I'd like that."

They both spoke the same time. She said," Hi, I'm …" He said, "This is …"

When they laughed, the smile brightened her face, and Colt felt another thrill.

"Sorry," she said. "What were you going to say?"

"That this is a beautiful place you have here. The views ..." He hesitated imperceptibly. "Are magnificent."

"I fell in love with it the first time I saw it."

Colt noticed that she didn't mention Ed.

They stood in silence as the sun finished dropping behind the mountains.

A small creak behind them made them turn around. Brady stood in the doorway. "Mom, when are we going to eat?"

Lindsay looked at her watch. "Oh, for Heaven's sake! It's almost eight o'clock. I'm sorry, Brady." She started for the door. Before she went inside, she turned back toward Colt. "Are you coming?"

Back inside, Colt's head whirled over what had just happened, but a glance into the web screen slammed him back to reality. The fighting continued to take lives, and he had to do something about it. He felt a growing anger at whoever had blown up the *Invincible*. "I'm beginning to really dislike these guys," he commented to no one in particular.

He pulled out the business card he had gotten from "Dennis O'Toole" and scanned it for a web address. After several false starts he got to a protected login. He entered his full name and answered some very personal questions. When the AI on the other end was satisfied with who he said he was, it gave him an address for future contact and brought up a communication form. Just as he finished typing out a brief message, Lindsay walked in. He cleared the screen.

"Dinner's ready," she announced, looking at the screen. "What are you doing?"

Colt signed off the link, stood up, and started walking with her to the dining room. "A friend of mine is a 'spook.' He's here on some mission. I left him a message to pass on to the Admiralty about what happened, and I told him I need a job that won't prevent me from looking for the rest of my crew. I also asked him for a new identity to use for the time being."

"Why do you need a new identity?"

"As soon as I can, I'm going to have to get back to work. Right now I don't know what I'll be doing, but for the time being it'll be easier if I can pass for a local; especially if my fingerprints and retinal pattern agree with a local identity." He hesitated, "It'll be safer for you and Brady as well."

"Safer?"

"It isn't likely, but rebel troops might come around and find me. If they have my full name and description, a local identity won't matter, but they wouldn't know you have any idea who I am so they should leave you alone."

A little over an hour later the website had an encrypted message from Fitzhugh: "To William August. Took care of missing ID. Congratulations on new job. No subspace. Out of contact with headquarters. Have about thirty folks from your office working for me. Looking for your other friends."

Peering over Colt's shoulder, Lindsay looked baffled. "What does all that mean."

"Basically, it means he has put a new identity for me in the system. I think the reference to the new job and the subspace says I'm working for him for now. It appears about thirty members of the *Invincible* crew, besides the ones who were with me, have been found. I don't know what he has them doing."

Colt logged in to the government website as "William August" and downloaded a temporary ID to Lindsay's printer. Other than the overprinted word "Temporary" it looked like a standard ID including a driver's license, a flyer's license, and a pilot's license. Although neither ground cars nor airplanes were that common any more, either might be useful at some point.

Colt pushed back from the terminal. "Now all we have to do is convince Brady that my name is Mr. August."

Chapter 17

That night he slept in the guest bedroom, which Lindsay and Brady had cleaned out earlier in the day. When he woke in the unfamiliar bed the next morning, it reminded him of a different awakening five years before.

Princess Jana Stewart had been standing beside the bed in a nightgown and robe, looking at him. Her light tone contrasted with the disturbing expression on her face. "Up and at 'em, sailor. I need you in the kitchen in five minutes."

He had been too groggy at the moment to even wonder what was going on. He had thrown on a robe, and hurried out into the corridor. Because of his job his cabin had been next to the royal suite. Jana's husband, David, had answered the annunciator. His expression had been grim when he had let Colt in. Jana had been sitting at the table in the nook, a piece of paper on the table in front of her. She stood and took both his hands. She said, "I'm so sorry," and when she handed him the sheet of paper, the content had hit him like a physical blow.

His reverie ended with a flood of painful memories. That piece of paper had been the notification about the accident Rachel and Caitlin had died in, and he had been out escorting a princess around her domain. If he'd been home …

Jana had been highly supportive. She immediately made arrangements for him to be transported back to Earth. She even recognized that he felt guilty and tried to tell him it wasn't his fault.

He shook his head as if to clear it. Why did he still feel guilty? But he knew. He had made a decision in favor of his career and had let Rachel and Caitlin down.

As he got up he could hear Lindsay busily at work in the kitchen. He checked the red blood cell sensor on his arm. It registered near normal. Testing, he found he was strong enough to walk without his crutches. He quickly dressed and went into the kitchen. Lindsay was fixing something at the counter. He walked around to her side. "Good morning," he said quietly.

She turned and smiled up at him. "Good morning. You look bright eyed this morning. Help yourself to breakfast. I have to get Brady ready for school."

"Can I help you clean up?"

"I can take care of it. When you get through with breakfast, why don't you go feed the livestock?"

Later, as he fed the animals, he kept coming back to how he was feeling about Lindsay. *Have I somehow stumbled onto someone I can care about? If so, what can I do about it?*

He had finished feeding the animals and stopped in front of Sarah's stall. He stood gazing at the big draft horse. "Well, Sarah," he said. "Looks like I'm about done here, The only question is what do I do now? I don't want to leave. Every time I look at her, it takes my breath away. I haven't felt this giddy since I was dating Rachel. But, dammit, that's not an excuse to not go back to work."

He leaned against the partition and reached out to scratch the big horse between the ears. "I should probably get back to First Landing and report to the governor general. Of course, I outrank his navy liaison. And the honor guard at the palace is the only permanent Republic unit on this planet. They must have all of twenty troops."

He thought for a second. "I suppose I can do as much good here as I can in First Landing." He smiled as he looked at Sarah. "Yeah, I know. I'm rationalizing. Still, I need to do whatever I can to complete the *Invincible*'s mission. I can work on disrupting the rebels until reinforcements arrive, and I can try to find the bastards who blew up the *Invincible*. I can do that from here as well as anyplace else." He paused. "The first thing I need to do is get in touch with Fitz to find out exactly what kind of help I've got: what's happened to the *Clermont* crew and what are the other *Invincible* crew members doing?"

Lindsay's voice behind him said, "That sounds like an awfully serious conversation for a horse to understand."

He spun to look at her. "I was just thinking out loud about what I need to do next. I don't particularly want to leave, but I have to report in. I can't just sit around with a war going on."

Lindsay looked dismayed. "Are you well enough to leave?"

"At the rate I'm recovering, I suspect I will be by tomorrow or the next day. Of course Doctor Strauss will have something to say about it."

"Are you really in such a hurry?" She asked. "I'm getting used to having you around."

He hesitated. *Does that mean she feels something too?* "I don't want to leave, but I have a job to do."

"Well," she said, "If you want to stay, the spare bedroom is yours."

"Thanks. I appreciate that. In fact, if my friend doesn't have something specific for me in First Landing, it would probably be better for me to stay away from the Governor General. I just need to get a plan together."

She smiled.

"Goodnight, Sport."

"Goodnight, Gus. Goodnight, Mom."

Somehow the day had passed in a flurry of activity. One of the irrigation ditches had sprung a leak, and Colt, despite still being weak, had spent several hours repairing the leak. The containment field around the chicken enclosure had failed while he was working on the ditch, and he had taken time off to help run down the chickens and get the field working again. Lindsay had a visit from her neighbor to the south that took more than two hours. By the then it was time for dinner. Afterwards Colt had helped Brady with his homework. Now they were alone.

"Are you up for a walk?" Lindsay asked. "I haven't been down to the lake in ages."

"I think I could handle that. But don't expect me to hurry."

She laughed. To Colt it was almost musical.

Outside, because Selene was so close to Corona, in its first quarter it shone nearly as brightly as the moon on the Earth. Lindsay stared at the little moon for a moment. "Beautiful, isn't it?" she said.

Colt was looking at Lindsay. "I'll say."

She looked at him, eyebrows raised. Then she smiled. "I was talking about Selene, but thanks." She led off.

Because she was walking slowly, Colt caught up after a few steps. "I hope I didn't embarrass you. I didn't mean to stare."

She laughed again. "You seem to be the one who's embarrassed," she observed.

For a while they walked in silence through an open field. In the distant north a thunderstorm towered. Lightning danced silently between the clouds and the ground. Lindsay stopped and stared at the light show. "You know," she said almost to herself, "Ed and I used to go down to the lake in the evening." She resumed walking. "We'd sit and talk for hours. Of course that was before Brady. Now he's old enough for Jeffrey, our AI, to watch him as long as I'm close, but Ed ..." She stopped speaking.

Colt looked at her. Her eyes were dry, but even in the half light from Selene he could see the discomfort in them. "Are you sure you want to go to the lake?" he asked.

For a second her pain remained. Then she smiled faintly. "Ed's gone. Nothing I can do will bring him back. I'm still learning to face those old memories, so yes, I want to go to the lake." She smiled and took his hand.

Colt realized she was compensating, but he held her hand as if she meant it. He decided to change the subject. "Where'd you get your degree?" he asked.

"I graduated from Hudson University. That's where I met Ed." Without hesitating she continued. "I was making spending money by tutoring. I was finishing up my post-graduate work, and Ed came to me for tutoring in organic chemistry."

She smiled. "It was almost comical. I was in the student union studying my notes when Ed came charging up. He was out of breath and in a hurry. He asked me to tutor him but didn't have time to stick around for my answer. I barely heard his name before he was gone."

She looked at him. "How did you meet your wife?"

"We were high school sweethearts. We met in history class." Colt grinned broadly. "To this day I think she arranged it because my girlfriend at the time somehow ended up in the other history class."

They strolled the rest of the way to the trees that surrounded the lake, talking about whatever came to mind but deliberately avoiding the rebellion. When they came out of the trees, a short, grassy verge ran down to the edge of the lake. Lindsay sat down in the grass and patted the ground beside her. Colt carefully lowered himself next to her.

"It's been so long since I've had someone I could really talk to." Lindsay was looking out across the lake. "I've missed it."

Colt drank in the cool evening air before responding. "So have I," he said. "Of course, I've never been a great conversationalist, but Rachel seemed to draw me out. You do too." He lay back in the grass with his arms behind his head.

Lindsay picked a rock out of the grass and flipped it toward the lake. It skipped twice before digging into the water. "This lake is named after one in western North America: Flathead Lake. I understand the name came from a misinterpretation of the name of a tribe in the area."

She nattered on for a while, and her voice faded from Colt's consciousness.

###

The next morning Colt woke to sounds from the kitchen. "He what?" Lois' voice broke into laughter.

Lindsay's voice answered. "He went to sleep. At least he doesn't snore loudly."

Colt hurriedly dressed while the conversation continued. He made his way to the kitchen.

"Well, here's sleeping beauty," Lois said with a smile. "Lindsay pours her heart out and you sleep through it."

Colt's eyebrows went up. He looked at Lindsay. "My gosh, I'm sorry."

"She made that part up," Lindsay cut in. "But it was funny."

"I can imagine." Colt gave her a weak grin. "I guess I was more tired than I realized. At least I was able to walk back here."

Lindsay handed him a plate. "Lois is here to give you a final checkup so I invited her to breakfast. We'll be in the dining room."

Colt helped himself to a farmer's breakfast and carried his plate into the next room.

Lois sized him up. "You don't look all that bad," she commented. "You couldn't handle a walk to the lake?"

"I over did it yesterday," Colt admitted, "but I feel pretty good."

"I'll be the judge of that." She grinned. "After breakfast."

###

Colt tucked his shirt back in. "So what's the verdict?"

"Your red blood count is almost normal so you don't need this anymore." Lois removed the monitor from his forearm. "After last night – yesterday – I do think you should take it easy the next few days. At least, don't go repairing anymore irrigation canals."

She looked at him for a moment.

"What?" Colt blurted.

"So what do you think of Lindsay?"

"What kind of question is that?" He frowned.

"I saw the looks you were giving her." She closed up her bag. "Don't get me wrong. I approve." She looked up at him. "You do realize what you have here, don't you? Lindsay's beautiful, intelligent, and one of the sweetest people you'll ever meet. I knew as soon as you were conscious and talking that you and she were perfect together."

"I've noticed her, believe me, but she's still grieving over Ed."

"And you're still grieving over Rachel. Lindsay told me about your loss." She paused. "I suppose the hurt will always be there, but sharing your life with someone helps. I don't know where I'd be without Andrew."

"Andrew?"

"My husband. He's down at the south pole, taking core samples of the ice. Atmospheric study."

"You said you don't know where you would be ..." Colt trailed off.

"We lost our son," she said matter-of-factly. "Andrew kept me from becoming a basket case."

Colt nodded. "I'm sorry to hear that."

"It was thirty Earth years ago. Right after we settled here. It's still hurts a little when I think about it, but I've moved on. You need to do that to. You and Lindsay could do it together."

Colt turned serious. "I definitely like what I see in Lindsay. Unfortunately, since the accident every time I've tried to have a relationship with another woman, I start feeling guilty about what happened."

"Why would you feel guilty?"

"It's a long story." Colt looked at his hands. "I have this unshakable feeling that I'm responsible for Rachel and Caitlin dying. If I hadn't been out pursuing a promotion, I would have been there. Things would have been different."

"How would that have helped? Would the transport not have crashed if you had been aboard?" Lois questioned.

"Well, no."

"Did anyone survive the crash?" She persisted.

"No."

"So, in other words, if you had been there, things would have been different because you would have either died with them or been at home when they died."

She looked him in the eye. "What would that have gained anybody? I guess if you had been with them, you, at least, wouldn't be alive to feel guilty. No, I shouldn't be flip. But you can hardly blame yourself for what took place."

"I know, and there's something special about Lindsay. Still, I don't want to push her — or me for that matter."

"Well, if it counts for anything, you have my blessing."

Lindsay stood up, her face radiant, when Lois and Colt walked into the kitchen. "I gather he's going to live," she said to Lois.

"Yep, he can leave any time — if you want him to."

Lindsay's smile faded. "That's good," she said quietly. "But he's welcome to stay as long as he needs to."

Lois winked at Colt.

Colt spent the rest of the day helping out where he could and resting often. He walked the perimeter of the farm, lost in thought. For a while he sat by the lake skipping stones. He knew he'd have to face his personal demons sooner or later, and Lindsay looked to be the person to help him. He hoped he wouldn't hurt her in the process. Finally, he got up and slowly walked back to the house.

Lindsay met him on the porch. Her smile made his pulse race. "I'm tied up right now," she said. "Can you meet Brady at the bus?"

"Sure. See you shortly." He turned and headed toward the bus landing.

As he and Brady were walking back to the house, Brady looked up at him and said, "Do you love my mom?"

For a second Colt smiled. "I'm not sure, partner, but I like her a lot."

"Good," Brady spoke with the directness of childhood. "I think she likes you too, but she's afraid you're leaving."

"I'll be here a few more days for sure, but after that it depends on my job."

"What's your job?"

"To keep people from being hurt by stopping all this fighting."

"That would be a good thing." Brady nodded. "But will you come back after you're through? I don't want you to leave either."

For a moment Colt paused, trying to control the catch in his voice. *I want to be this boy's dad*, he realized.

Chapter 18

After dinner the web had a coded message for Colt. When he had decrypted it, it read, "I hope you don't mind, but I have two jobs for you. Give me a call as soon as you get this."

Colt brought up his link with Fitzhugh and waited. A few minutes later Fitzhugh was online with him in his Dennis O'Toole persona.

"Good to see you again, Gus. How can I help you?" Dennis asked.

"I believe I'll be fully recovered by tomorrow, so your offer of work came at the right time. I'm need to get back to business. Technically, I should report in to the governor general, but if you have a priority job, I don't see why it shouldn't take precedence. I figure I can accomplish more if I keep my head down and work with you." Colt measured his words carefully even though the feed was encrypted.

Fitzhugh dropped his Dennis accent. "As I mentioned in my message, I have two jobs. The bad guys got wind of my subspace transmitter and were pounding on my door before I could logoff. I had to destroy it to keep them from getting access to the special equipment in it. I barely was able to get away. I thought I had another transmitter hidden away, but the separatists have control of the city it's in, and one of my contacts said they had found and gutted it. I need some way of contacting my people back on Earth. I was wondering if you could help with that."

"What do you have in mind?"

"I want you to find an operational transceiver, if you can, and send a message out for me."

"That lines up with one of the things I need to do. Can you authorize me to work as a company representative while I'm looking into it?"

"Well, as a matter of fact, I've already put you on the company payroll."

Fitzhugh looked at a display in his hand. "The other job has to do with your friends. I've started looking into what's happened to them, but I don't have any reliable information. This rebellion is playing havoc with communicating with my operatives. I believe your crew is still alive and being held by the separatists. I have operatives looking for them, and when we do find them, we'll probably need to move fast, but I don't have the manpower to pick them up myself. I'll help as much as I can, but you'll probably have to arrange everything yourself."

"I can handle that."

"I understand you're staying with a certain beautiful farmer lady. Anything I should know about?" Dennis quizzed.

"It's complicated. I honestly don't know where I stand or how I want to deal with it."

"That sounds like love, me boy. Good luck to the both of you." Fitzhugh switched his accent back on as he broke the connection.

###

The next day Brady followed Colt in to check the early news webcast. Though it was doubtful Brady really understood the war, Colt could see he was fascinated by it. Lindsay went along to make sure he didn't watch too much. As they entered the room, the reporter was saying, "—skirmishes around Kyoto, the separatists apparently detonated a nuclear device in the heart of the city." The image switched to an aerial view. The crater appeared to be half a kilometer in diameter. Outside it, none of the major buildings were left, and most of the residences around the city were either flattened or burning. The reporter continued, "Sensor readings indicate that the weapon was probably a low yield, primary fusion device. There appears to be very little residual radiation, and the dust cloud is not radioactive." She put her hand over her ear for a second. "We're getting a feed from the separatist headquarters."

The image shifted to a weary looking Billy Hargety, "This wasn't supposed to be a fight, and nuclear weapons were definitely not an option. The men who were responsible have been arrested and are en route to the jail in Pretoria. They will be severely dealt with when this crisis is over." The reporter reappeared. She looked badly shaken.

Colt turned to Lindsay. "This keeps getting worse. I feel like I ought to be doing something. I've rested enough."

"What can you do? You don't have a ship, and you don't have a crew."

He nodded, "Obviously, if I'm going to get anything accomplished, I'll need to do it on my own." He stopped, "Or with help I can recruit here." He looked at her meaningfully but she didn't respond.

He continued, "I have two immediate goals, getting the word to the Admiralty so they can send another peace keeping force out here, and finding out what happened to my crew. Fitz has people working on finding my crew, and I figure he's in a better position to do that, so for now I can leave it up to him. That means my first task is to try to find a working subspace transceiver."

Lindsay shook her head. "I don't see how you can do that. From what I hear, all the remaining subspace transmitters are in separatist hands," she said. "You couldn't get near one."

"I've thought of another possibility," Colt answered, smiling grimly. "The shuttle I was on had a subspace transmitter. We were too busy trying to get down in one piece to use it. If the rebels haven't pulled it or used it for target practice, I can have the transmitter up and running in less than twenty minutes. Do you have a flyer?"

"Of course. I gather you want to use it to check out your shuttle?"

"Right now that's the best idea I have."

"I'm going with you," Lindsay announced.

"I don't know," Colt replied. "I can use your help, but the rebels are probably guarding it. Are you sure you want to help me?"

"You're still not completely healed. If I can help you, I want to. But I have to admit, I have mixed feelings about you getting orders." She touched his arm. "I'm in no hurry for you to leave, but I do want to help."

Colt looked down at his arm, and put his hand over hers. He was glad she was willing to help, but he wasn't anxious to leave either.

"What about Brady?" he asked.

"Lois watches him for me."

"Okay, let's call her up. This is probably a wild goose chase, but I'm tired of sitting around."

Interlude

McKillip rubbed her hand down her face in exasperation. "What's going to go wrong next?"

Quan shrugged. "It doesn't look that bad to me. Hargety took the blame for it, or at least one of his people took the blame. That should pretty well wipe him out, credibility-wise. That's one less problem for us to worry about."

"Until someone starts thinking." She looked at the view of Kyoto on the screen. "That was a military weapon, not something cooked up in someone's basement. The missile that flew it in was sophisticated enough to disguise its trail. The only people on the planet who have access to nukes are Home Guard and mercenaries. Not even the Home Guard has that kind of delivery system. Did someone else hire mercenaries? Or do we have a loose cannon working for us?"

"We'd know if someone else had hired mercenaries," Quan answered. He realized what he had said and for a split second his eyes went wide before he gained control of his expression.

McKillip didn't notice. "Exactly," she said. "Find out who could have been so heartless and stupid and drag him in here. We'll have a serious complaint for his company. Hell, I'd like to try him and execute him in public if we could."

"I think we'd be better off covering this up. If we go public with it, we'll be exposing our involvement."

"That's another thing. I'm not happy with being this hush-hush. I want people to know I'm involved with freeing the planet from Republic tyranny."

"I'm not sure the public would understand hiring mercenaries to conduct a revolution," Quan countered. "Right now your hands are clean, but as soon as you admit to hiring mercs, if any of them overstep their contract like whoever this was, you become responsible. No matter how harsh a punishment this guy gets, you'll be stigmatized. You won't be able wash your hands and expect to be exonerated."

McKillip buried her face in her hands again.

Quan continued, "In fact, you're better off never exposing this guy because he can probably be traced back to you."

McKillip sighed. "I suppose you're right." She slapped her hand down on the desk. "Well, at least we can take him out of circulation and make sure nothing like this happens again. Let me know as soon as you've found him."

In the corridor a moment later, Quan pulled out his communicator. "That did not go well. I had to improvise to keep her from figuring out what is going on."

Chapter 19

By the next morning, Colt had had time to think about his comment that this was a wild goose chase, and he began to wonder if it wasn't a total waste of energy. Still, he needed to do something. There was a slim chance that he could get a message to navy command this way. He joined Lindsay in preparing for the day's activities.

Lindsay had put together a picnic lunch, which they carried, along with a heavy blanket, to the garage. The flyer was a typical family van, room for seven passengers and a small load of equipment in back. As Colt stowed the picnic supplies in the back of the flyer, he said, "I still don't understand the purpose of the lunch. This isn't a real picnic we're on."

Lindsay smiled, "Always be prepared. Suppose there are guards. What could be more innocuous than two lovebirds on a picnic?"

Colt grunted.

When they had stowed the supplies, Colt said, "I'd better drive since I know where we're going."

Lindsay nodded in agreement. "In that case let me introduce you to Amelia."

As soon as Lindsay had introduced Colt to the van's AI, Colt took the controls. He eased the van out the garage door in ground mode. Lifting the van, he applied forward thrust, accelerating toward the canyon that the Lodaanii had taken to bring him to Lindsay's. As the van gathered speed, the terrain lock engaged and raised it to five meters above the terrain. It quickly steadied at 200 kph.

Lindsay placed her hand on Colt's forearm. He glanced at her, welcoming her touch but concerned she might disturb the controls. "If you want this to look like a picnic trip," she said, "you probably should take it a little easier – unless you're really in a hurry to get me alone."

Colt felt a brief electric shock. Did she want him? He immediately eased back on the controller, dropping the speed to 100 kph. "You're right. I guess I was rushing because of the uncertainty. I can't imagine the rebels leaving something behind I can work with, but I'm hoping."

"Do you think they took the transmitter?"

"It's a good bet. These guys may be undisciplined, but they have been thorough. But, there's still a remote chance the transmitter will be there and intact."

They entered the mouth of the canyon, and Amelia raised the van just enough to clear the treetops. The leaves rushed under the van like flowing water.

"So how are you going to get a transmitter if this one isn't available?" Lindsay asked.

Colt glanced at her. "For starters, I might have to break into one of the commercial transmitter sites the rebels are holding." he answered.

"You're not serious?" Lindsay stared at him. "Before you came, I had already heard that the separatists were disabling almost every transceiver they could find, and guarding the others like the family jewels. Surely any of them that might be useful will be heavily guarded."

"I know, but right now I can't think of any other way to do it." Colt continued to hold the van to the center of the valley as they followed it upward. In a few minutes he guessed they were coming up on the Lodaanii village. He wondered if he could see it from the air. Then a thin curl of smoke coming up from under the tree canopy caught his eye. Curiosity got the better of him. He slowed the van to a crawl and scanned the area.

After a few seconds searching, he saw the pond that the Lodaanii used to wash their clothes. He moved the van directly over the pond and came to a hover.

"Why are we stopping?" Lindsay asked.

"If they'll come out, I have some friends I want you to see."

With effort he spotted the town bell. For a moment he wondered why none of the Lodaanii could be seen, and then he realized they were probably deliberately staying out of view. He was about to leave when Ramaanii walked into the open.

Colt waved and was met with the equivalent of a broad smile from Ramaanii's face. She turned and shouted something back to the rest of the village. Uujii came running into the open. He waved to her, and she reached up toward him with both arms.

Lindsay was straining to look past him. "Are these the people who saved your life?"

"Yes, especially that one," he answered, nodding toward Uujii. "Do you mind if we stop to say hello? Then I can introduce you to them." He eased the van into the clearing by the pond and carefully set it down. Uujii ran up to it before he could get the driver-side door open.

"Colt!" She gave him a hug that was as human as any he had ever received.

"Hello, Uujii. It's good to see you."

After a moment Uujii recognized that another human was sitting beside him. She released her grip and stepped back.

Colt said, "Uujii, this is Lindsay. I've been staying with her."

Uujii looked directly at Lindsay and said, "Linsee, I am happy to meet you. Are you Colt's mate?"

Lindsay gave an embarrassed laugh, "No, I'm not."

Colt hadn't considered before what Uujii's attitude might be toward him possibly having a human mate. Then he saw the signs of a Lodaanii smile.

"How have you been, Uujii?" Colt asked.

"Bored," she pouted. "It has been very quiet here since you left."

"Sometimes bored is good," Colt laughed.

Several other Lodaanii hurried over to greet Colt.

"Ahlonjii, Jomara, I am glad to see you again," he said in Lodaanii.

"Colt," they responded in unison.

"Lindsay, these are Ahlonjii and Jomara, Uujii's mother and father." He then introduced Lindsay to them. He watched in mild amusement as Lindsay tried to deal with the simultaneous hand grip.

They talked for a few minutes catching up on what had happened in the village since he left and on what had happened to Colt.

Finally, Colt looked at his watch and realized that he had already wasted enough time. He reluctantly said, "Well, little one, we need to leave now. I'm happy to find you well even if you are bored."

Colt waved goodbye as he lifted the van into the air. When it was above the treetops, he turned up the canyon and accelerated.

"So that's Uujii," Lindsay commented. "She is interesting. She reminds me of a human teenager, and she obviously likes you."

Colt grinned. "She is special. She reminds me so much of Caitlin. She's bright. She's funny. And I get the distinct feeling that she has a mind of her own; as you said, a teenager. That's what Caitlin would be now." The last words came out so softly Lindsay could barely hear them.

Lindsay looked back toward the village. "That was the first time I've actually seen any of the Lodaanii."

"Really? I assumed everyone had seen them at one time or another."

"No," Lindsay replied, "They don't come out of the mountains very often. In fact, most of us have only known about them for a few years. I guess they have been regular visitors up in Birchland for quite a while, but the Birchlanders kept them secret until recently."

"That was when the separatist movement took off, wasn't it?"

Lindsay nodded.

"I wonder why it took the governor general so long to report them," Colt commented.

"He probably hadn't seen them. He and his staff hardly ever leave First Landing, and the Lodaanii don't seem to go there very often. If they're seen in any of the other cities, people say they are visiting from another star system."

Colt's eyes widened briefly, he murmured something unintelligible, and seemed lost in thought.

After a few minutes, Lindsay asked, "What was that about being back for the birthing?"

"Ramaanii will have a baby in 285 days. I promised to be back for it."

"That's awfully precise," Lindsay responded. "Do they really know the date that well?"

Colt nodded. "That appears to be the way it is. Once they mate they know the baby is on the way."

"Why do they want you back for that?"

"It's a long story, I'll tell you one day. Right now, let's land this thing."

While they had been talking, they had flown out of the heavy forest and Colt had spotted the trail from the crash site. Colt dropped the van down until the terrain lock engaged and proceeded up the trail at a leisurely pace.

136

"The *Clermont* went down just over that ridge," he said. "I'm going to set down before we get there just in case the rebels have posted lookouts. See any good picnic spots?"

Lindsay pointed past him. "There's a nice one on the left. Those trees will shelter us from the sun and there's plenty of flat surface to land on."

Colt swung the van around and eased over to the suggested spot. "Looks like we aren't the first ones to picnic here. There's a fire ring and a couple of drink containers." He set the van down a few meters from the fire ring with the back end against a natural hedge extending out from the trees. That way they had privacy on three sides. The fourth side faced an imposing view of the Bright Mountain Range with snow covered Mount Churchill dominating the other peaks.

They unstrapped and unloaded the supplies. While Lindsay picked up the containers and set up the table and chairs, Colt found some boughs, spread them on the ground, and then put the blanket over them. "There," he said. "That looks like we have something in mind besides lunch."

She glanced at him, looking surprised.

He hurriedly continued, "Not that we do."

"What's next?"

"First we need to check out the shuttle. After that it would be a shame to waste this setting."

For a second he wondered about taking her hand. Then he turned and headed for the trail. "Come on."

As they started up the slope, Lindsay asked, "How are you doing with the altitude? Are you going to need a nap after we get to the top?"

"That's not fair. I had worked myself ragged that day. I feel fine today. My red blood cells are definitely close to normal." He was casual about the comment, but he stayed focused on the path ahead as he spoke.

The well-used, smooth and shallow trail led over the rise. Just before they got to where they could see the top, Colt halted and signaled for Lindsay to wait. Then he eased up to the rim, keeping low. Several minutes of careful observation satisfied him that there weren't any lookouts. He walked back to Lindsay.

"The coast appears to be clear," he announced. He cautioned her, "The shuttle has probably been rigged with sensors that someone is monitoring somewhere, so just act as if we've stumbled upon it during a hike. In fact, they probably have video coverage so maybe you should take my arm."

Lindsay smiled and wrapped her forearm around his.

As they walked up the shallow depression toward the shuttle, Colt made a show of taking pictures with Lindsay's communicator. He was still amazed that the wreckage was in such good shape: the left wing lying up the slope in the crash scar, the right side of the shuttle against a stand of trees that pinned the wing nearly straight up against the fuselage, the nose crumpled and the windscreen blown out. He couldn't believe that he and Orsini hadn't been injured. Tony deserved a commendation when they got out of this.

"You walked away from that?" Lindsay said.

"Yeah. Tony actually made a great landing since we had almost no power. There's a lot less damage than it appears."

When they reached the wreckage, they walked around it, gawking at the damage, and commenting about the possibility of survivors. When they reached the open portside passenger door, they climbed in. "It looks like whoever was on board got out alive, but we should check," Colt said.

They went forward first. Except for the windscreen lying on the ground in front of the shuttle, the control cabin remained relatively undamaged, and Colt noticed by a few indicator lights that the power was still on. He also spotted a hidden sensor that was obviously broadcasting their presence. He couldn't tell without risking a deliberate look whether it was videoing them, so he decided to continue to play it as if they had accidentally found the shuttle. Walking back through the passenger compartment, he noticed more sensors. He also saw that the articles left behind by the diplomats had been removed. The hatch at the back into the engine compartment was jammed, but Colt put enough shoulder into it to open it part way. Inside, the equipment bay had been stripped of most of the electronics and anything left had been trashed. The subspace transceiver was completely gone. Colt thought to himself that the rebels' effort to jam the hatch might have kept some visitors out, but it was inconsistent with the ransacked equipment bay.

After he had looked around, he said, "Considering the outside of this thing, the inside is amazingly intact. I wonder what happened to the people who were onboard."

Lindsay said, "I don't know about you, but something about this thing gives me the willies. Let's get out of here."

From the outside they took a few more pictures. Then they started back down the trail to the picnic site. When he was sure they were out of sensor range, Colt said, "I don't know whether you noticed, but they had a handful of sensors planted in there. I imagine we'll have visitors before we leave."

When they got back to the van, Lindsay asked, "What do we do now?"

Colt said, "We wait."

She put her hand on top of his. "Didn't you say the separatists are probably coming?"

"Yes."

"Then we need to make this look as realistic as possible. Aren't you glad we brought a picnic?"

Colt laughed, "You're right. If we leave, the rebels might figure we know more than we let on. And come to think of it, I'm hungry. Let's get lunch out."

As they ate, Colt kept wishing he had a full range of sensors because there was no way to tell with the equipment in the van if someone was coming. All they could do was wait for the rebels to arrive.

"What the hell!" Colt swung around like he had been prodded with a hot poker. He found himself facing six men in camouflaged hunting clothes pointing high-powered blast rifles at him.

"Keep your hands where I can see them," one of them growled. Colt stepped between them and Lindsay.

"Lindsay?" One of the other men said.

She moved close to Colt to peek over his shoulder. "Jeff? What's going on here?"

"We'll ask the questions," the first man said. "What were you doing in that wrecked shuttle?"

"We saw it on our walk," Colt answered. "We were curious so we checked it out."

"And who are you?"

"I'm William August."

"Let's see some ID."

"I've got a temporary in my pocket, but you can check it online." He started to reach for his pocket. "May I?"

"Take it slow," the first man ordered.

Colt slowly reached into his right hip pocket. He produced a thin wallet and extracted the computer generated ID. He handed it to the first man.

The leader ran the ID through an optical scanner and watched the information scroll up the display film. Finally, frowning, he lowered his weapon and handed the ID back to Colt. "He's clean," he said. "Lippmann, do you know this woman?"

"Yeah. We came here on the same transport."

"Okay. Let's get out of here. Sorry to have troubled you ma'am, sir." He didn't sound like he meant it. He turned back to Colt. "By the way, take my advice and stay away from that wreck."

As soon as they walked away, Colt let out a long sign of relief.

The intruders had gone, leaving them alone. Colt silently reloaded the supplies into the van as Lindsay cleaned up the site.

"You're deep in thought," Lindsay said, breaking the quiet.

Colt stopped loading and turned to look at her. "I was just thinking. If the rebels were looking for me, those guys would have had my picture. Maybe it wasn't so smart to stick around and wait for them."

"Maybe not, but now you know they aren't looking for you."

"There is that," Colt agreed. "Just remind me when I'm about to do something that stupid again." He returned to loading the van.

The last chair slid into place, and Colt closed the rear hatch. He once again looked at Lindsay. "One thing I can say: this entire situation has me frustrated. I should be doing something useful, but this expedition was a bust." He glanced at the picnic area. "Let's get going. I've never had to deal with a situation like this. There must be some way to get a message off planet."

When they were airborne, Lindsay said, "I don't know if I should suggest this, but you did mention breaking into a commercial transmitter site, and there is a subspace relay station in Sykesville. It was shut down like all the others were, but it may still be in working condition. The trouble is the separatists control Sykesville."

Colt took an immediate interest. "That's a definite problem. Is it hard for people to get in and out of town?"

"It's not too bad. I went in for supplies a few days before you showed up, and they had a no-fly zone over the whole town. I had to park in a temporary landing area out of town and ride a ground shuttle to get to the stores. I had to show an ID at the reception center to get on the shuttle and again at a gate they had set up, but that was all."

"I don't think this will be a one day job. Is there some place to stay in town?"

Lindsay considered for a moment, "Sykesville's not very big, but the old settlers' dormitory is still operating. They call it the Sykesville Plaza Hotel. You can get a room there fairly easily, especially with this rebellion going on."

Colt considered for a moment and rubbed his chin. "This actually sounds like it's worth a try. At least it's handy. Now I need an excuse for going there."

"I can give you two. The irrigation pump for the northwest section is just about shot. I've been unwilling to replace it myself without Ed to help, but with you here the two off us can actually get it fixed, if you don't mind."

"Sounds good to me. So what's the second excuse?"

She smiled, "To arrange our wedding."

The flyer lurched. Colt swallowed hard and turned beet red. When he had regained his composure, he said, "What are you talking about?"

She laughed. "After that invasion of privacy up on the mountain, people are bound to find out that I'm living under the same roof as a man. If that man were my fiancé and we'd set a wedding date, then the talk would be harmless and die out in a hurry. And you don't have to worry," she added. "Even if we did go through with the ceremony, it wouldn't be valid because you'd have to use your phony ID."

Colt hesitated. "You make a good point, and please don't take my reaction wrong. I know you've gotten over me being in the navy, but for a second I thought you'd suddenly developed feelings for me."

"What if I had?"

He didn't need to look at her to tell she wasn't joking. "I don't know. I haven't sorted out my feelings for you yet." It wasn't a lie, just not the whole truth. "I think I'd like it. Have you developed feelings for me?"

"I brought this up, didn't I?" Lindsay smiled crookedly. "To be fair, I guess I owe you an answer. So far I like what I see in you, but I'm not sure I'm ready for a new relationship yet."

Colt started to respond, but Lindsay cut him off. She pointed over a final ridgeline ahead of them and said, "Lois's house is that way."

Colt banked right and lifted to 200 meters. Doctor Strauss's farm came into view behind the ridge. He circled the house once and landed gently on the parking apron. Lois and Brady were already standing on the porch. Colt and Lindsay got out of the van and walked up to the house.

Doctor Strauss smiled. "I see you're much better."

Colt nodded. "Almost one hundred percent. I really owe you one. Thanks."

"Not a problem. Are you taking care of my girl?"

Colt looked at Lindsay, who said, "Yes he is." She paused. "We're going to need you to take care of Brady for a couple more days. Will that be all right?"

"What will you be doing?" Lois asked.

"For starters we need to pick up supplies and schedule the wedding," Lindsay responded.

It was the doctor's turn to show surprise. "A wedding? You two are getting along better than I expected."

"It's cover," Colt said. "We're going to break into the subspace relay station to send a message."

"Won't that be dangerous?" Lois asked.

"I figure the odds of getting hurt aren't nearly as great as being shot down by the rebel militia — or maybe that's a bad example."

Colt turned back to Lindsay, "One last chance to back out. Are you sure you want to be involved? It's my job, but you don't need to take the risk. I don't want to be responsible for something happening to you."

"I thought male chauvinism died with The Event. Wouldn't it be more risky without me? This is my world, and I know my way around in it. I can keep you out of trouble."

"I'm not suggesting you can't handle yourself, but …"

Doctor Strauss broke in. "There's no use in arguing, Gus. I've known Lindsay for twelve years, and I've never seen her lose an argument. You might as well give up now and save yourself some stress." She turned to Lindsay. "When will you be going?"

"If I can get the things I need off the web, we'll probably be ready to go early tomorrow morning," Colt said. He looked at Brady. "Would you mind coming back here after school for a couple of days, sport?"

Brady beamed. "No, sir! And I'll keep my mouth shut too."

Colt laughed. "Actually, it'd be better if you were just normal. Your mother and I really are going in to Sykesville to get a new irrigation pump and some other supplies and to arrange a wedding."

"Are you really getting married?" Brady asked.

"That depends on how long I can stand her bratty kid," he joked. "No, Brady, we're not." He wondered why the question made him tingle.

Chapter 20

"That's the relay station." Lindsay said, pointing at a building in the wall monitor. As one of the original drop-off points for settlers on Corona, Sykesville followed the classic debarkation point design. New arrivals were housed in the settlers' dormitory until they could start homesteading on their own or build a place in town. Typically the dormitory was built in the middle of a park that had come to be called the Commons. The various support facilities such as the motor pool, local and subspace transmitters, the medical center, and the supply center were scattered around the Commons. The supply center in Sykesville had been torn down when the retail district was established. The medical center had become a full-fledged hospital and the motor pool had become a commercial garage, but the subspace relay station, a single-story structure at the north end of the Commons, remained essentially unchanged.

Colt examined the photo. It had excellent detail, but the image was over six months old. Lindsay saw him frowning and recognized the problem. "We haven't put any new satellite photos in the database since the insurrection started, but the last time I was there, the subspace relay building hadn't changed at all."

Colt leaned back in the chair. He steepled his fingers in front of his chin before he said, "I don't suppose any sensors the rebels have installed would be visible at this resolution anyway. The best we can do is to try to guess where they would put them based on the vegetation and the building design. I wonder—" he leaned forward and began typing out an encrypted message to Fitzhugh.

When he finished, he leaned back again. "Well, that's all I can do for now. Fitzhugh probably won't reply until tomorrow night. We'd better let Lois know about the delay."

###

The next morning Colt took Brady to the school bus stop.
"I sure am glad you're here," Brady said.
Colt smiled. "Why is that?" he asked.

"Mom really likes you. She's been smiling a whole lot more since you came. After Dad went off to be in the navy, she quit smiling. I like it better when she smiles."

"I like making her smile. I wish …" Colt caught a glint of sunlight from the school bus and stopped. "Well, here comes your ride."

The bus settled quietly on the pad in front of them. "See you this afternoon, sport."

Brady got up and joined the line of kids getting on the bus. Then he broke from the line, ran back to Colt, and threw his arms around him.

Colt returned the hug and said, "Don't miss your bus, partner. I'll be here this afternoon."

Brady ran back to the bus and climbed aboard. The driver waved at Colt, closed the door, and lifted off. Colt returned the wave. Then he stood and watched until the bus disappeared behind the orchard to the south. Smiling, he shook his head and began the hike back to the house. She likes me, he thought.

He spent the rest of the morning making the rounds of the farm with Lindsay, checking for anything that needed repairing or replacing. The irrigation pump was in bad shape. The casing was cracked and it was drawing more air than water. He also found several places where the electronic fences had gaps. Since the horses and cattle were being kept in a physically fenced area near the house, the gaps hadn't been a problem so far, but they would need to be closed before the animals could be let out.

After lunch he continued checking the fences while Lindsay made veterinary visits to local farms. During the inspection he got a good look at the lake near the property. He noticed a community landing with a boathouse. Inside were half a dozen canoes and two starfish class sailboats. Before he left, he made a mental note to find out more about them.

Back on his rounds he found a massive leak in one of the irrigation ditches. He spent over an hour shoveling dirt before he could seal the tiles back in place. When he finally trudged up to the house, he was exhausted.

Lindsay was standing on the porch. "You look beat."

"Now I know why I joined the navy. Farming is a lot of work."

"Well, come on in and take a load off."

He looked at his watch. "I've got one more thing that needs to be done first. Tell me, are the boats in the boathouse community property or do individuals own them?"

"Individual property. The blue canoe is ours."

"Great. I'm going to meet Brady."

###

As they walked home from the bus stop, Colt asked, "How would you like to take the canoe out this afternoon?"

"All right!" Brady responded eagerly.

"I suppose I should make sure you don't have too much homework."

"I promise I can get it all done right after dinner," Brady vowed, looking as earnest as he could manage.

"You won't let me down?" Colt asked, staring at him with feigned intensity.

"No, sir."

"Okay, let's drop off your books and tell your mother what we're doing. Do you think we ought to invite her along?"

"Naw! She has to fix dinner."

###

Colt let Brady help take the canoe out of the boathouse and carry it down to the beach to put it in the water. As Colt held the boat for Brady to get into the front, he asked, "Do you know how to paddle a canoe?"

Brady shook his head, "I was too little before Dad left, and Mom hasn't done any canoeing since then."

"Then I guess we'd better show you how."

Colt spent the next half hour showing Brady as much about boat safety as he could without overwhelming him. Then they took the canoe out on the lake. As they paddled around, Brady was too fascinated by the boating and the wildlife to ask any more questions about Colt and his mom. And Colt was too busy with the rowing and watching Brady to remember how tired he was.

Finally, they headed back to the boathouse. When Lindsay came down to the shore, Brady waved so vigorously that Colt almost had to remind him not to stand up.

"You're a fast learner, Brady. I bet your mom will be proud of you."

Brady beamed, "Really?"

Before Colt could answer, a blaster bolt shattered the quiet, striking the water less than ten meters away. Water exploded in a shower of heated droplets and steam. Acting instinctively, Colt rolled the boat over, throwing him and Brady into the water. He checked to make sure Brady's life vest was keeping him afloat. Then he said softly, "Keep down and stay close to the canoe."

He jerked back to look toward where the shot had come from. A dark blue private flyer was coming in low from the north swerving frantically. An olive-drab military flyer followed close behind and above it. The attacking flyer fired another shot, blowing out most of the back end of the private flyer. The stricken flyer pitched over and immediately plunged into the lake, throwing up a sheet of water that engulfed Colt and Brady and carrying the flyer below the surface. The attacking flyer circled the impact point and headed back north.

Colt shook the water from his eyes and checked on Brady. Then he caught the bow line and handed it to Brady. "Do you think you can tow the canoe to shore, Brady?"

"Yes, sir."

"Good." Colt turned to shout to Lindsay. She was already wading out to help Brady. "I'm going to check for survivors," he yelled.

He shucked off his life vest and swam to where the flyer had gone down. Taking a deep breath, he dove beneath the surface. The crash had roiled up enough mud that he could barely see. He was almost out of air when he finally felt a hard surface. He quickly swam to the surface, grabbed another breath, and dove back to the submerged flyer.

The canopy had ripped loose but was lying on the passenger compartment. He grabbed it and shoved it aside. He quickly found the pilot. He immediately checked the other seats. They were all empty. The pilot wasn't moving, so Colt released his restraints and got behind him to pull him to the surface. Before he could reach the shore, Lindsay had rushed back into the water to help drag the man in.

"My God, it's Howard Walker!" Lindsay gasped as they lay the pilot on the grass.

Colt began checking the man for signs of life. He found a thready pulse. "He's still alive. Go get the van. We'll need to get him to Lois right away." He didn't wait for a reply. He turned his attention to artificial respiration. Before he finished the first minute of mouth to mouth, the man had coughed violently and then threw up, almost before Colt could roll him over.

Walker was still unconscious, but breathing, when Lindsay returned. They gently lifted him and laid him on his side in the back of the van. Colt covered him with a blanket while Lindsay raised the van and headed for Doctor Strauss's.

"He's going to make it." Lois said, stepping out onto the porch where Lindsay, Colt, and Brady waited. "He has a couple of broken ribs and a lacerated spleen, but you got him out of the water in time to keep anything serious from happening." She wiped her hands on a towel, "So now you're going to be a local hero."

Colt was sitting on the top step. He turned to look at her, but he ignored the remark. "Has he come to?"

"Yes. You can talk to him if you want."

Colt rose to his feet. He walked into the house and down the hall to the bedroom Lois used as a makeshift operating room.

Walker, a medium built man with dark brown hair and a craggy countenance, lay in bed with his back elevated so he could watch the news on the webcast. He started when Colt walked in. Then he relaxed. "You must be Gus," he said hoarsely.

Colt offered his hand. "The same. Doctor Strauss says you'll be all right."

Walker shook the proffered hand, "Yes. Thanks for saving my life."

"I'm amazed you survived that crash. Why were they shooting at you?"

Walker stiffened, "I was organizing a resistance cell in Sykesville. We got a call just before the militia broke in on our

148

party. I managed to get back to the parking area and used a spare key to get into my flyer. I guess someone thought it was important for me not to get away."

Colt nodded. "The more I hear about these separatists, the more they worry me. I get the feeling that if they take over here, it won't be just for the duration."

Lindsay stepped into the room. "We need to leave. Brady still hasn't had his supper or done his homework, and Howard needs to rest." She spoke to Walker, "Your brother's on his way."

"Thanks. Nice meeting you, Gus. I owe you."

Lindsay caught Colt by the elbow and led him out of the room.

Chapter 21

An announcement came over the web: new mail for William August.

Colt opened the message, saw that Fitzhugh had sent it, and fed it to the decryption program. Inside were several surface level shots of the relay station and a close up shot of one of the sensors. The text said that all the visible sensors were Argus Type M511. Good, reliable optical sensors that had one unadvertised fatal flaw: they could be frozen by a specific radio frequency signal. The message had a wiring diagram for a simple adapter that would allow a standard personal communicator to generate the signal.

He cleared the decrypted material from the screen and stood up. He walked into the kitchen where Lindsay was loading the dish sanitizer. For a moment he stood looking at her, fascinated. She glanced up, wiped her hands, and stood with her hands on her hips. "You look thoughtful," she said smiling. The implied question appeared to be, "Do you like what you're seeing?"

He took a second to collect himself. The smell of the fragrance she wore made it hard to think. He shook his head to clear it. "Well," he finally answered, avoiding the real question, "I got the word back from my contact. It looks like we may have a chance, if the transmitter is still operational."

She continued to smile, but dropped her arms to her sides. "I would think that would be good news. Are you ready to lay out a plan? Or are we going to play this by ear?"

"I don't think playing it by ear will do the job. I have some ideas. Let's go take a look at them."

The next morning from the air, Sykesville stood out as a rectangular patch of green. Trees, mostly mutated Earth plants, studded an outer band of homes. Inside the residential band the stores, restaurants, and other commercial buildings of the business district stood out like chess pieces. Everything centered on the Commons, a park with its own trees and Earth grasses. A network of streets and alleys dating back to when flyers weren't common laced the business district and wandered aimlessly through the newer part of the residential area. The picture was one of small town hominess, until you noticed the armed flyers patrolling the airspace.

As they approached from the south, Amelia warned them that it had received instructions to land at a parking area on the outskirts of town. Lindsay followed a guide beam down to what amounted to a mowed pasture with a prefabricated building on one side. An armed flyer circled overhead as she floated the van up to the building. A sign by the middle door said, "CHECK IN HERE." She put the van on the ground in a parking space near the door. She and Colt climbed out and walked inside.

The building had been hastily set up to process visitors. The door from the parking lot opened onto a large waiting area outfitted with plastic couches and chairs and a few web terminals scattered about. A counter ran the length of the room. Behind it were half a dozen desks, each with its own processing screen and keyboard. They walked up to the counter where a bored looking man sat watching the web news. He appeared to be the only other person in the building, but there were several offices at one end that might have been occupied. He looked up as they approached. With a sigh he casually got to his feet.

"Sorry, folks. We have to maintain security. IDs, please."

Colt and Lindsay handed over their identification. The man's eyebrows went up slightly when he saw Colt's, but his voice didn't change. "Purpose of your visit?"

"To pick up supplies and arrange a wedding," Colt answered.

"And to have someone else cook dinner," Lindsay added.

The man smiled wearily and handed them two data-entry tablets. He said, "Fill these out while I process your IDs."

Other than the vehicle ID and purpose of the visit, the clipboards asked nothing but questions that would be answered by web queries. Colt assumed they would be looking for inconsistencies. The only question he had difficulty with was the size of his cash account at the local Republic Bank and Trust. He wrote down CR 5000, but the ID check said CR 49,987. The clerk accepted that as a simple typo. He handed them a parking permit. Then he said, "Mr. August, since your ID is temporary, if you want to go into town, you'll have to wear this locator." He held up a simple silver wristband.

Colt didn't flinch. He stuck out his right wrist for the clerk to put the bracelet on. The clerk tightened the wristband snugly and touched a sealing key to it. He glanced at a digital display on the wall. "Overnight parking is in the far lot. The shuttle will be there in ten minutes. They run every half hour. Have a nice day." The clerk dismissed them.

"Thanks very much. You too," Colt said. He walked Lindsay to the door and held it open for her.

Once they were outside, Lindsay had the good sense not to say anything because of the bracelet, but she was clearly upset. Colt took her hand and smiled. For the moment, at least, she seemed to be relieved.

"I guess we'd better get parked and get our gear together," Colt said. Lindsay moved the van out in ground mode and followed the markers to the parking area. The van raised a faint trail of dust as it bumped across matted, dry grass. Joining a handful of flyers parked in the long term parking area, she took the first space he came to.

They picked up their backpacks and sealed the van. Then they walked the few meters to a shuttle stop, a sloping roof mounted on four wooden posts driven into the ground. As they walked up, a small annunciator hanging on one of the poles pronounced in a slightly mechanical voice that the shuttle would arrive in two minutes.

Almost immediately a cloud of dust appeared near a break in the trees at the edge of the field. Moments later the shuttle itself swung into sight, trailing dust. Except for its rounded corners it looked like a rectangular box made out of dust-covered white plastic. It rolled on black rubber tires that continued to kick up dust from the parched field. The driver was visible through a clear windscreen that wrapped around the front. Broad, dust-covered windows dotted the sides. The display over the windscreen announced in large lighted letters "13X – Market Street."

It braked to a halt in front of the shuttle stop. The dust drafting behind wrapped around Colt and Lindsay, the only waiting passengers. The door slid open, "Howdy folks. Climb on in so I can shut out the dust."

The shuttle driver, a slightly overweight man, wore civilian clothes and a billed cap lettered, "Tour Guide." His thinning gray hair included a short beard that covered his face. Colt estimated that he was at least eighty standard years old. The only other people on the shuttle were a younger couple, both looking somewhat dazed.

"You folks got lucky. I usually wait at one end of the line or the other until somebody shows up, but these two are headed back to their farm. As soon as I drop them at their flyer, I'll take you into town."

A moment later the shuttle glided to a halt. "Here's your flyer, youngsters."

When the couple had disembarked, the driver swung the shuttle around and headed back toward town. They had to stop briefly to show their ID cards to a bored guard at the gate. As soon as they passed through the break in the tree line, the driver began to live up to his "Tour Guide" label.

He described many of the residences as they passed them, explaining their significance to the town. "On your left is Captain Miriam's home. He commanded the crew that conducted the first survey of this planet. In fact, he's the one who named it Corona. He retired here when he left the survey service." The home was a large, brick two story dwarfed by the trees that surrounded it. As the shuttle passed, a gray haired woman looked up from working on a flowerbed. "That's Miriam's granddaughter." He yelled out his side window, "Mornin', Elise." The woman smiled and waved.

With no other traffic on the road the shuttle moved along rapidly. Once they reached the commercial part of town, the traffic, almost all pedestrian, was heavy enough to get in the way. Still, only a few minutes later the shuttle drew to a halt in front of the middle building of the old settlers' dormitory. The sign out front said, "Sykesville Plaza Hotel."

"This is it, folks, your home away from home," the driver said.

"Thanks for the ride," Colt said as he stepped off.

"My pleasure. Hope you folks enjoy your stay."

When they reached their room, Lindsay opened the door, and Colt carried the packs in. He tapped his wrist band, making sure Lindsay saw it. Then he looked around. "For a made-over dormitory this isn't bad." He headed to the bedside table that had a paper tablet on it.

"I think this is one of the more expensive rooms," Lindsay said, walking to the window. She drew back the curtains. The Bright Mountain Range stood out above the trees. She put both hands on the windowsill and leaned forward until her breath fogged the transpex of the window. "That's still a breathtaking sight."

Colt walked up and placed the tablet on the sill. "It is, isn't it? I wish we had more time for sightseeing."

She turned to face him, her mouth in a mock pout. "Spoil sport!"

He pointed to the pad and began writing. Out loud he said, "Time to get to work." He wrote on the pad, "This thing probably has a pickup, which I gather you thought of. It means we'll have to play this like we're really lovey-dovey."

She smiled. He continued on the tablet, "*At least, out loud.*"

The smile became a smirk. She said, "Let's get going then. We've got a lot of supplies to pick up."

Colt's and Lindsay's first destination was an electronics store they had passed on the way in. Colt needed parts to repair the force field fence, and he needed to replace his communicator. He also needed some other parts that the local militia would be interested in when he hooked them up. They left the hotel and casually made their way back to the store on foot.

They entered a small but well-stocked showroom. Colt's first objective was to select a new communicator. Then with the clerk's help they rapidly got all the other parts together, including some that Colt had to explain because they weren't exactly standard. The clerk had been uneasy when they walked into the store, but he brightened noticeably when Colt's ID paid the bill without a hitch.

Stepping out of the store, Colt said quietly, "I wonder what was eating him."

Lindsay pointed at the locator bracelet on his wrist, "Probably this."

Colt laughed shortly, "I'll bet you're right." He looked at his watch. "Okay, what's next?"

"We need to go to the veterinary supply store and the livestock store on the west side of the Commons," Lindsay responded. "It's a three kilometer walk unless you want to take a cab."

154

"I'm up for a walk," Colt replied.

A few blocks north they came to a small jewelry store. Colt stopped and looked at the sign. "Now this is an interesting coincidence. Let's go in."

As they walked into the store, Lindsay said pointedly, "You knew about this, didn't you?"

"The web has its uses."

A well-dressed man with a slender mustache hurried up from the back of the store. "Mister Ackerman?" Colt asked. The man smiled and nodded. "I'm William August and this is my fiancée, Lindsay Hansen."

"A pleasure to meet you, ma'am," Ackerman said. "Will you follow me?"

At the back of the store Ackerman reached into one of the display cases and pulled out a tray filled with a blue velvet cushion that had half a dozen engagement rings inserted in slots. "These are the only blue diamonds we have in stock. If you have a little more time, I can get more in from First Landing."

"Blue diamonds? Gus …" Lindsay started.

When they left the store, the diamond on Lindsay's left hand flashed brilliantly in the sunlight. She mouthed, "What's this all about?"

He pulled her close to him. "Got to make it look real," he whispered.

A few minutes later they came to the veterinary supply house. Lindsay quickly collected all the supplies she needed for the farm plus an extra supply of tranquilizer and some replacement darts. "Sarah keeps getting through the fence, and herding her with the family van just makes her panicky," she explained.

They stopped briefly at the farm supply just across the street to buy a new pump and arrange to have it delivered to the parking lot in the morning. Colt also bought two one meter lengths of plastic pipe, which he took with him.

The relay station was just across the loop road at the north end of the Commons. They strolled slowly by it so Colt could take in the security measures. It was a single-story, L-shaped building. The subspace array was in a fenced enclosure behind the building. He counted only two guards outside the building, and neither of them was paying much attention. That didn't surprise him. He felt sure no one had tried to break into the building since the rebels had taken it, and the building had two sensors on every corner. It was impossible to confirm Fitzhugh's report about their type without being obvious, but they appeared to be the same ones in the photos.

Back in their room Lindsay turned on the webcast. While she was watching the news, Colt pulled out assorted pieces of electronic gear from the shopping bag. He spent a few minutes twisting wires and components together, then dropped the gadget and a battery into his pocket. He opened the back of his communicator and attached a micro-oscillator across two exposed contacts. Finally, he sealed up the bag and placed it on the floor by the packs.

He walked up behind Lindsay. "Any signs that sanity is returning?" he asked, looking over her shoulder.

"Nothing definite. Most of the fighting seems to have died down. I think both sides are licking their wounds, trying to figure out what to do next."

"Why is it that people continue to believe that they can solve problems by force? In all the time I spent in the navy, I never saw one problem that couldn't have been worked out better by honest negotiation."

"But how can you negotiate when the rules are stacked against you?" Lindsay asked.

"There is that," Colt acknowledged, recognizing she was referring to the laws about not colonizing inhabited planets, "but I'd be willing to bet that there are legal ways around the rules. What we need to do is find out a way where the rules don't apply."

Lindsay looked at him questioningly. "Do you really think we can do that?" She asked.

Colt hesitated. He didn't want to raise false hopes. "I wish I could tell you yes, but frankly, I don't know. The trouble is I can't even check until we have subspace communication again."

"In other words we need to get you," she hesitated. She appeared to have noticed how dark his expression had become, "on the Republic web as soon as a relay station is available."

He mouthed, "Nice recovery." Then he said aloud, "Look at the time. We should make a reservation for dinner. I'll call."

She held her hands over her gaping mouth, still shocked at what she had almost said.

"Say, while I'm doing that, why don't you call the church and confirm our appointment with the minister this afternoon?"

Colt took in the details of the church as he and Lindsay walked up to its massive granite structure. The building stood out among the manufactured buildings that occupied the rest of inner city Sykesville. He saw that the twin belfries gave easy access to the roof and an emergency ladder led down from the peak to a fire escape on the second floor. The church, the school, and the parking facilities took up an entire block, making it unlikely that anyone would see activity on the roof in the dark of night.

He and Lindsay walked up the stone steps to the narthex hand in hand. A sign inside the doors pointed to the minister's office in the south wing. On the way Colt looked around carefully and ducked in and out of the door of the stairway to the southernmost belfry. In a moment they stood in front of the minister's youngest daughter, a small brunette, who served as the receptionist. She immediately recognized Lindsay and burst into a radiant smile. She jumped out of her chair and hurried around the desk. "Mrs. Hansen, how are you?"

"I'm fine, Victoria. How are you?"

Victoria beamed and held out her left hand. The diamond on her ring finger sparkled brightly. "Ray, Raymond Woolsey asked me to marry him."

Colt chuckled. "It seems to be going around. May I offer my congratulations?"

Victoria continued to smile. "Thank you, Mr. August. Daddy is waiting to see you. Please go on in."

Bill Riemann was an athletic-looking man with close-cropped brown hair and hazel eyes, whose face and physique belied his age. Colt found it hard to believe he was old enough to be the father of the young woman in the next room. He stood up and walked around his desk when Colt and Lindsay came into the room.

"Lindsay!" he said. He wrapped his arms around her and gave her an enthusiastic hug, "It's so good to see you!"

He turned to Colt and extended his right hand. "Mr. August, it's a pleasure to meet you."

"It's a pleasure to meet you, sir, but please call me Gus."

"All right, Gus. Then you can call me Bill." He looked Colt up and down. "You a swimmer, Gus?"

"A deck hand," Colt responded. "I developed my shoulders by hoisting sails and climbing the rigging when I was a kid."

Riemann got right to the point. "So what can I do for the two of you?"

"We were hoping you could preside at our wedding," Lindsay said.

Riemann smiled and said, "I'd be delighted. When did you have in mind?"

They spent the next several minutes setting up the ceremony and other details. When they finished, Riemann asked, "So, Gus, how long have you been on planet?"

Colt hesitated very briefly before saying, "Only a few weeks."

"Was that on the *Sunbird*?"

Again Colt hesitated almost imperceptibly. "No, I came on the *Invincible*. I had arranged to retire as soon as we arrived here. I spent several days wandering around before I made my way into the province."

Riemann looked aghast. "Then you haven't heard what happened? The reports from First Landing were that there was a nuclear explosion just as one of the shuttles was approaching the *Invincible*. When the ionization dispersed, none of the sensors could detect either vessel."

Colt did his best to look horrified, "My God!"

Without smiling Riemann said, "Indeed. God does seem to be looking after you."

The AI cut in, "Your next appointment is here, Bill."

"Thank you, Jeremiah." Riemann stood. He shook hands with both of Lindsay and Colt and escorted them to the door.

Before they left the church, Colt insisted on taking an unguided tour. With the security bracelet on he couldn't explain, but he used the tour to set up a reason for returning that evening. On the way out Lindsay stuck her head into the outer office and waved goodbye to Victoria. Then they strolled back to the hotel to get ready for dinner.

Chapter 22

A broad, spiral stairway covered with a deep red carpet rose through the center of the building to the rooftop restaurant. Heavy, highly polished brass railings ran the length of the stairs on both sides, adding to the air of opulence.

"Are you sure we can afford this place?" Colt whispered when they entered the building.

When they reached the roof, Colt saw that most of the tables were occupied by brightly dressed couples or families. It was hard to believe that the planet was in a state of civil war.

A hostess hurried over to greet them. She smiled brightly, found their reservation, and ushered them to a table. A live waiter took their order. Since they were having wine with dinner, as soon as the waiter had left, Colt took a Buzz-Off tablet from the table dispenser and passed it across to Lindsay. Then he swallowed one himself.

Colt turned to look toward the Bright Mountains. Corona's sun had slipped most of the way behind one of the peaks, making the peak look as if it were on fire, lighting the edges of the clouds in a golden glow. When he turned back, the glow was bathing Lindsay's face, and he felt his heart jump in his chest. He considered reaching across the table and taking her hand. He wondered how she would react and reluctantly tried to chase the thought from his mind.

The uneasiness must have shown in his face because she said, "Is something the matter?"

He glanced down at the table and then back up at her. "I was thinking …" He stopped, looking at the unwanted bracelet encircling his wrist. He realized he would have a hard enough time under normal circumstances. How could he say what he really felt without giving something away through a possible bug in the device?

A voice from the head of the stairs said, "Lindsay?"

They turned to look. Jeff Lippmann, the rebel who had vouched for Lindsay, was walking toward them in civilian clothes. As he came up, both Colt and Lindsay stood. Lippmann's first words were, "I'm sorry about the other day. We have orders to check out everyone who goes near that wreck, and Grainger is a jerk of an ex-marine who doesn't trust his own mother."

He reached out and shook Colt's hand.

"You don't have anything to apologize for," Colt said. "Thanks for getting us out of there with no trouble."

"You two haven't been properly introduced, have you?" Lindsay said. "Gus, this is Jeff Lippmann. Jeff, this is William August, Gus for short. Can you join us?"

"Sure, for a few minutes. I'm expecting my wife, Rebecca." Lippmann took a seat.

For a moment all three sat in silence. Trying to appear as casual as possible, Colt finally said, "I have to admit that raid on our picnic made me wonder. What's the big deal about a wrecked shuttle?"

Lippmann clearly tensed in his seat.

Colt recognized his unease, "Maybe I shouldn't have asked. I've been in the navy so I know how the military can be about civilians wanting to know things they're not supposed to know."

"No, it's not that. It's just that the higher ups really didn't tell us very much. They just said that almost everyone survived, and that the navy crew was in protective custody. They told us they wanted to find out who got curious about the wreck."

Colt managed to keep a bland expression. "Well, I have to hand it to the pilot who got that thing on the ground. From the looks of the site, he must have had to dead-stick onto that plateau. That had to be tough. How many were killed in the crash?"

"Actually," Lippmann said, "No one was killed during the landing. They lost a navy commander while they were trying to get down the mountain. He fell off a cliff. By the time they could get to the bottom the next morning the body was gone. It looked like one of the local carnivores had dragged it off. Maybe a Banshee, but I suppose that's not the sort of thing to talk about just before dinner."

Colt nodded and smiled. "I suppose you're right."

Lippmann quickly changed the subject, "So, Lindsay, how do you know Gus?"

Lindsay's face twisted briefly into an unrecognizable expression that Colt suspected was a cross between sorrow and amusement. "Believe it or not, he was out hiking and had an accident. He managed to make it to my farm before collapsing. While he was recuperating we got to know each other ..." She paused, looking at Lippmann's expression.

160

"Oh, you don't know," she said. She continued in a measured pace, "Ed died two years ago. He was killed protecting some students during a riot."

Lippmann's face fell. "I'm sorry."

"That's all right," Lindsay replied. "It was tough at first, but I'm getting on with my life. Gus has been just what I needed."

"We're getting married," Colt added a little too hurriedly. "We're here in town to make the arrangements."

"Well, congratulations. When's the event?"

"We've set the date for the sixth Sunday in July," Lindsay said. "You and Rebecca will have to come. How can we reach you?" Once again Colt marveled at her presence of mind.

"Jeff and Rebecca Lippmann at Dragonshead Mail Service," he replied. "I look forward to it."

At that moment a tall, slender, blonde woman wearing a long white sheath stepped onto the landing. As she spoke to one of the hostesses, Lippmann saw her and stood. He said, "That's Rebecca." She looked in their direction and waved. She nodded to the hostess and walked toward them. When she saw Lindsay, she broke into a broad smile and began walking faster.

Colt and Lindsay also stood as Rebecca greeted them, "Lindsay Hansen, is that you?" and threw her arms around Lindsay. She pulled back, still grasping Lindsay's arms. "It's great to see you. It's been years. I never expected to see you again after school, but here you are. I mean, I knew you were on the same planet, but what are the odds of both of us being in Sykesville at the same time? I just can't believe it. How've you been? I mean, I heard about Edward. I'm really sorry. I … Oh, listen to me, sometimes I don't know when to stop." Finally, she became aware of Colt standing nearby.

"Rebecca, it's great to see you too," Lindsay said. Then turning to Colt. "This is my fiancé, William August." She held up her hand, displaying the ring.

"Congratulations, Lindsay," Rebecca said, gaping at the ring. Then she turned to Colt. "It's a pleasure to meet you, Bill." She extended her hand.

Colt smiled and said, "My friends call me Gus."

"Gus. I hope you realize what a treasure you have here. We were dorm mates at Hudson. If Lindsay hadn't been so wrapped up in her studies, she would have been the most popular girl on campus."

She turned to Lippmann and kissed him passionately. "It's good to see you, too. I've missed you, honey. When are you going to get out of this military business?"

Lippmann didn't answer her directly. Instead he took her hand, turned to Lindsay and Colt, and said, "Nice seeing you again, Lindsay, and nice meeting you, Gus. We'll be waiting for that announcement." Then he led Rebecca away from the table.

Before he sat back down, Colt said, "Fascinating. I feel like we were just hit by a typhoon, but somehow she's actually quite likeable."

Lindsay smiled broadly. "She has that effect."

"You know, this bracelet sure makes it hard to talk," Colt said as he and Lindsay walked out onto the street.

"Tell me about it," Lindsay agreed. She glanced at the engagement ring on her finger.

Colt struggled to keep his expression bland, but he winced inwardly. He stepped in front of her and turned to face her. For a moment he took both her hands and looked directly into her eyes. Then he dropped her hands, and put his finger to his lips.

Reaching into his pocket he pulled out a battery and the crumpled wiring gadget he had put together after lunch. He held it next to the bracelet on his arm and touched the wires protruding from the gadget to the exposed battery terminals. There was a bright spark and smoke rose from both the gadget and the bracelet. "I'll be right back," he said.

He raced down a nearby alley, tearing the gadget into pieces as he ran. When he reached a dumpster, he scattered the pieces about inside. Then he ran back to Lindsay. "That should take care of this bracelet." He held up his wrist with the no-longer functional bracelet. "Now, let's get out of here before the separatists show up to check on what happened to it."

As they hurried away, Lindsay said, "You were about to say something back there. If that bracelet isn't working any more, you can say it now."

"I wish …" He stopped speaking but continued walking in silence. His mind churned. *Here I am a fearless warrior, and I can't tell a beautiful woman how I feel about her.*

When he looked back, Lindsay had halted and stood watching him. He walked back to her. Taking her hands and looking into her eyes, he said softly, "Let's keep walking. I want to put as much distance between us and where I blew out this tracker as we can before the rebels arrive."

"Not till you answer me."

"I'll answer you while we walk," he said. "I'm just having a hard time saying it."

When they were walking again, he started, "I've spent the past five years grieving over Rachel and Caitlin. Because I blamed myself for their deaths — I know, I didn't do anything to cause them, I've avoided getting involved with women. Then I met you."

He looked at her. "I really like what I see, and once you got past my being navy, I think you like me too." He paused. "This is where you tell me how you feel."

She laughed. "Yes, I like you, but I'm not ready to commit to anything long term. Ed's memory is still too strong — No, that's not it. I think I'm afraid to open up, afraid of being hurt. And I have some reservations. Navy people, even when they're stationed somewhere, don't stay around for long. They spend more time away than they do in port. I'd want someone who would be there for me. On top of that, I've invested enough years in the farm that it's my home, and I'm not ready to give it up. Of course, the natives may have taken care of that." She gave him a brilliant smile. "But I am open to getting to know each other better."

Colt stopped and took her hands again. "Okay, then we'll leave it at that for now." He hesitated. When he spoke it was almost a whisper, "Except I have to say I'm glad you're a part of my life, however briefly." He dropped her hands and in a normal voice said, "Now, we need to get moving."

He began walking again, and, after pausing, Lindsay hurried after him. "What exactly are we doing?" she asked.

Colt led the way across an empty bridge that spanned the Sykesville Creek and stepped off the road into the Commons. "That was one of the problems with having this bracelet hot. We couldn't really talk about what we're going to do. Fortunately, other than short-circuiting this thing, we haven't had to do much improvising.

"Now, we're going to walk back to the other end of the park, go to the church to look for the stylus you dropped, switch into our night gear, and try to get inside the relay station."

"I didn't drop a stylus," Lindsay objected.

"Check your handbag. It fell out while we were touring the church this afternoon."

She quickly searched her purse, frustration obviously growing. "That stylus, Ed gave it to me for tutoring him. I can't believe I dropped it."

"Actually, you didn't. I did, and I know where it is. I needed an excuse to go back to the church, but I couldn't tell you while the bracelet was live."

He switched gears. "As for what we're doing. I have a device that will, hopefully, freeze the sensors that are protecting the relay so that anyone watching the monitor screens won't be able to see us. All we have to do is avoid the live guards. At a guess, they depend almost entirely on the sensors, so they probably aren't too careful with their foot patrols."

They hurried up a pathway that circled the lake about fifteen meters out from the shore. Random trees, shrubs, and flower gardens grew around the path. Flocks of birds in or near the water, many of them of Earth origin such as the Canadian geese, flapped and squawked noisily as they passed. The pale glow of Selene shining through clouds in the east shimmered and broke into thousands of flickering points on the choppy surface of the lake.

Several minutes later they reached the loop road and followed it to the street that led to the church. Colt had to consciously slow down and walk in as if this were a routine visit. Once inside they checked in with Victoria to tell her they were there to look for Lindsay's stylus and not to worry about them. At the end of the hall Colt checked to make sure no one was watching and tried the closed door to the south belfry. It opened easily. They stepped inside a stairwell and closed the door. Colt went behind the stairs and brought back the two plastic tubes he had bought at the farm supply.

"Are you sure you're a naval officer and not a magician?" Lindsay asked. "I saw you come in here, but I didn't see those tubes."

"We could hardly have carried these into the restaurant," he commented.

He looked up the stairs. "This is where it gets tricky."

"Shut up and get going," Lindsay gibed.

At the top of the stairs was a small square storage room. Along one side, the amplifiers and switching relays for the internal sound system stood in a rack. Each wall held a small window, and a metal ladder in one corner led to a trapdoor in the ceiling.

With only the ghostly light of Selene coming in the eastern window Colt quickly stripped off his evening clothes down to a full bodysuit of black nylon. He stretched the sleeves down to his wrists and covered his legs to the tops of his dark socks. Donning black gloves, a black stocking cap, and black slippers, he prepared to climb the ladder. Meanwhile Lindsay undid the tab under her left arm, split the left side of her dress, and let it drop to the floor. For a moment Colt eyed her appreciatively. "Don't look," she demanded and then grinned.

Something scuttled into the corner behind the boxes. Lindsay jerked at the sound. "Zealots!" she muttered.

"What about zealots?" Colt asked.

Removing a small plastic bag from her purse, she replied, "They're like Earth spiders only bigger. Obnoxious, but not dangerous. They like churches because they eat paper, and churches are one of the few places you can still find real paper." She opened the bag and took out her own dark clothing, gloves, cap, and slippers and was soon also dressed all in black. "Ready," she said.

"One more thing," Colt said. "Those tranquilizer darts."

Lindsay pulled the packet of darts and tranquilizer out of her purse.

"Great! Fill them with a strong enough dose to knock a man out without killing him."

"How big a man?"

"The size of an average guard."

"That's not a lot of help. How many are we going to need?"

"If we have to deal with more than a couple of guards, it's all over," Colt responded. "Make it four, in case we miss."

She drew a half cc into each dart, reinstalled the covers over the points, and handed two to Colt. He handed her one of the improvised blowpipes he had made from the plastic pipe.

They tucked their clothing into bags and left them behind the boxes. Then Colt led the way up the ladder. He said, "Maybe the zealots will scare the curious away from our clothes."

At the top of the ladder, he unlatched the door and pushed it open. He climbed out onto the belfry platform surrounded by a railing with four corner posts supporting a sharply peaked roof. A weatherproof loud speaker system nestled under the center of the roof hung like an enormous bat.

The ridgeline of the south wing roof came up to the platform, level with its surface. Colt climbed over the railing and turned to stand with his feet on either side of the ridge. He offered to help Lindsay over the railing, but she ignored his hand and climbed over on her own. Colt nodded approvingly and maneuvered along the roof to the end of the building where a single metal ladder led down to the second floor landing of a fire escape.

When Colt lowered the fire stairs they squealed. In the quiet it sounded like a siren. He stopped and looked around to check if someone had heard. Then he started again, lowering them centimeter by centimeter to avoid making noise. Once he and Lindsay were on the ground, he attached a fine black wire to the bottom and eased the stairs back up. The black wire blended into the shadows, disappearing from sight but waiting to bring the stairs back down when they returned.

At that moment a ground vehicle rounded the northwest corner of the park, its headlights swinging toward them. "Down!" Colt half shouted. They both dropped to the grass. The lights swept over them and stopped.

Chapter 23

A voice from the vehicle carried across the open space, "Nope. Must have been my imagination. I don't see a thing."

The vehicle continued on. As soon as the light had cleared away from them, Colt looked up in time to see an open troop carrier with a couple of men seated in back. It drove away down the street until the church blocked it from view.

"Do you think they saw us?" Lindsay whispered.

"I hope not, but we'd better move while the church blocks us from view." Colt sprang to his feet. "Let's go." He sprinted for the street.

Moments later they arrived at the L-shaped relay building. They approached it from the north using a neighboring building as cover. The relay building sat back from the north loop road and the centerline road far enough to have a broad, dense flowering hedge on all sides. Lying at the bottom of the hedge they were out of the light and out of view of the sensors on the building. Two guards walked into sight from in front of the building, carelessly flicking the beams of their lights from side to side, clearly not paying much attention. Colt waited with increasing impatience as they took almost fifteen minutes to complete a circuit.

The second time the guards moved back to the front of the building, Colt activated the sensor-freezing device. He signaled to Lindsay, and they jumped to their feet. They raced to the back door of the building. The message from Fitzhugh had indicated that there had never been a reason for locks on the building, and there were none now. With Lindsay watching behind them Colt opened the door a crack and quickly checked inside. The hallway stood empty and quiet. They slipped inside, closing the door behind them.

A sterile, gray-walled corridor led to a brightly lit but empty reception area that occupied the front of the building. On either side of the hall closed doors stood every three or four meters.

Half way up the hall the door to the transmitter room proclaimed, "Authorized Personnel Only." Despite the warning, it had no lock. Colt cautiously opened the door just enough to look inside. The room was dark and unoccupied. Using the light from his communicator screen, Colt led the way between racks of communicator relay transceivers and web servers to the back of the room. The subspace transmitter had its own rack and a small workbench next to it.

The bay that normally held the transmitter was empty. "Damn!" Colt muttered. Checking the workbench to the right of the rack, he found the transmitter. It was partially disassembled. No way could they put it back together in the short time they had. In fact, time had run out.

Colt heard voices in the corridor. He waved Lindsay behind a communicator relay rack and turned off his communicator screen. The door from the hallway opened, flooding the transmitter room with light. Two guards stood silhouetted in the door for a moment. Then the shorter one announced, "All clear," and started to close the door.

The guard's communicator crackled, "Hey, Dubresky, who are you guys trying to fool? The door didn't open."

"What do you mean the door didn't open?" The taller guard asked.

"I mean I'm looking at the room on the monitor and you haven't opened the door. There's nobody in it."

"That's ridiculous," the tall man responded. "We're both standing just inside the door, and it's wide open."

"Son of a—," the communicator said. "You're right. The hall sensor shows the door open, and I see one of your backs."

"There must be something wrong with the room sensor," the shorter man said. "We'd better take a closer look." He switched on the room lights. His eyes went wide just before the dart caught him in the throat. The other guard was already sagging to the floor.

"Good shot," Colt whispered. "Let's move."

On the way out of the room he leaned over both men and retrieved the darts. Then he and Lindsay headed down the hall, running silently to the outside door. As they started to open the door, they heard the guard's communicator, "What the hell? Dubresky, are you guys okay? Dubresky?"

Colt pushed the door open and checked outside. "You're clear. Go." he whispered to Lindsay. She darted out the door and ran to the bushes, plunging into them as the surveillance lights flared. Colt dashed out right behind her, slamming the door behind him. As he sprinted to catch up with Lindsay, he said a fervent prayer that Fitzhugh was right about the range of the sensor interference. He grabbed her hand and shouted, "Move. We have to get out of the light before someone sees us."

Sprinting between buildings, Colt had a hard time keeping up with Lindsay. Both of them were gasping by the time they reached the road north of the relay station. Exhausted, Colt pulled Lindsay around the corner of the building and into its shadow and collapsed onto the grass. He was tempted to stay there and rest, but he knew the militia would be on them in minutes. He struggled to his feet and for several seconds they both stood with their hands on their knees trying to get enough air. When he could wheeze out a few words, he urged Lindsay on and, still panting, led the way toward the church at a fast walk.

When the station was out of sight, between gasps Lindsay nervously laughed, "God, I was scared."

"Hang on, sweetheart. We're not out of the woods yet. Let's get to the church first."

A few minutes later, Colt saw lights rapidly approaching and hurried Lindsay into a gap between buildings. They both dropped to the ground and held their breath as the ground car swept through the intersection and continued down the street. They could hear it slowing as it approached the relay station.

As soon as the ground car had passed, Colt and Lindsay got to their feet. Colt signaled Lindsay to stay back and, keeping flat against the wall, eased up to the corner of the building. From the shadows he watched the car pull up at the station. Six men carrying assorted weapons scrambled out and headed for the building. Two went inside. The other four fanned out around the building.

As soon as they were out of sight, Colt barked, "Now!" They ran across the street and halfway down the next block. Then they slowed to a panting walk. Before they had gone far, they heard another ground car rush up to the station, but no one came near them. In a few minutes they were climbing back up to the roof of the church.

By the time they had changed back into their regular clothes and emerged from the stairs to the belfry, it was after 9:00 in the evening. They picked up the missing stylus from under one of the pews, briefly showed it to the minister, and made a point of walking out the after-hours door of the church arm in arm. They headed back to the hotel. The C wing of the hotel had the only movie theatre in Sykesville. When they reached the hotel, Colt paused to examine the marquee. It listed "The Return of Zorro" as the late show. He inserted his ID card in the charge scanner and led Lindsay inside. "That's to make sure anyone who is looking for me will know where I am," he said.

After the movie they stopped long enough to ditch the plastic pipes and darts under some shrubbery. Then they walked arm in arm back to their room. Colt opened the door.

A voice from inside said, "Come in, we've been waiting for you."

Colt froze in the doorway, staring at the three men inside the room. He threw out his right arm to block Lindsay from entering. Each of the men wore khaki-colored uniforms and had a stunner on his hip. The man nearest the door had a star shaped badge, apparently a town marshal.

A quiet voice behind them said, "Go on in. We don't need a scene."

Lindsay looked back to see a fourth man, also wearing a badge, standing behind them. She turned furious. "What right do you have to break into our room while we're gone? Citizens have rights, or have they been suspended for the duration."

The man inside the room closest to the door looked uncomfortable and took a step forward. "Ms. Hansen, please calm down and come in the room. We're not particularly happy to be here either."

"Not until you tell me what this is all about," she shot back.

The man looked apologetic. "I'm sorry we have to trouble you, but we have no choice. Please come in, and we'll explain."

Lindsay continued to look angry, but she stepped into the room. Colt followed her, keeping an eye on the deputy behind them.

"I'm Deputy Marshal Owen Tucker." He flashed his ID. "These are Deputy Marshals Ho, Breitmann, and Czerwinski. Where were you around 8:50 tonight?"

170

"You haven't told us what this is about," Lindsay demanded angrily.

Colt held up his right hand. "It's okay, Lindsay. These men are just doing their jobs."

Tucker nodded at him. "Thanks, Mr. August." He turned back to Lindsay. "We got a call from the Commandant's office that told us to find out where you were. Apparently Mr. August's tracker has stopped working and they want to know why. When the Commandant tells us to do something, we don't have to like it, we just have to obey orders."

Colt pulled his sleeve back, showing the bracelet.

Tucker said, "I thought so." He nodded to Breitmann who produced a multiscanner. Colt held out his wrist, and Breitmann put the scanner next to the tracker for a half second.

"The circuits are fused. Looks like an EM pulse of some sort." He looked at Colt and asked, "Were you near any heavy duty medical equipment this evening?"

"We were at the Bright Mountain restaurant and the First Universalist Church," Colt answered. "We had gone to the church earlier to talk to the minister and schedule a wedding." He looked at Lindsay. "Our wedding. After we left, we discovered Lindsay's stylus was missing. We went back to the church to look for it."

"How long were you there?"

"I don't have any idea. While we were in the church the first time, we wandered around the whole facility. When we went back, we had to look under and behind a lot of things before we finally found the stylus. By the time we left and walked back here, we barely had time to catch the last movie."

"Do you have any witnesses?"

"Well, we checked in with the receptionist when we started looking and with Reverend Riemann when we left, but we did the searching by ourselves."

Tucker nodded, "That's easy enough to check, and you're obviously wearing the tracker. If you're going to be hanging around after tonight, you'll need to get another at the reception center. Otherwise, just turn this one in when you leave.

"I had a feeling this was going to be pointless. Sorry to have bothered you folks. Let's go, boys."

The four men walked out of the room. Colt nodded to each of them as they left and closed the door quietly behind them. Then he plopped down on the bed. Mindful of possible bugs in the room, he said, "Well, that was a bust, but at least we know now."

Lindsay nodded. "So now what? I don't know about you, but I'm up past my bed time. Where ... ?" Seeing him looking strained, she stopped abruptly.

"After that episode," Colt said, "I need a breath of fresh air before I go to bed. Care to join me?"

Once they were clear of the hotel, Colt whispered, "I'm concerned that there may be a bug in our room. I think we'll need to sleep in the same bed and pretend to be loving partners."

"How far do we have to go?"

"A simple good night, darling, with a kiss is all."

Somehow the simple kiss turned into something far more passionate.

Colt raised up on an elbow and looked at Lindsay lying next to him. Memories of the previous night rushed back to him, and he stared at her face, aware once again of how beautiful she was. She stirred and her eyes opened. "Good morning, Sleepy Head," he said. He leaned over and kissed her.

She wrapped her arms around his neck and returned the kiss enthusiastically. "Good morning yourself. Did I dream last night or was it real?"

"It was real, and we need to talk about it, but not here."

Chapter 24

Lindsay was silent on the way to the parking area, and Colt couldn't read her expression. After she lifted off the van Colt broke the silence. "I don't do one night stands," he said, "if that's what's bothering you."

Lindsay turned to look directly at him. "What exactly did happen last night?"

Colt shrugged. "If you don't know …"

"I don't mean that way." She slugged his right arm. "We were supposed to make loving sounds, not make love. What set us off?"

"I'm no psychologist, but I'd guess it had something to do with the adrenalin rush from breaking into the relay station."

She smiled. "I'm glad it happened, and if it happens again, I won't object. But I'm still not sure I'm ready for something permanent. I mean, it happened so impulsively."

"I know, making love and being in love aren't the same," Colt said. "But it was a first step."

"We'll see. I'm glad you're with me, yes, but I need time to unscramble how I feel."

Colt turned to face forward. "I'm no expert on love, and I've never been very good at expressing my emotions. In a way I was lucky. Rachel and I were high school sweethearts, and at some point she became the most important person in my life. But I never really thought about how I felt. I just knew she was the one." He looked back at her. "Now I know you're the one."

"Please don't rush me," Lindsay said. "This happened too soon. Last night I let passion take over, and I liked it, but I don't know whether you're the one for me."

"I'll accept that for now. The last thing I want to do is rush you, but the door is open."

Doctor Strauss met them on her porch. "Lindsay, why don't you go on in? Toby Walker's inside. I'm sure he'd be glad to see you."

She caught Colt's sleeve as he started to follow Lindsay. "Gus, I need a word with you."

Colt looked at her, waiting.

"The way you're grinning, I assume something happened on your trip," Lois said. "And I don't think it has anything to do with finding a useable subspace transceiver."

"I admit I'm walking on air, but am I that obvious?"

"So what happened?"

"Let's just say we made some progress — no commitments yet but promising."

"Good. Just continue on. It'll happen soon enough." She smiled. "You'll see. Now let's go inside."

As they entered the house, she said, "Toby and I have been friends for over twenty years. I'm his son, Jake's, godmother. Lindsay has known him since she and Ed moved here. I can't speak for Lindsay, but I'd trust him with my life. He came to me a few days ago saying he was organizing a local defense team to keep the separatists from taking over the valley. He said he could use someone who could whip untrained recruits into shape. When I was sure he was serious, I suggested I knew someone who might be able to help."

Colt shook his head, thinking. "I'm not an advocate of involving private citizens in war," he said. "But it may fit in with what I'm planning to do. I'll hear what he has to say."

Inside, he found Lindsay talking to a tall, heavyset man with a weathered face and thinning brown hair. Colt immediately saw the resemblance to the younger Howard. They both noticed Colt and stopped their conversation.

"Gus, this is Toby Walker, Howard's brother," Lindsay said.

Walker extended a calloused hand, "Real pleasure to meet you, Gus. I can't thank you enough for pulling Howard out of the lake. I've heard good things about you."

"Lois speaks highly of you as well," Colt responded.

"Then she's probably told you why I'm here."

Colt grinned. "Yes, she did. And even though I don't favor involving civilians, I think a self-defense force can be a good idea as long as it's handled correctly." He paused. "However, I'm beginning to believe that the rebels aren't the real problem."

Walker cocked his head, "What do you mean, the rebels aren't the problem?"

"Right now it's just a gut feeling. Too many things aren't adding up. For instance, there was an attempt on Billy Hargety's life a couple of weeks back. All the evidence pointed to the rebels, but since he's the rebel leader, that doesn't make any sense.

"Then there was the nuke used on Kyoto. Either Hargety was genuinely out of the loop on that, or he's a much better actor than I give him credit for. On top of that, it was a really bad move for the rebels, so why did they do it? Who gave the order?"

"No one said the rebels know what they're doing," Walker said.

Colt barked a short laugh. "True, but the whole situation looks suspicious. I'm beginning to wonder if someone is using the rebels, and I don't think that most of the rebels even know it."

Walker considered that. "Interesting concept. Can we sit and discuss this further?"

"I'm afraid not right now. We just stopped by to pick up Brady before we go home and unload our supplies."

As if on cue, Lindsay walked into the room with Brady. "If you two have finished talking business, we need to get home."

Colt looked at Walker. "Give me a call later this evening, and we can talk."

That evening, when Lindsay returned from putting Brady to bed, Colt had just connected on the web to Fitzhugh in his Dennis O'Toole guise. He broke into a broad grin when he saw Colt. "Gus, me boy, it's good to see you again. It's been ages. How're ye doing?"

"Can't complain, Dennis. How about you?"

"Doin' well, thanks." He looked approvingly at Lindsay, who had walked up behind Colt. "Is that the lass you'd be marryin'?" he asked.

Colt looked back at Lindsay. He waited a moment, deciding that their personal status didn't need to be aired, before saying, "That's the story for public consumption. We'll see how it actually works out."

He turned to Lindsay. "Lindsay, this is Dennis O'Toole. Dennis, this is Lindsay Hansen."

"It's a pleasure to meet you, ma'am. When's the big day?"

"We reserved the church for July fortieth. Are you going to be able to make it?"

"I wouldn't miss it." He turned back to Colt. "I looked into the things you lost in shipment. I believe they're on their way to a warehouse in Dixon on Baldric Avenue. They should be there by the weekend after next. It appears that they won't be available until then because of some personnel shuffling." A map popped up in a separate window. "That's the location. The proprietor is Margaret Gilford, and you can reach her at Dixon Central Mail Service."

Colt nodded. "That actually works. I met someone today that I think can help me get started on my original project here."

"And what would that be?"

"Some people around here are getting tired of this fighting and want my help settling things down," Colt responded.

"Good luck to you. We could stand getting back to peaceful times."

"Thanks, Dennis. I appreciate you getting back to me so quickly about my shipment. One other thing, have you heard from Jana?"

"Not a peep. It's like she dropped off the grid." Fitzhugh glanced at his watch. "Would you look at the time? It's been great talkin' to you, Gus. Next time you're in First Landing, we'll have to get together at McGinty's."

After the connection was broken, Lindsay said, "I thought you weren't supposed to hold conversations with him in the clear."

"Well, first of all it wasn't in the clear. It was encrypted. You were out of the room when Jeffrey announced it. Second, what would anyone make of what we said?"

"If they were doing something at the address he gave you, they would at least be suspicious."

"Ah, but they're not," Colt replied. "That's just where he's leaving the information."

"And some equipment," Lindsay surmised.

"You got it."

"What did he mean by 'personnel shuffling'?"

"My guess would be that the rebels are moving my crew around to keep them from being pinpointed."

She frowned. "You're going to Dixon to break them out, aren't you?"

176

"I have to," he said. "Back before The Event the military adopted a policy of 'Leave no one behind.' It's a good policy, and if my people are being held, I have to do what I can for them."

"Won't that be risky?" She looked concerned.

"It could be, but I won't do anything to get captured or killed myself unless it's absolutely necessary."

"What does that mean?" she asked.

"It means that I'm going to avoid being captured, and especially killed, unless it will improve the military situation here from the Republic's standpoint. I can do more if I'm unrestricted, so unless my sacrifice would put a division of Imperial Marines on the ground to end this situation, I plan on staying alive and free. I'll be careful. I value my life. But I knew there were risks when I signed up for this job."

"I know." She wrinkled her brow. "Is it okay if I worry?"

"Does this mean you're developing feelings for me?" He resisted the urge to brush his fingers across her forehead to smooth away the wrinkles.

"I already said I like you. You'll have to settle for that — for now."

"Ah, there is hope."

"When are you leaving?"

"It should be easier after dark, so probably the following Saturday around sunset." He paused. "I need to contact Toby. I wasn't able to commit when he mentioned the town meeting Friday night. Now I know we can make it, and I have some ideas I want to discuss with him. If we can organize a resistance in the province, it will help put a stop to the rebellion."

He stood up and stretched. "I'll talk to him in the morning. Meanwhile, I have a pump to install tomorrow and a fence to repair. I think it's time to get to bed."

"After last night there isn't any point in using the guest room," she said. "You're welcome to sleep with me."

"What about Brady?"

She paused. "That is a problem, isn't it? We'll think of something."

Chapter 25

Two nights later, the school gymnasium was filled with families from all over the southern half of the province, a few from as far away as Sykesville. All the chairs and bleachers were taken, and an overflow crowd stood at the back of the room.

Toby Walker stepped onto the dais and surveyed the audience. When he cleared his throat, the AI focused the sound pickup on him. There was a brief squeal of feedback as it adjusted the level. Then Walker spoke, "Neighbors, you all know why we're here tonight. There're some people who are trying to take over the planet and kick the Republic off by force. Right now they only hold a few places." He looked at the couple from Sykesville. "Bonny and Vince can tell you what it's like living under them, but so far it's been mostly restrictions on movement. One thing we've noticed; they don't like people disagreeing with them. I'm sure you've heard about Howard's little adventure.

"A lot of us are getting worried that they may try to move in on us next. We can either stand by and let them take over, or we can tell them to stay out. If we tell them to stay out, we have to be ready to back it up. Also, I've been talking to some people who have the feeling the separatist militia won't just pack up and go home if the Republic leaves. I personally don't want to trade Republic citizenship for a military dictator. If we want to stay free, we'll need training and organization. We'll need someone with serious military experience to guide us."

He stepped back from the edge of the platform. "I only know one person in the province who fits that description, and he's here with us tonight. He was a full commander before he left the navy to join us in homesteading. He's already shown me a thing or two that tells me he knows what he's talking about. For those of you who haven't met him, here's William August. Come on up, Gus."

Colt bounded up onto the platform, and the AI focused sound pickups on him. "Thanks, Toby." He turned to the families gathered in the gym. "Folks, I'll get right to the point. The people who are holding Sykesville are led by professionals. Most of the militia are made up of civilians, but they take orders from people who know what they're doing. If you find yourself facing a large contingent of them, you have three choices: run, hide, or surrender. Do not try to fight them. They will kill you."

Low murmurs and shuffling filled the gym.

"I know that's not what you wanted to hear, but it's essential that you understand what you're up against. Follow that rule and you'll have a much better chance of staying alive. But that doesn't mean we can't stand up for ourselves." The murmurs began to die down.

"First of all, I don't believe the people who are holding Sykesville have enough professionals to mount a significant widespread attack. They want to focus on the control points: the cities and larger towns. Even that will spread them thin. Farmland will be their lowest priority, and as long as more or less normal commerce takes place, it'll probably stay that way."

Someone in the audience spoke up, and the AI focused a pickup on him. "You mean we should just sit back and ignore this mess?"

Colt looked at the man. "That may well be all you have to do. I certainly hope so, but we don't want to completely ignore the issue and be unprepared. The question is, what can we do and how do we go about it?"

Colt looked over the audience and could see his message was sinking in. He continued, "Back on Earth before The Event, a type of fighting called guerilla warfare was developed. Small groups of men and women working independently of other groups would attack and harass enemy forces in quick raids and then blend back into the countryside. Some groups would set traps for the enemy forces. Others would attack and destroy their supplies and communications. The basic idea was that using hit and run tactics to strike the enemy made it difficult or impossible for them to effectively strike back."

He paused again. "Here, though, we have to consider two things. First, the separatists, for the most part, aren't our enemy. When this thing is over, we're going to want to go back to being friends with many of them. In other words, we want to avoid injuring or killing unless they threaten us. Second, guerilla warfare was developed when sensors were much less sophisticated. From my observations, some of these militia units have the most up-to-date equipment. That means that it will be much harder to simply fade into the countryside or even to set a trap. In fact, unless we have similar sensor capability, we won't even be able to tell when we're being watched."

He held up his hand to ease the rumblings from the crowd. "It's not quite as dire as that. For one thing, they don't have enough sensors to watch everyone all the time or to even watch a few people all the time. For another, most of the sensors we have to worry about can be spotted easily once you know what to look for. Your chances of actually being observed are pretty remote.

"That said, there are a lot of things that keep us from outright guerilla warfare. Being concerned about our friends is just one of them. Another is the question of what kind of attacks can we expect, if any?

"Since the militia is stretched pretty thin, I think it would be hard for them to simply march into the lower half of the province. The most likely attack would be more along the lines of house-to-house searches for weapons accompanied by webcasts pointing out how useless resistance is. That sounds pretty harmless, but once they take control of your homes, they're not likely to give them back unless you agree to their terms. In the end they have control of the province. If we're going to keep them out, it will help if we can keep them occupied in their own half of the province."

"You mean take the battle to them?" someone asked.

"Something like that, but I'm thinking more along the lines of tossing apple wasps into the middle of a bivouac or broadcasting static on their operating frequencies or sending nonsense-encrypted messages using their comm channels. Things to disrupt their operations. Let's do some brainstorming to come up with effective, nonviolent ideas."

The meeting broke up an hour and a half later. Most of the ideas had been impractical, but teams were assigned to work on some of the ones that seemed most feasible, and other teams were put together to get the information that would be needed to put them into operation. The demand for a marksmanship class was overwhelming, so Colt finally gave in to teaching it. "Use it only for self-defense and then only as a last resort," he said as he stepped off the platform.

A voice from the crowd was familiar. Colt and Lindsay both turned to see Jeff Lippmann and his wife, Rebecca, working their way through the crowd toward them.

Colt extended his hand. "Jeff, Rebecca. It's good to see you. I didn't expect you to be here."

"You know I belong to the militia," Jeff said. "And I have to report this."

"No, actually you don't," Colt replied. "Let's find a place to talk."

A moment later they were seated in the teacher's lounge. Colt wasted no time. "Everyone who came here tonight is concerned about protecting their own homes and personal freedom. I assume the same is true for you. In fact, the other night I got the distinct impression that you weren't totally committed to the separatists."

Jeff hesitated and then nodded.

Colt continued, "I've seen something in military history books like what's going on here. People who had genuine concerns started a rebellion, and others took over the movement for their own purposes. Ever hear of the Takahara Revolution?"

"No."

"About two hundred years ago the royal family had a dimwit son who kept getting into trouble on Earth, so they had the Colonization Board send him to Takahara as the governor. It was supposed to be a sinecure position, but he decided it gave him absolute power and became a repressive dictator. The citizens revolted, but a local politician subverted the revolt and took over the planet. The citizens ended up worse off than with the royal as governor."

"What's that got to do with this situation?"

Colt paused. "I think that's happening here. I keep seeing things that just don't add up. Hargety and his separatists aren't that well organized, but the militia is. I believe someone else is pulling the strings, and like the woman who took over Takahara, they plan to take over 'for the duration.'"

"I don't see it."

"Think about the militia. It's clear that some of the militia are professionals, your sergeant for instance. Where'd they come from? They sure aren't settlers."

"Yeah, now that you mention it, there are a lot of officers and several NCOs who seem too professional," Jeff agreed.

"Then of course, why cut off subspace communication unless you want to keep the Republic out of the fight until it's too late to matter?" Colt added. "I could go down a long list of things I've found out since I started looking into it, but it all points to someone who is in a hurry to take control."

Lippmann simply nodded, looking grim.

Colt regarded him for a moment before he said, "I have to admit I don't know what the Colonization Board will do with this situation. If we do have to move, there is a fund that's supposed to cover all the expenses."

"But the whole point is that we don't want to move. This is our home."

"I know. It would be a tragedy to have to leave here. Perhaps we won't. When we have subspace communication again, I know several people who are good at finding loopholes in the law. Maybe they can help. If they can't, well my loyalty goes with the Republic. I'll bet that despite being a separatist yours does too."

After a brief hesitation Lippmann nodded. So did Rebecca. Lippmann finally spoke, "Making noises about seceding was supposed to give us better bargaining power, but you're right, it looks more and more like a serious attempt to secede. That isn't what I signed up for. Trouble is when I start talking about getting out, people keep telling me we'll all be tried for treason if we don't succeed." He stood up and started pacing.

"Fortunately, that isn't true. Ever since the Expansion started, the Republic has had an official policy that citizens' first loyalty is to their home world. Planets can secede from the Republic. Of course, if the separation is by force, the Republic can decide to restore colonial government unilaterally, like they did on Takahara. All it takes is a valid complaint from a citizen, but even then they don't punish anyone. They leave that to the local government."

"In other words, the militia is setting us up to fail?" Jeff questioned.

182

"That I can't say," Colt answered. "We're far enough out that the Republic may not believe we're worth the bother. Even if it does and uses force to take the planet back, only a handful of individuals will be prosecuted. Personally, I'm more concerned with what will happen if whoever is behind this pulls it off."

Lippmann stopped pacing and stared at Colt for a moment. "You're sure that only a handful will be prosecuted?"

"Yes. The Takahara Revolt established the precedent. The only people who were prosecuted were the ones who diverted the revolution. The rest were given blanket pardons." Again Colt paused. "So you see why I said you don't have to report this."

Lippmann looked relieved. "As soon as I get out of here I'm going to call Grainger and tell him to stuff it."

"Before you do that, I have a request." Colt stood up. "You know what we're planning. We need to find out what's going on before it's too late. Maybe these professionals really are in it to keep us from having to give up the planet, but I don't buy it. I believe we need to keep tabs on what they're doing, so we could use someone on the inside."

"Me?" Lippmann shook his head. "I'm no spy."

"No, and I won't ask you to be. I have something else in mind, which should be much safer."

"Some of those ideas were really interesting," Lindsay said. They were walking arm in arm across the school parking lot to the van. "Will we really be able to do any of that?"

"That's the beauty of this approach, all of these proposed attacks are just pranks that many of us did in school, but these will be carried to the extreme. We may really be able to keep the militia off balance enough that they can't get organized for a serious move into this part of the province – at least for a while."

They reached the van and the doors slid open as they approached. Colt escorted Lindsay to the passenger side to help her in. "You realize that what you just did is absolutely archaic," Lindsay noted.

Colt laughed. He walked around the front of the van and climbed into the driver's seat. "I still can't believe that stunt Robby and Jean signed up for. What are those critters, again? Skunk caterpillars?"

"That's what we call them. School kids play tricks with them all the time. Of course, they're only in season at this time of the year."

Colt pulled up the thrust lever and eased the van forward as he lifted it out of its parking space. As soon as they were above twenty meters, he said, "Doctor Strauss, Amelia."

Amelia responded, "Very good, sir," and took control of the van.

Five minutes later they reached Doctor Strauss's house, and Colt landed the flyer. Lois came out with an eager Brady who ran up to them.

"How come you guys took so long?" Brady demanded.

Colt dropped into a crouch so he could look Brady in the eye. "We did take a while, didn't we? Sorry, partner. It was important."

"How'd it go?" Lois asked.

"Gus gave them something to focus on," Lindsay replied. "I think it'll help make them less anxious."

"That sounds mysterious," Lois said. "Come on in and tell me about it."

"It wasn't that complicated. I just gave them some things to do that will make it harder for the organized forces up north to pay attention to us. If our people can pull off half the missions they signed up for, the northern forces will be too busy to do anything but clean up messes. I figure most normal citizens aren't enthusiastic about fighting battles, but they do worry about protecting their homes. If they're thinking about how to cause mischief, they won't have as much time to fret."

"Now there's an interesting concept," Lois remarked. "So what did they sign up for?"

###

On their way out Lois stopped at the door. "I like the sound of this. It will tie Billy and his goons in knots."

Colt stopped and looked back at her, "You know, I'm not sure Hargety has anything to do with Sykesville. He may be arrogant, but I don't think he meant to get into any kind of real conflict. Yes, he's taking credit for militia action, but it's mostly bluster."

"Well, whoever is leading it, the rebel militia around Sykesville is going to have their hands full. I wish I could be there tomorrow night. You will be recording it, won't you?"

"Of course, that's it!" Colt brightened. "We can stream it live and put the recording on the web as soon as it's over. Great idea, Lois. See you later." He turned and followed Lindsay and Brady down the front steps.

As Colt slid into the driver's seat of the van, Amelia announced. "I have a voice message for Mister August."

"No visual?"

"No, sir."

"Strange. Okay, play it back."

"Interesting town meeting, Gus," an electronically altered voice said. "You don't really think it will have an impact, do you? Say hi to Lindsay and Brady for me." The message ended.

"What was that all about?" Lindsay asked.

"It was a threat. They mentioned you and Brady so I'd know that. They didn't say what they wanted, so we'll probably hear from them again."

"What are we going to do?" she said, concern showing on her face.

"We need to be extra careful getting Brady to school and back until we get the next message, and we need to keep our eyes open. That's all we can do."

Chapter 26

A crowd had congregated outside the small bivouac area where the Sykesville militia trained. Many of the citizens of Sykesville and the surrounding countryside had turned out and were milling around, waiting for something to happen. The rumor campaign had worked. Colt could see one of the militia members standing on the steps of the headquarters trailer, bewildered by the growing number of people assembling in the gathering darkness. After a moment of what looked like puzzled contemplation, he went inside.

As soon as the door shut behind him, floating lights came on over the crowd and one of the local bands struck up a popular song. Couples near the band began dancing to the music. In another area a comedienne began telling jokes using a portable amplifier. Several resourceful vendors worked their way through the clusters of people, selling everything from lemonade to sandwiches. The throng took on a decidedly festive atmosphere.

"You're sure Jeff isn't in there?" Lindsay asked.

Colt unrolled his computer display, switching it to map mode. "If the locator code we got from him is right, he's out on patrol." He pointed to a red dot on the map of Sykesville. "That patrol doesn't get back here until 11:30. That's well after this show is supposed to be over."

"I'm surprised the folks inside the compound haven't tried to shoo us off," Lindsay said.

"I'll guarantee the commanders are convinced something is going to happen. They probably saw all the rumors on the web," replied Colt. "Ah, here we go."

Two squads of militiamen came stumbling out of the community tent, many of them still stuffing their shirts into their trousers. The squad leaders hustled their squads into two ground troop carriers, and they immediately headed for the gate nearest town. The citizens in front of the gate slowly gave way as the carriers pulled out of the compound. Then they closed in behind the carriers as they moved through the crowd. There were a few catcalls but mostly friendly waves.

"Drop off!" Jean's voice signaled in Colt's ear piece that the caterpillars had been dropped. He looked up knowing he couldn't see the two sailplanes and hoped that the patrolling flyers couldn't detect them either. He started his timer, "This should be interesting."

Then he spoke to the display AI, "Flash the lights, twice." The AI obediently complied, and the floating lights flashed briefly. The crowd immediately went quiet and turned to look at the headquarters trailer. The troop carriers halted, and the militiamen piled out, still a bit bewildered.

When the timer hit forty-five seconds, Colt whispered to the AI, "Start the drill."

A siren went off, and the compound loud speakers began blaring, "Attack drill! Attack drill! All hands to your battle stations!" Immediately the troops began pouring out of their tents. In less than thirty seconds every militia member in the compound was out and on the ground, weapons ready for an attack.

The speakers were still blaring when a rain of small objects began falling out of the sky landing all over the compound. The militiamen immediately started brushing at their clothes. The siren and loud speakers abruptly cut off, and militiamen could be heard swearing loudly.

In the next second several voices began shouting, "Skunk caterpillars!" and the whole crowd erupted in laughter.

"Our job here is done. Nice work," Colt said to the display. "Film at eleven." He and Lindsay began walking away from the compound as he rolled up the display and slipped it into his jacket pocket.

###

A babble of voices filled Lindsay's common room. The video of the caterpillar drop was playing for the fourth time on the big screen. People were standing and sitting around the room, still laughing at the militia frantically brushing off the evil smelling creatures. Robby and Jean stood arm in arm, beaming. Everyone congratulated them.

Colt walked over, "Great job, kids." He glanced at his watch. "It looks like it's time to hold the debriefing." He turned to the group and said, "Everybody get comfortable and let's get started. First of all, I want to congratulate you all for making this mission successful.

I have a few improvements for future operations, but I'll start by asking for your feedback. Toby?"

Toby Walker stood up. "I have to say I wasn't very comfortable when the militia came out and trained their guns on everyone. What would have happened if one of those guys had been trigger happy?"

"I have to agree," Colt said. I know they're supposed to have their weapons unloaded, but it would only take that one person who forgot to squeeze his trigger. I have to take the blame for that. I should have come up with a safer way to get them out of their quarters. Larry?"

"It was funny, but do you think it'll do any good?" Larry said.

"Probably not by itself. It might have them looking over their shoulders for a while, and if we keep up the low level pranks, they'll stay on edge. However, to have a long-term effect, we need to start disabling their equipment, interfering with their communications, and so forth. I believe we had some good ideas at the town meeting. For instance, they're using rotating offset cryptography to encode their communications. If they change the baseline and the offset frequently, it will take about five minutes to break the code. Usually, by then they will have finished the communication. On the other hand, we know they're using Jensen-Allworth engines to encode and decode. If we can rig one of theirs to burst transmit every time it receives or sends a message, we can break their codes as fast as they can change them. We have someone on the inside that should be able to do that for us. Obviously we can't give out names." Colt looked around the room to see everyone nodding in agreement.

"There are also other ideas being put to work to degrade rather than disable their equipment and to keep them from getting sleep and several other unpleasant but non-lethal problems."

"Emilio?"

"What about setting fire to their encampment? Wouldn't that discourage them a lot more than stink bugs?"

"It might, but keep in mind these are your friends and neighbors who happen to have a differing opinion. Burning down their camp could cause somebody to get hurt, maybe killed. I don't think any of us really wants to risk that. Besides, that would give them a reason to track down anyone involved."

Then Colt considered briefly. "Most of the farms around here have electronic fences, don't they?"

A murmur of agreement filled the room.

"Have you ever noticed how when you start a fire inside an electronic enclosure, the smoke accumulates until it spills over the top?"

"Yes, That's why we shut down the fences when we burn off a field," Emilio replied.

"How hard would it be to cap an enclosure? Emilio, can you look into that?"

Emilio brightened. "You're thinking the militiamen will all have penetrators so they can just march across the fields."

"Right. Smoke won't stop them unless they don't have breathing gear, but it will slow them down. And you don't have to burn the fields, just something that gives off a lot of smoke."

An hour later, after the meeting adjourned, Amelia broke in, "A voice message just came in for Mr. August."

"Let's hear it," Colt responded, frowning.

Once again the voice was electronically altered. "Congratulations, Gus. The first blow for the loyalists. Tell whoever dropped those worms they did a super job!"

Colt stood silent for several seconds. Finally, he said, "I was afraid of this. Whoever it is has us under surveillance; otherwise, he or she wouldn't have known when our guests left. On the other hand, it also means that even though he's keeping track of us outside the house, he doesn't have any bugs planted inside. At least, he didn't show any sign of knowing what we talked about tonight." He paused. "Right now all he's trying to do is make us uncomfortable."

"Well, he's succeeding," Lindsay responded. "I'm really worried that he'll come after Brady."

"Yeah, I know," Colt answered. "Still, I get the feeling that as long as he doesn't believe he's being threatened by us, he'll be content to watch … for now. We need to be alert though."

"Isn't there anything we can do?" Lindsay asked.

"I'm going to look into that. I can think of several possibilities, and maybe Fitz has some tech stuff that will help."

Chapter 27

Toby and Howard Walker had set up the firing range around a sharp bend three kilometers back from the open country farmland in one of the narrow collateral valleys that led into the foothills. They had worked for two days to plow up a three meter high berm and install baffles over the target area for safety. The shooters had just finished their last timed fire session.

"Clear and ground your weapons. Then step back from your positions," Toby Walker barked. In a few seconds all the weapons were on the tables at the firing positions, and all the shooters had stepped back.

"Weapons are cleared. The firing line is safe," Walker announced. "Everyone go forward and retrieve your targets."

As the targets were brought back behind the firing positions, Colt had a chance to look at them. He had to be careful not to show his dismay. Out of fifteen shooters only three had a decent score. He realized that most of them were probably unfamiliar with slug-throwers, but he was looking more for consistency than accuracy. After practicing all morning they were still producing wildly random patterns.

When the group had assembled in front of him, Colt said in a calm, low voice, "Take a look at your targets. I believe you can see why we are not ready for a gunfight right now. Only the three hunters show any proficiency with these rifles."

"That's not fair. Nobody uses rifles anymore," one of the shooters complained.

"It may not be fair, but do you want to risk your life on your shooting skill? This has nothing to do with fair. It has to do with keeping you alive in a fire fight."

"But we won't be using hunting rifles, will we?" another spoke out.

"I don't want any of us fighting at all, but if we have to, I want us to be able to hold our own, at least briefly. The military still trains using rifles. They do it to teach new recruits discipline under fire."

Colt paused and looked the shooters over. "Hopefully, you've learned some range safety. I expect you to put in at least an hour a day working on your proficiency, but don't practice alone. Get together with one of the hunters. And for Pete's sake, be careful. These guns may be archaic, but they're also deadly."

A glint of light from the northern ridge caught Colt's eye. Without turning to look he keyed his communicator, "Bogey on Rialto, fifteen meters from the top."

"That's near me," Howard Walker's voice came from the communicator.

"Remember he's probably armed."

Colt turned to the shooters as if nothing had happened. "Ladies and gentlemen, we've done a good day's work. As soon as you police your brass and clean your weapons, you can head for home."

"That's another reason for using a blaster," someone grumbled as the shooters moved off.

A flyer broke from the trees on the other side of the ridge where Colt had seen the glint. Almost immediately his communicator erupted with Howard Walker's voice, "Damn! I almost got to him but he got to the flyer first."

"Did you get a look at him?" Colt asked.

"Not really. He was in camouflage, face painted, and wearing a hat. I got pictures but they probably won't tell us much."

"What else?"

"He was carrying a tripod and a parabolic mike. My guess is he heard us discussing him and lit out."

Colt murmured, "You're probably right. Any information from the tracks to suggest size and weight?"

"Sorry, too many tracks were rubbed out."

"Okay, thanks. All hands, you might as well bring it in."

Colt walked over to Lindsay's van. "What did you pick up from his transponder?" he asked Amelia.

"His transponder was disabled," Amelia answered.

A few minutes later Howard Walker trotted out of the brush at the base of the ridge. When he reached Colt, he plugged the nanodrive from his helmet camera into the flyer's dash and brought up the video. "A black Fischer Comet with a sliding bubble canopy," Colt observed.

"There can't be more than five or six hundred of those on the planet," Walker said. He leaned forward and pointed toward the back end of the flyer. "That ding ought to be pretty easy to identify, if we can find it."

"Unfortunately, he probably won't be so careless next time," Colt said.

Amelia announced, "I just received a burst transmission for Mr. August."

"Play it back, please."

"That wasn't very nice, Gus. Do you know where Brady is?"

###

Colt flew all the way back to the farm with the thrust grip twisted to full, despite the speed governor engaging at 200 kph. Several times he started to call Lindsay, and then stopped. He didn't want to panic her. As soon as he grounded the van, he bolted for the house.

He almost ran into Lindsay as she opened the door. "Where's Brady?" he asked, trying to keep the tension out of his voice.

"He's playing with a friend. Why?" she asked. The expression on her face turned to alarm.

He wrapped his arms around her, holding her tightly for several seconds. "I got a message from our anonymous caller. I think I made him mad. We had better get Brady home right away."

Her face went white. "My God, is he in danger?"

"I hope not, but we need to get him now."

"I'll call Ramona and get her to bring him home." She reached for her communicator.

"We should probably go pick him up. Just tell her we're coming for him." He turned and headed for the van. "You drive since you know where we're going."

Lindsay called Ramona Commager while they rushed to the van. As she was getting into the driver's seat, the van relay responded with, "Hi, Lindsay. Is it time for Brady to come home already?"

Lindsay pulled the door shut. "We're on our way over to pick him up. We'll explain when we get there."

Lindsay lifted the van off the pad and turned it toward Commager's farm to the east. Without taking her focus off the terrain in front of them, she demanded, "How did this happen?"

"The snooper was spying on us at the firing range. We took him by surprise and almost caught him," Colt answered. "I'm hoping he was just trying to scare me as payback."

They quickly crossed the lake, and moments later Lindsay set the van down on the Commager's pad. Ramona, a plain looking woman with dishwater blond hair, came out on the porch while Colt and Lindsay were getting out. She waved and hurried down the steps. "Jason and Brady went down to the grove to play in Jason's fort." She nodded at a clump of trees a few hundred meters away. "Vince left to get them as soon as you called."

Colt broke into a run toward the grove. Before he had covered ten meters, a flyer rose from the trees and swept in a small half circle toward him. Colt stopped, pulled out his communicator, and used it to take several pictures. The flyer swung away and headed north, barely clearing the tree tops. Colt began running again.

When he reached the grove, he found Commager sprawled on the ground, not moving. Jason was crying, prodding him. "Daddy! Daddy! Are you all right?" he sobbed.

Colt dropped down next to the two of them. He quickly checked Commager. When he found that Commager was breathing, he put his hand on Jason's shoulder and said as calmly as he could, "Your dad's going to be okay. Where's Brady?"

It took Jason several seconds to overcome his sobbing enough to say, "They took him."

"They took him? There was more than one?"

Jason nodded, but before he said anything else, Commager twitched and groaned. Colt said, "Let's get your dad back to the house."

Commager was a large man. With Jason's help Colt managed to get him into a fireman's carry and started walking toward the house. After a few dozen meters, Commager twitched violently, and Colt almost dropped him. After a few more meters, Commager mumbled, "I'm all right. Let me down." Colt lowered him to the ground. He was so wobbly that Colt almost tried to pick him up again, but with his left arm over Colt's shoulder he was able to walk shakily.

Ramona saw them as soon as they stepped out of the trees and headed for them at a run. "Vince, Jason, are you all right?" she shouted. Commager waved weakly.

When she got near, Colt said, "Looks like a stunner. There shouldn't be any lasting effects." She threw her arms around Commager, forcing them to stop.

Lindsay ran up right after Ramona did. "Where's Brady? I don't see Brady. Where is he?" Her voice was approaching hysteria, and tears ran down her cheeks.

Struggling to help Commager stay on his feet, Colt could only say blankly, "They took him."

"Who took him? Who took him?" She demanded, sobbing.

Jason had regained some of his composure. "Two men. And they shot daddy."

Brushing at her tears, Lindsay turned to Commager. "Did you see them? Can you describe them?"

Commager drew himself up as best he could. "I saw them. Two men in hunting camouflage. One was about my height and thin. Brown hair, light-colored eyes. The other was shorter and heavyset. Black hair and dark eyes and a beard."

Colt could see that Lindsay was near the breaking point. "Lindsay, you and Ramona help get Vince to the house. I'm going to call the marshal." He moved Commager's arm to her shoulders, and Ramona took the other arm.

The call went through immediately. "Marshal's office, Deputy Marshal DeVry speaking. How may I direct your call?"

"This is William August. I need to report a kidnapping."

There was a pause. "Yes, sir. Just a moment, please."

A few seconds later a new voice came over the communicator. "This is Deputy Tucker. You say there's been a kidnapping?"

Colt recognized the name as one of the deputies that had questioned him and Lindsay in Sykesville. "Owen, this is William August. Mrs. Hansen's son, Brady, was taken just a few minutes ago from the Commager's farm southeast of Sykesville. I have some pretty good images of the flyer he was taken in, and Vince Commager and his boy can both describe the men."

"Right, Mister August. I remember you and Mrs. Hansen. Sorry about the other night. Do you know what kind of condition Brady was in?"

Colt looked at Commager. "As far as we know he was unharmed. Are you ready to download the images?"

"Ready." When the images had been transmitted, Tucker said, "I can make out the registry number in this image. Let me run it."

A few seconds later he came back with, "It belongs to Morgan Hildreth. He reported it stolen late last night. Uh oh." He paused, "This is strange. The whole record just disappeared. Now I'm getting an interdiction message. This record has been sealed from public access. That doesn't make any sense, unless …" Again he paused. "Let me call you back in just a second."

It was closer to a minute when Colt's communicator buzzed. "Mister August, I'm on my personal communicator. I have to apologize. I've been instructed to erase all evidence of your report and our conversation. Direct orders from the Commandant."

"What!" Colt exploded. "What the hell is going on here?"

"I wish I knew because this isn't right. I may get in trouble for it, but I was able to recover what was in the stolen flyer report. I'm sending you the information I captured." He paused. "Now I'm getting a message that the marshal's office isn't supposed to respond to any more calls from outside Sykesville. I can't do more right now, but I'll try to drop by after I go off duty this evening to see if I can help in any way."

By then they had reached the porch and Lindsay and Ramona were able to let Commager sit down. Lindsay saw Colt's expression. "What is it?" she asked, her voice shaking.

"Apparently we're on our own," he said flatly.

"What do you mean?" Lindsay demanded.

"Tucker was given direct orders not to help us by the military governor of Sykesville." Colt answered.

"That can't be all there is. We've got to get Brady back." She wrapped her arms around him and buried her face in his shoulder. "We have to!"

"Tucker said he'll stop by after work to see if he can help. He also sent me some information that may help, but I'll need to have a workstation to follow up on it. We'd better get home."

They flew most of the way back to the farm in numbed silence when Lindsay finally said, "This was my fault, wasn't it? I shouldn't have let Brady out of my sight."

Colt put his hand on her shoulder. "It's not your fault. He was with friends. He should have been safe. Don't blame yourself."

"What are we going to do?"

"We're going to have to find him ourselves. The information I got from Tucker was that the stolen flyer has a built-in tracking device. Even if the local constabulary isn't allowed to track it, we have the ID and should be able to get my spook friend or the Home Guard to run it down. The trouble is Dennis may take hours to get back to us, and I don't know how fast the Guard can react either. Their software is classified, no public access."

"I probably shouldn't tell you this," Lindsay hesitated, "but Howard Walker is a notorious hacker." She looked quickly at Colt. "Don't get me wrong. He doesn't do any harm. He just does it as a game. He claims there isn't a computer system on the planet he can't break into."

By the time they landed a few minutes later, Walker had agreed to help and was on his way to Lindsay's house.

###

"That's where the flyer is right now." Walker pointed to an open field in the monitor screen. "From the looks of the countryside around there, they just ditched it. I don't see any place they could be holding Brady."

"You mean we can't find him?" Lindsay demanded.

"There is a possibility," Walker added. "According to the report, the flyer's tracking device logs where the flyer has been. If they dropped Brady off and then ditched it, we should be able to backtrack and find out where else they stopped. The trouble is the flyer doesn't transmit the log. It's only available on the console monitor."

"In other words we have to go to where the flyer is," Colt said.

"It's a little more complicated than that. It requires a user's identification coded into an access fob or a communicator," Walker said.

"It looks like it's time to call on Morgan Hildreth," Colt said. He picked up his communicator. After a brief delay a woman's voice answered, "Morgan Hildreth."

"Ma'am, this is William August. We need your help. My fiancée's son has been kidnapped, and the kidnappers used your flyer."

"My flyer was stolen last night," she said.

"Yes, we've located it and will be happy to take you to it, but we'd need you to give us access to the last few hours of the trip log before you take it home."

"I can certainly do that," she said.

Jeffrey interrupted, "There is a flyer approaching the landing pad. It identifies itself as belonging to Owen Tucker."

"Perfect timing," Colt said. "Let's get moving."

Tucker stepped out of his flyer as they walked out of the house and onto the porch.

"Owen, thanks for coming. We found the flyer the kidnappers used. We're on our way to pick up Ms. Hildreth and take her to it so she can give us access to the trip log. Do you want to come with us or follow along in your flyer?"

"Should I ask how you found it?" Tucker asked.

"Probably not," Colt replied.

"I'd better take my flyer. If we catch these guys, I should bring them in, and my flyer's equipped for transporting suspects."

Morgan Hildreth was a middle-aged woman in her nineties and a great grandmother. The only indication of her age was her flowing white hair. She expressed her sympathy for Lindsay as she heard the whole story of the kidnapping.

The abandoned flyer nestled under trees in a canyon north of Sykesville. Tucker took his time looking it over before he let anyone else approach it.

Morgan Hildreth spoke to the ship's AI using her communicator, "Jessica, do you know who I am?"

"Yes, Morgan."

"Did the people who took you do anything to you?"

"I don't know, Morgan. I've been inactive until you spoke to me just now."

"Typical," Tucker said. "An active AI would 'scream its head off' to the local authorities when it was stolen."

"Jessica, do you detect anything hazardous in you?" Morgan asked.

"My outer fusion cylinder is approaching its contamination limit," the AI responded.

"We don't have to worry about that," Tucker commented. "Let's see what that trip log has to say."

While the others looked on, Morgan activated the trip log and played back the entries starting from when the flyer was stolen.

"There it is," Colt said, pointing at the monitor. "It's the only stop they made between Commager's and here." He rolled out his display and laid it on the hood of the flyer. He called up a map of the area and put a marker on the spot the flyer had landed. "They must be in this house. It'll be dark soon. If we come in low and land in this canyon to the north," he pointed at the map on his display, "that'll keep us out of sight. Then Howard, Owen, and I can go up to the house on foot."

"I want to go too," Lindsay said.

"No," Colt responded. "You won't be able to help, and you're already on the verge of hysteria. I've been trained for situations like this, and I'm having a hard time keeping from screaming myself."

"I don't like it."

"I know, but if anything goes wrong, you may be our only lifeline. We need you at the van."

Lindsay wasn't placated and fumed all the way to the canyon. She checked her communicator along with Walker, Tucker, and Colt. Then she gritted her teeth and watched as they started the trek out of the canyon

Tucker waited till they rounded the first bend before he said, "I'm not completely comfortable letting civilians be in this operation, much less lead it. I'll be responsible if anything happens to either of you."

"I'm more than happy to let you lead," Colt said, "as long as it doesn't involve waiting for reinforcements."

"No reinforcements, but we will need to take a few minutes to survey the situation and figure out what we're up against. Especially we'll need to have some idea of where the boy is and where the kidnappers are. And I don't want to stumble on a lookout."

"I understand," Colt acknowledged. "I'm not suggesting we ignore the possibility of lookouts or sensors, but I believe this kidnapping was spur of the moment. They probably haven't set up anything yet. Commager said two men kidnapped Brady. We have to assume they have backup here. We know they used a stunner on Vince. That suggests they're not killers, at least when it isn't necessary. The rest we'll have to find out when we get there."

In ten minutes they had reached the end of the valley. By then Aurora had completely set. The only light came from the stars and a rapidly waning Selene. They stood behind a clump of bushes that stood about a hundred meters away from the house. The only light they could see in the house came from a room in the back.

Before they could determine anything else, Tucker tensed. "There's a flyer on the other side of the house," he said. "Howard, take up a position near it so you can keep them from getting away. Gus, I'm going around back. You set up in front to stop them if they try to come out there."

They had just started to move into position when Howard called, "Flyer coming in low from the south. No lights. Take cover."

Colt was about ten meters from the front door. He dove under a large shrub. Looking up, he spotted the flyer, a dark spot with no running lights against the rapidly darkening sky. He kept it in view as it approached until it landed behind the house. Moments later the back door to the house opened and a familiar voice yelled, "What the hell did you brainless son of a bitches do?" The voice moved into the house. "Can't you obey a simple order?"

"But, Colt almost caught me. We had to teach him a lesson."

"All you did was make him mad, and you left enough clues that it won't take long before he finds you. Where's the kid?"

"In the basement," another voice answered. "Want me to get him?"

"You've already done enough," the first voice said.

"Hey! Wait!" one of the voices frantically shouted.

Colt heard two blaster bolts, and the lights in the house went out. He was on his feet charging through the front door before he thought. A dim form in the next room turned toward him and raised its arm. He dove to the side and hit the floor rolling. A blaster bolt shrieked past, barely missing him. A large part of the front wall burst into fiery particles that showered into the front yard. He continued to roll to keep out of the line of fire, but there was only the single shot. He looked up in time to see a retreating back hurrying out of the other room.

Surging to his feet, Colt pulled out the hunting pistol Walker had given him. He sprinted into the next room, tripping over a body lying on the floor. As he hit the floor, the silhouetted figure fired at the back door, blowing out the door and the wall around it. Colt scrambled to a crouch and cautiously moved toward the hole. When he reached the smoldering back wall, the shooter was already in his flyer with the canopy coming down. He looked Colt's way.

For an instant Colt saw Grainger, the sergeant in charge of keeping tourists away from the Clermont. Then the canopy closed and the interior lights switched to flight mode. The flyer immediately rose from the ground, turned away, and began climbing and accelerating. Before it could disappear into the deepening murk, Colt was dazzled by the distinctive purple beam of a Franklin two-phase that sliced through the flyer cutting it in two. The halves tumbled in the air and smashed into the ground, bouncing and knocking down trees until they came to rest.

Tucker came trotting around the building, holstering his blaster. "Damn, I wanted to take him alive, but I couldn't get in position."

Colt said, "Maybe it's better this way. He was a professional militiaman named Grainger. You probably wouldn't have been allowed to hold him." He turned back to the house. They had said Brady was in the basement. "Owen, do you have a light?" He grabbed the light and ran for the basement door while the others checked the two bodies in the kitchen.

He ran down the stairs. "Brady!" he shouted.

"Gus?" Brady's voice trembled. "Gus. Is that you?"

Colt made a beeline for his voice and found Brady tied to a support beam. Making quick work of the knots, he freed the boy, picked him up, and hugged him.

"Am I glad to see you!" he said.

"Me too, but be careful. I need to go really bad."

Charging up the stairs with Brady in his arms, Colt fumbled for his communicator. He flipped it open to call Lindsay. "I've got Brady. He's okay. See you at the landing pad."

After a brief delay they walked out the front door and started down the path toward the landing pad. Tucker and Walker joined them. "I presume this crime scene is in your hands now, Owen. Do we need to stick around?" Colt asked Tucker

"I know where to find you," Tucker said. "Off the record, thank you. I don't know what's going on between you and the commandant, and I'd just as soon not know. The militia may not like it, but you helped solve a major crime today."

They were waiting by the pad when Lindsay set the van down. Colt put Brady on the ground and let him run to her waiting arms. Smiling, but with tears streaming down her cheeks, she held his hand as she walked up to Colt. "I think it's time we all went home," she said.

On the way back to the farm, Colt gave control of the flyer to Amelia. He turned to Brady who was sitting in his mother's lap. "So, partner, were you scared?"

Lindsay shook her head, frowning at him.

"He'll be okay. The sooner we get him talking about it, the sooner he'll get over it," Colt told her. She was still frowning but nodded hesitantly.

"How about it, Brady? It's all right. I sure was afraid."

"Yeah …" Then, "Why did they do that, Gus?" Confusion wrinkled his face.

"I wish we knew, Brady. I wish we knew. Can you tell us what happened?"

"I was playing with Jason in his fort when these two guys flew up. They got out, and one of them said, 'Hey, which one of you kids is Brady Hansen?' Jason pointed at me. The guy said, 'Brady, you have to come with me. Mister August said to bring you home.' I didn't believe him." He stopped.

He looked down as if ashamed. "I was going to run away, but Mr. Commager came up and said, 'What's going on here?' and they shot him."

"Yes, but he's all right. It was a stunner," Colt assured him. "It just put him to sleep. What happened next?"

"I couldn't run." He paused again. "I was too scared. Was that okay?"

"Yes, Brady. You did the right thing."

Over the next several minutes Colt got Brady to talk about being taken to the hideout and being tied up in the basement. Colt was careful not to make it too serious, but he still wanted to make sure that Brady knew to be careful in the future. Talking seemed to help because by the time they landed Brady had settled down and was dozing off.

Colt was tight lipped as he and Lindsay returned to the common room after putting Brady to bed. Inside he was raging. When he stopped, he stood silent for a moment before saying, "I'm sorry I got you involved in this. It was supposed to be a relatively safe way to put stumbling blocks in front of the rebels. Then they kidnapped Brady." He paused. "I don't know what Grainger would have done if we hadn't arrived."

"You think he would have killed Brady?"

"He might have planned to get rid of any witnesses, or he might have dropped Brady off here with a note about how easy it had been. I don't know, but I don't want to put you and Brady in that position again"

"What can you do about it?"

"I'm going to have it out with this so-called commandant," he said.

"What do you mean, have it out?"

"I'm going to walk into her office and tell her enough is enough."

"Are you crazy? You won't get within twenty meters of the commandant. You'll probably get yourself thrown in prison, or worse, killed."

He took her hands. "Look, I got you and Brady involved in this, and I don't want to risk anything more happening to you. I will be taking a chance, but I don't believe the separatists would want the bad press if something were to happen to a 'concerned citizen.' All I need to do is get the media involved, and I know just how to do that."

"But if your image gets on a webcast, someone could recognize you."

"I have to take that risk. This harassment has gone on long enough. I can't have you and Brady in danger because of me." He led her to the couch and sat down beside her. "Grainger killed the two kidnappers because they weren't supposed to kidnap Brady — at least, not then. They'll take at least a few days to get organized to start harassing us again, but just in case, I'm going to get a reliable guard to stay with you and Brady while I'm gone. I'm going to make sure you and Brady are safe, and I'm going to make certain it stays that way."

She sat in silence, her emotions playing over her face. "But what about you?"

"Look, something about this rebellion shouts there's more going on than they want the public to know. If I go in with live video coverage, they won't be able to do anything without exposing themselves. As long as I stick to discussing the harassment, I can get in and out without forcing them to do anything drastic."

He got up, walked over to the web terminal and started typing. A few minutes later he received a coded message back from Fitzhugh: Dave Cavanaugh is Jana's cameraman. I'll contact him and Martha Fletcher of Corona News Service, tell them your story, and have them in Sykesville by 9:00 a.m. tomorrow. Good luck.

Colt beckoned Lindsay over and showed her the message. "That should take care of me. Now I need to contact Toby to help me find a guard."

Chapter 28

The next morning Walker flew Colt Sykesville. "Are you positive this is the best way to do this?" Walker asked as they approached the reception center.

"No I'm not, but it's all I have for now," Colt answered.

As they were touching down, Walker glanced at the flyer's clock. It showed 9:00 am. He frowned. "I don't see anything that looks like media."

"Don't worry. They'll be here. I trust my contact." Colt got out of the flyer. "Thanks for the lift. I'll call Lindsay when I get done."

"You're sure you don't want me to wait?" Walker asked.

Colt nodded, waved, and turned toward the reception building. Inside the same clerk was behind the counter. He stood up from his desk. "Good morning, Mr. August. In for more farm supplies?"

"I'm here to see the commandant."

"Excuse me?"

"I'm here to see the commandant," Colt repeated.

"Do you have an appointment?"

"I assume she has a time for seeing disgruntled citizens."

"I'll have to check. Please have a seat over there." He walked back to his desk and sat down in front of the web phone.

Colt started toward the indicated chairs. "By the way," he turned back to the clerk, "have Mr. Cavanaugh or Ms. Fletcher shown up yet this morning?"

The clerk looked at him over the video unit. "No, you're the first out-of-towner today." He turned away from Colt and started talking to the video.

Colt watched as the clerk made the calls. Although he couldn't see the display, it was clear that the clerk had to talk to several different people. Midway through his conversation, he stopped and glanced at Colt, "Yes, sir. I understand, sir." He continued to talk, glancing furtively at Colt several times. Colt got the uncomfortable feeling that something was wrong and started looking for the nearest exits.

A few minutes later the entrance door opened, and four militiamen came in with stunners drawn. The clerk nodded toward Colt. The militiaman with corporal's stripes said, "Mr. August, you'll have to come with us."

Colt carefully stood up. "What's going on? I'm here to see the commandant. I don't need an armed escort."

By then the militiamen had surrounded him. The corporal addressed the man on Colt's right, "Pat him down and shackle him."

Colt protested, "Hold on. What is this?" He turned to face the man who was approaching him. He glanced at each of the militiamen, realizing that the corporal was the only one who had actually armed his stunner.

Without taking more time to think, he grabbed the approaching militiaman and swung him into the corporal, knocking the stunner out of his hand. He dove and picked up the fallen weapon, bringing it up and firing as he rolled. He stunned all four of the militiamen before they could react. Standing up, he faced the clerk, "Sorry, my friend." He thumbed the charge to its lowest setting and fired.

He started for the door but paused. A set of video displays in the back of the room caught his eye. Vaulting over the counter, he trotted back to the displays. They were for cameras monitoring the parking lot and the reception building. He realized someone was probably watching what had just happened and had a unit on its way to recapture him.

Taking a quick look at the control panel, he began switching off the cameras and the transmission circuit. Then he began searching for the building's power module. He wanted to make sure the sensors couldn't be restored by remote control. There was no circuit breaker panel visible inside the building, so he dashed out the front door to look for the access on the outside. He found it on the end of the building. He pulled the master switch, powering down the entire facility. Then he threw the stunner down by the front door of the building and headed for town at a trot.

He had barely gotten away from the reception center when he heard the trolley approaching. He ducked behind a parked flyer, swearing under his breath. He impatiently watched as the driver pulled up to the loading shelter. He could see the driver pull out his communicator to transmit his arrival to the clerk but the man didn't seem concerned when there was no answer. Instead, he leaned his seat back and pulled his cap bill over his eyes.

Keeping flyers between him and the driver, Colt ran in a crouch toward the north end of the lot. About halfway there he saw the gate guard walking rapidly toward the reception building. He ducked down behind another flyer to avoid being seen. Colt heard him mumbling about the power cutting off in the middle of a webcast. When the guard cut through the parked flyers, Colt dashed to the gate and out of the parking lot.

He had entered a newer part of town. Trees and shrubs provided sparse cover, but the roads wandered, making it harder for anyone who might be pursuing him to see him from any distance. As soon as he had gone around a bend and was no longer visible from the parking lot, he straightened up and began walking briskly. He deliberately followed streets that angled him north and westward, away from the direct route to downtown.

He pulled his communicator out of his pocket and removed the battery to disable the tracking locator. More than once he passed someone on the street. He waved casually and maintained his power walk pace. In a few minutes he reached the older part of town. When it had been built, the Colonization Board had a single design for all debarkation points, laying the streets out in a rectangular grid. He looked back frequently to be sure no one was following him. Ten minutes later he guessed he had covered about a kilometer. He pulled out his communicator and reinstalled the battery. He dialed a personal number. "Tucker," the voice said.

"Owen, this is Gus. I'm trying to get in to see the commandant, but I just realized I don't know where her office is."

"Gus! My God, what's going on? The militia has orders to shoot you on sight."

"Wow! Someone really doesn't want me to talk to her." He glanced around to see if anyone was closing in on him. "I'm not sure what's going on. When I checked in with the reception clerk, everything seemed to be going fine at first, but before long four militiamen charged into the building with stunners drawn. They were getting ready to clap me in irons. I was lucky to get away. So how do I find the commandant?"

"She's the mayor so she's using her own office on the east side of the Commons, but I don't recommend you get anywhere near her. Shoot on sight is no joke."

"I understand. Thanks for the info. I won't take any unnecessary risks. I'll give you a call when I'm through." When he switched off the connection, he dropped the battery out of his communicator and pocketed it.

He was still in a residential area, but he could see the roof of the hotel through gaps in the trees. He estimated he was only six or seven blocks from the Commons on the west side, and he knew exactly where he was going.

Just then a flash of movement caught his eye. A troop carrier a little over a block away was coming slowly up one of the cross streets. Colt dodged behind a densely flowered bush. He held his breath as he listened for an indication that the militiamen had seen him. The carrier stopped. When it started up again a few seconds later, Colt realized the militiamen were going house to house to canvass the local residents and he didn't have much time to get out of sight.

He sprinted to the next intersection, only slowing down long enough to make sure there wasn't a carrier coming up that street. He turned into the side street and continued sprinting. Two blocks farther, he spotted another carrier moving rapidly toward him. He ducked back and looked around. The only cover was a dense hedge around the house he stood in front of. He rolled under the hedge and crawled as far back as he could without coming out the other side.

As he watched, the carrier turned at the corner and offloaded two militiamen. The one who took Colt's side of the street walked within a meter of him. Colt held his breath as the man stopped and turned back toward the carrier. "Hey, Grimaldi, when does Meyers get to do the house to house?"

A voice from the carrier said, "Shut up and get on with it, Taylor." The carrier continued slowly down the street, while the militiamen went house to house.

Colt was getting ready to crawl out the back side of the hedge when a deep voice behind him said, "I gather you're the one they're looking for."

Colt rolled out from under the hedge. He looked up at a dark haired man frowning at him. "Why shouldn't I call that militiaman back?" the man asked.

"Because they have a shoot on sight order out for me."

The man took a step back, "What for?"

"I'm trying to talk with the commandant, and the militia doesn't want me to."

"Why not?"

"I'm not sure, but I suspect it has something to do with the fact that a couple of renegade militiamen kidnapped my fiancée's son yesterday and the militia is hushing it up for some reason."

"Can you verify that?" the man asked.

"Call Deputy Marshal Tucker."

The man extended his hand. "If Owen trusts you, that's good enough for me," he said, helping Colt to his feet. "I think you'd better get moving." He pointed to an opening in the hedge beside the house. "You can use that gate without being seen by the militia."

Colt thanked him and hurried toward the shops on the west side of the Commons. He had a particular shop in mind.

Ackerman, smiling, met him at the door of the jewelry store. "Mr. August, it's a pleasure to see you again, sir. What can we do for you today?"

"I don't know my way around Sykesville very well. I was wondering if you know of a place where I can get a costume for Brady's birthday party."

Ackerman continued to smile. "I'm afraid we don't have a costume shop, but a traveling theatrical troupe is in town. Perhaps they could help you."

The troupe had their vans in the old motor pool parking lot, too close to the patrolling militiamen as far as Colt was concerned, but he couldn't see any other way to try to get an effective disguise. He approached the motor pool around the south end of the Common's lake and stopped at the door of one of the vans. The side of the van was decorated with playbills.

An attractive woman in an unfamiliar period costume answered his knock.

"Hi. I know this is going to sound weird," Colt said, "but if possible I need to borrow a costume for a few hours. Is there someone I can talk to?"

"Come on in," she said to his surprise. Then she leaned back inside the van, "Hey, Matt, we've got a live one."

As Colt stepped inside the van, she said to him, "That has to be the most unique come-on I've ever heard."

"Pardon?"

"Your excuse for getting to meet us." She turned as a tall, thin man with a black beard came out of one of the rooms in the back of the van. "Meet Matt Striker," she said, and then turned to Colt. "I didn't catch your name."

"William August."

"Pleased to meet you, Bill. I'm Delores Quinton."

"Please, call me Gus," he said as he shook Striker's hand. "I remember you. You were Christian in Mutiny on the Bounty. You played for us my graduating year at the Academy back in '43."

"Ah, yes, the good old days. One of my favorite roles. Are you here for an autograph?"

"I'd love to have one, but I really am trying to find a costume I can borrow."

"What's the occasion?" Delores asked.

"I'm trying to get to see the commandant, and the militia is patrolling the street to keep me out."

"You're not that dastardly William August, are you?" Delores said with a twinkle.

"Dastardly, no. William August, yes."

"We were told you had a vendetta against the commandant and were trying to kill her," Striker said.

"I don't have anything against the commandant," Gus said. "Other than a couple of militiamen kidnapped my fiancée's son yesterday. I'm trying to talk to the commandant to make sure it doesn't happen again, but the militia seems to be determined to stop me."

"Why shouldn't we turn you in?" Delores asked.

"A shoot on sight order?" Colt sounded incredulous. "That's what you do to someone who has something potentially damaging to say. I don't expect any good citizen to obey it, so I don't expect you to turn me over to someone who might."

"An interesting turn of logic there," Striker laughed. "And you're right, we won't turn you in." He beckoned and started toward the back of the van. "Come with me."

When Colt emerged twenty minutes later, he had red hair and a beard and was wearing garishly bright clothes.

"All I need is a clown nose," he said.

From the motor pool parking lot he walked up the east loop road, deliberately gawking at the militia patrol in the street.

"Move along fellow. This isn't a circus," one of the militiamen said.

He continued up the street, trying to figure out how he could get by the guards and into the city building, when one of the guards caught his eye. It was Jeff Lippmann. He turned back and walked over to Lippmann.

"Excuse me," he said loudly. "What the hell is going on here? Why are you guys patrolling the streets?"

Lippmann recognized Colt and looked at him quizzically.

"Jeff, I'm surrendering to you," Colt said quietly. "Have me lie down so no one has an excuse to shoot, and invite the commandant's guards out to lock me up in the municipal jail."

"What are you doing?" Jeff asked.

"I don't have time to explain," Colt said. "Just do it."

Lippmann drew his blaster and pointed it at Colt. "On your face, now," he ordered. Colt immediately dropped to the ground. Lippmann waved to the two nearest guards to come over. Then he pulled out his communicator and made the call.

The first militiaman arrived with his blaster drawn. "What's up?"

Lippmann closed his communicator and put it away. "This is William August. He surrendered to me of his own free will so there's no need to shoot him. Just in case keep a blaster on him while I shackle him."

"How do you know he's August?"

"I've met him before," Lippmann answered. He finished locking the wrist bands of the shackles. Before he had completely patted

Colt down, four of the commandant's guards rushed out of the city building and down the steps. Lippmann stood up. "He's all yours fellows."

"Hey, wait a minute," said the first militiaman. "Shouldn't we be taking him in?"

"That's what these guys are doing. What do we want him for? The commandant will probably have some questions for him, but we caught him. Our job is done."

The commandant's guards pulled Colt to his feet and propelled him toward the city building. As they were leading him inside a carrier rolled up. A sergeant jumped out, drew his blaster, and pointed it at Colt. He swore loudly, stuffed the blaster back in his holster, and yelled, "What have you meatheads done? He was to be shot on sight!" The doors closed on Colt and the guards.

The city building only had one cell and it was empty. As the guards released his shackles and closed the door on Colt, one of them asked him, "What are we locking you up for?"

"Beats me. I just wanted to see if I could have a few words with the commandant. Would you see if she has time?" Colt thought about the guard's question. They obviously hadn't gotten the shoot on sight order, which meant the commandant hadn't issued it. When she found out about it, she would want to know who had and why. Someone wanted to keep him away from her, probably because it would tell her something she wasn't supposed to know. Whoever it was, it was becoming increasingly clear that the militia had two chains of command at work.

Colt had just finished pulling off the wig and fake beard when one of the guards returned. "The militia has word that you plan to kill the commandant."

"Does that make sense to you? I surrendered of my own free will, and I'm unarmed. Ask them where they got that information."

The guard returned a few minutes later. "They said it was passed down through channels."

"In other words no one is taking responsibility for it. Did it come down through your channels?"

"Well, no."

"Makes you wonder who's in charge here, doesn't it?" Colt questioned. "Are there any off-world ex-military in the commandant's guards?"

"Just one, Corporal Jennings. Why?"

"That means you didn't hear about the shoot on sight order when it went out. You just heard about it a few minutes ago, right?"

The guard nodded agreement.

"That had to be a last ditch effort to keep me from talking to the commandant." Colt paused. "Okay, let me tell you what I want to talk to her about. You can pass it on and she can decide whether to talk to me. Fair enough?"

When the guard left again, Colt reclined on the cot and stared at the ceiling, wondering over and over if he had done the right thing. Eventually he dozed off.

He woke to voices coming from outside the cell area. "We came here to interview Mr. William August," A woman's voice demanded. In a moment a blond, older man carrying a video camera came in accompanied by a guard. He reached through the bars and shook Colt's hand. "Sorry we're so late. I'm Dave Cavanaugh. Martha is getting scanned and will be here in a minute."

Cavanaugh began setting up sound pickups around the cell. "Before we could leave First Landing, we had to cover a group of protesters outside the governor general's palace," he explained. "By the time the dust settled, it was already late. Then, when we got here, the blokes at the reception building wanted to confiscate our equipment. If I hadn't already been transmitting, they probably would have."

At that moment Martha Fletcher, a professional-looking brunette, walked in accompanied by another guard. The guard said, "We just got word to release you, Mr. August. We're sorry for the inconvenience. Also, the Commandant has time to see you now. Ms. Fletcher and Mr. Cavanaugh you're welcome to video the discussion if Mr. August doesn't object."

Her Honor, Susan Winsock, Mayor of Sykesville sat behind a heavy wooden desk. . Somehow, she didn't look out of place in the camouflaged fatigues. She rose and extended her hand. "Mr. August,

212

please accept my apologies for your recent treatment." She turned to Fletcher and Cavanaugh. "Ms. Fletcher, Mr. Cavanaugh. Feel free to set up any way you see fit," she smiled and shook their hands.

Returning to Colt she nodded toward a chair. "Mr. August, have a seat and tell me what I can do for you."

Colt spent several minutes describing the veiled threats he and Lindsay had been subjected to and Brady's kidnapping. He concluded with, "Naturally I'm concerned about the safety of two people I love, and after this episode, I can't be confident that harassment won't turn nasty again. If you have any control over it, I want you to call off the dogs."

Winsock bristled, "I understand your concern, Mr. August, but I honestly have no knowledge of any attempts to harass you or anyone else in the southern part of the province. Also, my office had nothing to do with calling off the official search for your fiancée's son."

"Ma'am, I believe you," Colt responded, "But someone who has access to your office's web server definitely sent out the message. Whoever did it also had a spider on the web looking out for traffic related to the kidnapping. That's the only way they could have responded so rapidly."

Winsock nodded. "I see what you mean."

Colt continued, "I'd recommend having your IT person do an immediate security check before the perpetrator has a chance to erase his or her tracks. You may also want to review who you trust because someone is using your authority behind your back."

"Point taken. Roberta Nguyen handles our IT work." She spoke to her AI, "Winston, get Roberta on a secure line and interrupt us as soon as she responds." She leaned back in her chair and placed her finger tips together in a thoughtful pose. "I have to admit I've noticed some unexplained activities going on, but since they've generally been effective and this is a civilian militia, I let them pass as field commanders taking the initiative." She looked thoughtful. "Now that I think about it, maybe I was deliberately being bypassed — someone else higher up issuing orders."

She straightened up. "Wait a minute. Corporal Jennings was assigned here by direct orders from the regional commander. If anyone is channeling orders from higher up in the chain of command, he'd be the one. Winston, find Corporal Jennings and have him report here immediately."

Colt frowned, "One other thing. The shoot on sight order was to keep me from getting to you. Now that I've spoken with you, I hope I haven't put you in real danger."

"This feed is going out live, so the whole planet knows about what's going on here. I don't think anyone would be stupid enough to come after you under the circumstances," Martha said.

At that moment Winston interrupted, "Dr. Nguyen wasn't available on a secure line so I left her a message to call back as soon as she could. Also, Corporal Jennings has just arrived. Shall I send him in?"

"Please do," the commandant responded.

The door opened, and Corporal Jennings stepped in. "Corporal Jennings reporting as ordered, ma'am."

"At ease, corporal. Have a seat."

Jennings started to take a chair, but when he saw Colt, he said, "August!" and reached for his blaster.

"Don't do it, corporal. You're live on the web," Colt commanded.

Jennings hesitated. "But there's a shoot on sight order."

"It's been rescinded, and blasters make such a mess indoors," Colt responded wryly.

"Just sit down, Corporal," Winsock ordered.

Jennings sat down stiffly in the chair. Commandant Winsock looked directly into his eyes. "Corporal, have you been using my web account to send out orders I didn't authorize?"

Jennings' face stayed frozen. "No, ma'am."

"Don't lie to me, corporal."

"Ma'am. I ..." His voice broke.

"The truth!"

"I ... Yes, ma'am," he hesitated. "I was assigned here to issue orders in your name when the regional commander sent them to me." Again he hesitated. "I'm sorry, ma'am, but you're a civilian and a politician, not a real officer. Headquarters put me here to make sure effective orders were issued on time."

"I see. Did you issue the orders that had Mr. August being watched?"

"No, ma'am. Those went directly from the regional commander to Sergeant Grainger."

"This just keeps getting better. How many of the militia are issuing orders that bypass this office?"

"I don't know, ma'am."

"Make a guess. How many do you know of personally?"

"Four of us now that Grainger is dead."

"Mercenaries?" Colt asked.

"Yes, sir."

It was nearly five o'clock when Lindsay and Brady picked up Colt at the visitor parking area. "You made it!" Lindsay gloated. "I watched the interview on the web. Do you really believe she knew nothing about the harassment?"

Colt beamed at her. As he strapped in and the van lifted off, he said, "I'm sure of it. When I talked to Evan afterwards, he said he had just gotten word that she had been replaced as the Sykesville Commandant." Then he looked back at Brady. "Hi, sport."

Interlude

Quan paced back and forth in front of McKillip's desk. He had just given her a report on another successful militia operation. A voice from the wall screen interrupted his thoughts.

"And now a strange story out of Sykesville. Our field reporter, Martha Fletcher, is on scene."

McKillip looked up at the webcast from the report. She briefly tried to rub the haze of fatigue from her eyes, as the image switched to the office of the Mayor of Sykesville. A man dressed in garish clothes was taking a seat across from the mayor's desk. Martha Fletcher stood in the foreground. She said, "This man is William August. Just a few minutes ago he was released from the city's jail, where he was being held because he allegedly had threatened the life of the mayor. The local militia unit had been ordered to shoot him on sight, but he was able to surrender to one of the militiamen who turned him over to the mayor's guards rather than shoot him. A shoot on sight order is virtually unheard of these days. This one was rescinded as soon as the marshal's office confirmed his story. Let's listen in." She vanished from the image.

The man spoke of militiamen kidnapping his fiancé's son and how he was threatened when he tried to talk to the mayor, who was also the local militia commandant.

When the newscast broke from the report, McKillip looked at Quan. "What the hell is this all about? Who gave that order?"

Quan scowled and shook his head. "I don't have any idea." He looked at his display. "But I will say we'd have been better off if the order had been carried out. That man is the one I've been telling you about. He's starting to become a real threat, organizing the locals in the southern half of the province to resist the militia."

"I don't approve of assassinations," McKillip pointed out. "And that's what that would have been. I also disapprove of involving children – in any way. What's this about kidnapping?"

Quan looked thoughtful for a moment. Then he said, "We had people keeping an eye on August, but they were supposed to harass him, not kidnap the kid."

Quan looked at his display again. "This says the men who kidnapped the boy were killed by a merc named Grainger, and an off-duty Sykesville marshal shot him down. Grainger died in the crash. I met Grainger a while back. He had a hair trigger, but I can't see him ordering a kidnapping. I'll look into it."

"And what about this shoot on sight order?"

"Apparently someone had bad information and was trying to protect the mayor."

"But the order would have to go through her, and Winsock was clearly as surprised to hear about it as I was. What's this about a separate chain of command bypassing Winsock?"

"Again, I don't know. Clearly something is fouled up. I'll have to check into that too." He rolled up his display. "I need a secure net. I'll be back when I get the query started."

Outside in the corridor, he opened his communicator. "Now what?" he growled to himself. When the communicator showed "connected," he said, "We have to talk."

Chapter 29

The following morning Colt took Lindsay aside. "I'm going over to Toby's to check on the command post, and I'll be gone most of the morning. After yesterday I don't anybody will be harassing you, but just in case, if you see or hear anything suspicious just say the name Delilah. I've instructed Jeffrey to immediately call me and hook me up to his audio and video pickups if you say that. I'll be on my way in thirty seconds or less."

"Do you think that's necessary?"

"I hope not. I think it'll at least take the militia a little time to recruit someone new for the job. Plus with the news coverage, if they start harassing us again — the wrong people are likely to start investigating. Still, I'd rather be prepared."

"We'll be all right." She stepped back, as if to shield her doubt from his eyes. "See you this afternoon."

The "stink bug committee" had set up a command post in Toby Walker's basement. From there, teams of observers kept constant watch on the messages flowing back and forth among the militia units, compiling a stack of potential intelligence. Nothing had seemed threatening for the first few days, but that changed shortly after Colt arrived that morning.

"Gus, these messages I'm decoding don't look good." Troy Mercer looked up from his desk monitor. "Even when they're translated, they're still cryptic." He switched to the latest message and the image on the monitor changed. "Look at this one. It says they're preparing for practice maneuvers, but the coordinates are right on our northern border with militia controlled territory."

Colt studied the message for a few seconds. "This has them moving into position before sunup on Thursday. With neither Selene nor Luna up, that would be a good time for the militia to slip into position without being seen. We'd need night vision to keep a watch out for them. Looks like they're preparing for a real attack. I think it's time to assemble the troops."

He called across the room to Walker, "Toby, it's time for a war council. Apparently the militia aren't going to give us time to pull any more pranks."

An hour later everyone was in agreement. Colt listened in as innocuous sounding comm calls went out, all with the keyword "Peacemaker." The volunteers invited friends who were also volunteers over for dinner or a game of cards. Colt knew that to outside observers the gatherings that would take place that evening would seem like normal visits. What they wouldn't see was that when the flyers returned home after the visits, not all of the visitors would return. The men and women who stayed behind would deploy after dark to set up their defensive positions.

Two days later the attack came.

The spring wheat had been harvested, leaving much of the valley covered with dry, brown stubble that ran for kilometers in all directions, broken only by the occasional stream, road, and farm buildings. The militia, wearing night-vision goggles, headed directly toward several of those buildings. One was the house of the widow Hansen.

Hidden by the dense bayberry shrubbery, Colt watched the approach from in front of the porch of Lindsay's house. He wanted to be in the open in case any of the militia members got through and he had to stop them. He whispered into his communicator, "How are we doing? Are any of the squads still out of the containment fields?"

"This is Len. I've got one squad still hanging out on the road. I can't see any reason for the delay."

"We'll give them another two minutes. Let me know if they move," Colt announced. "Anyone have squads that will be out of position by then?"

There was no response. Two minutes later Colt keyed his mike and said, "Okay, troops. That's it. Light 'em up!"

Immediately fires broke out all across the occupied fields. The stubble near the force field fences caught fire first, and a few militia stragglers were singed. Most of the militia was already well away from the field borders and wearing fireproof fatigues, so no one was seriously hurt.

The leader of the squad that had been approaching Lindsay's house was the first to recognize that the smoke was only rising about three meters and was rapidly spreading out inside the force field. He signaled his squad and broke into a run for the middle of the field.

Colt heard him calling on the militia frequency as he ran, "The farmers have capped the force fields and the smoke can't get out. Get to the middle of the field and get down. The fire will burn away from the force fences quickly. When it does, we can run through the flames to the perimeter."

It didn't turn out to be that easy. The fires were sucking up the available oxygen rapidly. By the time the stubble near the force fences had burned out, the air was full of smoke and the oxygen had been depleted to the point that the fires were dying down on their own. Not a single shot had been fired, but the militiamen had been overcome by the combination of smoke, carbon monoxide, and lack of oxygen.

The sky was brightening rapidly as Colt trotted through a gap between the fences. When he neared the road, he slowed to a walk. The smoke kept him out of sight, but he didn't want to risk startling anyone from the stranded squad and being shot. Before he got to the road, the sound level had started changing as the force fields shut down. A stiff breeze out of the west began dissipating the smoke and blew it across his path. He had to hold his breath for the last ten meters to avoid inhaling it, but by the time he reached the road, the air had almost cleared.

One of the militiamen saw him. "Hey! Stop right there," he shouted, swinging a blast rifle around to point at Colt.

Colt stopped. He said, "What the hemlock do you think you're doing? I'm unarmed. Point that thing somewhere else."

The militiaman looked at the squad leader. She nodded, and he lowered his weapon.

Colt turned to the squad leader, a green-eyed blond with three stripes on her sleeves. "Sergeant, we can use your help. As you can see, the rest of your division is on the ground."

He swept his arm around, indicating the open fields where the provincials were gathering weapons and checking the downed militiamen for vital signs. As they were watching, several provincials signaled for assistance and other provincials trotted over with litters. The litter bearers quickly loaded the inert forms of militiamen and hustled them to the nearest farm house.

"We need to make sure no one was seriously hurt, and do so as rapidly as possible so we can get you folks on your way back home. You can help speed things up if you'll leave you're weapons here at the carriers and start checking the downed troops in that field. There's a med station in that farm house," Colt said.

"Leave our weapons?" the sergeant asked warily.

"The litter bearers have been instructed not to approach anyone with weapons, and even if you carry the ones needing treatment yourselves, the med station won't allow you in with weapons."

The sergeant hesitated.

"Those troops need your help, sergeant. Get moving," Colt ordered.

The squad members looked at their sergeant for direction. She removed her rifle and ordered, "Do it! Alpha patrol, take the west side. Bravo, take the east." She dropped her rifle and pistol in the carrier. The rest of the squad followed suit. "Move out!" she ordered.

As Colt watched the squad work its way among the downed militiamen, Toby Walker approached on the road. "That was too easy," he said, grinning.

Colt nodded. "If they decide to try again, they won't make the same mistake." He started walking toward the farm house.

"They can't make the same mistake," Walker agreed. "We don't have any more stubble to burn."

"I mean underestimating us," Colt responded. "A ground attack was just plain arrogant. They knew that the hick farmers in the south half of the province couldn't put up an effective fight, and their leadership wanted to give them an easy victory." He paused. "My main concern right now is that our troops remember that these people are still our friends and neighbors. We don't want to do anything to them that they'll resent later."

The militia squad called for litters several times before Colt and Walker reached the farm house. By the time they arrived, the ambulatory casualties were straggling up the front steps. Colt stood on the porch until the squad leader, trailing the last of her troops, approached supporting a groggy militiaman.

Colt jogged over to her. "Let me help you with him," he said, wrapping the man's left arm around his neck and shouldering some of his weight.

"Thanks." The sergeant looked back where the carrier was parked. "What are they doing to my carrier?"

"They're putting it away."

"But …"

"Don't worry. We have buses coming to get you home." He forestalled her next question by holding up his left hand. "If the carrier is personal property, leave a physical address and we'll get it back to you."

"It isn't, but out of curiosity, how soon?"

"We'll try to get all the personal items back to their owners tomorrow, but it will depend on how much we have to return."

"What about the weapons?"

"Sorry, if nobody claims them, the weapons and other equipment go into storage."

"But the pistol is mine."

They had reached the med station and paused a moment to turn the dazed militiaman over to Doctor Strauss. She had him lie down on a gurney and ran a scanner over him. She eyed the results on the monitor, produced an injector, and gave him two quick shots. "The first shot was to clear all the contaminants out of your blood. It'll take a couple of hours, and your blood will be good as new. The second shot was for your heart. It will take care of you for now, but I don't recommend you play any more war games until you get your heart repaired."

Colt looked back at the sergeant. "Personal weapons will be sent back to their owners by delivery service. C.O.D. Again, just leave your address."

She laughed. "You have this all worked out, don't you?"

"We just wanted to make sure that no one got hurt."

She laughed again and extended her right hand. "I'm Diane Feldman."

"William August. My friends call me Gus."

"So Gus, what is going on here? You were obviously prepared for us."

"The way we see it, we're not enemies," Colt answered. "We simply have a difference of opinion. So we wanted to avoid doing anything that would make you mad at us. By disarming you and sending you home, we hope you'll not try to bother us again."

"That doesn't seem like much of a military strategy."

"I'm former navy, and the navy is called 'Peacemaker' for a reason. Why do battle if there's another solution? Of course, if you happen to have a bigger club handy, it helps."

"I don't think I want to know what that was."

A few minutes later a provincial Colt didn't know stuck his head in the door and shouted, "The first bus is here. If you're able-bodied, please help someone who isn't and load up."

"Well, Gus, that's me. In its own weird way, it was a pleasure to meet you. You know you're on the wrong side, don't you?"

"What makes you say that?"

She took the arm of one of the still dazed militiamen sitting in the hall, wrapped it over her shoulder, and lifted him into a standing position. "Lean on me, soldier, and we'll get you out to the bus." She looked back at Colt. "This is our home. We're going to be forcibly removed from it if we don't break away from the Republic."

Colt helped another militiaman to his feet, and followed her toward the door. "You mean because of the Lodaanii?"

She stopped and stared at him with her mouth open, "What else?"

"If it were that simple, you wouldn't need to use force. I suspect that whoever is giving orders has more in mind than simply declaring independence."

"What do you mean?" She began moving ahead again.

"How about setting himself or herself up as in charge for the duration? I've noticed that durations don't seem to have time limits."

"Oh, please!" They both helped the militiamen into seats on the bus.

"Something to think about," Colt responded. "See you around, Diane Feldman."

When he got off the bus, she was pensively chewing her bottom lip.

Interlude

Quan was still smarting from the latest confrontation on his communicator. McKillip looked at his dark face and said, "Why the scowl?"

He caught himself before giving anything away. "This guy August is becoming a major problem. He was responsible for the debacle in southern Salish province. I'm trying to get a handle on him. One of my sources says he's the Commander Colt who was supposedly killed trying to escape after the shuttle crash."

"He survived?" McKillip asked.

"Apparently."

McKillip frowned. "I'm developing serious reservations about this pompous ass, Dixon. I thought he reported Colt was eaten by banshees."

"I know what you mean," Quan agreed. With an effort he brightened. "If it is Colt, maybe we have a way to get him out of circulation."

"I'm listening."

"Dixon is holding the crew of the shuttle. If we could leak their location, Colt might make an attempt to free them. All we have to do is make sure he's caught when he tries it."

McKillip frowned. "The way things have been going for Dixon lately is there any real chance that will work?"

Quan allowed himself a brief smile. "We'll put mercs in charge of the operation and have them report to him as if he were running the show. That way there won't be any screw ups."

"So how do we get the message to Colt?"

"If my source is right, Colt is in contact with a spook named Fitzhugh, and Fitzhugh has his own sources that are on the lookout for Colt's crew. All we have to do is pass an unprotected order to Dixon to move the crew to an accessible location."

"Should we bring Dixon in for a debriefing so he's out of the way when it happens?"

"Normally I'd say that was a good idea. Unfortunately, Dixon may have an ego, but he's not stupid. If we take him out of circulation while this is going on, he'll know we aren't being straight with him."

McKillip smiled faintly. "So you think it would be better to play him with false information?"

Quan caught the irony. "As I said, he's an egotist, and it's easy to play an egotist as long as you keep him thinking he's in charge."

"I suspect you're right. Does that apply to me too?"

Quan blanched enough that McKillip could see it. He swallowed and said, "What do you mean?"

"I mean how much am I in control and how much am I being played?"

"Nobody's playing you."

"Oh, come off it. You've been playing me the whole time. I went along because you were leading me where I wanted to go. Now I'm beginning to wonder. The way events have been going sour lately are we beating a dead horse? We'll need to discuss this later. For now see if you can get August or Colt or whatever his name is out of our hair."

Quan started to argue and then thought better of it. "Okay, I'll get a team together and assign them to Dixon on paper. Then I'll send Dixon a secure order about the team and what they're doing."

"Make sure you come up with a solid reason for him to not get directly involved."

Quan nodded. "I'll get back with you as soon as I get everything out." He headed for the door.

Quan stopped briefly when McKillip said, "This conversation isn't over."

He held off using his communicator until he stepped into the men's room. "Okay, I backed your plan in, and she thinks I'm just now ordering it instead of it already being underway. But we've got problems, she suspects that I've been playing her. I hope you didn't put Dixon in actual charge of this operation."

Chapter 30

The stink bug committee continued to monitor the militia transmissions. By Saturday, it was clear that dissension was spreading in the ranks and that their lost weapons weren't being resupplied. The few weapons that were left were being used to hold a few key communities.

Colt spent the day doing farm chores. After dinner he and Lindsay went out to the barn to keep their discussion away from Brady.

"I'm not comfortable about you going after your crew by yourself," Lindsay said. "If Dennis knows where your crewmembers are, why doesn't he rescue them?"

"He doesn't have the manpower. Almost everyone who works for him is some kind of informant, not a real operative, and they aren't trained for a rescue operation."

"Are you?"

"Well enough."

"What about Dennis?"

"He has too many responsibilities to risk being compromised in a rescue attempt."

She wasn't placated. "What about us? Brady and I have gotten used to having you around. What if you are caught or killed? And don't you have some responsibility to the people of the province?"

"That's not fair. As long as I'm in the navy, duty comes first. The military can't work any other way."

She hung her head. "I know. It's just that . . . Dammit, I think I'm in love with you."

Colt had to struggle not to say, "You mean that?" He held her while she buried her face in his shoulder. Then she straightened up. Her eyes were red, but there were no tears. With a hoarse voice she said, "Let's go take Brady to Lois's and get this over with."

Lindsay lifted the van a few meters above the ground and headed back to the farm. Colt stood by the side of the road and watched her disappear into the twilight murk. He'd told her to wait until she was at least five kilometers away before turning on her running lights. When she was out of sight, he turned around and started to briskly walk down the road toward Dixon, less than a kilometer to the south.

The farm sounds drifted toward him on a gentle breeze. They reminded him that he had become at home here, and it wasn't just Lindsay and Brady. The whole planet seemed to have a grip on him. He grinned as he remembered Lois's comment, "Wait till you've lived through a six-month winter!"

As soon as he entered the city of Dixon, the dusty dirt road gave way to a paved street, and streetlights lit the way. He slowed his pace to look as if he was simply out for a stroll and made his way toward the center of the town. No one challenged him, and as far as he could tell, no one had even noticed him.

Bigger than Sykesville, Dixon had never been a colonist point of debarkation. The residential streets had evolved rather than been planned out, which made for random intersections and, in many cases, winding roads. Still, even here an abundance of trees towered around the homes.

He passed a small square park with a statue of Radcliff Dixon in the middle. Dixon was the first planetary governor and had stayed behind to homestead when his term of office was over. He later became one of the first delegates to represent Corona at Parliament on Earth. He was instrumental in getting Parliamentary approval to form a local government, which was why he was elected the first prime minister. The statue showed him as a heroic figure over three meters tall, although in real-life he was a stout, unimposing man. Colt stood looking at the statue for a moment. Then he headed down Central Avenue.

He had only walked a few blocks from the park when a flyer in ground mode and with its top retracted slowed to his pace. The driver called to him, "Can I give you a lift?"

Briefly, Colt was struck by how that offer, an almost alien concept on Earth, was simply the action of a good neighbor here on Corona. He smiled, waved, and responded, "No thanks. I'm just out to stretch my legs."

The driver nodded. He waved and accelerated to street speed. Colt continued straight ahead until the flyer was out of sight. He discovered that he had walked past Baldric Avenue. He had to retrace his steps for half a block. In less than a minute he was standing in front of the street door to the warehouse. He touched the annunciator plate at the side of the door. An AI responded, "May I help you?"

Colt used the name he had gotten from Fitzhugh, "I'm here to see Margaret Gilford. I believe she's expecting me. Gus August."

"Certainly, sir. Just a moment please."

Almost immediately the door lock clicked and a woman's voice announced, "Please come on in, Mr. August. We're at the top of the stairs."

Inside a well-lit stairway Colt made his way to the second floor and a door marked Dixon Moving and Storage. He tried the handle, and the door opened easily.

"Commander Colt!" gasped a familiar voice.

Colt froze. They know who I am? As he turned toward the speaker, Billy Hargety rose out of a waiting area easy chair, extending a hand. "My God! We thought you were dead. It's good to see you."

Colt stood dazed and mechanically took the politician's outstretched hand.

"Margaret. This is Commander Colt of the *Invincible*. We thought he had died." He stopped and looked at Colt. "I'm sorry, this has got to be shock for you. Please, sit down, and I'll try to explain. Hey, and don't worry. You haven't been captured again."

As Colt sat down, Margaret Gilford, the owner of Dixon Moving and Storage, walked from behind the counter with a mug of coffee in her hand. She was a willowy blonde, obviously several years Colt's senior, but remarkably attractive. She offered the coffee to Colt, who took it gratefully.

"It's a pleasure to meet you, Commander." As she sat down, Margaret said, "Tell me more, Billy."

"Well, it's a long story. I'll try to cut it down some. You probably haven't heard about the shuttle crash a few weeks back. Commander Colt was ferrying a group of us to what was supposed to be a peace conference in First Landing. Something happened to the shuttle's drive." He looked at Colt.

"Saboteurs had put a time-released vial of acid on the power bars," Colt filled in. "We lost all power to the drives. Somebody apparently wanted to head off the peace conference, and Mr. Hargety here was on the suspect list at the time."

"Hey, I want to be able to continue living here, but I'm not ready to die to do it." He paused. "That doesn't make sense."

Colt grinned. "Actually, it does. From what I've found out since the crash, you aren't the self-sacrificing type, much less suicidal."

"I suppose I deserve that. I've been a politician ever since I got here, but I really have had the public's interest at heart."

"So, why did your people sabotage the Clermont shuttle?"

"My people didn't have anything to do with sabotaging the shuttle. Most of the passengers on the shuttle were personal friends of mine, separatists and loyalists."

"I notice your man contacted the force that captured us and the commander deferred to you — took you out first."

"Dubrovich isn't my man. He was a last-minute replacement when Alex Komarov couldn't make it. And I don't have any control over the commander. I'm surprised you didn't recognize him. He's Radcliff Dixon III."

Suddenly, Colt remembered why the name on the statue was familiar. Dixon the Third was thrown out of the Academy about five years before Colt graduated. As the commander of a new cadet summer squadron, he had pushed his unit so hard that one of the fourth classmen fell off a cliff during an overnight march. The board of inquiry found that the death was caused by fatigue brought on by Dixon's relentless pressure. Due to the circumstantial nature of the evidence and the family name, no charges were filed but he was dismissed from the Academy.

"So you don't have anything to do with my crew members being held here?" Colt asked.

"Absolutely not. I found out they were here through one of my contacts and came to see what I could do for them. I couldn't get past the front gate, but I did find out that Dixon is in charge. He was willing to see me, but flat-out said no to letting me even talk to your people. It was after I talked to him that your man, O'Toole, contacted me and said I should be here tonight to meet a William August. I presume that's you."

"Billy, from my brief experience with you, I had you figured for a self-centered, power-hungry politician."

"Guilty."

"Who would do anything to further his own agenda."

"Not guilty. My people and this world come first."

"That I'll believe when I see it, but if O'Toole sent you here, I'll trust his judgment. Yes, I'm William August. You don't need to justify yourself to me," Colt responded.

"Yes, I do," Hargety disagreed. "Too many people have invested their lives on this planet to just yank them off it and resettle them somewhere else. I wanted to put us in a position where that couldn't happen. It hasn't worked out at all like I had planned."

"From what I've seen, so far all you've established is chaos."

"Unfortunately, you're right," Hargety replied. "None of this was supposed to happen. There weren't supposed to be any deaths."

"That's almost unavoidable when you march armed troops into unwilling communities."

"Those troops were only there to protect the citizens," Hargety argued.

"Was protecting Kyoto part of that plan?"

"Look, we made some serious mistakes," Hargety pleaded. "I know that. But none of the separatist forces had anything to do with that."

"As I recall, you reported that the culprits were under arrest. You didn't suggest they were loyalists."

"They weren't. We didn't arrest anyone. We still don't know where the nuke came from. It came in from the north, but we weren't able to backtrack to its point of origin. I knew there was no point in us denying responsibility. I figured making up a story about arresting someone would be more believable than saying we didn't do it." He looked up at Colt, "I don't suppose you'd believe that's the truth."

Colt looked Hargety in the eye, "Actually, that makes some degree of sense. I can't see how nuking anyone would have helped your cause."

"And I still say there weren't supposed to be any killings. We haven't yet figured out how these fire fights started."

"Because someone else has been interfering?" Colt asked.

230

Hargety stopped, his mouth gaping. "You're right. That's exactly what it looks like."

"When you're primed for battle, all it takes is for someone to fire a weapon, especially with green troops. It would have been easy for someone who wanted to cause real trouble to get things started."

Hargety nodded.

Margaret took advantage of the opening. "I won't ask you two to kiss and make up, but you did leave me hanging. What happened to the shuttle?"

Hargety picked up his narration, "The shuttle made an emergency landing in the mountains. The pilot did a remarkable job. The shuttle was destroyed, but no one was seriously hurt. We were eventually all airlifted out, except for Commander Colt. He escaped and fell off a cliff. The shuttle crew was 'taken into protective custody.'"

"Obviously you survived," Margaret said. "How did you manage to do it, Commander?"

"A group of locals found me and gave me medical treatment until I could return to a human community."

"Then you've met the natives," Hargety said. "It was bound to happen eventually. That's why it's so essential to establish ourselves as an independent world immediately. As soon as that gets back to the colonization board, they're going to demand we get off-planet."

"The colonization board already knows about the Lodaanii," Colt responded. "While that bothers me, it's not my concern right now," Colt said.

"So what, exactly, are you planning to do?"

"Get my people out and see if I can make contact with the Admiralty. I have one man who can build a subspace transmitter from parts, if it comes to that."

"Which brings us to this. O'Toole sent it for you, Commander." Margaret pulled a meter-long tube from under the counter and handed it to Colt.

He unscrewed the cap on one end and slid out three secure communicators, a blank badge, a pistol-shaped object, a plastic bag with a gray, claylike brick, two black capsules, and a clear sheet of display film about 60 centimeters by 80.

Hargety picked up the bag, "What's this?"

"My guess is plastic explosive," Colt answered. "The black capsules would be detonators."

Hargety gingerly put the bag back on the counter.

Colt unrolled the film and spread it out on the counter. Hargety and Margaret stood on either side of him, curious. Colt pressed his thumb to a small opaque square in one corner. The film display switched on and showed a floor plan for a large warehouse. The address was for a building only six blocks away. The warehouse occupied the entire block with the center of the block serving as a landing pad and open parking for transport vans. A note on the display said, "Closed for Renovation."

Colt spent several minutes studying the floor plans getting familiar with the layout, especially the exits. Then he selected the electrical system plan and worked his way down to the security system. The security circuits weren't encouraging. They were the closest to foolproof he had seen. The primary sensors had nearly every square meter of the warehouse covered, and they were top of the line, virtually invulnerable to jamming. Their only weakness was that they relied on external power. However, a central monitor somewhere else in town pinged the security system at random intervals, so simply shutting off the building's power wasn't the answer. Once the power was off, he had to be able to get the crew out before reinforcements could arrive.

Fitzhugh had included comprehensive notes with the plan. Colt scrolled through them. He noted that the sensors could be deactivated if he had the three-level password, but Fitzhugh had neglected to include it. The last item caught his eye. Patrols: only two guards at night. One watches the monitors, the other patrols the warehouse corridors around the holding cells. With that he saw the reason for the badge. He picked it up and looked at Margaret. "May I use your link?"

"Certainly." She walked over to the wall display, "Unlock, please." The screen lit up with the AI's image, a gray haired man resembling Margaret. "One time, unlimited access for William August. This is William August."

"Mister August," the AI said.

"Secure mode," Colt said. "I'll provide the keys manually." The screen cleared to a light gray. A small text box appeared near the bottom, and Colt typed in a series of letters and digits, and a new screen popped up. He quickly worked his way through several screens. Then he slid the badge into a slot on the keyboard and clicked on the submit button. A moment later the completed badge, including Colt's real name, popped out of the slot.

"You're going to use your own name for this?" Hargety asked, clearly puzzled.

"If something happens, I don't want them to be able to trace me back to William August," Colt replied. He turned to Margaret. "Can you deactivate your AI without rousing suspicion?"

Margaret responded, "Maxwell, excuse us please." She looked at Colt. "He's in hibernation until I reactivate him."

"Thanks." He looked quickly back and forth between them. "Here's how this is going to work."

"I'm going to replace the next guard that goes on. The building AI will check my badge against the list before letting me in and this program has already added me to the access list. I'm counting on the guards not all knowing each other, or at least that they'll accept a newbie as long as he gets by the AI."

He turned to Hargety. "Billy, I'm assuming O'Toole sent you here to help. Your job will be to turn off the building power when I get to the cell block. I'll have to work fast to be sure the remote security team doesn't detect the power failure and send help before I get my crew out.

"The building runs off the city grid, and since city power is so reliable, there's no backup generator." Colt switched the display from blueprint to map mode, showing the city immediately around the warehouse. "The main transmission lines run under Syracuse Street. There's a manhole here that gives access to the transmission tunnel." He touched a spot on the map about a block from where they were. It immediately expanded to a close up view.

"What good will that do?" Hargety asked.

Colt handed Hargety the pistol. "Have you ever played with a squirt gun?"

Hargety examined the pistol. Colt continued, "This one is filled with a special acid. It's pretty much harmless, but it will eat through a transmission line in less than a minute. All you have to do is hold the trigger down and wet the cable thoroughly in one place. Then get out of there."

Colt switched the display back to floor plan and turned to Margaret. "One of your jobs is to tell him when to start. You can track my movement on the floor plan, but I'll try to call you when I'm ready. As soon as I get to the corridor outside the cells, here, if you haven't heard from me, call Billy on this communicator." He handed her one of the communicators and handed another to Hargety.

Colt paused, "I never like to go into a tight situation without a safety net. Do you have any vans?"

"I have several. How large?"

"Just enough for the fourteen of us," Colt answered. "Can your vans fly themselves without humans aboard?"

"None of my vans have onboard AIs, but Maxwell has flight programming."

Colt considered the significance of that for a split second, then said, "Okay, bring him out of hibernation please."

Margaret recited a string of letters and digits. Maxwell immediately appeared in the display. "Mister August has a mission for you, Maxwell."

Colt told Maxwell to be prepared for takeoff with only a moment's notice in case the plan went sour. "You'll fly as fast as your programming will allow and set down in the central quad of the warehouse complex." He concluded with, "There should be fourteen of us. As soon as we're aboard, you're to lift off and head due north at top legal speed. Anticipate being fired upon."

"Shall I employ countermeasures, ma'am?" Maxwell asked.

"Only as necessary to make certain neither you nor any of your passengers is compromised," Margaret responded.

"Very well."

Margaret looked up from the floor plan. "So, assuming nothing goes wrong, you plan to just walk out of there?"

"That's the plan. The fire codes for Dixon require all internal doors to fail safe to unlocked in case of emergency. We should be out the back door before the power goes back on."

He looked back at Hargety. "Billy, I assume you can find the manhole into the transmission tunnel."

"No problem."

Colt picked up the last communicator. He returned the film to full map view, touched a command, and it immediately showed a bright red dot in Margaret's office. "Do you have any questions, Margaret?"

She toggled the display back and forth between map and plan mode. "Piece of cake," she answered.

"Okay, Billy. Let's move. We have just over seventeen minutes before the next guard is due to check in."

Before Colt and Hargety separated at the next corner, they both called Margaret to test their communicators. Then Colt headed up the street toward the warehouse. As he turned the corner the replacement guard was walking up to the entrance of the warehouse. Was he too late?

Chapter 31

"Hey!" Colt shouted. "At last, another human being!" He broke into a trot toward the other man. The guard stopped and stared at him. "Can you help me?" Colt called breathlessly as he ran up.

"I don't have a lot of time," the guard said, perplexed. "What do you need?"

"I have spent the last two hours trying to find Transcon Shipping. I'm about ready to give up and go back to the hotel. Can you tell me where it is?"

The guard laughed and looked up at the unlighted sign above the front entry door to the warehouse. Colt followed his glance, noting the name on the sign and no visible sensors on the front of the building. "You're standing in front of it," the guard said. "The place is closed for renovation. There's nobody here except us guards."

Colt struck without warning. A blow to the back of the guard's head knocked him unconscious with barely a sound. Colt caught him as he collapsed. He threw the guard over his shoulder and carried him across the street into an alley where he carefully laid him down behind a dumpster. Colt quickly bound and gagged the man. Then he checked the time and hurried back to the entrance.

The entry scanner was on the right side of the door. It recognized his badge, and the door lock clicked open. Colt stepped inside. As soon as the door closed interior lights came on providing just enough light to find his way. A voice said, "I don't recognize you."

"I'm new today. This is my first shift. I'm William Colt."

There was a brief pause. "Ah, found you. Welcome aboard."

"How do I get to the command center?"

"Straight ahead to the first cross corridor. Then hang a right. First door on the left."

There were two guards in the command center. The voice belonged to Garry Marks, a hulking man with bone crushing handshake and a ready smile. The other was a thin, red haired, sour looking man who introduced himself as Woody.

After the brief introduction Marks said, "Well, Bill, since you're here, I can leave. You girls have fun."

236

As soon as Marks left, Woody said, "You'll need to get used to the layout, so you can take the first patrol." He pulled up a floor plan on the main monitor. "This is where we are." He traced a route with his index finger, leaving a glowing yellow trail on the display. "The stairs are right around the corner. The prisoners are here." He jabbed at two rooms almost directly beneath them. "All you need to do is run a headcount and check all the doors in this section of the corridor." He pulled a communicator off its mount on the wall and handed it to Colt.

"Do I need a weapon?"

"The prisoners are locked up and disarmed. There's no way for anyone to get in without being detected. No weapons needed."

"Okay." Colt turned and walked out of the room.

As soon as he had gone down the stairs, he keyed the connection to Margaret. "I'm in and ready."

He heard Margaret speak to Hargety. As he waited for the lights to go out, he walked down the corridor checking doors so he wouldn't look suspicious. It quickly became apparent that something wasn't working as planned. Then he heard Hargety's garbled voice come through Margaret's communicator.

"There's a glitch," Margaret announced. "The power cables are covered with some kind of insulation that isn't being melted by the acid."

"Tell Billy to get out of there. Now!" Colt ordered. "And alert Maxwell. I'll need him in fifteen minutes over the quad."

When he returned to the cell doors, he hesitated briefly in front of them for a moment, aware that the crew would recognize him and might react, giving him away. To cover for the pause he keyed the communicator, "Anyone near the door?"

"Negative," Woody responded

Colt unlocked the door and stepped inside for the headcount. Each of the men showed varying degrees of shock but said nothing. Because the video camera was at their backs, Woody was unable to see the surprised expressions. Colt silently breathed a sigh of relief. He repeated the process with the women's cell. Again, the prisoners showed astonishment but held their tongues.

He calmly finished the patrol. "All clear down here," he reported to Woody looking at his watch. "The time is 8:07 PM."

"Roger. See you in the command center."

Colt already figured that he was in a trap, and something in Woody's voice confirmed that. Colt started for the stairs and stopped suddenly. He keyed the communicator and said in a near whisper, "Hey, I saw some movement at the end of the corridor. Do you have anything on your sensors?"

"No, there's nothing on the sensors. There can't be anyone in the halls. Get on up here."

"Strange. I'm sure I saw something. I'm going to check it out."

"I said, 'Get up here.'"

"You know better than that. Sensors sometimes act up. I wouldn't be doing my job if I didn't check it out." Colt said. He started down the hall at a soft trot. Just before the cross passage at the end of the hall, he stopped and carefully checked both ways. Then he turned to his right and entered the stairwell.

"Now what are you doing?" Woody asked annoyed.

"This door clicked as I came up. I think someone just entered this stairwell."

"I didn't see anything on the monitors, in the hall or in the stairwell."

"Just the same, I'm going to check."

Again he looked around as if for possible intruders. He hurried down the stairs and warily opened the door.

The layout on sub-basement level was essentially the same as on the upper floors except the air ducts and plumbing were exposed. Wiring ran through large diameter conduits that Colt traced to a massive circuit breaker panel. Still watching for a possible intruder, he trotted toward the panel. Just as he reached it, he pretended to stumble, banging into the panel. Surreptitiously he brushed his left hand along the bottom of the panel, depositing the glob of explosive and a remote detonator. Holding his arm as if he'd injured it, he trotted toward the next stairwell. Just as he reached it, the door opened and two men stepped out, pointing blasters at him.

"Upstairs," one of them he recognized as Marks ordered. "We know who you are, Commander Colt. Let's not play games." Colt didn't bother to raise his hands as he led the way up the stairs.

In the command center, Woody asked, "Did you really think you could get away with this costume party?"

"Did you really think I would be this easy to catch if I hadn't let you?"

Woody looked uncomfortable. "Your game is over, not mine."

Colt glanced at his watch. "We have a couple of minutes, why don't you tell me what you had in mind to do with me."

"You're bluffing."

Colt smiled. "I really would like to know before I leave."

"All right, wise guy. If Brigadier Dixon had his way, we'd throw you in with the other prisoners until this little conflict is over."

"That's consistent, but why bother?"

"We don't want you guys fighting for the loyalists."

"The movement is falling apart, is it?"

Woody frowned. "You won't have to worry about it. We have orders to ship you to headquarters in First Landing. A flyer's on its way now to pick you up."

Colt again glanced at his watch. "Would you look at the time? It's been entertaining, boys, but I've got a ride to catch." He tapped his pocket, and an explosion rocked the building plunging them into pitch darkness.

Marks immediately grabbed for him just snagging his shirt sleeve. Colt swung around, hitting Marks in the neck with his other forearm. He followed through by slamming into the other guard as Marks collided with the door. He whipped his freed forearm back, trying to connect with Woody. The blow hit a pistol, sending it flying. As it left Woody's hand, the pistol fired. The bolt blew a hole in the wall and left a glowing perimeter. In the wan glow he immediately dove for Woody, ramming into his midsection. For a moment they rolled around on the floor. Woody savagely fought back. Then Colt managed to get behind him and put him in a choke hold. After a short struggle Woody went limp. Colt checked to make sure he had a pulse and stood up.

He felt his way to the door, stepping over the guard he hadn't met and moving Marks' limp form out of the way. The streetlight shining through the front door of the building faded into murky shadows by the time it reached the hallway outside the command center, but it fluctuated enough that Colt realized that someone was coming up the steps. He turned and raced down the hall to the other stairwell. Descending the stairs in complete darkness he nearly missed the landing. Hanging on to the railing with all his strength, he managed to regain his balance.

He yanked open the stairwell door at the next floor and ran down the hallway counting doors as he skimmed his hand against the wall in darkness. Just before he reached the men's cell, he fell over a body.

A familiar voice yelped.

"Sergeant Jiracek?" Colt asked.

"Commander Colt?"

As they both stood up, Colt said, "Is everyone out here in the hall?"

There was a jumble of answers, which Colt took for a yes.

"Everybody, follow my voice. We're getting out of here." He pushed his way through the group. To make sure everyone stayed with him, he began talking nonstop, "There're loading doors at the end of the next corridor. If we can get there before the rebels know what we're doing, there should be a van waiting to pick us up. We're turning right. The door is fifteen meters ahead." He continued talking until he reached the door.

With no power, the loading door rolled up using a noisy and slow manual chain. As soon as the door had enough clearance under it, Colt and Orsini slid out and scanned the quad in the faint light of Selene passing through the planetary penumbra. Almost immediately they heard a rush of air overhead and rolled under cover. Looking up, Colt spotted Margaret's van against the stars. He pulled out the communicator and punched the speed button for the van. Maxwell answered immediately. "Are you ready, sir?"

"Land near the west edge of the quad. We're coming out now."

As soon as the last of the crew made it under the door, Colt released the chain, and the door rolled rapidly shut. He dashed to the van and clambered in right behind the last crewman. He turned and slid the door closed. "Maxwell, take us out of here, low and fast."

Once they were clear of the warehouse and were certain no one was shooting at them, Colt took a deep breath. "Is everyone okay?"

The crew members murmured that they were all right.

Petty Officer Juneuil had taken the driver's seat, watching in fascination as Maxwell piloted the van, staying at roof top level as they headed out of town. Colt slid into the right seat and began scanning the airspace in front of them. They were passing over the residential district when the master caution light flashed on, and the van dove toward the ground. Juneuil immediately grabbed the flight stick, pulling the nose of the craft up and applying upward thrust. She managed to stop the descent just as the van crashed through the top of a tree. When they were climbing again, she tapped the master caution light to turn it off. The computer link warning stayed on. "It looks as though the AI link was severed."

When they reached the edge of the town, Colt pointed at a clearing visible in the low light head up display. "Land us there so you and Orsini can switch places. We have to be ready to evade."

Juneuil turned her attention to the clearing. As they neared the ground, she switched on the landing lights. Not visible in the head up display, a guide line strung across the middle of the clearing whipped by just underneath them. "Hemlock! That was close!"

The van settled into rows of freshly plowed earth and came to rest.

Juneuil got out of the driver's seat, and Orsini slid into it. "Great job, Chief," he said. Colt brought up the map display. He pointed to a valley that snaked off to the west of them. "Let's go up this valley, and stay below the radar."

Orsini lifted the van clear of the trees and rapidly accelerated to the low altitude speed limit. Colt looked toward the back of the van and spotted Chapman. "Harry, can you disable the transponder on this thing?"

"Let me look," Chapman replied. He shooed the rest of the crew away from the middle of the van and checked the floor. "There's the access panel." Kneeling, he pulled the release handle and opened the panel.

He stared for a moment before he noticed wires that were obscured by the sealed primary unit and ran under the control lines. He got up, dropped the cover back in place, and walked to the front of the van. With his fingertips he felt beneath the lip of the dashboard, found a hidden switch and clicked it on. Immediately the master caution light came on, and the "Transponder Out" light glowed red. Orsini punched off the master caution.

Colt muttered, "That fits with the lack of an onboard AI. Clearly, Margaret does some things she doesn't want anyone else to know about." He smiled, "Of course, she does work for Fitz."

In a few minutes they were well up the valley, away from human intrusion. Watching the map display, Colt said, "Tony, slow us down to a crawl. Then see if you can find a small clearing we can get into."

Orsini pointed to the head up display as the van came to a virtual stop. "How's that one look?"

"Great! Take us into it but don't land."

In a few seconds they hovered a meter above the clearing, well beneath the tree tops. Orsini rotated the van slowly counterclockwise. "There," Colt said. "Take us into that opening under the trees and back us in."

As soon as they were on the ground, Colt clapped Orsini on the shoulder. "Now shut everything down; and I mean everything."

"We'd better open the windows first," Orsini noted. "I suspect this van is space-worthy. I wouldn't want to suffocate."

"So, Commander, what next?" Chapman asked.

Colt turned in his seat to face the crew in the back of the van. "I'm not convinced we got away clean. We're going to lie here doggo and powered down for a while. If you want to stretch your legs, do so, but no lights and don't go far. Be ready to hustle back. As soon as we're sure we're not being tracked, we'll head for a safe house."

"If this van is space-worthy, why don't we just take it up to the *Invincible*?" Ensign Leslie asked.

Colt paused, "We don't know where the *Invincible* is right now, or whether she's intact. There was a nuclear explosion near her about the same time we lost drive power. We haven't been able to make contact since."

The interior lighting went out as Orsini switched off the fusion power plant, and silence fell. Someone announced, "I'm going out." The latch for the right side door clicked, but before the door slid open, Orsini murmured, "Hold on. I hear something."

A whooshing sound came rapidly up the valley, rushing past, leaving a wake of roiled air that agitated the leaves and branches overhead. Since it was without lights, Colt concluded it was a flyer trying to find them. Colt remembered the armed flyer that had shot down Howard Walker. A minute later a second flyer swept up the valley.

"That's two, Commander," Orsini whispered. "Think there'll be more?"

"Let's wait awhile to see if any more are coming or these two double back."

After a few minutes conversations started up sotto voce in the back. Colt leaned back in his seat and stared out the windscreen at the blackness. Gradually he began to make out shapes and movement as a light breeze stirred the leaves. A faint sound caught his attention. "Quiet!" he commanded under his breath. The crew immediately went silent. A branch snapped nearby, followed by a curt hiss.

Thoughts of commandos wearing night-vision goggles sneaking up on them invaded Colt's mind. He fumbled under the driver's seat. Sure enough, a flashlight was stuck to the carpet. He winced as it loudly tore free. He swung it around to point at the open window just as the sounds outside reached the door. He flicked the light on. The beam lit a huge green face at the window with an equally huge mouth that let out a piercing scream, echoed by several voices inside the van. Then the face was gone.

"What was that?" Orsini gasped.

Suddenly, an image of a dark robed Lodaanii flashed in Colt's mind. It couldn't be! He acted quickly. Leaning out the window, he shouted in Lodaanii, "Jontaro, is that you?"

A moment later the tribal leader of the Others shuffled up to the van. "What Lodaanii is with the small mouths?" he asked.

"There are no Lodaanii in here," Colt responded. "Do you not recognize me from Lodaro's village?"

"All small mouths look the same," Jontaro sniffed.

"Perhaps, but how many small mouths have challenged you and left you unable to find a champion?"

Colt expected a growl, but instead he recognized the sound as laughter. "You did well. Now three of my warriors will walk through water. Perhaps you would like another challenge."

"No, but I no longer have to use crutches so do not think I would be easy to defeat."

"Why are you here, so far from small mouth lands?" Jontaro asked.

"My friends were being held captive. We were able to get away, but we are being hunted. They have weapons, and we do not. We are waiting for them to give up the hunt, before we move on."

A tiny Lodaanii voice emanated from somewhere on Jontaro. "Jontaro, this is Leleaanii. Many small mouths are headed up the valley in your direction. They have weapons and are moving with great stealth."

Colt was surprised. He knew that Lodaanii had radios, but he'd never seen them use personal communicators. "How far away are they?" he asked.

Jontaro repeated the question. The answer translated to about three kilometers. As the transmission ended, one of the unlighted flyers whooshed by overhead again.

Colt hesitated a moment, but he knew he had to act and hoped this strange being could help. He looked at the shadowy form in the darkness. He chose his words with care, "We believe it would be best if my friends are not captured again. Could some of your people lead us over the ridge into the next valley before the other small mouths arrive?"

"You ask me for help after keeping me from taking what I should have from Lodaro's village?" Jontaro growled. Then he laughed again, "Why not? We are not finding enough gellen to make hunting worthwhile. Perhaps there are more herds in the next valley."

Colt immediately grasped the opportunity. Gellen were pig-like native animals. He offered pigs as a replacement. "Or perhaps we can arrange a trade. I will bring leto-gellen animals to you if you guide us."

Chapter 32

Jontaro called his team together using high-pitched whistles. As soon as the team assembled, he and two Others led the way into the brush at a rapid but silent pace, with Colt and his crew struggling to keep up. The rest of the team followed behind, keeping watch and covering the trail the best they could. Colt hoped the pursuers were relying on IR sensors. If they had sniffers, the escapees would be easy to follow.

Half an hour later one of Jontaro's team radioed that the small mouths were fanning out to search the local area where the flyer was parked and weren't pursuing Jontaro and his group. Jontaro turned to Colt. "Your small mouths are having difficulty keeping up. We can slow down now. Then my people will not have to work so hard to cover the trail you leave."

"Perhaps that would be best," Colt agreed.

After taking a moment to catch his breath, Colt asked, "I did not see personal communicators in the village. Where did you get them?"

"We traded twelve gellen for them at Lamanaro's village. They are all that are left that work. They have made hunting easier."

"I can imagine. Are many of your devices breaking down?"

"Yes, for instance our fire guns can be charged but the fuel chambers are empty and common dust does not work to fuel them. Our weaponeers say that the material that fuels them is very pure and dust has very little of the fuel in it."

Colt considered for a moment. Most man-made blasters were fueled with cesium oxide. The Lodaanii probably used something similar. The Lodaanii weapons and communicators were getting old and not being replaced. Why was that?

At that moment they broke out of the brush onto a well-worn trail, and Jontaro picked up the pace. With the more open surface the humans had an easier time keeping up. Even so it took another hour to cross the ridgeline and start down the other side. Before they had gone far, Orsini caught up with Colt. "Who are these people and where do they come from?"

"They live in these mountains."

"You mean they're natives?"

"It appears that way, but something about them doesn't ring true."

"How did you learn to speak their language?"

"When I escaped from the rebels, I fell off a cliff, and some of these people from another village rescued me. I spent a little over a week with them. One of them spoke some English, so we taught each other."

After a brief pause, Colt said, "This whole situation doesn't sit right with me. Billy Hargety helped me get you and the others out of that warehouse."

Orsini gave a short, barking laugh. "That doesn't make any sense. He's supposedly the separatist leader."

"Is that what they told you while they were holding you?"

"Actually, no. They let us watch the news, and that was what several reporters said."

"Well, apparently there are competing factions among the rebels. The guy who was holding you was Radcliff Dixon the Third, and Billy has no control over him."

Orsini sounded stunned, "The Radcliff Dixon? The one who got thrown out of the academy?"

"So it would seem."

They walked on in silence for a while. Soon Colt noticed that the trees were thinning out and the sky was becoming visible. It was also rapidly growing light.

The trees abruptly ended, and the party found themselves at the edge of a meadow between two east-west ridges that sloped down to the valley where Lindsay lived. Looking across the open plains in the morning light, Colt could see several farm houses and a glint of sunlight off the distant Flatwater Lake.

"This is the rendezvous point," he said to no one in particular. He turned to Jontaro, "Thank you for your help, Jontaro."

"You welcome my help now?" Jontaro asked. "It comes with a price. Do not forget, small mouth."

"On my world we thank those who help us, whether they are paid or do it out of kindness."

"We speak of pay. Where are the gellen you promise?"

"It will take several days to get the gellen," Colt hesitated. He was unsure how a Lodaanii would react to the necessary delay. "How will I contact you?"

"Lodaro will find me." Jontaro raised his left arm, moved it in a small circle over his head, and, turning to face up the valley towards the mountains, brought it down sharply to point straight ahead. Without another word he and the other hunters walked away from the humans and faded into the forest.

Colt turned to the crew. "Take a break. We'll be here a while."

Reaching into his jacket pocket, Colt pulled out his communicator, turned it on and said, "Call Lindsay."

A few seconds later the communicator blurted, "Gus! Where are you?" Lindsay's voice was both anxious and relieved.

"We're at the mouth of Wildcat Canyon."

"You got your people out? That's wonderful! I was terrified that something had happened to you when you didn't get home last night."

"We ran into a few problems, but fortunately we got some help. I'll tell you about it later. In the meantime I need you to pick us up."

"I'm on my way."

"Wait," Colt interrupted. "You'll need the trailer. There are fourteen of us."

"I can do that. I'll be there shortly."

"See you in a few minutes."

The trek through the forest had taken its toll on all of them. Colt turned to Orsini, "Tony, set up a perimeter and have everyone relax. I'll stand watch for our transport."

Colt plopped down in the tall grass about twenty meters from the tree line, looking out toward the open valley.

The wait was shorter than Colt had anticipated. Orsini heard it first, "Gus, incoming traffic from up the canyon!"

Colt sat up. "Everyone get under cover!"

He jumped to his feet and started running for the forest. He didn't make it. A blaster bolt ripped the ground in front of him. He jumped out of the way, veering sharply to the right. Another bolt struck in front of him. The shots were too well placed to be accidental misses. He stopped and stood where he was and raised his hands.

The flyer was almost directly overhead. Its external speaker barked, "Good decision, Commander. Stand where you are."

The flyer circled him and landed less than two meters away, the canopy already open. From the back a man wearing camouflaged fighting gear waved a blaster to signal him toward the right front seat. He said, "Get in." Colt immediately noticed the professional competency. These weren't home grown rebels.

Colt approached the flyer slowly. Just as he was about to climb in a voice shouted, "Duck, Commander!"

Colt immediately dropped to the ground. A small object arced into the cockpit, and immediately a deafening blast shattered the air. Ears ringing, Colt stood up shakily and peered into the flyer. Both men were unconscious, blood streaming from their ears, noses, and mouths.

Chapman came running up. "Are you okay, Commander?" he shouted.

Colt shouted back without realizing it, "What the Hell?"

Chapman held up a stun grenade. "I didn't just sit around while we were waiting for those flyers to go by last night," he said. "It's amazing what you find hidden in a 'legitimate' shippers van."

Orsini trotted up with the rest of the crew. They quickly pulled the two men from the flyer and checked them to be sure they were breathing. Then Orsini began patting one of the men down. He signaled for Buchanan to do the same with the other man.

"Tony," Colt shook his head to clear it. "Be sure to check both of these guys for communication devices and beacons as well as weapons. Then tie them up with whatever you can find."

Colt waved Chapman over and spoke in a more normal volume as his hearing began to return. "Harry, I'll guarantee this flyer has a locator beacon. Can you find it and disable it?"

"Will do," Chapman responded and climbed into the cockpit. In a moment he tossed out a roll of industrial tape. "This might help with the prisoners."

Colt ripped off a meter long piece and flipped the roll to Orsini. Then he walked over to Buchanan who was completing his search of the other man. He quickly bound the man's wrists and ankles. He nodded to Buchanan, "Let's get this guy out of the hot sun."

Soon both men were securely bound to a small tree. "These guys probably homed on your communicator," Orsini observed. "They may have backup on the way."

Colt nodded. "Good point. You're our best pilot. As soon as Harry finishes, take the flyer up and keep an eye out for inbound traffic," he paused. "Just don't shoot Lindsay down."

"How do I recognize her?"

"She'll be flying a dark blue van with a trailer module attached."

He turned to the pile of electronics they had pulled off the men. Besides their personal communicators, a rolled up computer, and their watches both men had two button-sized audio transmitters and military grade micro-beacons. Colt dumped everything into a pile. Then, using one of the blasters, he melted the pile into slag. "That should stop any transmissions except for locator beacons the flyer has."

"Had," Chapman announced as he climbed out of the cockpit. He looked at Orsini, "She's all yours, Lieutenant. I had to disconnect the AI so you'll need to rely on the manual sight for the blasters."

"Thanks, Harry." Orsini climbed into the flyer, closed the canopy, and looked back at Colt, who gave him a thumbs up.

Over the next twenty minutes Colt paced impatiently. He had to keep reminding himself that it took time to hook up the trailer and fly from the farm to the canyon. Finally, Orsini announced over the loudspeaker that he had the van in sight. "I'll lead her in."

A moment later both flyers landed in the clearing. Lindsay jumped from the van and ran to Colt. She threw her arms around him and kissed him. "I'm so glad you're alright," she said. "Oh my, I think I'm in love with you." She kissed him again.

She looked back at Orsini approaching from the other flyer. "When he pulled up beside me, I was scared to death. I thought sure the militia had gotten you, but he smiled and waved."

Had she really said she loved him? Dazed, he managed to mumble, "Yeah, we had a run in with a couple of mercenaries, but we took care of them." He pointed at the two men secured to a tree at the edge of the clearing.

Still overcome, he turned to the crew. "Let's load up," He said.

Before they lifted off, Colt cut the mercenaries loose to walk out of the canyon, and in a minute the two flyers were airborne.

Flying back to the farm Colt sat in the passenger seat in silence. He wanted to say something to Lindsay, but he couldn't find the words. She glanced at him. "You're awfully quiet."

"Sorry," he temporized. "I got my crew free, but I haven't been planning far enough ahead. I'm trying to figure out what's next." He broke off and looked at her.

"Did you really say you love me?" he asked.

"I said I think I love you." She smiled, "but, yes, I do love you. I hope that's alright."

"That's better than alright. I'm crazy about you. I just didn't want to push."

"Amelia, would you take the controls and get us home." Lindsay released her seat restraints. She looked back at the passengers in the van and the trailer module. "I guess we'll have to keep it clean," she said.

On the approach for landing realization hit Colt. "Someone knew what I was going to do from the start. They were waiting for me!" he said, his voice rising. "The whole thing was a deliberate trap. How did they find out? You and Fitz were the only ones who knew what I was doing, and I know you didn't tell anyone. And I'd trust Fitz with my life." He stopped for a moment, mouth open and eyes wide. "That's it! I know where the leak is."

Once on the ground at home Lindsay took charge. She immediately called Doctor Strauss and set about making the crew feel at home. "Who's second in command here?" she asked, looking around the common room.

"I am," Orsini responded. He got up from his seat on the floor. "What do you want me to do?"

Lindsay smiled, "We have two showers but the bathrooms aren't big enough to handle everyone at once. I'll leave it up to you to figure out who goes in what order."

She looked over the rest of the crew, "Whoever isn't in the shower, I can start serving breakfast to you almost immediately. Anyone object to eggs, bacon, and toast?"

Turning to Colt she said, "You're going to be the waiter and busboy for this. You know where the dishes are. There should be enough for everyone, but you'll have to expand the table."

For the next half hour while Colt carried food and dishes back and forth, he watched Lindsay admiringly as she flitted about between the kitchen and the common room. She continued to wear a cheerful smile as she answered questions and settled disputes. No, she didn't have enough clean clothes to go around. Yes, there were plenty of towels. No one was going to be shorted. Yes, the clothes cleaner could handle all their clothes, but unless they wanted to go nude, the only thing she had was bed clothes to wrap up in. "Ma'am, we're a coed military these days, but I'm not sure how it would affect your son," Orsini observed. "Perhaps we could use the sheets and blankets."

When Doctor Strauss arrived, Lindsay turned her attention to helping out as the doctor checked each of the crewmembers for lingering effects of their imprisonment. As Lois put away her med-scanner, she announced, "These bed clothes aren't going to do. I'll bet we can get some clothes from the neighbors." She pulled out her communicator and began calling. She soon had an assortment of clean clothes on their way for the crew. After finishing her calls, she cornered Colt.

"You're not planning to have your people sleep on the floor are you? And you certainly don't expect to put them up in Sykesville, either."

Colt looked down. "I've been thinking about that. Technically we should all go back to First Landing. The guard barracks ..."

She interrupted, "We could use your people here, you know. Putting professionals in charge – sounds like what the separatists are doing so well."

"What do you have in mind?"

"This whole operation, not just the 'stink bug committee' command post, could definitely use people in key positions who know what they're doing, and I'll bet your marines could handle small arms training, taking that load off you. You see where I'm going with this? And Toby would have a lot of ideas that could use your crew. After all, what would they be doing in First Landing besides sitting on their duffs?"

"I can't argue that," Colt responded. His expression abruptly changed. "Wait a minute. That's it." He began pacing.

Lois looked at him but said nothing.

When Colt stopped pacing, he said, "I'm damned tired of always being one step behind. It's time to take the offensive."

"What do you mean?" Lois' bafflement showed on her face.

"I mean I'm pretty sure I know who's pulling the strings of the militia, and I'm going to throw an enormous monkey wrench in his plans." He smiled as he looked at her. "Did you have some specific idea of where my crew could stay?"

"A lot of the families who volunteered clothing have spare bedrooms. I don't think that should be a problem. Let me call Toby, and I'll start contacting people."

Toby scratched his head and frowned faintly. "You've got a crew of twelve sailors and marines and one civilian you're putting at our disposal? Who gave you the authority to assign service members?"

"What?" Colt could only gape.

"You're retired, right? Where do you get the authority?"

Colt hesitated, realizing what Walker was talking about. "Ah, I see," he responded. "No, I'm not retired. Let me explain. It's a long story, but I'll try to keep it brief."

Colt quickly explained what had happened to the Clermont and what followed up until he met Walker. Trying to avoid giving away anything classified, he carefully told how he had contacted an operative he knew to help him free the crew and how he got permission to help in the province with self-defense while things developed.

"You're working with Imperial Intelligence?" Walker scowled. "Were you sent here to spy on the provinces?"

"No, I'm not spying." Colt glared at Walker for a moment. "To put it bluntly, I'm trying to help with maintaining a semblance of stability while this thing gets sorted out, and helping the province stay out of militia hands is part of that."

Toby stood silently for a moment, continuing to frown. "But you still have to report the natives, right?"

"Not necessary. The Colonization Board already knows of their existence."

"They already know?" Walker stared directly into Colt's eyes, daring him to prove his statement.

"I didn't want to discourage anyone at the town meeting, so I didn't bring this up. Governor General Remarque may seem like a pompous bureaucrat, but the man is sharp, and I'll guarantee he has eyes and ears all over the planet. There's no way he could have overlooked evidence of the Lodaanii. He sent a message to the Colonization Board over a month ago." He held up a hand. "I've seen it. I imagine he's waiting on word from them on what to do. Fortunately they're bureaucrats, and they aren't used to handling complicated situations like this." Colt flashed a brief smile. "And, of course, sub-space communication is shut down."

"You don't seem to be too concerned about the natives," Walker noted.

"Don't get me wrong, I'm concerned about them," Colt answered. "But there's not much we can do. You have people looking for legal loopholes to stall and hopefully block the Colonization Board from kicking the colonists off the planet. I have every hope they'll succeed, but right now I'm more concerned about putting this rebellion to rest. It doesn't serve any useful purpose, and I believe we can do something about it."

Walker considered for a moment. "Okay, then what're your troops going to be doing?"

"They'll be helping keep the southern half of the province out of separatist hands. In fact, that's just the first part. The next part is to free the northern half of the province, and I think I know how to do it."

Walker relaxed and smiled. "This I've got to hear."

After Walker left an hour later, Colt muttered to himself, "I need to talk to Fitz." He stepped over to the computer terminal and said, "Call Dennis O'Toole."

Chapter 33

A lively crowd greeted Colt when he arrived at McGinty's pub the next day. Fitzhugh was already seated at the bar in his O'Toole guise. As Colt approached, Fitzhugh stood up and slapped him on the back. "Good to see you again, commodore. There's an empty booth. Why don't we sit back there?"

"It's good to see you again, Dennis," Colt replied heartily as they walked toward the booth. He lowered his voice, "Did you find her?"

"The lady was elusive, but, yes, I found her. She'll be along in half an hour. I didn't want her to see me," he smiled broadly and slid into the booth.

"Are we talking about the same woman?" Colt asked.

"I certainly hope so. I had a devil of a time …" He paused. "You didn't think I was talking about Jana, did you?"

"I just wanted to be sure."

McGinty showed up with a pint. Fitzhugh picked it up and said, "Many thanks, Seamus. It's dry I am." He took a healthy swallow from the glass.

Colt shook the publican's hand before sitting. "I'll have the same, Seamus."

When McGinty had moved off, Fitzhugh handed Colt a piece of paper with the royal seal on it. He continued in a whisper, "This is the paperwork you wanted. I hope she's worth it."

Colt tucked the paper in his jacket. "Thanks, I know she is, and I hope … no, believe, this will be enough."

"So what the Hemlock are you planning to do?"

"Start a chain reaction," Colt replied.

"How's that?" Fitzhugh took another swallow.

"I'm pretty sure I know who's pushing the buttons in this rebellion. I'm planning to smoke him out by breaking up his organization."

"All by yourself?" Fitzhugh asked.

Colt smiled, "Of course not. I'll need help. That's where she comes in."

"Still, just the two of you? What if she doesn't cooperate?"

"Oh, she'll cooperate. Besides, I have plenty of additional help. I've got my crew. I've got my insider. I've got the mayor of Sykesville." He put his forearms on the table and leaned forward conspiratorially. "And you have what's left of the *Invincible* crew." He paused. "Look, I've seen enough of the militia to know the locals are already disaffected. All it will take is a little push in the right places and the whole organization will fall apart." He leaned back. "Here comes Seamus."

McGinty put the glass of ale on the table. "Looks like you two are up to something."

"Can you keep a secret?" Colt asked.

"Not a chance," McGinty answered.

"In that case let's just say we've discovered something else we have in common."

When McGinty had left, Fitzhugh took another swallow. "If it was anyone but you, I'd laugh. All I can say is watch your back."

"That's another part of it. I need you to do me another favor."

Fitzhugh cocked his head. "Go on."

"Don't tell anyone what I'm doing, not anyone. That's important." He stared at Fitzhugh, frowning. "If anyone asks what was going on tonight, just tell them I was boiling mad about nearly being captured and vented to you."

"If I'm good at anything, I'm good at keeping secrets," Fitzhugh responded. He glanced at his watch. "I'd better get out of here. Your guest will be here soon."

About ten minutes later she appeared at the door to the pub. When she saw Colt, she immediately walked over to the booth. He stood up as she approached. She said, "Commander, it's a pleasant surprise to see you again."

He shook her hand. "It's nice to see you too, Sergeant Hess. Please have a seat."

She slid into the booth facing Colt. "So, why am I here?"

"I need your help, but if you accept my offer you'll probably be blackballed by all the mercenary companies. I'm hoping your allegiance to the Crown and the Republic will be enough to sway your decision." Colt produced the document Fitzhugh had given him. "The person responsible for getting you here has the authority to issue certain official documents. This one exonerates you for all

256

the charges you were court martialed for and removes them from the records. It restores your rank and term of service. To make it official all you have to do is sign it in my presence. It's yours regardless of whether you accept my offer."

Hess studied the paper for a moment. "This is real?"

He nodded.

She put the paper down and looked Colt directly in the eye. "First. I don't owe the mercenaries any allegiance. My company fired me as soon as they found out I had let you live and I told them I draw the line at murder." She paused. "Second, what's the catch?"

"None. I admit I'll be disappointed if you choose not to work with me, but it's your decision."

"I don't get it. Why are you doing this?"

He returned her gaze, smiling, and said, "The last time we saw each other, I said I couldn't officially condone what you did, but since then I've studied your case and changed my mind. I can condone it. I probably would have done the same thing. You made a command decision that the hostages' lives were more important, and I agree." She returned the smile briefly.

"On top of that I need your knowledge," he continued. "There's more going on here than meets the uninformed eye, and I believe you have a better idea of what it is than I do. And, yes, you saved my life, so I owe you."

Colt heard the front door of the pub open and swung around as four men walked through. Their appearance and actions immediately put him on guard. Entering the pub, they spread out, moving with a distinct combat posture. Colt lowered his voice, "Don't look now but I think we have company." Turning on the communicator camera, he punched in the number on O'Toole's business card. He made a quick but unobtrusive sweep of the four men and put the communicator on the table, leaning it against the wall so it had a clear view as the men approached the booth.

Sergeant Hess pulled a small mirror out of her purse and used it to take a quick look at the men. "I recognize three of them. All mercs. The one with the shaved head is Gregor Malinowski. A mean son of a bitch."

Malinowski looked in their direction. His eyes widened briefly, and he started toward them, moving at a brisk pace. As he approached, his face brightened with a smile that almost seemed genuine. "Nancy Hess. Is that you?"

The other men turned and hurried toward the booth. Their smiles were more predatory.

Colt and Hess stood to face the approaching men. "Well, Greg. Fancy meeting you here. I thought you were in Woomera," Hess responded. Her expression was neutral, but her eyes blazed.

"So, who's your friend?" Malinowski stopped centimeters from the table.

"Commander Gus Colt. Gus, this is Greg Malinowski."

"Let's cut the bull," Malinowski lowered his voice. "You two are going with us."

"I don't know," Colt responded. "The odds don't seem very fair. After all, there are two of us and only four of you."

Malinowski pulled back his jacket, exposing a Franklin two-phase in his waist-band. "A wise guy, huh?" he smiled. "This little feller evens the odds. Now, move."

Colt looked at Hess. "What do you think, should we take this outside?"

"Knock it off and get moving," Malinowski growled, reaching toward the blaster.

"Well, when you put it that way." Colt stepped out of the booth, smiling. "After all, we wouldn't want any of the bystanders in here to get caught in the crossfire."

As they walked toward the door, Hess hissed, "You know, Commander, one of these days your mouth is going to get you in trouble."

"It already has," he responded, but he continued to smile. "I've got Malinowski. I hope you don't mind me leaving the others to you."

"You two shut up," Malinowski commanded through clinched teeth and a false smile.

At the door Colt deferred to Hess, signaling her to the hinged side of the door with his eyes. He stepped out to the opposite side.

Malinowski followed before he realized what was happening. The edge of Colt's right hand caught him in the throat. He went down choking, but he still tried to get to the blaster. Colt grabbed him as he fell and yanked him away from the door. At the same time

Hess kicked the door closed in the faces of the other three knocking them backwards. They stumbled over each other as they fell.

Colt grabbed the Franklin from Malinowski and pointed it at the door. The three struggled to their feet. The one in front pulled out his blaster and started to swing it toward the door. Colt waggled the Franklin and pointed behind them. McGinty was bringing what looked like a shotgun to bear on the three. When the one with the blaster started to turn toward him, McGinty squeezed the trigger and all three men collapsed.

"Sorry," Colt said, "There were three of us, not two." He turned back to Hess. "My apologies for taking the fun part."

The police arrived five minutes later and took the four men into custody. After they had questioned Colt and Hess and taken statements from the other customers, Colt gave them his communicator as evidence. The police left with a friendly wave to McGinty.

McGinty walked over to the booth where Colt and Hess had reseated themselves. "That's about as much excitement as we've had around here in a quite while … unless you count the pair who tried to jump you a few weeks back. What was it all about?"

"I was trying to convince Sergeant Hess to return to active duty, and apparently someone didn't like it," Colt answered. "To be honest, Seamus, someone has been trying to get me out of circulation ever since they found out I didn't die on Mount Chamberlain. And I'm bloody well sure they didn't want Nancy here to sign up with me. She knows too much. I suspect they've had a detail following her ever since her company fired her."

"I had that feeling myself," Hess admitted.

"By the way, thanks for taking those three out," Colt nodded to McGinty. "That stunner of yours looks like a MacArthur twelve gauge. Where'd you get it?"

"I had it made. It seems like an appropriate thing to have under the bar in case trouble pops up." McGinty looked up. "I see I have some paying customers. You'll have to excuse me."

When McGinty had left, Colt looked at Hess. "So, do you need some time to think about this or are you ready to get back in uniform, at least figuratively?"

"Where do I sign?"

"Was she pretty?" Lindsay asked, closing the lid to the dish sanitizer and turning it on. Colt had just finished telling her about the meeting with Sergeant Hess and the intrusion by the mercenaries. By the time he and Hess had been debriefed by the First Landing police and he had flown back to the ranch it was after dinner time.

Colt laughed, "Are you jealous?"

"No, I'm just curious," she sniffed.

Colt pulled back slightly. He thought for a second. "Am I attracted to her? No. In civvies she would rate as handsome rather than pretty. Nancy is a senior NCO in the Marine Corps. I tend to see her that way first. You'll get to meet her tomorrow and see for yourself."

He paused. "Do I like her? Yes. I admire her. She had the personal integrity to disobey orders that would have gotten some civilians killed for no good reason and got cashiered because of it."

She flashed a brilliant smile. "So what happens now?"

"Tomorrow we have our first strategy meeting, but what happens now is I'm going to bed. Are you joining me?"

The next morning Toby Walker was the first to arrive. The others trickled in. Promptly at ten o'clock Sergeant Hess walked up the porch stairs. Colt introduced her to Lindsay, whom she immediately called ma'am. Then Colt ushered her into the common room.

"The first thing we need to do is introduce ourselves so everyone knows who they'll be dealing with. Let's start on the left with Toby Walker, a local farmer and resistance organizer."

Walker introduced himself briefly. He was followed by Diane Feldman, the militia sergeant who helped with the cleanup after the militia's abortive attack. Beside her was her husband George Feldman, a platoon leader in the militia and a civil engineer. Next was Susan Winsock, the mayor and former commandant of Sykesville, followed by Deputy Marshall Owen Tucker. Finally, Sergeant Hess introduced herself as Master Gunnery Sergeant Nancy Hess, Royal Marines, and immediately sat down.

"For those of you who don't already know, I've been using a lame alias since I arrived here. I'm Commander William August Colt. I was the first officer on the *HMS Invincible* before she was scuttled. I want you to know right away that my allegiance is to the Crown and the Republic."

Diane frowned. "So as soon as you can contact your superiors back on Earth, we'll all be without homes." Bitterness almost choked off the words.

"To be honest I don't know what's going to happen. The Colonization Board already knows about the Lodaanii, but bureaucracy doesn't come to conclusions very fast, and this situation isn't nearly as cut-and-dried as it seems. Toby has lawyers looking into ways around this Colonization Board regulation, and we believe there is hope. Here's the big thing. We do know for sure even if Corona declares its independence, it won't make any difference to the Republic. They'll either evict the whole human populace by force or allow you to stay, regardless of your declaration of independence."

"In other words we're damned if we do and damned if we don't," George Feldman grumbled.

"I hope not," Colt responded. "But pulling out of the Republic as a means of getting around the Colonization Board is definitely wasted effort. In my opinion all the fighting that has taken place, the people who've lost their lives, the city that was destroyed – none of that was worth the cost, and any further fighting needs to stop – now. That's what this meeting is all about."

"I gather you have a plan," Walker prompted.

"I have the start of one." Colt looked at each of them. "I think we can easily convince enough of the separatists of the futility of further fighting. The trouble is, the militia is full of mercenaries, and we don't know who they're working for. The question is why go to all that expense? Anyone who has that kind of resources …" He paused. "They must have another motive, and I'm betting it's to get control of the planet before anyone knows they're being taken over." He looked at the mayor. "Why else would they have a military governor – commandant – for the province?"

Susan nodded. "It makes sense. They want a force in place when all the fighting was over," she answered. "Probably to impose martial law."

"They also want someone in charge locally they can count on to take orders," Tucker noted. "That's why they replaced you, mayor."

"Of course, I was a figurehead anyway. They were bypassing me to issue orders directly to the militia units. I'm sure that meant I would have been replaced sooner or later."

Diane squirmed. Looking at Colt, she said, "This seems like speculation. Why should we believe you? After all you represent the Crown."

"Just think about what I've said. I know this isn't comfortable for you. I don't like it either. But you can't deny that once the Republic decides what to do about the Lodaanii, whether you claim independence or not, they will do it."

Diane raised her voice, "They can't! The law says that if a colony declares independence, the Republic has to honor it."

"Unfortunately they can. That law you're talking about has been overridden more than once for the good of the Republic. The Takahara Revolution is an example. In fact, there are articles in the law that specifically gives the government that authority. Our best hope is to put our resources into finding a legal loophole. In the meantime we have to call a complete halt to the fighting."

"You've made your case," George Feldman responded. "But why are we meeting now?"

"I want you to help me dismantle the militia, starting with Sykesville. Here's what I have in mind ..."

Two hours later the group separated. The counteroffensive had begun.

Chapter 34

The next day the bivouac area at Sykesville looked much the same as it had the night of the caterpillar drop. As they drove up to the gate in the mayor's official ground car, Colt wondered briefly what had happened to the smelly creatures. The driver held out everyone's ID cards and said, "Mayor Winsock, Commander Colt, Sergeant Feldman, and Sergeant Hess are here to talk to the commandant. Please inform him that the mayor wants all military presence removed from Sykesville without delay."

Bending his knees to look at Susan in the front seat, the guard, a civilian militiaman, stammered, "Ma'am, I can't do that."

She leaned across the seat and said, "Sure you can, young man. Say, aren't you Bruce Lidke? I spoke to your wife just two days ago at the farmers' market. We were both concerned about the fact that the fresh produce is in short supply because the farmers are avoiding town with the militia controlling it. Just pass the message on to the commandant and let us in. Wouldn't you rather be doing something besides guarding a gate?"

Hesitantly he raised his communicator. "Sergeant Frasier, the mayor is here. She wants to talk to commandant." He paused. "About pulling the militia out of town." There was a choked off laugh from the communicator.

Lidke's uncomfortable expression said it all. "Ma'am, I can let you in but Commandant Gradishar probably won't see you. You'll have to go to the assembly tent and wait." He pointed to the tent that served as a mess hall and briefing room.

"Thank you, Bruce." The ground car rolled smoothly forward.

As soon as they were inside the tent, Colt unrolled his computer display. He spoke to the AI. "Announce commander's call starting immediately." He rolled up the display and stuck it back in his jacket.

"Attention in the area. Attention in the area. All personnel assemble in the mess hall immediately for commander's call. I say again, all personnel assemble in the mess hall immediately for commander's call."

263

The tent was over half full when Commandant Gradishar stormed in, his face crimson. "What the hell is going on here?" he demanded, looking around the tent.

Colt waved from the briefing stage. "Commandant Gradishar, we were hoping you could make it. Come on over here so I can introduce you around."

Gradishar stomped his way to the platform. He leapt onto the stage and signaled to a group of militia men wearing guard arm bands. "Who the hell are you, and what are you doing here?" he raged.

While the guards forced their way through the growing crowd, Colt grabbed Gradishar's hand and started shaking it. Smiling broadly he said in a stage whisper, "This is going out live on the web, so be pleasant."

"What!" Gradishar exploded. His face rapidly drained of color as he saw his image on the display behind Colt.

Colt indicated the mayor and the other members of his party, and introduced them to Gradishar as if this were a social occasion. When he finished he said, "Why don't you have a seat, commandant. I have a few words to say to the assembled troops."

Visibly shaken, Gradishar sat in the chair and stared dumbly at the web feed with the Corona News Central logo in the lower right corner.

Colt stepped to the center front of the platform. "Ladies and gentlemen, if you'll take a seat, we'll get started." The AI faithfully amplified his voice, and the noise level began rapidly dying down. The guards arrived before there was complete quiet. Colt turned away from the pickup and directed them to seats in front. They looked confused, but sat down just as the babble faded away.

Over the next twenty minutes Colt explained the futility of the rebellion, the presence of the mercenaries, and his interpretation of the intent of the people who had hired the mercenaries. When he threw the discussion open to the audience, many of the questions were about the mercenaries. He had Sergeant Hess address most of those. She identified every mercenary she recognized in the tent and finished with, "These are all good men, doing their jobs, but they're loyal to their employers and not to the rebellion."

Colt resumed his position at the front of the platform. After several more questions, Colt summarized and said, "The mayor of Sykesville has asked that all military operations in Sykesville and the surrounding province be shut down immediately and that the bivouac area be restored to its owners. You militiamen have an option. You can collect your gear and go home or collect your gear and go with the mercenaries you've been introduced to today."

Again there was a flurry of questions. When they were all answered, Colt came to attention and commanded, "First Sergeant, dismiss the troops."

The first sergeant, a mercenary, jumped to attention. "Battalion, 'ten-hut!'" He paused as the assembled militia men and women stood to a quasi-military attention. "Dismissed," he said. Except for a few stragglers the militia hurried out of the tent, talking excitedly.

Gradishar rose to his feet, his face again bright red. "You can't do this," he grated.

Mayor Winsock smiled. "Look around you, colonel," she replied. "We just did. Now here's what we want you to do."

A half hour later most of the volunteer militia had already gone home. The team left a dazed Gradishar at the briefing table and headed for town.

Hess looked Colt in the eye. "That was too easy, Commander," she said. "How did you get away with it?"

Colt chuckled. "Two things. I already knew that the volunteers in the militia were disenchanted. All I had to do was to give them a good excuse to walk. The other is to always keep your opposition off balance. Do what they don't expect and do it with flair."

"And it doesn't hurt to do it with authority, even when you don't have any," Hess' jaw dropped. "That's why you're such a wise-ass in a tight situation."

Colt laughed out loud. "It is indeed."

The mayor's driver broke in, "I'm not sure what it means, but there's a military vehicle of some kind following us. It pulled on about three intersections back." Everyone swiveled in their seats to look behind. A few seconds later he warned, "Another military vehicle just pulled into the intersection ahead, and it's blocking the street. Shall I try going through someone's yard?"

Hess responded first, "Don't bother. They'll just ram us if we try to get past them. We expected this. Perhaps it's time to put Commander Colt's technique to work."

The driver brought the mayor's ground car to a stop about five meters from the vehicle in the intersection. Nine men in combat gear jumped out of it and started running toward them, waving blast rifles in their direction. At the same time the vehicle in back pulled in blocking their retreat. The driver started to open his door.

"Don't!" Colt commanded. The driver froze. Looking up he found himself staring into nine blast rifle muzzles. He swallowed hard.

Colt said quietly, "Everyone be calm. Just sit still and wait. These guys are mercenaries, and they know we're leading the opposition. All it would take is one suspicious move, and there could be a blood bath."

The first man reached the driver's door. He yanked it open, banging it against the stops. He grabbed the driver by the arm and pulled him from the car, sending him sprawling across the pavement. The other mercenaries opened the other doors and reached for the other passengers. Hess' reaction was immediate and painful. The merc jumped back, holding his forearm. "You broke my arm," he growled, glaring at her. He started to bring the blast rifle up with his other arm. Hess swung out of the car using the grab handle over the door. One foot connected with the rifle. It clattered harmlessly to the ground. The other foot struck the man in the chin. He lurched backward, fell to the pavement, and lay still. The merc who had opened Colt's door swung her rifle toward Hess. Colt mumbled, "Dammit," and jerked the woman's arm down. "Ah – ah – ah!" he said into her purpling face. "Your buddy got what he deserved. Now, back off. If you want us to get out of the car, let us get out of the car." She stepped back and pointed her rifle at Colt.

An authoritative voice interrupted, "You heard the man, Swanson, back off. Keep them covered, but let them get out on their own. Just make sure they don't try any more funny stuff."

The mercenaries stood the mayor's party against the outside of the car and searched them one at a time, removing their repeller field units. "No weapons, Lieutenant, and these things are useless against blast rifles."

"Just out of curiosity, what do you think you'll gain from this?" Colt asked. "After all, you're no longer welcome here."

The lieutenant laughed, "What's welcome got to do with anything. It's power that counts, and we have it."

"Power?" Colt snorted. "By my count there are barely enough mercenaries on the planet to fill a platoon. Together you might be able to hold a town. Individually you can be a major nuisance, but frontier people figure out how to deal with nuisances in a hurry."

The lieutenant stepped in front of Colt and glared at him. "Just because you were able to talk some bored colonists into going home, doesn't mean they all will. We still control half the towns and cities on this dirt ball."

"You'll probably want to check your facts," Colt stared back at the man but remained expressionless. "The separatists never controlled half the communities on Corona, and not all the ones they did control were in militia hands." Colt paused. "But, come on, you haven't answered my question. What do you expect to gain by holding us at gun point?"

The lieutenant studied Colt for a moment. "The brass was right about you. You are a threat to our operation. To answer your question, we don't plan to hold you at gun point. We have orders to execute you, and that's what we're going to do." He turned to one of the other mercenaries. "Swanson."

Hess murmured, "Okay, let's see how you talk us out of this one."

Colt smiled faintly but addressed the lieutenant. "You don't want to do that. You know as well as I do that your company will lose its license if you execute any prisoners, not to mention members of the royal armed forces."

"How will anyone know?" The lieutenant smirked. "There won't be anyone left to tell the story. Oh, even if the car's AI is trying to broadcast this little scenario, its signal is being jammed. Of course, we'll destroy the AI as part of the mop-up."

The lieutenant turned to Swanson. "He's first. Take him away from the vehicles so they don't get damaged by any blaster leakage."

Swanson poked Colt with her rifle muzzle and then swung it to point down the road.

Colt looked at Hess and said, "Protect the mayor with your life."

"Get a move on," Swanson ordered.

"Why should I hurry? You're going to shoot me anyway. I'm in no rush."

She prodded him again. "You want me to do it here?"

Colt started moving slowly. "I suppose you're right, there's no point risking a perfectly good Interceptor 4000," he said, indicating the ground car.

"Stop gabbing and start walking." Colt complied without enthusiasm.

Passing the blocking vehicle, Colt calculatingly bumped into one of the towing hooks and tripped, sprawling forward onto his face. Swanson prodded him in the back with the rifle. "Get up."

Colt rolled over sweeping Swanson's legs out from under her. As she fell, he reached for the rifle and snatched it away. He lunged behind the vehicle as a blaster bolt evaporated the pavement where he had fallen. He immediately heard the sound of a struggle including that of a heavy body colliding violently with the side of a vehicle. Next he heard the lieutenant command, "Drop it, Sergeant. Do it now!"

He took a quick look around the front of the troop carrier, and watched Swanson scrambling to get away. He heard Hess say, "I can't do that, Lieutenant. You heard my orders."

Colt jumped in front of the troop carrier and brought the rifle to bear on the lieutenant. "Don't do it, Lieutenant," he ordered. "You drop yours." At that instant he realized that the other mercenaries had scattered. He heard sand scratching the pavement behind him and started to swing around. A sledgehammer blow struck him between the eyes.

"He's coming around." The voice was weak and fuzzy. He opened his eyes. A swirl of blurred images greeted him. "Gus, can you sit up?" Another voice, this one clearer and louder. Then he became aware of his stomach. "Oh Hemlock," the first voice said. It was also clearer, but Colt wasn't listening. He was too busy emptying his stomach on the pavement.

When he had finished retching, the second voice said, "Sorry about that, Gus. We had to use the max setting on our stunners because they were wearing armor."

Colt turned his head to the side and looked up to see where the voice was coming from. Tucker was bending down to offer him a hand. He continued, "Sorry we were so late. There was another group of mercs guarding the approach and we had to take them out first. We were monitoring the transmissions from the mayor's car like Sergeant Hess recommended. The satellite relay was a great idea, but by the time we arrived you were in a standoff. Our only choice was to stun all of you."

Colt's head was beginning to clear. He looked around at the other marshals loading the mercenaries into vans. "You heard what Jamal said about having orders to execute us?"

"Isn't that against the mercenary code?" Tucker asked.

"It is, but it's happened before with these mercenaries." He nodded at Hess who had already recovered and was walking toward them. "That's why Nancy is on our side."

He shook his head to clear it and immediately regretted doing it.

Hess stopped in front of them. "Are you okay Commander?"

"I'm recovering, thanks to you. Setting up monitoring via satellite was a great idea."

She nodded.

Colt continued, "Owen and I were just discussing the order to execute us. You're old company was New Castle, right?"

Hess nodded again.

"I know from personal experience that they're a solid, ethical company. Yet someone in the chain of command said to kill me and the order was passed on to you. I'd be willing to bet that the orders were issued by someone outside the company. And, of course, there are always jerks like Jamal who are willing to follow orders."

He looked at Tucker. "Owen, I think I know who's issuing these orders, and I'm going to find out for sure."

Interlude

"The first thing I want to know is, are you're working on your own or for someone else?" Quan was standing stiffly in front of McKillip's desk when she asked the question. He had tried to avoid this confrontation, but it had been inevitable. Now he had to tell just enough truth to keep from losing his grip on McKillip, tenuous as it had become. He forced himself to relax.

"Corey Anne, how long have we known each other?"

"I told you, don't call me that name." She stood up, glaring at him. "Just answer my question."

"We've known each other for over ten years. I was the one who recognized your potential and pointed you to Corona so you could take advantage of it. This planet was ripe for someone with your political savvy. Together we got you into parliament and into a ministerial position in record time. Isn't that what you wanted?"

"That doesn't answer my question."

"Yes, I've been guiding you, but I've been trying to take you where you want to go. These people need your leadership, and my job is to make sure they get it."

"You almost make that sound reasonable. You expect me to believe that you're working on your own and you're doing it for me?"

"Take a look at what's happened since I've been working for you. Have I steered you wrong?"

"Up until lately your advice has been good, but recently things have been going wrong more than right. Are you really working for me? A straight answer this time." She locked her eyes on his, daring him to tell a lie.

Without breaking his gaze he started, "Of course I am. … " The urgent news alarm from the webcast cut him off.

The AI turned on the audio, and an announcer said, "The mayor and former commandant of Sykesville, Susan Winsock, and several other concerned citizens have just called the local militia into a meeting. Mayor Winsock told our reporter that they were going to order the militia out of town and asked us to carry the feed live.

Mayor Winsock stated, 'It's time the citizens took back their city and their lives.'"

Both Quan and McKillip watched in stunned silence as Commander Colt stepped onto the briefing stage in the dining hall and took control of the gathering. McKillip found herself snickering despite her dismay when Colt silenced Commandant Gradishar. When the broadcast ended, both she and Quan stood shocked for several seconds.

When McKillip found her voice, she said, "That man just defeated a whole battalion of militia without firing a single shot. What are we up against?"

Quan was equally bewildered. "I'm not sure. That was the Commander Colt we tried to trap in Dixon. I'm beginning to realize how dangerous he really is. We have to get him out of the picture."

McKillip had rapidly composed herself. She asked, "What do you have in mind?" with a commanding voice.

"I'll think of something. Let me talk to some people. I'll be back soon." He headed toward the door.

He halted briefly when McKillip said, "I still want a straight answer to my question, and I will get it."

Out in the hall he flipped his communicator open. "We've got real problems, and I'm not sure which is worse," he said.

Chapter 35

"Well, Mayor. You have your city back, and I don't think anyone will try to take it from you again. Thanks for your help." Colt was standing by Lindsay's van in the rapidly emptying visitor parking area.

"Thank you, Commander. Are you sure I can't help on this next job?"

"You have work to do here getting Sykesville back to normal. However, I do need as many experienced troops as I can get for this next operation and I could use more of them. If any of your marshals are willing to help, I can use them."

"I'll see what I can do."

"Don't sugar coat it," Colt advised. "This operation will probably be dangerous."

"I'll let them know. Watch out for yourself."

"I'll call you when it's over." Colt said with a half-smile. "If you don't hear from me, you'll know it went south."

Lindsay wasn't as understanding. "You're going to what?" Her face was pale.

"I'm going to lead a raid on militia headquarters in Dixon to capture the provincial commander. I'm confident he knows who's really running the militia."

"You'll get yourself killed."

Colt knew better than to lie to her. "That's possible, but I've got a lot more help this time. I believe it's worth the risk."

"I don't," Lindsay countered. "I've already lost one man. Can't you let someone else lead the raid?"

"No, it's my job. I can't send people in where I won't go myself."

She dropped her head. "I know, but, dammit, I don't want to lose you."

"Believe me, I want to be certain I come back to you, but it has to be this way."

"I'm not sure I'm going to want you back. I don't know whether I can take it anymore."

"You don't mean that — do you?"

For a second she stood silent. Then she took his hands. "Please come back in one piece," she whispered.

With the six deputy marshals Mayor Winsock had recruited and the thirty-one members of the *Invincible* crew that Fitzhugh had released, Colt had fifty-three members in his team including Toby and Howard Walker. It was after sunset when they landed their eight vehicles on the outskirts of Dixon and drove into the city in ground mode. The streets were completely deserted, making Colt feel uncomfortably exposed as he dropped off Harry Chapman and the Walkers at the city power plant. Leading the team toward the downtown complex that the militia was using as headquarters, he kept a constant lookout.

Several blocks from the city center they stopped and assembled for a final briefing. Colt unrolled his portable display and stuck it to the van's side window. "Let's keep this simple. We're going up against trained military, so this could turn ugly in a hurry. I've set up a distraction that should get us in, but we still have to watch our step."

He pointed at the center of the display. "The mercenaries control the center of the city, and there are about as many of them as there are of us. These buildings are their compound." He indicated four buildings facing the town square. "Quarters here and here. Armory here. Headquarters and combat operations center here, and that's where we'll find Dixon the Third. I know I'm repeating myself, but we want him alive and able to talk."

He changed the display. "Here are the known threats. Fitzhugh's intelligence says these four gun mounts are manned. They're primarily for airborne targets, but they cover most of the surface approaches. These additional mounts are remotely operated. Altogether they don't leave many areas on the ground that aren't covered. We'll be approaching in the power tunnels, but if we have to surface for any reason and we start taking fire while we're in the open, these areas in green are about as safe as we can get. And keep in mind that the only way out of them is through the building walls."

He looked at them. "Hopefully we won't come to that. As far as Fitz could determine, there are no surveillance sensors in the outer buildings, but we're assuming that the tunnels near the headquarters are rigged with video and perhaps acoustic and IR sensors. The team at the generator station will cut power on my signal, but don't count on the sensors being out for long. As soon as the power goes off, disable as many of the sensors as you can. The power outage may bring the guards, but our distraction should have tied up most of them above ground. The ones in the tunnels will approach slowly because they won't know how many of us there are. We can take them out with stunners and stun grenades. Blasters are a last resort." He paused.

"Once we're in, your job will be to neutralize any guards you run into and set up force fields to block all the approach tunnels. When they're secured, Tony, your squad will join Sergeant Hess and me inside the command center, and as soon as we have Dixon the Third in custody we'll announce to the mercenaries that it's over and they are dismissed."

Green belts that ran down either side of Central Avenue forced the squads to walk in the open for the remaining distance. They broke into small groups and did their best to look as if they were out for a stroll. Colt kept looking over his shoulder, expecting to be spotted by a militia patrol. He was right. Before they reached the city center, a troop carrier heading from downtown rolled to a stop beside Colt's group. The militiaman in the shotgun seat opened the door and glared at them. "What the Hemlock are you violating curfew for?" he growled.

Colt glared back, "Since when can't citizens walk their own streets without some jerk in uniform hassling them?"

"You know bloody well that the brigadier ordered a walking curfew tonight. Are you looking for trouble?" The militiamen signaled to the troops in back and got out of the carrier. "Perhaps you'd rather spend the night under lock and key."

The other militiamen vaulted to the ground with their weapons ready. They quickly surrounded Colt and the others. Colt backed down, "Look, I apologize if I offended you, but aside from your guns, what authority does the brigadier have to declare a curfew?"

"Aren't our guns enough?"

"No, damn it. We're free citizens and Dixon isn't at war with anyone that I'm aware of."

"Like I said, aren't our guns enough?" The edge of the militiaman's mouth quirked upward.

"Nancy?" One of the other militiamen lowered his weapon.

"Bryce? I heard you'd been killed."

"You two know each other?" The first militiaman asked.

Hess replied, "I used to work for New Castle, but I got fired. Bryce was in my platoon. He never could beat me at hand to hand."

"I can now!"

"Let's see you prove it." She glanced at Colt.

"I'll hold your coat," he said. As she shucked her jacket and handed it to him, he carefully made sure her weapons weren't exposed.

Bryce looked at the first militiaman, who nodded. He took off his jacket and handed it and his weapon to another militiaman. The two combatants stepped into the center of the circle that had formed, assuming a ready position. Bryce said, "Corporal Steig, would you do the honor?"

The first militiaman nodded. "This will be a fight to the first take down," he said. "Fighters ready? ... Begin!"

Bryce immediately went on the offensive, delivering a side kick that almost connected. Hess grabbed for his leg but missed. She jumped back to avoid a left hook that came with surprising speed. This time she hacked at his arm and met muscle. He jerked his arm back, swearing. Before he moved far Hess delivered a kick that hit his knee, but he was moving away from the blow, and it glanced off.

For the next five minutes the battle went back and forth, neither combatant doing serious harm to the other. As the fight continued, the rest of Colt's team drifted up and joined the circle of watchers. Several of them positioned themselves behind the militiamen as if there wasn't enough room in the circle.

Orsini commented to the man next to him, "I'm betting on the blonde."

"No way. Five quid says Bryce takes her." The other responded.

Orsini took out his wallet and fished out a five credit note. "You're on."

As soon as Colt saw his team was ready, he caught Hess's eye. She slipped under Bryce's roundhouse as if to attack his mid-section. Instead he swept the arm down and inward striking her neck with his forearm. At the same time, he thrust out his leg. Hess fell forward onto her hands and knees. Bryce was immediately on her back with an arm around her throat. She reached up with one hand to pull his arm away. He took advantage of her unstable position and rolled her over onto the ground. He threw up his hands and yelled, "Down!"

Seven stunners fired simultaneously, and the standing militiamen all slumped to the ground. Hess swung her right hand up and caught Bryce's. "Nice job, Bryce," she said as he helped her to her feet. "You've definitely improved." She stepped aside as Colt fired his stunner.

Moments later they were on their way again. Orsini and his team had taken the carrier with the unconscious militiamen to get to his entry point. The rest of the team meandered toward downtown.

Colt signaled a stop two blocks from their objective to survey the situation. The militia complex occupied squat, municipal government buildings facing the town square. All four buildings stood clad in stark pseudo-marble with columned porticos in front. Heavy barricades had been dropped in the streets so surface traffic had to slow down and snake around them to reach the square.

"Looks like they're expecting trouble," Ensign Leslie whispered. "Do you think they know we're coming?"

"I wouldn't be surprised," Colt responded.

He quickly reminded the team of their assignments and was finishing up when from the back of the group Buchanan, one of the lookouts, shouted to the group. "Everybody down! We've got company!"

Colt hit the pavement, drawing his stunner as he dropped. Raising his head he saw movement down the road. A crowd had spread completely across Central Avenue, emerging from the shadows as they moved toward Colt's team. When they passed beneath a street lamp, Colt recognized them. He quickly rose to his feet. "Our distraction is here. Everyone get to your positions and signal me when you're in place."

In a few minutes over one hundred Lodaanii, male and female, wearing gaudy ceremonial garb had reached Colt. They stood silently as he climbed onto a parked flyer to address them in Lodaanii. Colt finished off, "I am indebted to you for being here. You know what you are to do. Again, thank you."

Colt jumped down from the flyer, landing next to Jontaro. "You know we do this for leto-gellen," the Lodaanii reminded him.

"I do," Colt responded. "Let us go."

The Lodaanii immediately moved out into the street and started toward the city center. They picked up a brisk pace. Staying close together in the middle of the street, they began a song which reminded Colt of Mardi Gras music. Sure enough, within seconds they had started dancing, a powerful, hypnotic dance that swirled and surged down the street.

For a moment Colt followed them with his eyes as they reached the barricades and flowed around them, continuing the song and dance. Glancing toward the roofs of the buildings on either side of the street, he watched uneasily as the live gunners there pointed their guns at the crowd, but they all seemed more amused than concerned. They tracked the Lodaanii erratically, pausing on one group or another from time to time but stayed away from their triggers.

Colt had already located the nearest manhole. He slid the cover off, and in a few seconds his communicator began beeping as signals came in that the other units had reached their positions. After the last one, he keyed his communicator briefly to alert the team at the power station. The whole city went dark. He and Hess slid on their night-vision goggles, and Colt led the way into the power tunnel below.

With the power off, the night-vision goggles had to rely on infrared to pick up images outside the circle of starlight that came through the manhole. Climbing down the ladder, Colt was instantly aware that he and Hess would be spotlighted targets. As soon as he cleared the roof of the tunnel, he began watching down the tunnel toward the headquarters building. At the bottom of the ladder he detected movement. As his feet touched the fused earth floor of the tunnel, he realized that one of the moving objects was bringing a weapon into firing position. He jumped up and grabbed Hess around the waist, yanking her off the ladder. They both fell backwards into the opening of a cross tunnel as a blaster bolt struck the ladder, sending a spray of molten metal in all directions.

Chapter 36

The bright flash from the bolt overpowered their night-vision goggles momentarily. It also blinded the militiamen who were moving up the tunnel. As Colt and Hess struggled to crawl into the side tunnel out of the line of fire, the militiamen fired a volley. Bolts struck all around them, creating clouds of dust and spraying them with pieces of fused earth. Before they were completely clear, the roof of the tunnel collapsed dropping large, broken chunks on them.

Gasping in the dust Colt pulled his shirt over his face and drew in a breath. When his goggles clicked back on, he saw from the infrared image that Hess wasn't moving. He reached toward her, "Nancy, are you all right?"

She coughed. "I'll survive, but my legs are trapped under the rubble."

"Let me see what the situation is." Colt stood up and flicked on his wrist light briefly. The flash showed him that the entire entrance to the side tunnel they were in was blocked. He turned the light back on to get a better look. Hess was lying on her back in the shallow drainage ditch that ran through the tunnel. A slab of ceiling lay across the ditch, pinning her legs but not crushing them. "Give me your hands. Let's see if we can get you out from under there." He reached down and grasped her hands, noting how powerful they were. "Yell if this hurts."

He began pulling, gently at first and then harder as she failed to move. He was sweating profusely when she lurched forward a half meter. "Damn," he swore.

"Don't quit," she grunted. Struggling as he pulled, she managed to drag her right knee up and get her foot against the slab. With her pushing and him pulling, her other leg came free. Her trouser leg was shredded and her leg was red with blood.

"You're bleeding." He knelt to examine the leg. "You've lost a lot of skin. How's it feel?"

"It hurts like hell," she answered. "Let's see if I can stand on it."

He helped her to her feet and held her up as she tested the leg. Carefully she let go of him and took a tentative step, then another. "My ankle hurts, but nothing is broken."

"Are you able to carry on?" Colt asked.

"Yes sir."

"You're sure?"

"Commander, we have work to do. We can't stand around arguing over a minor injury. We can clean my leg up when we have Brigadier Dixon in custody. We need to move."

"We certainly can't go back into the main tunnel," Colt commented, examining the wall of debris that filled the side tunnel entrance.

"And there's no way to get to the other side of the main tunnel from here," Hess pointed out. "How do we get to the command center?"

"We go back to the surface, and move through the buildings. We need to get out of here before these guys figure out we may still be alive." Colt set off down the tunnel toward the next intersection. "I've got point."

In his night-vision goggles light flared in the tunnel ahead. "Oh, sh…!" he heard Hess whisper.

"They've already switched to backup power at the command center," Colt said. "We need to get out of here fast. If the guards are smart, they could be halfway up the next tunnel, looking for us."

His wrist light picked up an access tunnel a dozen meters ahead. He hurried forward and peered into the tunnel. It stopped at a blank wall. Hess hobbled up. "We could blow our way through that."

"Yeah, but the guards would notice." The wall opposite was blank. "Looks like we'll need to go farther down."

Hess turned off her wrist light. "Commander, if they haven't seen our lights already, we'd better turn them off."

Colt switched his light off. He could see the other tunnel clearly but not anything nearby. "You take the left side. I'll take the right." Dragging his right hand along the tunnel wall, he took off at a trot.

The next access tunnel ended in a metal door. Colt switched on his light to examine the lock. "This should have released when the city power shut down." The handle resisted his efforts.

Hess tapped him on the shoulder, "Let me try." She unholstered her blaster and set it for low power and full dispersion. Blue fire coruscated off the door around the handle. Using the sleeve of her jacket for insulation, she twisted the handle until the lock clicked. The door moved but didn't open. Colt began pulling with her.

A voice carried down the tunnel, "This is the cross tunnel. If they weren't buried, they're probably in here."

Colt tensed but kept pulling. The door moved as if stuck in tar. Finally, it was open wide enough to squeeze through. Colt could hear the guards approaching as he followed Hess through the door. "There's an access tunnel on the left. Be careful, they're probably armed. Don't give them a …" The door shut silently. Colt slowly released the handle, praying that the lock wouldn't make any noise. It clicked.

Colt drew his stunner and pointed it at the door. The handle didn't move.

Hess switched on her wrist light. She signaled Colt to move out. He nodded and headed toward the nearest stairwell. He opened the door carefully, listening for any telltale sound. He led the way silently up the stairs, with his stunner pointing ahead of them, constantly looking for a target. In a matter of seconds they were on the ground floor.

Colt peered out a window. None of the lights were on, but starlight showed Lodaanii in the street being herded away from downtown. Colt did a quick count. "I make out twenty militiamen trying to prod the Lodaanii out of the area," he told Hess in a whisper. "That's half the force, and there were six in the carrier."

"I'll bet the rest are down in the tunnels looking for us," she answered.

"They're going to be running into the rest of our team. I hope our people are better prepared for them than I was."

Colt looked out the window for another second. "It looks like it's time to move. The militia are focused on the Lodaanii for now. If we go right away, we can get across the street before they notice us."

The side door opened without a sound. Cracking it open, Colt peered into the alley. He nudged the door further open and eased his head out. A voice from behind startled him. He jerked his head back. Guards were coming up the stairs.

Hess whispered, "We can take them out with stunners."

Colt nodded. "But if one of them gets a shot off, it's all over. Our backup expects us to be in the headquarters building, not here."

He opened the door and, stunner drawn, stepped out into the alley. Hess followed, silently closing the door behind them.

Hugging the building they approached the corner. The militiamen in the street were still concentrating on the Lodaanii, and the Lodaanii had decided to sit down in the middle of the street. Colt heard someone ask, "Now what do we do?"

Before Colt could pull his head back, one of the Lodaanii saw Colt and smiled. She jumped to her feet, and for a second he was afraid she would point in his direction. Instead, she started another impromptu song and dance. The other Lodaanii quickly stood up and joined in. Their voices drowned out anything the militiamen were saying. Colt realized it was as much of a distraction as they were going to get.

He signaled Hess and dashed into the street, not taking his eyes off the militiamen. Halfway across the street he heard a blaster bolt shriek by uncomfortably close. He jumped to the side, turning and firing in mid-jump. His stunner caught two militiamen coming out of the front door of the building Colt and Hess had just left. They pitched forward, unconscious, and tumbled down the steps onto the sidewalk.

The racket the Lodaanii were making covered up the sound of the blaster, but some of the Lodaanii saw the men fall and stopped dancing. Several militiamen turned to follow their gaze, looking away from Colt and Hess who sprinted the final few meters to the next building.

Once they were out of sight behind it, Colt slowed down, but he knew they had only seconds before someone came to the alley to check it. The only cover was a dumpster at the back door of the headquarters building. He and Hess dropped behind it, pointing their stunners toward the street. "If we let them get far enough into the alley, the others won't know right away that we took them out," Colt advised. "We might have time to get into the building."

"Or they might see us and start firing something more lethal than a stunner."

"So we take them out as soon as they come in sight?"

"No, I think you're right, but it is risky," she answered.

The first militiaman came around the corner within seconds. He scanned the alley with a blast rifle, moving forward slowly, watching for any sign of movement. A second militia man followed a few meters behind. Colt realized that if they were too spread out, the first would be almost on them before they could fire. He focused his stunner for long range and signaled Hess to take the closer targets. The third man rounded the corner with a fourth on his heels. Colt whispered, "Fire!"

All four men were down. Colt signaled for Hess to cover him and dove down the stairs to the alley door into the basement of the headquarters building. As he swung the door open, he found himself looking into the business end of a blaster. "Ah, Commander Colt, we've been waiting for you. Won't you and your companion come in?"

Chapter 37

Colt barely caught the flicker of the stun grenade as it flew past him into the open door. He heard Hess yell, "Duck, Commander!" Using the door handle he swung himself out of the way and slammed the door on the extended blaster. The partially closed door absorbed some of the blast from the grenade, but his ears still rang as Hess threw open the door and dragged him inside. A blaster bolt slammed into the outside of the building as the door closed.

"That was close!" Hess shouted.

"Thanks. I owe you another one," Colt responded. The lights were on inside the building, so he pulled his night-vision goggles down and surveyed the damage. Five militiamen lay on the floor. They would be unconscious for at least a half hour. Looking up he saw that the video camera had been ripped off its mount and was hanging by its transmission line. "Let's get out of here."

Halfway down the hall to the command center Hess looked back suddenly. Another squad of guards was emerging from a cross corridor behind them. She shouted, "In here," and dived into a doorway, pulling Colt with her. Blaster bolts filled the air where they had been. Chunks of dust and flaming debris filled the air in the corridor.

"Cease fire, you idiots. Are you trying to burn down the building?" Colt heard the squad leader shout, despite the continued ringing in his ears. "The brigadier wants them alive."

Colt signaled Hess, and they dove out the door to land facing opposite directions with their stunners aimed down the hallway. A blaster shot grazed Colt's arm as he rolled to a stop. He fired his stunner, dropping the entire squad.

"Clear!" Hess announced.

Colt scrambled to his feet. He looked at his arm and commented, "Just singed."

Leaving the squad and their weapons, they dashed the final few meters down the hall to the command center. The door had an electronic keypad lock. "We could blast the door down," Hess suggested.

Colt shook his head. "It's probably backed up by a force field." He spotted a fire bottle attached to the wall nearby. "Let's try something."

With Hess on one side of the door and him on the other, he swung the fire bottle down on the keypad, knocking it loose from the wall. He yanked the wires out of the unit, but before he could touch them together, a voice from behind said, "Hold it right there. Get your hands up."

Colt and Hess raised their hands and turned around slowly. The guard was out of reach and pointing a blaster at them. Colt recognized him as one of the guards they had stunned. He showed signs of being unsteady but not enough to justify an attack.

The guard pulled out his communicator with his spare hand. "Ops, this is Sergeant McAllister. I have Commander Colt and his companion at gunpoint outside the COC door. Colt just broke the access pad so someone will have to open the door from inside."

A moment later the door eased open. Two guards with handguns drawn stood just inside. As soon as they confirmed McAllister, they stepped aside. McAllister maintained his distance and said, "Go on in, both of you."

Inside was chaos. Monitor images were blacking out as Colt and Hess watched. At the communication desk two radio operators were frantically calling different squads but getting no answers. Colt smiled to himself. His team was isolating the command center.

A man wearing a star on each shoulder was bent over a monitor console, stabbing at the keyboard without effect. When he straightened up, Colt recognized Radcliff Dixon III. Ignoring the guns trained on him, Colt stepped forward and extended his hand. "Well, well, well. Dix, fancy meeting you here." He grabbed Dixon's hand before Dixon thought to jerk it away. "I'd like you to meet Master Gunnery Sergeant Hess, my assistant for this operation."

Looking bewildered, Dixon shook Hess' hand.

Colt started working his way around the room, introducing himself and Hess. After his third introduction, Dixon shouted, "Enough! This isn't a social occasion. You're both our prisoners, not our guests. We finally got you. You have been a tough bastard to nail down."

Dixon turned to the guard who brought them in. "Toss them in the holding cell down the hall. I'll get to them when we get this mess straightened up."

The guard stepped forward, reaching for Colt with his empty hand. Hess chopped down on the guard's neck, sending him sprawling to the floor unconscious. "Not nice," she said as she kicked his blaster out of the way without trying to retrieve it.

"Really, Dix. Is this any way to treat someone you haven't seen in over a month?" Colt asked. "But I suppose we ought to get down to business. We're here to find out who's giving orders. We figured you'd know. I mean, we know it couldn't be you. Who gives you orders to pass on?"

Dixon's face was rapidly turning purple. "What?" he sputtered. "I'm in charge here."

"It's okay, Dix. Your men know you're just an intermediary."

"I'm not an intermediary!" Dixon raged. "This is my command!"

"Oh, come on, Dix. You can be up front. It won't affect your command. We just need to know who you're getting your orders from."

Dixon exploded. Waving at the other two guards, he screamed, "Get them out of here!"

The guards hesitated. One of the technicians on the tactical board said, "Why not just shoot him and get it over with?"

Dixon started to speak and froze with his mouth open. Colt waited knowing Dixon had orders to deliver him alive. Finally Dixon said, "That won't be necessary." He glared at Colt. "Just lock them up."

A noise came from the corridor, and the door disintegrated in a brief flash. Orsini looked into the command center. "We're mopping up now, Commander," he said. "Any orders?"

Enraged, Dixon pulled his blaster. As it cleared the holster, Colt kicked it out of his hand. Dixon charged at Colt, swinging wildly. A few of the militiamen tentatively reached for weapons, but Orsini raised his left hand and held up his index finger. All the hands reaching toward weapons halted.

Holding off Dixon who was now swearing incoherently, Colt said between parries, "Tony, let Harry know to turn the power back on and have these men and women collect all the weapons in here and take them over to the armory for storage. Then you can go over to the Coventry Inn – it's on the other side of the square – and buy them a beer on me. I have some serious questions to ask Dix."

"Aye, sir." Orsini glanced at Hess. "Sergeant, can you handle this?"

"Yes sir."

"Good." He looked at the command center staff. "Ladies and gentlemen, start collecting weapons. I haven't had a cold beer in a long time."

As soon as Orsini and the staff walked out the door, Colt turned serious. Dixon had him in an ineffective choke hold. "Dix, I have to admit, you're an interesting fighter, but this has gone on long enough." He swung his right arm down, moving aside so it went between Dixon's legs and struck him solidly in the groin. Spinning around he drove his left fist into Dixon's solar plexus. Dixon doubled over, and Colt slammed his right knee into Dixon's chin. Dixon collapsed to the floor, moaning.

Colt rolled Dixon onto his back, took a glass of water from a nearby console, and threw it in his face. He woke up swinging, but everyone had moved out of range. He staggered to his feet, looked around the room, and stood there slumped.

"Are you ready to answer questions now, Dix?" Colt asked.

"Perhaps we can make a deal," Dixon said.

"What do you have in mind?" Colt managed not to frown.

"I know where Princess Jana is." Dixon let a faint smile flicker across his face.

Colt froze. "That Jana is missing is not general knowledge. How did you find out about it?"

"I have contacts." The smile lingered a little longer this time.

Colt grabbed Dixon's shirt in both hands, lifting him off the floor and bringing Dixon's face within centimeters of his own. "Where is she?" he demanded.

"Ah! Ah! Ah! Not very nice," Dixon smirked. The smirk faded and his face turned white as he saw the rage on Colt's face and felt Colt's grip tighten on his shirt. His voice shook when he responded, "I'll tell you, but I have to get something in return."

Colt put him down, but his reply was a growl, "What do you want?"

"Let me go."

"That's not going to happen, and you know it. Up until now you were an enemy combatant. I could have released you if I thought it was reasonable. Now, you're a co-conspirator in kidnapping a Royal. I don't have a whole lot of latitude."

"Now wait a minute," Dixon protested. "I didn't kidnap her. I simply found out about it."

"But you didn't report it to the governor general."

"How was I supposed to do that? As you just said, I'm an enemy combatant."

Interlude

Both the outer office and McKillip's personal office were completely empty. Even the carpets had been pulled up and removed. Quan suspected that every trace of DNA had been scrubbed out of the rooms. Cringing, he pulled out his communicator. With an unsteady voice he said, "She's gone. Vanished."

A voice exploded from the communicator, "What?"

Chapter 38

Colt and Hess walked into the Coventry Inn with Dixon in tow. Orsini saw them as soon as they entered and hurried over. "Commander, we weren't expecting you here until later. Has something changed?"

"I need an armed escort. Brigadier Dixon has agreed to lead us to Princess Jana, and I want to be prepared for contingencies." Colt looked around the room. "I need two armed marines to go with Sergeant Hess and me, and at least four more armed personnel to follow in the van."

While Orsini rounded up the escort, Colt took the time to settle up with the barkeep and to call Lindsay's van with instructions to land out front. Then he made a quick call to Fitzhugh and left a message about Jana. Orsini returned with the full contingent of marines from the Clermont and two navy petty officers.

"I also got volunteer offers from several of the mercenaries," Orsini reported. "And I'd like to go along as well."

Colt spoke to the mercenaries. "Thanks for your offer, ladies and gentlemen. I believe we have enough for this job."

He turned to Orsini. "You'll be in charge of the van contingent. We don't want to come in like a strike force. The people holding Jana might panic and do something stupid, so you'll stand off a kilometer or so and observe from the air. If something looks like it's going seriously wrong, use your discretion. Otherwise, come down when I call you."

Colt looked at Dixon. "Now, call your bloody flyer."

Colt walked to the command side of Dixon's flyer. Before he got in, he growled at Dixon, "Tell your AI that you are relinquishing all command to me."

"What? I can't do that."

Colt glared at him. "Yes you can. I don't want any funny business. Do it."

Dixon frowned. "But …"

"No buts, and make it clear that you are doing so without duress."

Dixon grumbled, but said, "Sergeant York, I am voluntarily relinquishing all control of you and this flyer to Commander Colt. This is Commander Colt standing beside me. Confirm your orders."

The AI responded, "Commander Colt now has all control. What are your orders, Commander?"

"First, do you understand that Brigadier Dixon is giving up control of his own free will?"

"He does seem to be under stress."

"That's because his freedom after this operation depends on its success. Is that not so, Brigadier?"

"Yes," Dixon answered.

Colt again spoke to the AI, "Was that answer the truth?"

"Yes, sir."

"So do you accept my command unequivocally?"

"Yes, sir."

"Good. Let's get moving."

Less than half an hour later they settled on a landing pad of a farm house several dozen kilometers east of First Landing. Luna was full, lighting the countryside so brightly colors were discernible. Colt looked overhead to locate the van with Orsini and his crew and then climbed out of Dixon's flyer.

As soon as Dixon was out of the flyer, he immediately yelled, "Protocol 53!" and sprinted toward the house. Hess immediately started after him, limping as she ran.

The AI responded, "Protocol 53. Self-destruct in five seconds."

Colt shouted, "Sergeant York, belay that order."

The AI responded, "I can't, sir."

Colt bellowed, "Run!" and sprinted away from the flyer. At four seconds he caught up with Hess. He threw his left arm around her shoulders and took her to the ground just as the flyer exploded. The blast was deafening, and for a moment pieces of metal fell all around them.

Colt jumped up to chase after Dixon, but a volley of blaster bolts near his feet stopped him. Three men in mufti were pointing blast

291

rifles at him as Dixon closed the distance and mounted the steps to the front porch.

He turned around and called back to Colt, "Princess Jana really is here, and she is obviously no longer of any use to us, so we'll make you a trade."

"What do we have that you want?" Colt demanded.

"I want you," Dixon answered. "Drop your weapons where you're standing and walk here with your hands in the air."

"I have a better idea," Colt responded. "Send the princess out and when she reaches this position, I'll start walking."

"You're in no position to dictate to me."

"I disagree. You'll notice three trained sharpshooters behind me, and they all have you in their sights. Personally I'd prefer no one gets killed in this confrontation, so send the princess out."

"Don't go anywhere," Dixon said. He turned and went into the house.

A minute later Dixon and Jana Stewart appeared on the porch. She started walking toward Colt. When she stepped off the porch, he caught the flash of her red hair in the moonlight.

"That's her. Orsini will be on his way down by now. Sergeant Hess, as soon as he lands, get the princess aboard and take her directly to the governor general's palace," Colt ordered without turning his head.

As Jana approached, she recognized him and broke into a run. Colt stood paralyzed, hoping none of the marksmen on the porch decided to stop her. "Gus Colt!" she cried. "Is that really you?"

Reaching him, she wrapped her arms around his neck and sobbed, "Thank God you're here."

"I'm glad to see you too, but you need to keep moving. There are men with guns trained on us right now, and I want you behind my marines in case they change their mind about not shooting. Get! I'll talk to you when I have the chance."

Glancing back Colt saw that Hess had taken up a position to shield Jana and was escorting her out of the way. He dropped his weapons onto the ground and raised his hands. Slowly he walked the remaining distance to the farm house, intensely aware of the guns pointing at him. When he reached the porch, one of the marksmen pulled his arms down and behind his back and wrapped a restraint around his wrists.

Dixon looked at him smugly. "Check him for hidden weapons and take his communicator." While Colt was being searched, Dixon pulled out his own communicator. "Call Alpha One." Colt couldn't hear the other end of the conversation, but he heard Dixon's reply, "I've got him."

As they led Colt into the house, one of the gunmen fired his blast rifle. He shouted, "That was a warning shot. Stay where you are."

Colt didn't see Orsini land, but he got a running commentary from Dixon's gunmen, "The other flyer just landed and they're loading the princess in. It's moving away on the ground, but the three marines have taken cover and they look like they don't intend to leave. The flyer has moved off beyond the clump of trees over there. It's not leaving either."

Colt noticed that Dixon didn't seem to be concerned. Instead, he was looking out the back of the house. About thirty minutes later something caught his attention. He spoke to his communicator, "Alpha One." Again, Colt couldn't hear the other voice, but Dixon responded with, "There are seven military shooters in front of the house. Land in back and turn on your shields if you have them."

A few minutes later a black flyer descended to hover over the backyard. Dixon and his hired guns hustled Colt outside and stood waiting for the flyer to land. Instead, it continued to hover and rotated until it was pointing directly at them. "What the ...." Dixon started. It was the last thing he ever said. A blaster bolt caught him in the chest. Colt dove for the ground as withering fire took out the rest of the gunmen.

The flyer landed close by. A man wearing a Home Guard uniform stepped out of the back door on Colt's side. The guardsman kept a blaster leveled on Colt as he stood up and stared at the carnage around him. The guardsman said, "Thanks for getting out of the way, Commander. It made our job easier." He roughly frisked Colt, examining the restraints on his wrists, and ordered him into the flyer. Before he got back into the flyer, the guardsman checked all the bodies. One of the shooters was still alive. The guardsman used his blaster to complete the job.

Seconds later the flyer was airborne, accelerating rapidly toward the west. The guardsman grinned maliciously at Colt, "You're the only one we want, Commander. Relax and enjoy the ride."

As the flyer accelerated to altitude, Colt looked back and caught sight of Lindsay's van. It was rapidly falling behind. The guardsman smirked, "This baby has the military overrides, that flyer will never keep up with us. The speed governor won't let them." He showed his teeth at Colt. "Besides, what could they do if they caught us?"

The guardsman turned back to watch the struggling van. "Hey! Now they're trying to climb above the governor setting. It'll take them too long. We'll be out of range before they can get high enough."

In minutes the van had disappeared from sight.

"You're very quiet, Commander. I heard you're big on bravado. Not so brave now?"

Colt's mind seethed. He looked at the guardsman. "I was just thinking. Someone has been trying to haul me in ever since Brady was kidnapped. I don't suppose you'd know anything about that, would you?"

The guardsman snorted.

Colt continued, "Whoever had the Clermont sabotaged and kept the crew prisoners tried to set me up. They fed me what I needed to know to break the crew out. Then they had a team ready to catch me when I tried. Luckily, we all managed to get away."

"Do I care about this?" the guardsman grunted.

"Something to pass the time. You've got me, so humor me."

The guardsman snorted again. "Go ahead, I like a good story as much as the next man."

"Someone was obviously monitoring my communicator. When I called Lindsay, they homed on the signal. We managed to stun the two men they sent to pick me up. I presume they got back safely."

"Safely is a relative term. I understand after they got back to First Landing they were shot for botching the job."

"That's doesn't sound like the mercenaries I know. I gather New Castle doesn't know you've gone renegade?"

"We're just following orders," the guardsman snarled.

"Right. When subspace is restored, tell that to New Castle."

The driver looked uncomfortable.

The flyer began slowing down as it approached First Landing airspace.

Colt resumed thinking out loud. "The thing is that whoever is pulling the strings, knew virtually everything I was doing, but the only people I was talking with were people I trust implicitly. I finally realized it had to be someone Fitzhugh reported to, and it had to be someone on Corona."

"Who's Fitzhugh?" the guardsman asked.

"A friend of mine who regularly reports to the governor general. However, I've met Remarque face to face, and no way could he be involved in treason of any sort. So who does that leave?" Colt stopped because he knew there could only be one answer, the one person on Remarque's staff who had full access to the same classified information Remarque did.

They had arrived in First Landing airspace. The flyer entered a descent corridor, bleeding off both speed and altitude. It leveled off in an air corridor, turning into a northwest corridor when they passed the center of the city. Minutes later it descended onto the landing pad for the governor general's palace. A half-dozen palace guards were standing by the pad when the flyer touched down.

As Colt stepped from the flyer, the guards surrounded him and silently escorted him up the steps to the portico of the palace. As he entered the building, he mumbled, "Where's Zorro when you need him?"

Chapter 39

"Well, well, well, Commander Colt, so good to see you alive and healthy. Won't you join me in my office?" Wallace sounded cordial enough, but his face remained expressionless.

Colt pulled his right hand out from behind him far enough that his restraint was visible and looked at it pointedly. Wallace nodded at the guards. One released the restraint. "Will you be needing us anymore, sir."

"No, I can handle him. You're dismissed."

Once the door to Wallace's office was closed, Colt asked, "Do they know who they're working for or did you convince them I was a threat to the governor general?"

Wallace looked at him coldly. "Have a seat, Commander."

Colt picked a chair to the side of Wallace's desk. Wallace sat on the front edge of the desk and stared at Colt for several seconds. Colt stared back, unruffled.

Finally Wallace said, "You've become a problem, Commander. Frankly, I don't know what to do about you."

"But it's such a great plan. Surely you had all the contingencies covered."

Wallace frowned. "Perhaps you don't appreciate how precarious your position is."

"Oh, I have a pretty good idea. The trouble is your plan's falling apart around you. The loyalists weren't supposed to put up so much resistance. And, of course, they don't even have to win. All they have to do is keep you from taking over long enough for the fleet to figure out that they need to intervene."

"Unfortunately, in a way you're correct. There was supposed to be complete chaos after the explosion in Kyoto."

Colt smiled. "Backfired, didn't it?" He changed the subject, "Help me out here. You don't strike me as a power-hungry politician. Why are you doing this?"

"It's a long story."

"Apparently I'm not going anywhere."

"I don't know why I should tell you. I certainly don't expect to recruit you."

"I always like to know my opponent's motivation. It helps me decide how to handle them when I take them out."

Wallace snorted. "Then perhaps I should be interrogating you." He stood up and began pacing back and forth in front of Colt. "I'll tell you what. I'll exchange information with you. You tell me what you know, and I'll tell you why I'm doing it."

"Why should I tell you?"

"Well, there's a certain Mrs. Hansen."

Colt glared.

"Oh, come now, Commander. I suppose it was in poor taste to threaten the love of your life, but we can share information with each other. After all, what harm can it do to tell me where I fouled up?"

"All right. Let's see how well I've figured this out. You're planning to take control of the planetary government and secede from the Republic. I feel certain the separatists were poorly organized and had no intention of actually rebelling. Your people either prodded a few splinter groups or started battles themselves. Come to think of it, it almost had to be your people who took the subspace relays out and that would account for most of the battles. It didn't turn into the ground swell you had hoped for, and the nuke at Kyoto pretty well took the fight out of both sides. I presume you're working on plan B now."

"Not bad. Of course, I know these people. I knew an armed rebellion wouldn't have a chance. The nuke did just what it was supposed to. It got that oaf, Hargety, out of the way. Nobody trusts him now."

"You strike me as more of an idealist than a petty tyrant. All right, it's your turn. What's your reason?"

"In case you hadn't noticed, the Republic is collapsing. Soon enough all the colonies will be independent. We're just hurrying the process."

"So you expect me to believe you're simply power hungry and want to rule a whole planet," Colt remarked dryly. Wallace frowned, but Colt continued, "Have you sent your demands yet?"

"No, we haven't been in contact with her majesty yet."

"You know they'll laugh in your face."

Again Wallace frowned.

"Oh, come on, Wallace. You've been in the business long enough to know the Crown doesn't negotiate with rebels. The most you can hope for is time to consolidate your grip." For a second his jaw dropped. "Wait a minute! You've known all along this wasn't going to work, haven't you? What were you really up to?"

This time Wallace's eyes widened.

"That's it isn't it? You helped set this up, but you planned all along for it to fail. You've been careful to make sure that none of your operatives know you personally. I'll bet the men who brought me in don't know anything about your involvement in this little insurrection. They probably think they're doing undercover work for you. What do you get from being the hero and unmasking the real conspirators?"

By now Wallace's face had become ashen. He looked away from Colt and composed himself. "I knew you were too dangerous to leave on the loose."

He swung around and pointed a finger at Colt. "Does revenge seem like a strong motive to you?" He was looking Colt directly in the eye.

"I considered it once. Fortunately, there was no one to take revenge on."

"Ah yes, your wife and daughter. Well, this too is about revenge." Wallace went back to his pacing.

"Several years ago, after almost two years of painstaking work, I had put together an ironclad case against Ernst Prochaska for drug trafficking using military personnel. I even had a video of him handing over money to a navy CPO for drugs. I got a warrant and brought him in. Then things started turning sour. First, the video and all the backups disappeared. Then the witnesses all ended up dead or missing. Finally, at the trial, the DNA evidence turned out to be corrupted. On top of that, the defense brought in a surprise witness, Senator Corey Anne McKillip, who swore she was in bed with Prochaska at the time of the exchange. As you can imagine, Prochaska walked."

"The Admiralty doesn't take kindly to getting egg on its collective face, does it? You're trying to get revenge against the Admiralty?" Colt asked.

"No, not the Admiralty. As it turned out, Prochaska had enough damaging evidence on Senator McKillip to send her to jail for several years. Even though it meant the end of her political career, she perjured herself rather than go to jail."

"You found this out how?"

"Before Prochaska mysteriously vanished, he confessed most of his varied crimes to me. Unfortunately, none of it was admissible in court.

"Immediately after the trial McKillip dropped out of the government and disappeared from sight. I finally was able to trace her. She had had bio-sculpting to change her looks and had changed her name to Maryanne Phillips. I had an operative convince her that there was opportunity here on Corona, and she's been rebuilding her political career ever since. When Remarque sent the message about finding natives to the colonization board, I made sure she saw a copy. With a little prodding, she started the separatist movement. When Hargety, with his moderate approach, emerged as the separatist leader, she broke off a group who wanted action rather than talk and started the militia.

"Which worked right into my plans. I've been working to set her up. My agents carried out all these incidents—Kyoto, the Guard barracks, Pretoria and dozens more—so they trace directly back to her. We left enough evidence for Hargety's people that they'll get the credit for finding her out. She was going down hard!" Wallace winced.

"Ah, but something else went wrong," Colt said.

"That she-witch disappeared again," Wallace growled. He took a moment to calm himself. "She won't get away this time. She can't get off the planet without me knowing it."

"I gather the governor general doesn't know what you're doing."

"No, he doesn't."

"Aren't you concerned he may drop in on us when he hears I'm here?"

"Remarque is out for the moment. Just before you got here we received a call from the *Invincible*. He went to the spaceport to welcome Captain Wessler and find out from her firsthand what happened."

Colt's eyes widened.

Wallace continued, "I see you were aware there was an incident."

"Incident? It was a nuclear explosion."

"Apparently the ship survived, but for some reason went incommunicado. They were lucky."

"Are you trying to pretend you had nothing to do with the blast?" Colt glared at him.

"There isn't a shred of evidence connecting me with the explosion, so, yes, I categorically deny having anything to do with it." Wallace allowed himself a faint smile. His glance strayed to something on the wall to Colt's left. Colt followed his gaze. He had to fight to keep his expression neutral.

He looked back at Wallace. "I'd say there is evidence." He stood up and walked over to the wall. The revolver hanging on the wall on a highly polished piece of teakwood had a tarnished bronze placard at the bottom that said, "Colt 45 Peacemaker."

"The serial number on this piece is 357849. It happens to be mine. You can see the implications, can't you? After all, how did you get it?"

Wallace frowned faintly. "I suppose I owe you that. Lieutenant Von Hagen got it for me. She took it to prove she was earnest about working for me."

"And how did you get in contact with Magda?"

"I could say I had information that she was a Dissolutionist and needed to see if she was a danger, which is true. She turned out to be useful, however. She volunteered to disable the *Invincible* for a price."

"Was the nuke her idea or yours?"

Wallace smiled again, "It was her idea, but I provided it."

Colt nodded. "I can't imagine that anyone would fall for a limpet mine after the one on the Clermont. What did you use?"

"It's called a wake follower. It follows along in the wake of a ship under power."

Colt nodded. "Until the drive cuts off. Then, kaboom!"

"You're aware of them?"

"That's why the ship survived. All navy pilots are trained to shut off the drives momentarily on approach. The *Invincible* must have had its shields up. Perhaps enough of the pulse got through to disable the electronics, which would explain the comm blackout."

"That sounds possible. We'll know soon enough."

"So where's Magda now?"

"She was aboard the shuttle that blew up and took the *Invincible* out of commission."

"She knew too much to let her run free, I see. What about me?"

Wallace's face remained expressionless, "You know I can't let you leave here alive."

Colt nodded, "I suppose that makes sense." He pulled the Peacemaker free from the plaque, and pointed it at the security chief. "You know that this weapon is just as deadly as a blaster at this range."

A brief, faint smile crossed Wallace's face. "I also know it isn't loaded."

With his free hand Colt opened the loading gate. Then he pulled back the hammer to the half-cocked position and spun the cylinder. "What do you know? You're right. By the way, when your men searched me, they didn't even recognize this bullet." He eased the bullet from his pocket and slid it into the open chamber. Before he could close the loading gate, Wallace was on him, knocking the gun from his hand with a vicious right-handed chop. Wallace followed with a knee to Colt's solar plexus, and when he doubled over, Wallace chopped the base of his neck. The blow stunned Colt, and he dropped to the floor. He watched dazedly as Wallace closed the loading gate and pointed the gun at him.

"I hate to do this," Wallace said. "You've been a surprisingly formidable opponent, but I have no choice. What an irony that it's your own weapon." He squeezed the trigger. Colt struggled to roll out of the way, but he could barely move. The gun didn't go off. With the hammer in the half-cocked position it wouldn't fire. "What the hell?" Wallace wondered aloud.

He looked at the gun more closely and then pulled the hammer all the way back. He squeezed the trigger again. This time Colt was able to move a little more, but the hammer fell on an empty chamber, and the gun didn't go off.

"What?"

Wallace squeezed the trigger again in growing frustration. Nothing happened. He pulled the hammer back. This time the gun fired, but Colt kicked Wallace's legs out from under him as the gun was going off. The bullet struck Colt in the right side.

Despite his injury Colt struggled up from the floor. Wallace scrambled to his feet just as Colt hurtled into him, crashing him into the wall. Dazed, Wallace fought back. He shoved one forearm into Colt's throat and the other behind his neck. Colt hammered him against the wall again. Then, using all the strength he could muster, he slammed Wallace onto his desk and landed on top of him.

For a moment Colt lay unable to move, and Wallace opened one of the drawers, pulling out a Franklin two-phase. The gun came up and pointed at Colt. For an instant Colt stared death in the face, but Wallace moved too slowly. Colt's hand found the geode that was the only decoration on the desk. He bashed it into Wallace's head, and Wallace slid to the floor, spreading papers as he fell.

The room became hazy and began to spin, but Colt could make out Fitzhugh walking across the room toward him. He tried to get up but fell to the floor, barely conscious. Fitzhugh spoke into his communicator, "Officer down, governor general's outer office. Get a medical team here pronto." He picked up the revolver from where it had fallen on the floor. "Sometimes I wonder about you, my friend. You seem to have more tricks up your sleeve by accident than I have from twenty years of field experience and preparation. Just lie there. Help is on the way."

He carefully rolled Colt onto his back. "It's a good thing Lindsay knew how to contact me when Orsini told her you had been taken. Can you talk?" He asked.

To Colt the voice came from far away, but he was able to croak out, "Yes."

"What happened? Where the blazes did the bullet come from?"

As he passed out, Colt murmured, "I always carry one for good luck."

Chapter 40

Colt woke in a hospital bed with several tubes attached to him and Lois Strauss looking down at him. She said, "It's about time. How do you feel?"

"Like someone who was just shot."

"You'll get over it," Lois stated. "The bullet shattered one of your ribs. The nanites have a harder time repairing bones than they do soft tissue."

"So I've noticed," Colt agreed. "But, what are you doing here?"

"I sometimes work here and happened to be on hand when the Guard brought you in."

"And how long have I been out?"

"They brought you in yesterday morning."

"When can I leave?" Colt asked.

"You could leave right now, but you'll be uncomfortable walking around until that rib is completely knitted. What's your rush?"

"As soon as I've talked to Lindsay, I need to do some research."

"What are you going to research?" Lois asked.

"I don't want to say anything just yet, so if you don't mind, I'll wait to answer that question."

"Hmmm. Mysterious." Lois smiled. "Okay, let me introduce you to the hospital AI. Florence, this is Commander Gus Colt. He has full access."

A woman's voice said, "Yes, Dr. Strauss."

Lois turned back to Colt. "She can provide whatever connections you need for research, and she can call Lindsay. Now, let me get these tubes out of you."

As soon as Lois had left the room, Colt addressed the AI, "Ms. Nightingale, I need to place a call to Lindsay Hansen." He gave the number.

The AI responded with human sounding surprise, "You made the connection. I'm impressed. One moment please."

After what struck Colt as an unnecessary delay, Lindsay appeared in the screen. She looked at him for a moment before speaking. "You survived. I'm glad." She didn't look happy.

"The *Invincible* wasn't destroyed after all, and I'm going to be recuperating here in the hospital. I don't know when I'll be able to come back to you. Can you come here?"

"Don't expect to see me there, and don't bother to come here," Lindsay responded. "If there's anything here you need, make a list, and I'll send it to you."

Stung, Colt stammered, "What's this all about?"

"You know. I can't go through this again. It tears me up." A tear started down her face. As she wiped it away, she said, "And don't call me again. It hurts too much." She reached forward, and the screen went blank.

Colt lay there stunned for a minute. Then he found his voice. "Florence, could you ask Dr. Strauss to come here when she has a moment?"

"Certainly, Commander."

"Thank you. In the meantime I have some research to do. Please connect me to the *Invincible* subspace relay."

Colt logged in to the *Invincible*'s computer system and used the subspace transceiver to access several databases on Earth. He spent the next fifteen minutes scanning data. Finally he found what he was looking for. As he was finishing up, Lois came in. "What's up?" she asked.

"I've upset Lindsay and she won't talk to me."

"What did you do?" She frowned at him.

"My job."

"And you nearly got killed in the process. You don't expect her to be exactly thrilled that you willingly stick your neck out like that do you?"

"I know. But I need to talk to her — see if we can iron things out. Can you get her to come see me here?"

"I'll try, but I can't guarantee any results."

"Thanks, Lois."

As Lois walked out of the room she said, "You can go in now."

Colt looked up and felt his breath catch. The first person in the door was a tall, beautiful redhead with a broad grin on her face. "Hey, sailor, it's good to see you again!"

"Jana, what're you doing here?"

Jana Stewart leaned over the bed and kissed him squarely on the lips. "Thanks, Gus. I owe you."

"How's David these days?" referring to her husband.

"I just got through talking to him. He's fine and he passes on his thanks as well."

Then he saw the second woman. She looked like Magda but somehow not Magda. He stared at her in puzzlement. The third person to enter was Fitzhugh.

Fitzhugh walked up to the bed and shook his hand, "I see you two have already met. They tell us you're going to pull through. Personally, you look like—" He stopped and stared at the image in the screen. "Great Hemlock!" He breathed. "Is that what I think it is?"

"Yes, Fitz. I'm pretty sure it is," Colt answered.

Fitz stared at the image for a moment and then breathed, "I'll be damned."

Colt returned his gaze to the Magda who wasn't Magda and demanded, "Would somebody tell me what's going on here?"

She stepped forward, "Sorry for the confusion, Commander Colt. I'm Angela Gonzales. I'm an Imperial Intelligence agent, and this was my first field assignment. In a nutshell I was called in to get Mr. Wallace's confidence and collect evidence so we could arrest him. Sorry I had to steal your pistol to convince him." She smiled briefly. "You seem to have done a better job of getting the information than I did."

Fitzhugh said, "Angela was aboard the shuttle that supposedly was blown up. As a matter of fact, she kept everyone aboard safe."

"What do you mean, supposedly was blown up?"

"Angela warned the shuttle pilot about the wake follower and had him contact the *Invincible* about it. Gunners on the *Invincible* blew it up far enough from both the shuttle and the *Invincible* that it couldn't do any harm. The explosion produced the ionized cloud that interfered with sensors. To make it look as if the attack was successful, the *Invincible* and the shuttle jumped out of planetary sensor range and went radio silent."

Colt raised a hand. "I get the picture." He looked at the screen. "I'm really glad to see all of you. Don't leave, but I need to talk to this guy." He nodded at the image.

###

Half an hour later Colt broke the connection. "Well that certainly puts an interesting twist on things, doesn't it?"

"It certainly does. I'll need to let my people know as soon as I leave here," Fitzhugh responded.

Colt turned to him, "For the record, I wonder how it happened that Imperial Intelligence turned up just in time at the governor general's palace."

"We've known for several months that Wallace was up to something – that's why we called Angela in, and we had the palace bugged as you know. After I passed him the word that Jana had been rescued and you had been taken prisoner, he was so riled I made a point of going to the palace to listen in. I was there when you arrived. I literally had to run from the surveillance room to his office, and I still didn't get there in time to help."

"That explains it. I knew Magda — Angela — was faking her passion for the Dissolutionism," Colt nodded. He sagged back into the bed. "You know, Fitz, I've earned a month of shore leave."

There was a knock at the door. Colt looked up to see Captain Wessler standing in the opening. She said, "You've earned the Victoria Cross. Her majesty wants to present it herself."

Colt was stunned. "What?"

Wessler walked over to the bed and nodded at Jana. "We would have never found Princess Jana even with the clues she left. Her majesty figures you saved Jana's life and wants to honor you. The Reliant has been dispatched to bring a division of marines and you're expected to be on her when she leaves. About three weeks."

She looked down at him. "How're you doing, Gus?"

"Getting better by the minute."

There was another knock. This time Lindsay stood framed in the door. Colt felt blood rush to his face. "Lindsay, come in," he said enthusiastically.

He introduced her around, starting with Jana.

Lindsay looked flustered and bowed her head slightly, "Your highness."

"Please, call me, Jana," she said. "If you're marrying Gus, you're practically family."

Lindsay glanced at Colt, but he continued the introductions. When he finished, Fitzhugh said, "I wish we could stay to enjoy this, but you two have quite a bit to talk about, and I don't want to get in the way." He turned to Colt, "Talk to you later, Admiral. I want a complete debriefing. Nice to see you in person, Lindsay. Maybe we'll have more time to talk later." He offered Wessler his arm. "Won't you join us, Captain."

Lindsay looked after them for a moment as they walked out of the room. She turned to Colt. "Wow, I just met Princess Jana. That was really her, wasn't it?"

Then she turned serious. "Dammit, Gus Colt, the only reason I'm here is because Lois insisted. Look at you. Every time I turn around you stick your neck out because it's your job. Yes, I'm in love with you, but I can't stand by waiting, not knowing whether you'll come back in a body bag. It will hurt less if I never see you again." She turned to leave.

"Wait." The word hung in mid-air. She reached the door before she stopped and turned to look back at him.

"I've been doing a lot of thinking about us. " Colt said. "If you'll listen to me, there's something I want you to hear. After losing Rachel I never expected to meet another woman I could care for, but you happened. I knew immediately — even when you couldn't stand me — that I wanted you more than anything else."

Lindsay stood with tears in her eyes. "Thank you for telling me, but it doesn't mean anything if your next assignment gets you killed."

"It means I love you too. And by the way, we need to move the wedding date up."

"What? The wedding? Why?"

"I have to go to Earth to receive the Victoria Cross in three weeks, and I want my wife and son to be with me. Will you marry me?"

Her tears flowed freely now. She swallowed, "I just told you I can't live with someone who is always putting his life in danger."

"My career? I admit I did have my sights set on admiral's stars, but there are things that are more important. There's a young man who needs a father right now, and there's his mother whom I couldn't bear to be separated from. I'm not sure I'm cut out to be a gentleman farmer, but this world needs teachers, and I have a masters in political science. I'd love …"

"…But we're going to have to leave!" Lindsay interrupted.

"I can't imagine why."

Lindsay put her fists on her hips and tried to glare at him. "You know very well that the Republic doesn't allow colonizing an inhabited planet!"

"I know that you're concerned, but I've been doing some research. Actually, the rule is that we can't colonize a world that has a native sentient race," He paused and looked at her.

A mixture of emotions flitted across her face. "But …"

"The Lodaanii fail that test."

"What!" She almost shouted. "What do you mean?"

"They're not native. It seems that the Lodaanii are part of a star-faring race called the Nidacheen. The Lodaanii are the descendants of a group of outcasts from a desert planet who were dumped here just about the time the first human colonists landed. So they don't qualify as native any more than humans do."

"You're sure?"

"I spoke to the Nidacheen foreign office just before you came in. The sub-deputy I talked to was amused by my accent, but she was more than willing to tell me the whole story."

Lindsay sank down on the edge of the bed as if her legs were giving out, "We can keep the farm?"

"We can keep the farm. Everyone can keep their farms."

She leaned over and kissed him, a long, warm kiss. "I love you," she murmured. "And, yes, I'll marry you."

He hesitated. "There's one other thing. It seems the Nidacheen haven't yet outgrown their caste system. They won't associate with anyone who is socially equal with the outcasts."

"You're saying they won't establish diplomatic relations with the Republic?"

"Not exactly. They already have diplomatic relations with the Republic. They won't establish diplomatic relations with Corona."

"But we're part of the Republic."

"Not for long. The central government will disown Corona officially once they know the full details. That doesn't mean they'll hang us out to dry or break off trade or any such thing. It's just that it will all take place unofficially. In the meantime, we have to form a full-fledged government and start running our own affairs."

"So the separatists could have won this whole rebellion without firing a shot?"

Colt nodded.

Chapter 41

"Hey! You're getting me wet!" Brady complained, wiping water from his face.

"I thought you humans liked water," Uujii countered, splashing another handful on him.

Brady dipped his hand into the water swiftly flowing past the bow of the little cat boat and threw a handful on Uujii. Uujii sputtered and the water fight began in earnest.

Colt dropped the sail and let the boat slow down. He watched the progress of the battle from the tiller with an amused look on his face. Uujii was staying with them to go to school, at least until one could be set up for the village. Initially she had been reluctant to deal with the water, but Colt and Brady had been adamant about spending time at the lake. Over the past few months Colt had slowly encouraged her, first to wade, then to swim, and finally to go out on the lake in the boat. The hardest part had been teaching her to handle the boat capsizing. Colt was pleased that the Lodaanii fear of the water was taught rather than inherited because Uujii had blossomed as her confidence grew. Now she was comfortable on the water.

"Kids! Kids! That's enough. You two are acting like a brother and sister."

Uujii produced a near-human looking smile, "Brother and sister? I like that."

Colt smiled inwardly. Going to a human school, Uujii had grown remarkably human-like. She spoke the local human dialect with just a trace of an accent. She had become close friends with several of her human classmates and adopted the mannerisms of a human teenager. Fortunately, she had not entered the rebellious phase, but Colt was almost sure that wasn't a Lodaanii trait.

Uujii worked her way to the stern and plopped down beside Colt at the tiller. "Are you still going to be at the birthing?" She asked, hugging his arm.

"I wouldn't miss it."

"Good. I get the day off from school. You can fly us both to the village."

Colt began pulling in the sheets to raise the sail. "Would it be proper for me to bring Lindsay?"

"She's your wife. Of course she should be with you. And Brady too."

The sail billowed out and the little boat plunged ahead.

From the bow Brady called back, "Hey! Are we headed in?"

"Fair is fair. It's your mother's turn. Besides, with you and Uujii brawling I'm afraid you're going to capsize the boat."

As they approached the beach, Uujii asked, "Now that you're retired, what are you going to do?"

"Well for now I'm learning how to be a farmer. It's not nearly as hard as it once was, and it gives me a feeling of having accomplished something." Colt paused and smiled. He added, "I suspect it will get boring pretty quickly, but so far I'm enjoying it."

"What will you do when it becomes boring?"

"I have some options. I can teach. And I've been talking to some people who want Corona to have its own navy. It would probably be a one ship operation, but they want me to put a plan together. I'd likely end up as the chief of naval operations and get my admirals stars. Or maybe I'll get into politics. The Republic has given this system independence, so we're in the process of setting up our own government. The parliament makes the laws and ..."

"I just read about that in school," Uujii interrupted. "It's sort of like our village council, only bigger."

"That's a good analogy. Anyway, we already have a parliament, but a lot of the humans that are in it don't want to be in the new one. Also, we need to make room for Lodaanii representatives. So we're having a planet-wide election to choose new representatives. In fact, Jontaro is planning to run as a Lodaanii representative."

They were close enough to shore that Colt again dropped the sail. Then he hauled up the dagger-board. The hull of the boat ground against the lake bottom, bringing them quickly to a halt. Colt jumped over the side with the bow line in hand and waded to shore. In a second, both Brady and Uujii were also wading to shore.

Lindsay hurried down to the water to meet them. "You have a call. It's the chief constable of First Landing." She nodded toward the picnic table where his communicator lay. "I'll tie you off," she said.

Colt walked to the picnic table and picked up the communicator. "Re-call the last caller." In a few seconds he was speaking to the chief constable, who seemed bemused. "Do you know a Lodaanii MP candidate named Jontaro?" He asked.

"Yes."

"Well, he raided the livestock auction earlier this morning and stole some pigs. Other than scaring a few people, no harm was done, so I returned the pigs to their owner, and I was getting ready to let the Lodaanii go, but he demanded I call you. He said the pigs you gave him were too small and you would pay for what he took. — Sir? I'm sorry, sir. I can't understand you. You're laughing too hard."

TELEPORTAL

Chapter 1

Day 1: 10:00 a.m.

"Troy, don't!" Melissa Kim shouted. She jumped to her feet, watching in horror as the man reached toward the torus.

"Bzzzt!" A brilliant electric discharge arced from the torus to Troy Santori's hand, and a vicious, invisible force tossed him away from the makeshift worktable. He spun around and fell face down on the concrete floor of the garage. The flash from the arc left a blue afterimage on Melissa's retinas, and the rasping sound of the discharge reverberated off the walls and ceiling. Troy didn't move.

For an instant Melissa stood stunned. Then from the opposite side of the test rig, she heard Greg Masterson's voice, "What the —"

It cut into her paralysis. She shoved her chair back, barely missing Greg who was rounding the table. Dashing to the inert form, she left Greg to toss the offending chair out of the way. She dropped to her knees beside Troy. The odor of ozone and burned flesh assaulted her nose. "Oh my God!" escaped from her lips.

Melissa stared at Troy, her thoughts in a whirl. "No, this can't be happening. Oh God. Oh God," she whispered. *Is he dead? He can't be!* She called up her CPR training and grabbed the big man's shoulders, shaking him like his life depended on it. "Troy, are you okay?" she recited. Greg dropped to a squat on the other side of their partner's motionless body.

Troy didn't respond. Melissa strained to turn him over, but he was tall and heavier than he looked. Greg touched her hand. "Let me do that."

Thoughts of Greg's and Troy's supposedly private nickname for her, "General Patton," raced through her mind in response to the offered help. She hated the name, but it was important. As a petite, attractive—she saw no point in denying it—Asian woman she knew people didn't take her seriously. She had to earn their respect by being decisive and forceful.

Staring down at Troy, Melissa's concern almost overcame her self-control, something she knew she couldn't allow. Instead, she took a deep breath and called on General Patton to take command. She frowned at Greg and shook her head. She could do this. "I've got it." With a final heave she rolled Troy onto his back. She took a hurried look at his hand and whispered, "At least he didn't get cut on the razor," referring to the sharp edge of the interface between the two connected portals. She put her ear next to Troy's mouth and listened for breathing noises.

"Not good. He's not breathing," she said, fighting to sound in control. Her fingers belied her tone, trembling as she fumbled for Troy's carotid to check his pulse. Angry with herself, Melissa glared at Greg and let her irritation come out in her tone of voice. "No heartbeat! Call 9-1-1! I'll start CPR." As Greg rose to his feet she saw him wince, but she stifled an apology.

She directed her attention back to Troy and began chest compressions. Greg pulled out his phone and made the call. The phone had barely rung when a woman's voice responded, *"Phoenix Police Department. What's your emergency?"*

Melissa could hear Greg's military experience in his matter-of-fact response. "This is Greg Masterson. We're at 11844 South Sunflower Drive. We're in the garage. We need immediate medical help. My friend got hit by an electrical discharge. He's down and has no pulse."

"Don't touch him," the emergency dispatcher directed. "Is he in contact with any wires?"

Melissa almost smiled at the scripted instructions that she could hear from her position beside Troy.

Greg continued calmly. "No. He was hit by an electrical arc. He's not touching any wires." Melissa saw him take a quick look at her efforts to resuscitate Troy.

"Okay. I have you at 11844 South Sunflower Drive in the garage." The emergency operator paused only briefly. "The response team is on their way. Are you performing CPR?"

"Melissa is, and we've both been trained."

"Great. Do you have a defibrillator?"

"No reason to have one. We weren't supposed to be dealing with high voltage." Greg stared at the offending torus as if he were trying to spot a flaw.

"That's okay," the dispatcher assured him. "If you want to take turns with the person who's with you, do so, but one of you should stay on the line with me until the team arrives."

Greg lightly covered his cell phone mike with a finger and asked Melissa, "Are you doing all right, or do you want me to take over for a while?"

"I'm okay for now." Melissa had regained some of her composure and dropped the "General" from her voice. She paused the chest compressions long enough to signal Greg to mute the phone.

He touched the button and nodded at her. She said, "You have work to do."

He seemed puzzled.

"In a few minutes we're going to have a garage full of curious people. I'd just as soon they don't get overly inquisitive about what we're doing here."

"Oh, right. I can't argue with that," Greg acknowledged.

"We don't need outsiders snooping around right now. We're too close to getting this thing right, and if the word gets out…"

"Got it, but I don't have time to hide all this stuff." He gestured at the jury-rigged table, a sheet of plywood sitting on sawhorses. At each end of the table a twelve-inch-diameter torus—a wire-wrapped ring—stood in a base. Power cables and control wires connected each to its own control panel, which was in turn connected to the computer Melissa had been monitoring. Papers, pencils, and tools littered the surface around the rings.

She shook her head. "No need. Turn everything off and disconnect the computers from the equipment." Then she indicated the three video cameras stationed around the room. "But be sure to get those cameras out of here. We could have people asking to see what happened. You can put them in my bedroom."

Greg put the phone on speaker and set it down beside her so she could monitor the dispatcher. "You're up," he said. He started working his way around the table. When he had shut down the computers and disconnected the cables, he tucked the cameras under his arms and carried them into the house.

A moment later he returned. He knelt down on the other side of Troy from Melissa and picked up the phone. "That's about all I can do. Shall I take over here?"

Troy chose that moment to cough.

Melissa pulled back and murmured, "Thank God." She checked Troy's pulse and rolled him onto his side. She examined her shaking hands before speaking to Greg. "He's still out, but he's breathing. You go outside and direct the EMTs in here. I'll keep watch on him."

"Yes, sir, General." Greg stood up and mock saluted, continuing a routine he and Troy had started early in the project. Despite the seriousness of the situation, Melissa had to wrestle with an urge to laugh at the silly salute. Or was it the release of tension now that Troy was breathing again? She sobered at the thought he might have critical internal damage.

Greg trotted to the front of the garage, updating the dispatcher on his way. He pushed the garage door button and stepped back. A burst of Arizona sunlight and stifling air rushed in.

Melissa could hear the approaching siren over the clanking chain of the opener hauling up the door.

Moments later the ambulance rolled into the driveway, and its blaring siren cut off with a chirp. Melissa sighed with relief. One of the EMTs rushed up, dropped his bag beside Troy, and began examining him. "How'd this happen?"

Feeling weary Melissa stood up and stretched. "We were running an ultra-powerful electromagnet." She indicated one of the wire wrapped rings on the lab table. "Troy got too close, and it arced. Apparently, it generates static electricity as well as a magnetic field."

While she spoke, the other EMT rolled a gurney into the garage. He approached the nearest ring. Melissa cautioned, "We haven't had a chance to ground those since the accident, so I wouldn't get too close."

He jumped back, staring at the ring. After that both EMTs warily avoided getting anywhere near the table.

About the author

When Gordon was in third grade, he saw an army recruiting poster in which a "true" spaceship hurtled across a star-strewn backdrop. That image reached out and grabbed him. He wanted to be on that ship, exploring the solar system. A few years later he discovered science fiction in the form of Astounding and Galaxy magazines and was immediately hooked.

He entered the Air Force Academy at seventeen, and graduated in the second class of the Air Force Academy. His twenty years in the Air Force taught him both the value of applying the right amount of force and the importance of not having to apply it. He recognizes that finding and working with common interests is the win-win situation even when it has significant risks.

His service in the Air Force and eighteen years as a software engineer kept him busy, but all that time he read every piece of science fiction he could: Heinlein, Asimov, Clarke. He was especially taken by Zenna Henderson's People series. Eventually he got into writing, and Poul Anderson became his guiding light. In fact, one of Anderson's short stories, "A Live Coward," inspired the development of his protagonist, Gus Colt. The result is *Peacemaker*, in which wits and daring are more important than strength of arms. In *Peacemaker* his hero applies what Gordon has learned to deal with crushing difficulties and a determined, well organized adversary.

Gordon lives with his wife, Carol, in rural Colorado and as a Toastmaster would love to get feedback from readers. Visit his website at gordonsavage.com and check out his second book, *Teleportal*.

Acknowledgments

I had considerable help putting this story together. I'd like to start by thanking my wife Carol who has contributed so much to my happiness over the years. I'd also like to extend my appreciation to Joe Sabah who has been both a friend and a mentor and to Diana Hall who kick started me on this journey. She connected me with my accountability team and inspired me to make it work. And definitely to my accountability team, Helle Hill and Zuzana Tauvinkl, who advised, challenged, and encouraged me and kept me moving. Additionally, I owe a debt of gratitude to Karen Reddick, my editor, for her "flowing red pen" and for teaching me how to write a novel. Finally, I want to thank my daughters, Kathy and Shannon, for their thoughtful feedback, much of which has been incorporated into this latest revision.

www.ingramcontent.com/pod-product-compliance
Lightning Source LLC
Chambersburg PA
CBHW061537170626
46811CB00001B/13